WELCOME TO

The Abyss line of cutting-edge psychological horror is committed to publishing the best, most innovative works of dark fiction available. ABYSS is horror unlike anything you've ever read before. It's not about haunted houses or evil children or ancient Indian burial grounds. We've all read those books, and we all know their plots by heart.

ABYSS is for the seeker of truth, no matter how disturbing or twisted it may be. It's about people, and the darkness we all carry within us. ABYSS is the new horror from the dark frontier. And in that place, where we come face to face with terror, what we find is ourselves.

"THANK YOU FOR INTRODUCING ME TO THE REMARKABLE LINE OF NOVELS CURRENTLY BEING ISSUED UNDER DELL'S ABYSS IMPRINT. I HAVE GIVEN A GREAT MANY BLURBS OVER THE LAST TWELVE YEARS OR SO, BUT THIS ONE MARKS TWO FIRSTS: FIRST *UNSOLICITED* BLURB (*I* CALLED *YOU*) AND THE FIRST TIME I HAVE BLURBED A WHOLE *LINE* OF BOOKS. IN TERMS OF QUALITY, PRODUCTION, AND PLAIN OLD STORY TELLING RELIABILITY (THAT'S THE BOTTOM LINE, ISN'T IT?), DELL'S NEW LINE IS AMAZINGLY SATISFYING . . . A RARE AND WONDERFUL BARGAIN FOR READERS. I HOPE TO BE LOOKING INTO THE ABYSS FOR A LONG TIME TO COME."

—Stephen King

Please turn the page for more quotes

HIGH PRAISE FOR

KRISTINE KATHRYN RUSCH

AND HER FIRST HORROR NOVEL

FACADE

"A must read!" *

"RUSCH SHOWS SHE'S EVERY BIT AS ACCOMPLISHED AS A NOVELIST AS SHE IS AS AN EDITOR. . . . HER WORDS ARE SPARE, AUSTERE, TO THE POINT, BUT NEVER STINTING IN EMOTIONAL LOAD."
—Edward Bryant

"Rusch has been an author . . . to watch for several years now, and is continuing to do excellent work."
—Tom Whitmore, *Locus*

"Intrigue, suspense and unexpected twists . . . if you enjoy this type of reading, [*FACADE*] is a must read; just don't read it alone in a dark room. Rusch uses the element of psychological horror in a fascinating manner . . . add[ing] a deeper element of psychological suspense. [A] journey into the mind and its mysteries."
—*Fordham University Ram* *

"A MASTERFUL WRITER . . . FRESH, SURPRISING."
—*Pulphouse*

Also by Kristine Kathryn Rusch

FACADE

SINS OF THE BLOOD

KRISTINE KATHRYN RUSCH

A DELL BOOK

Published by
Dell Publishing
a division of
Bantam Doubleday Dell Publishing Group, Inc.
1540 Broadway
New York, New York 10036

Parts of the first section of this novel appeared in altered form as the short story "Children of the Night" in *The Ultimate Dracula* edited by Byron Preiss and published by Dell Books in October 1991.

ISBN: 0-440-21540-4

Printed in the United States of America

Published simultaneously in Canada

December 1994

10   9   8   7   6   5   4   3   2   1

For Jenny,
who understands how fiction can
break the silence

Acknowledgments

Thanks on this one go to Tony Gangi and Jeanne Cavelos for their enthusiasm, to Richard Curtis for supporting me even though I wanted to write a vampire novel, to Nina Kiriki Hoffman for all that pizza and the use of her VCR, to John Betancourt for forcing me to think of this idea in the first place, and to Dean Wesley Smith who looked beyond the short story and saw the novel hidden in each sentence.

"Suitcases?"

He stood at the door, holding the cut-glass knob, the rich iron taste of his evening meal still warm on his tongue. Laura put the baby in the wooden bassinet, her hands shaking. A slamming door down the hall let him know that their daughter had already hidden.

The dining room looked the same. The new oak table was set for company—as it always was—with a lovely linen tablecloth protecting the surface. The collectibles hid in the matching china hutch, and the hardwood floor was bare.

Except for the suitcases.

And Laura, huddling protectively over the bassinet.

It was only midnight. He had arrived home early—usually he barely escaped the dawn—because the atmosphere in the house had been tense. He hadn't slept much the past few days, listening for odd noises. He had known that Laura was planning something, but he didn't know what it was.

Twice he had caught her in the middle of the afternoon, clothes strewn about her feet, crying as she rocked the baby.

He pulled the front door closed behind him and kicked at the molded plastic Samsonite luggage he and Laura had bought for their honeymoon. The large travel case slid along the floor, scratching it, and banged into the leg of the oak table he had bought just last week. The delicate bone china rattled.

"Are we going somewhere?"

Laura shook her head. Her trembling hand brushed long, dirty hair away from her white face.

"The suitcases are full."

In two long steps, he was across the room. He grabbed her shoulders. They felt thin and bony under his palms. She wasn't eating well. She had to keep eating to keep him strong.

"What were you planning, Laura?"

"Nothing." Her voice came out in a whisper.

"Nothing?" He took her chin between his thumb and forefinger. "My son is wearing his traveling clothes. There are suitcases on the floor, and I wasn't due back until dawn. That doesn't seem like nothing to me, Laura."

She tried to pull her head away, but he tightened his grip. A little more effort and he could snap her jawbone. He liked the strength that was coming to him. He liked the power. He had thought she would too.

"We were going to go see my mother. Please—"

He let go of her head and she stumbled back.

"I would have let you know." Two bruised spots already appeared on her jaw.

"When? Next week? Next year? You were going to take my son, Laura." He brought his hand back and hit her across the mouth so hard she stumbled into the table. The wood cracked. She grabbed the tablecloth, trying to remain upright, but instead it and the bone china his father had brought from Germany slipped to the floor. Dishes clattered and broke, and the baby started crying.

He picked up a shard of china and tossed it at her. Then he took her collar and pulled her to her feet until her face was inches from his. "You are my wife, Laura. You go nowhere without my permission and you go nowhere without me. Is that clear?"

She nodded. The baby's wails grew louder.

"Good." He flung her away from him. She hit her head on the wood and slid to the floor as the cloth had done. As he crouched over her, he saw a small blonde head peek around the doorway.

"Go to bed," he said.

The sound of a door closing the second time meant that his orders had been followed. The baby's cries turned into deep bellows. Maybe he should have his daughter return and take care of her brother. Laura couldn't.

Laura never did take care of him properly.

Blood matted the hair on the back of Laura's head and stained the tablecloth. He sank his hands in it, feeling the warmth, the richness. It was time. She had betrayed him. He saw no trace of the woman he had once loved in the white, bruised face. He wished her eyes were open, so that she would know what he was going to do.

But he couldn't wait. The coppery scent teased him like a lover.

He bent over her and sank his teeth into her neck. They went in easily—how he loved cows—and he sucked, sucked, sucked until there was nothing left.

When he'd finished, he leaned back on his heels and rubbed the back of his hand over his mouth. The baby was still crying, but the sound didn't bother him as much as it had earlier.

He stood and walked over to the bassinet. His son had a round face and wide blue eyes. When the baby saw him, the crying stopped. The boy reached up. He put his hand on his son's cheek and stuck a blood-covered thumb in the baby's mouth, smiling as the boy sucked.

"You are mine, now," he said. "All mine."

PART ONE

Chapter One

The address Cammie had memorized placed the eradication in the new development behind West Towne Mall. She repeated the address to Whitney, then climbed in the back of the white minivan to pull on her gloves and prepare the equipment.

The van rumbled as Whitney turned the key in the ignition. His freckles stood out against his skin, his bright red hair reflecting the sunlight streaming in the windshield. He drove cautiously over the speed bumps in the Center's parking lot.

Cammie turned her back on the front seat. She hated watching the neighborhoods go by. That was why Whitney drove, even though he had more experience. Other teams usually put the partner with the least experience in the driver's seat. But early on, Cammie had learned that if she watched the roads she traveled every day, she would see nothing but threat in her off-hours. She rarely went out after dark as it was, and when she did, she always brought her emergency case.

Whitney didn't seem to mind this quirk or any of the others that Cammie displayed. He had a few of his own. Red foods made him ill. He rarely went into Italian restaurants and never ordered anything with marinara sauce or red wine. He preferred Middle Eastern cuisine, with its spicy brown and white sauces.

In the two years they had worked together, Cammie had never asked him about the roots of that prejudice, just as he had never asked about hers.

The windows in the back of the van were tinted so dark that it was impossible to see in or out. She flicked on the overhead light, grabbed the rubber band off her wrist, and scooped her hair into a ponytail. Then she pulled on her black gloves—the third pair she'd worn this month. She would have to put in an expense voucher for equipment, even though the Center hated that. The gloves were thick and heavy, made of black leather with a sheepskin interior, the best protection money could buy. She had barely been able to afford the last pair. She wouldn't get paid for another week, and the fifty dollars remaining in her checkbook had to last until then. Maybe if she was careful, this pair wouldn't get ruined.

The van bounced over potholes and swayed side to side as Whitney drove. Even though Cammie couldn't see out the windows, she knew where they were: the sharp curve on Gammon Road, heading the back way toward the mall.

Not much time left. She checked the pack, making sure there was a stake and mallet for her and another set for Whitney. The lock picks were inside, as well as the gun. Then she adjusted her necklace so the cross was outside her dark sweatshirt. She attached a vial of holy water to her belt and made sure the pouch of garlic was in her front pocket. Whitney always carried extra garlic. Like her, he didn't believe the religious symbols had much effect. The garlic seemed to work better.

Still, they carried the religious icons to cover their own asses. The Center's research had shown that a vampire, raised in a particular religion, would fear that religion's icons. According to his file, the subject of today's eradication had been raised Catholic. The vampire they had eradicated two weeks ago had been a Jew but apparently had stopped practicing long before his change. He had ripped the Star of David off Whitney's chest.

Cammie closed her eyes. She still dreamed about that eradication. The vampire had grabbed Whitney and pulled him so close that Cammie saw the flash of fangs against Whitney's neck. Fortunately, she had gotten there quickly enough to prevent the breaking of Whitney's skin.

"Ready?" Whitney's deep voice had a tremble she hadn't heard in a long time. He hadn't forgotten their last eradication either.

"As I'm going to be." Cammie brought the pack into the front seat, then sat down. She blinked in the bright sunlight, waiting for her eyes to adjust. Whitney had turned the van into the parking lot of a development of blue condos. Behind them, cars streamed along the Beltline. The whoosh added the comfort of civilization.

The condos had been built in mock-colonial style—with columned doorways and wide arched windows—and they had a look of understated elegance. Cammie sighed. She had placed her name on the list when the condos were first under construction, but when she found out the asking price, she quietly withdrew. Still, over six years later, she still felt a stab of envy for the people who lived there.

Until now.

"I thought there would be too much ambient light in these things," she said.

Whitney shook his head. "I had one here just after they were built. The middle condos are as dark as a tomb."

Cammie didn't laugh. Whitney had not intended the comment as a joke.

They pulled up in front of a middle condo, as Whitney had predicted. The numbers on the door were elegantly lettered in black script. The developers had added a number of touches like that, designed to make the residents feel that they lived in a house instead of a condominium complex.

Whitney shut off the motor and sat for a moment. His red curls framed his face like a halo and the mid-morning sunlight gave his green eyes a brightness they didn't normally have. Cammie rolled her shoulders to get the tension out of them. Mid-morning eradications were usually the safest, but there was still risk. Two months ago, another team had nearly died on an 11 A.M. job.

Cammie took his hand. It was cold and clammy. "I'll be there for you, partner," she said.

He nodded and squeezed her fingers. "I've been doing this too long."

She took a sharp intake of breath. Whitney had been her only partner. She couldn't do this with anyone else. "The last time just scared you."

He glanced at her. His freckles seemed darker than usual. His lower lip was chapped. He had been licking it—a nervous habit she wished he would break. "Every time scares me."

"Me too." She swallowed. Their attitude was wrong for an eradication. She made herself take a deep breath. "But we're tough, right?"

He grinned, obviously recognizing the tactic. He had used it on her numbers of times. "The most macho pair of eradicators I've ever met."

She nodded and handed him the pack. They were ready now. He got out and slung it over his shoulders. Cammie let herself out the other door. Its slam echoed through the entire neighborhood.

The air carried the scent of freshly mown grass. Cammie thought she saw a curtain move in an upstairs window on one of the side condos, but she wasn't sure. Even though a handful of cars dotted the street, the neighborhood had the deserted look left by nine-to-five professionals. Good. Cammie hated coming out of a job and explaining herself to the neighbors.

She adjusted her ponytail and tugged her gloves a final time. Whitney double-checked the address against the one he had written in his notebook, then trudged up the walk. Cammie followed.

Her mouth was dry. She had done nearly fifty eradications, counting the ones she had trained on, and still she felt nervous before entering a house. Whitney took the step up to the stoop and placed duct tape over the bell. No need to have some door-to-door salesman wake up their vampire. Cammie hated condos. They couldn't snip the phone lines: too many times a team would snip the line to the wrong apartment.

Whitney tried the knob, but it didn't turn. The door was locked.

Cammie mounted the step and unzipped the pack, pulling out the picks. Whitney took them from her. He selected the tools with an accuracy and precision she had yet to master. He slid the picks into the lock, jiggled them around for a moment, then stepped back as the door slid open.

The smell hit her first: rotting flesh, ancient blood. Cammie swallowed back nausea and followed Whitney inside, closing the door behind her.

The living room was not completely dark. A thin, filtered gray light from the arched window etched everything in outline. A matching couch and love seat faced an oversized television. A bookshelf stood in the back corner. Cammie walked over to the end table and took the black princess phone off the hook.

They followed the smell into the hall. The darkness grew, hiding the details of the photographs lining the walls. A thin, reedy sound that took Cammie a moment to identify as music bled in from another condo. She was suddenly glad she hadn't bought one, if the walls were this thin. She took the mallet, stake, and flashlight out of the pack and handed them to Whitney, then pulled out the second set for herself. Her heart was pounding.

She hated this moment, walking into the darkness. She was always afraid the vampire would wake up and attack her.

Whitney turned on the flashlight. It made a round hole in the gloom. The carpet was a beige weave and the walls were paneled, all designed to make the room darker. Cammie doubted that the paneling was in the original specifications.

A bathroom door stood open. Ahead, one more door was open, and two were closed, including the one at the end of the hall. The reedy music continued, adding an odd counterpoint to the brush of their footsteps.

Near the door to their right, the smell became overpowering. The rancid thickness of decay made Cammie wish she had brought a handkerchief to cover her nose and mouth. The nausea returned and she had to grip the wall for a moment, to keep dizziness at bay.

"You okay?" Whitney whispered.

Cammie swallowed and nodded. "Never better."

She would have to report to Eliason after this job. The nausea was growing worse. At the last job, she had been trying to prevent herself from getting sick when the vampire attacked Whitney.

Whitney grabbed the doorknob, turned it, and shoved the door open. Cammie turned on her flashlight and set it on the floor, adding enough illumination so that they could see, but not enough to wake the vampire.

The room was large, with its own bathroom off to the side. The closet door was open, and clothes were strewn all over the floor. The dresser had several open drawers and different kinds of jewelry winked on top. The mirror had been broken.

A California king-sized waterbed dominated the center of the room. It had no bedclothes. For a moment, Cammie thought it was a decoy until she realized that the mattress and plywood base were gone. The bottom had been cut out of the center of the bed. Beneath, where the drawers should have been, lay a naked man covered in a handmade quilt.

Whitney trained his flashlight on the man, careful to avoid his eyes. The light accented the whiteness of his skin. His lips were stained a dark red. One hand lay on top of the covers, his nails untrimmed and dirty.

Cammie clutched her mallet and stake. She had a better reach from her position. She took a deep breath, the smell not bothering her now. She leaned over, positioned the stake above the heart, and pounded with all her strength.

The stake pierced the flesh. The vampire roared up, fetid breath covering her, hand grasping for hers. Cammie pounded again, feeling the stake go in deeper. The vampire screamed, a harsh long male sound. Blood spurted on her, on the bed, on the paneled walls. Still she held her place, letting the ringing sound of the mallet serve as a counterpoint to the vampire's cries.

His nails raked her skin, and blood dripped off her face. The blood was fresh; he had only been asleep a few hours. He flailed, his legs and arms smashing against the wooden walls.

Cammie hit with the mallet one final time. The vampire arched, and fell still.

Whitney came up beside her. The body began to twitch. Then the skin started flaking. The smell of decay sweetened, then faded as the body fell apart. Cammie held the stake in place until the vampire was nothing more than bones.

Behind them, a light went on. Cammie jumped and turned. Light from the hallway spilled into the room, adding a false brightness. A little girl stood in the doorway. She had blonde curls and wide blue eyes. She glanced at Cammie, then took a step into the room.

"Daddy?"

Cammie looked around the room. She saw no sign of another human being. Whitney bit his lower lip. The little girl crept across the carpet, her tiny tennis shoes leaving no mark on the weave. She knelt in front of the bed, put her forehead against the wood and whispered, "Daddy." The airy, pain-filled sound was more plaintive than a wail.

The women's bathroom in Eliason's office had a large mirror that ran the length of the vanity. Above each wash station were small instructions taped to the glass. Every time Cammie came into this room, she found herself staring at the instructions for taking a urine sample, something she had never done in this office. (*1. Wash your hands thoroughly . . .*)

She was hiding in here, in the bright yellow bathroom, filled with fluorescent light and instructions for simple things, like urinating. She had never hidden before. Usually she had too much energy—so much that Whitney often had to tell her to sit still on the drive back to the Center. This time, she felt as if someone had punched her in the stomach. A heavy, cottony feeling of shock enveloped her—and that feeling had started when she first saw the little girl.

Cammie peered into the mirror. Three long scratches ran down her right cheek, looking like warpaint from a bad Western. Heather, Eliason's nurse, had taken samples from the scratches when Cammie arrived and then had dotted the wounds with hydrogen peroxide. It had stung and foamed—visible proof that the medication was fighting an infection.

Just as she was.

She looked tired. Deep circles ran under her gray eyes. Eliason had once told her that her eyes were her best feature—wide and innocent, changing color with her mood or her clothing. She never saw the color change, only the same dirty gray that she had seen each morning in the mirror.

Blood had stained her brown hair black. She pulled out her ponytail and finger-combed her hair. Some of the blood flaked away. She turned on the water in the sink and ran matted strands under it, watching the blood stain the yellow sink. She forgot how much she had needed a comb after an eradication.

Of course, she had never planned to come directly to Eliason's office. But Whitney had insisted. They had to make sure the little girl was okay.

A child. Whatever was that vampire doing with a child?

Cammie ran a paper towel over her face, then tossed it in the trash. The blood didn't show up on her black sweatshirt, but two long brown streaks ran across the front of her jeans. No wonder the child had refused to get close to her. Whitney had grabbed the girl's stuffed dog and placed them both in the back of the van. The child had seemed more comfortable in the darkness.

Cammie had tried to talk to Whitney, but he had put his finger to his lips. Whatever she had to say, he didn't want said in front of the child.

They brought the child to Dr. Brett Eliason. Eliason specialized in vampire cases and was on call for the Center. He also ran a general practice near Westgate, only a few miles from where they had been. Eliason had managed to open a large office in a building next to the Center. He was the only doctor, but he maintained a large support staff—three nurses, two receptionists, and his own lab technician. The lab tech was invaluable for her knowledge of rare blood diseases. Cammie had known Dr. Eliason since she started working for the Westrina Center, and in that time, his practice had grown from Center-related clients to others from the Westgate area.

She leaned into the mirror and ran a finger over the

shadows under her eyes. She could actually feel the sunken skin. The effect of not enough sleep.

Too many dreams of vampires.

This little girl wouldn't help.

Cammie sighed and pulled back the heavy bathroom door. She paused in the hallway, as she always did, disoriented. The design of the hall played some kind of spatial trick on her. She could find her way into the bathroom easily enough, but finding her way back to the waiting room was always difficult. She glanced left at the double doors and the open L-shaped hallway, then decided to turn right, not because it looked like the correct direction, but because it didn't.

She hated it when Eliason found her walking through his halls, searching for the reception area. After finding her on four separate occasions, he had given her a spatial relations test—psychology was his minor and his hobby—and she had flunked. He said she was the first bright person he had ever met who did not think in three dimensions.

Halfway down the hall, past the oversized scale and the blood lab, she saw a sign pointing to reception. An odd thread of relief went through her. Eliason wouldn't catch her this time.

A new receptionist sat behind the desk. She was young, maybe not even out of college. She wore a headset and spoke into it as she typed onto a computer keyboard. Behind her, the file room stood open, with rows and rows of file folders visible. Fortunately, they had arrived on a light day—Eliason only had two other patients in the office, and Heather had already taken them to the back.

The narrow hallway opened into the waiting room. It was cheerfully decorated in the warmest shade of blue she had ever seen. Modular furniture formed groupings throughout, some centered around a table covered in books, another around a box of toys, and a third around an oversized television with the sound on low. Cammie preferred the high-backed chairs in front of the mock fireplace. They gave her comfort.

Whitney sat on a modular unit, feet stretched out and crossed in front of him. His jeans were blood-spattered too, and the tips of his curls were wet. He looked older, somehow. There were worry lines around his mouth that Cammie had never seen before.

He was reading an ancient, battered copy of *Time* with a picture of the fallen Berlin Wall on the cover. He set the magazine on his lap when he saw her. "You okay now?"

No, she wasn't. She felt oddly light-headed and a strange fear had formed in her stomach. "How come they didn't tell us there was a kid?"

Whitney's expression hardened for a moment. "They probably didn't know. The report could have come from anywhere. Some woman he picked up or a grocery store clerk."

"But someone had to investigate. Someone had to know."

"Cammie, they knew we would take care of it. Kids aren't that unusual, you know."

Cammie sat on the edge of the unit next to Whitney. She didn't lean back. "Not unusual? I have done forty-eight eradications and I've never encountered a child before."

"They might have been in school. The Center tries to plan these things when no one else is home. This little girl is too young for school."

She was too young to see that, too. No child should have to witness that kind of blood-letting. Cammie put a hand to her forehead. A headache built behind her eyes.

"Cam, look. We go in, do our job, and leave. How many times have you stayed to investigate the house?"

"That's not part of my job."

"No," Whitney said. "It's not. So how do you know how many children you've encountered?"

The bloodstains were worse around his ankles and on the hem of his jeans. She wanted to lean against his shoulder, but didn't. "How many children did you see before you started working with me?"

"Three." His voice sounded odd, strangled. She looked up. His tongue was playing with his lower lip. He always did that when the memories got too bad for him.

Her headache had grown worse. "There can't be children," Cammie said. "Vampires are dead. Are you telling me they kidnap kids and keep them for some strange reason?"

"Jesus." Whitney closed his eyes. Cammie recognized the expression on his face. She had seen it once before—when a neighbor had stopped them on the street before an eradication. He knew something. Something he didn't want to tell her. He ran a hand over his face and then looked at her. "You need to talk to Anita, Cam," he said.

"Why don't you tell me? You're my partner. We're best friends."

He half smiled. The look didn't reach his eyes. "I can't."

"Why not?"

He rolled the magazine into a club, then unrolled it, flattening it against his legs. "Because," he said slowly, "I told Alyse."

Alyse. His mysterious first partner. The one he would never talk about. When Cammie would ask about her, Whitney would always reply, *She decided to leave for the same reasons most eradicators leave.*

Only Whitney had never left. He had stayed at the Center longer than any other eradicator. Some had gone into administration, but Whitney remained on the streets, fighting with his fists and his stakes for over five years.

The swinging door that led to the examining rooms opened, and Eliason came out, holding the little girl by the hand. He looked tall by comparison, his chocolate-colored skin looking black against the girl's. His lab coat was open, revealing a denim workshirt and well-tailored jeans. He looked, as always, as if he had just dressed for the day.

The little girl clutched her stuffed dog to her left side, its fabric head crammed against her heart. Eliason crouched, spoke softly to her, wiped a strand of hair from her forehead, and then smiled. He had the gentleness that Cammie always thought doctors should have. He had asked her out numerous times, but she had refused; she didn't want to learn that his gentleness was false, a pretense for patients and nothing more.

He stood, left the girl by the swinging doors, and came over to Cammie. "She's clean," he said. "Not a mark on her. Her blood is her own, and it's infection-free. She's well fed, well nourished, well cared for. She's also in shock. She might be one of the lucky ones. She hasn't said much, so maybe she'll forget all this. But I think you need to take her to the Center right away. They should be able to get her settled somewhere before the pain really starts. Those all her possessions?"

"She had a room full of stuff," Whitney said.

"Get that and bring it," Eliason said. He didn't look at Whitney. He was watching Cammie. "She needs as much of her home as you can salvage."

"Home?" Cammie choked the word out. A place that smelled of rotting blood, and filled with the presence of a man no longer human. Eliason was calling that home?

He put his palm against Cammie's face. She resisted the urge to lean into him, to let him comfort her as he had comforted the little girl. "Home, Camila," he said. "It's all she ever knew."

Whitney knelt and extended his hands. He looked like a big kid himself. Cammie had never suspected such empathy from her partner. "Come on, hon," he said. "I'll take you someplace safe."

"Her name is Janie." Eliason's thumb traced Cammie's

cheekbone. His dark gaze remained on her. He was one of the handsomest men she had ever seen, with high flat cheekbones that suggested some Native American blood, a broad nose above a sensitive mouth.

"Janie," Whitney said, hand still outstretched. "Come with me."

Janie wrapped both arms around her dog, rested her chin on the animal's head, and shuffled forward. She brushed near Eliason, but when she saw Cammie, she scooted away.

"It's okay," Whitney said.

Janie continued her walk, occasionally throwing Cammie a frightened glance. When she reached Whitney, she buried her face in his sleeve.

"I guess you've been elected to pick up her things," Whitney said. "I'll meet you back at the office."

Cammie nodded. She watched Whitney take Janie and lead her outside. Cammie watched through the window as the two of them went to the van. Now that Cammie was no longer riding with them, Janie chose to sit in front.

"First kid?" Eliason asked.

Cammie returned her attention to him. The slight callus on his thumb felt good against her soft skin. He smelled faintly of Ivory soap. "How did you know?" she asked.

"Because eradications usually don't shake you. They usually give you a strange kind of joy."

Joy. She would never use that word for the bouncy nervous energy she felt after she performed an eradication. Joy. She rejected the word. Eradication was state-sanctioned killing. She should not find joy in that, even if it was her job.

She didn't want to think about that. "How come you and Whitney weren't surprised by that girl and I was?"

Eliason ran his thumb across her lips, then let his hand down. "That's something you have to ask yourself, Cammie."

"No one said anything about children. In all those months of training, no one said one word."

"They didn't have to," he said. "You should have already known."

Chapter Two

The ferry let him off at Pier 52, a huge empty building that had the chill of a bus terminal. He walked down the ramp, along with families with children scampering in front of him, teenagers in prom clothes going into the city, and studious women carrying paperbacks and wearing the rubber-soled shoes of people who spent the evening on their feet.

The cold mist off Elliot Bay felt good. Lately sunshine made him uncomfortable. An itching started under his skin as though a thousand tiny ants were crawling through his veins. These days, his body felt as if it belonged to someone else. His sense of smell had grown stronger, and he could often scent the sickly, sweet odor of illness before he saw someone coughing around a corner. The new awareness made him uncomfortable, made him act in ways he wasn't sure he liked.

Like Candyce. He rubbed a hand over his face, trying to block the memory. Candyce. The reason he had come up here.

The ramp sloped to an iron railing that led to wide metal steps. Most of the ferry's passengers went inside to avoid the drizzle. He stayed out and took the stairs to street level.

The road was wider than he expected. Cabs parked

in a designated area, waiting for passengers. Ben doubted they would get many on a Saturday. He pulled the piece of paper out of his pocket, stared at the address, and debated. Then he decided that he wanted to walk.

He had spent the last two days exploring Seattle, always avoiding the downtown. The night before he had slept in a cheap roadside motel on Bainbridge Island, squirming at the light that leaked through the too thin curtains. The island was too suburban, too yupped for him. The neat row houses, the expensive cars in the driveway, the boats in the bay. He hadn't expected the Seattle area to be so clean. Even the university section, with its funky coffee shops and clothing stores, had an air of wholesomeness.

It made him uncomfortable, and he found that odd. Eugene, the city he had grown up in, was cleaner, smaller, and even less diverse. But he knew the city's darker regions. He knew the smoky underground bars, and the places along the river where people bought drugs. He knew how to find a hooker, and he knew how to find someone who had disappeared.

Like Steve. Steve had gone to Portland with men that Ben wouldn't associate with. Only now he seemed to have no choice. Less than a week ago, he had been a college graduate, at the top of his class, looking for work. Now he was wandering the streets of Seattle in search of a group of people he would have snubbed a few days before.

You got it, man. You got it real bad, Steve had said that last night. Ben had found him in a bar in Portland—the Keg. At least, that had been its name once. Someone had removed the sign, but the letters remained on the outside of the building in paint splotches brighter than the rest of the paint job. The interior was dark, cigarette smoke so thick it shaded the lights.

People sat at tables, staring into the Pit, where Steve

and his friends hung out. The Pit smelled of sex and cum and blood.

He had an erection the entire time he spoke to Steve—and Steve had noticed. He had smiled. *I know some sweet little bitch who can ease you.*

Ben had pulled away. Candyce was still too near. Her cry of pain and his powerful, shattering orgasm still echoed in his head. *I'm going to Seattle. I can't stay here.*

Steve had smiled. Ben couldn't see his eyes in the darkness. *Sure you can,* Steve had said. Ben didn't remember the Steve he used to know having such self-assurance. Ben had searched him out here because they had had similar pasts, similar outlooks. But sometime after Steve's disappearance, the outlook had changed. He didn't know Steve at all anymore. *Stay here. Free food. Great sex. All you got to do is sit in the Pit six nights out of seven. Not a bad life.*

Ben glanced around. Most people had a glazed look. In the corner, near the empty fireplace, a woman had pulled up her skirt and was sitting on a man's lap. He could hear her moans from across the room. The sexual excitement it aroused in him made him uneasy. He tugged on his jeans and adjusted his position on the chair. He couldn't stay here six nights out of seven. He had to go somewhere, do something. He hadn't spent all those years in school to throw it away because his hormones had run wild.

Steve seemed to catch the distaste Ben was feeling. *Running away won't change anything.*

I'm not running, Ben had said. *God, Steve. I got a future ahead of me. I can't spend the next year in a bar, letting someone else take care of me.*

Steve's smile had grown. *Yeah, right.* He bent over a bar napkin, took a pen out of his pocket and scrawled something down. *Look, you get up there and you feel lost, I got some friends who can help you. Show 'em this note. They'll let you join 'em. They're ambitious, just like you are. You'll fit right in.*

Ben had pocketed the note, thinking he would never use it. But he held it now, wondering how Steve's friends could help him. He hated being bored, and lost, and aimless. He had a B.A. from the University of Oregon in pre-law, with grades high enough to get him into any law school in the country, but the idea of continuing his education—walking across campuses in the sunlight—made him cringe. Maybe he could find a job as a waiter. Something he could do at night until his sensitivity to sunlight eased.

He would have to find an apartment, but he hadn't found a place in Seattle that welcomed him yet. He couldn't go back home and face his parents. Not after Candyce.

The steps finally brought him to that dark, wide road. Cars zoomed past him. A handful of other ferry riders stood at the crosswalk, staring down the curve in the road as if they could see where the cars stopped.

Candyce would have told someone by now. She would have to explain the bruises. He took a deep breath and shook his head. Even he couldn't explain the bruises.

He loved her. A man didn't treat the woman he loved that way.

Finally the stream eased enough that he could dodge across, passing the lonesome cabs, and jumping over streetcar tracks, until he was on a sidewalk that sloped up. Toward life.

A gray government building stood to his right, with a hotel to his left. As he walked, a tall, thin man flanked him. Ben resisted the urge to check his wallet.

"Hey!" the man called. "You just get off the ferry?"

Ben hurried to the cross street. Another block up, he could see people ambling down a tree-lined street.

"Hey!" the man called. "I'm talking to you."

Even from his position ahead of the man, Ben could smell the alcohol. Cheap stuff, overlaying the odor of the man's unwashed clothing and skin.

"Did you just get off the ferry?"

The crawling feeling had returned, even though the sunlight wasn't there. If he closed his eyes, he could see Candyce's shocked face, taste the warmth of her just before the orgasm pulsed through him.

"What's it to you?" Ben asked, more to banish the image than to get rid of the man.

"I just got off the ferry too. Somebody took my wallet."

That made Ben stop. He did check his back pocket and felt the familiar lump of the wallet there. The man hurried to catch up to him.

"I wouldn'ta bothered you if I knew what else to do."

"Report it to the police," Ben said.

The man's eyes were bloodshot. He had two days growth of beard, and most of it was coming in gray. "Look. I ain't got nothing. No ID, no cash. Can you give me some change just so I can make a phone call."

"The operator will let you call the police for free," Ben said, and walked away.

"Hey!" The man put his hand on Ben's arm. Ben pushed him against the gray wall of the government building, holding the man a few feet off the ground.

"Look, I didn't mean nothing." The man was squirming, his arms and legs flailing. Ben held him in place. "Look, you don't have to give me nothing. I just wanted to buy a drink, you know? What's wrong with that? Wanting a drink?"

The man started to cry. Ben dropped him. The man landed in a heap at Ben's feet. Ben had held him and it had taken no strength at all. His mouth was dry. Another change. He had never been that strong before.

He opened his wallet and pulled out a five, tossing it on the man. "Here," Ben said. "You might want to buy a cup of soup with that too."

The man's dirty hand slid out under his pea coat and snatched the money. "Thanks," he said, not looking up. "I'll get that soup. I will."

Ben turned around and walked away. The crawling feeling had gotten so bad that he was shaking. He wanted to go back to the wino, grab him, twist his neck to one side as he had done with Candyce, and suck . . .

God, what was wrong with him? He stopped on the corner of the tree-lined boulevard and leaned against an iron bench. Maybe he needed food. It had been four days since he had eaten anything, and even water had begun to taste bad.

He had to eat. But he didn't want to. Nothing had tasted good since he had been with Candyce a week ago. He had spent the last few days telling himself that his lack of appetite was an emotional response, but what if it wasn't? What if something else was going on?

He walked to the bookstore he remembered from an earlier visit, made years ago, with his parents. In the basement, they had a cafe. He went inside, followed the signs to the stairs, and walked down.

The book-lined walls soothed him. The crawly feeling had diminished. In the cafe, students read books on oak tables. Patrons sat with a pile of books around them, browsing through each as if they had discovered a feast. Some tables had two people, leaning forward in intense conversation. It reminded him of movies he had seen about Paris in the fifties. A great intellectual gathering place. A place where revolution was being born.

He grabbed a tray and got in line. The list of sandwiches sounded good in theory, but when he actually thought of putting one in his mouth, his stomach turned. He toyed with getting the chili, but stopped when he saw someone else take the borscht. His mouth watered. He had never liked beet soup before, but it looked good now. He ordered some, along with some bread and a glass of red wine.

He took a seat beneath a large wooden beam. The soup didn't smell as good as it looked. He sipped the wine. Finally, something that eased him. He gulped the rest down, not caring what it did to him. His stomach rumbled for the first time in days.

Then he picked up his spoon and tasted the soup. It tasted as if it had spoiled. He grabbed his napkin and spit the mouthful into it. The young man who had ordered the soup before him was shoveling it into his mouth one table over. Ben could smell him, the fresh clean tang of his after-shave mingling with the salty musk of his skin. Beneath it, he could hear the rustle of the blood moving through the man's veins—

Ben stood so fast that he nearly knocked the table over. The borscht splashed out of the bowl and spilled onto the tray. The redness intrigued him. He almost dipped his finger in it before he remembered how it tasted.

Remember, Steve had said as Ben was leaving. *I have a nice little cow. She's bleeding. You like them when they're bleeding, don't you?*

Ben swung past the tables, past the perfumes and the tang of good honest sweat. He ran up the stairs and out the front door, not stopping until he had taken a breath of fresh air.

Steve had been trying to tell him something all that night. *You're different now, Ben. Running away won't help you. It won't change who you are.*

His stomach still rumbled, but real food tasted no good. He patted the address in his pocket. Time to stop running. Steve's friends would help him. Steve had made that clear.

Ben would walk. He would avoid people he saw on the street, and he wouldn't get close to a cab driver. He didn't want to smell the freshness of their skin or hear the whisper of blood flowing through their veins.

It would bring the crawly feeling back.

Or it would make him crazy.

Chapter Three

i

Cammie had never returned to the site of an eradication before. She had been warned in training that she might have to return to a site, but she had never experienced it. It took the entire bus ride from Eliason's office to the Center, where she had parked her car, to remember the correct procedures.

As she drove down University, her hands shook. She had shifted into the wrong gear twice at separate stoplights, and the car had lurched forward. The Mazda was ten years old and not tolerant of this kind of mistreatment. It had been belching blue smoke since she turned on Gammon Road.

This time, she had to look at the houses as they passed. She had lived in Madison all her life; she could remember when this road was nothing but a few houses pushed back on fertile fields. During the late seventies and eighties developers had bought the farmland and built shopping centers, apartments, and condominium developments. The area now had a cheap, ready-made feel that looked as if the next tornado would blow it all over.

Beneath the buildings, she could still see those fields, remembered driving by on snowy mornings, seeing the brown dirt etched in ice.

She hadn't realized how many blue mock-colonial condos existed in this neighborhood until she had to search for one. It was as if the developers thought the buyers would notice that other condos with the same design existed a few blocks away. She was no longer certain that the condos she had admired when they were being built were the same ones she had performed the eradication in.

She hoped they weren't.

She turned on the side street and into the development's parking lot. The sun was still high—it was only two in the afternoon—and none of the nine-to-fivers had arrived home yet. Good. She didn't want to see anyone or answer questions on her own.

Cammie parked in the same spot they had used earlier. She sat for a moment, taking deep breaths, trying to collect herself. Because she and Whitney hadn't gone back to the Center and made an official report, the secondary team hadn't arrived yet. The vampire's body was still inside.

She wiped her palms on her jeans, then she opened the door and got out. The scent of mown grass had faded, leaving only the faint odor of lilacs. Someday she would like to have lilacs near her house.

They had left the front door slightly ajar. Careless of them. They had been so preoccupied with the little girl. With Janie. Cammie was glad the secondary team hadn't shown. A note about the open door would have made it onto Anita's desk.

With her right hand, Cammie pushed the door open and waited for the rotted flesh smell to assault her. The nausea rose at the thought. This time, as she went in, she flicked on the interior light.

A lamp went on beside the couch. A doll rested on one of the cushions and a child-sized blanket was crumpled on the center cushion. An empty wine glass sat on the end table beside the love seat, next to a large remote. The oversized television dominated the room, and

on top of it were Disney movies: *Beauty and the Beast,*
The Little Mermaid, Cinderella, Dumbo, and *Fantasia.*
Hardcover books filled the bookshelf, except for the
bottom two rows which had thin, battered—no, well
loved—children's books. The living room opened into a
formal dining room complete with chandelier. A glass-
enclosed china hutch revealed dusty dishes and clean
crystal goblets. An expensive stereo system, complete
with laser disk player, and twelve-disk CD changer covered the far wall.

Where had he gotten this kind of money? Vampires
set for this kind of eradication no longer had real-world
jobs. They had no contact with society at all. They
wouldn't be missed. Vampires with jobs faced a different eradication program, one employers were required
by law to cooperate with.

Cammie took a large garbage bag out of the kitchen
pantry and put the doll and blanket inside. The kitchen
was spotless. The stove looked like it had never been
used. A child-sized bowl sat next to the sink, a bit of
milk in the bottom. Cammie opened the dishwasher.
Cold water dripped down the sides. More child-sized
dishes filled its interior, along with cheaper wineglasses.
He must have turned it on before he went to sleep.

She slammed the door with a metallic bang. The
Center had dishes. She had come for child things.
Clothes and toys and books.

With a sigh, she went back into the living room. The
garbage bag wouldn't do. She would have to make a
number of trips. She stacked the books and videos near
the door, then took a deep breath and faced the hall.

The light was still on. Some blood stained the wall at
knee level. As she got closer, she saw that the print was
child-sized. The little girl had put her hands in the vampire's stolen blood.

The nausea returned and with it a deep ache that ran
from Cammie's heart across her chest. For a moment,
she had trouble drawing a breath. Children didn't be-

long with vampires. Didn't anyone see that? Why were Eliason and Whitney acting like it was normal?

She gripped the bag and headed to the only room with light coming in under the doorway. The door was made of a cheap wood and the latch didn't work properly. She pushed it open and stepped back in surprise.

The shades were up, revealing a lilac bush and a shrub-filled backyard. Sunlight flooded across a pink canopied bed. Stuffed animals lined the floors and walls. A record player sat in the middle of the floor, the turntable still revolving. No wonder she hadn't heard them come. She had been playing records. The thin reedy sound Cammie had thought came from the neighbors. If she had known about children, she would have looked.

She would have prevented the little girl from witnessing her father's death.

The rancid, bloody smell filled her nostrils. She had to have fresh air. She crossed the room in two strides and yanked the window open.

Cool spring air caressed her face. She had to stick her upper torso out before the blood odor faded. Lilacs and fresh green grass replaced it. Spring. How she loved it. Springtime meant lots of light. It meant the ability to stay outside until late. It meant freedom.

She blinked. She was an adult. She had the freedom to do anything she wanted.

When she wasn't working. And she had a job to finish. The quicker she packed the little girl's things, the better.

Cammie closed the window, grabbed a suitcase out of the closet and stuffed it with ruffly little-girl dresses, sweatshirts, and blue jeans. She poured the contents of the underwear and sock drawers on top, then added two winter coats for warmth. Janie had been well tended, physically.

She took the suitcase and an armload of stuffed animals to the front door and set them beside her earlier pile. If everything had not been covered in that rancid odor, if she hadn't seen the vampire's room first, she would have thought Janie well loved. She had everything a little girl could want. Pretty dresses, a nice room, toys.

Everything but parents.

A shudder ran down Cammie's back. She went back into the room, picked up the toy box, and carried it out. Then she packed the remaining toys in the garbage bag. When she came to the record player, she stopped.

The record player was an old model, the cheap kind that parents gave children thirty years ago. The record was a thick thirty-three with an orange label. In black ink printed in a half moon around the hole were the words *The Wizard of Oz.* Cammie put the needle on the edge of the record.

The hiss-hiss before the music started had a familiarity that she had almost forgotten. She only listened to CDs now. The record player had a small soundbox and it took her a moment to realize that the voices were supposed to sound that high and reedy. Munchkins. Celebrating the death of the witch.

She yanked the needle off without scratching the record. A lump had formed in her throat. Why wasn't Janie celebrating? That man had been the bad witch. That vampire. She should have hated him.

Cammie hit the off switch, then unplugged the player. She took the record off and placed it in its jacket. Then she stacked the records on top of the player, and stopped.

Janie wouldn't want that toy. It would remind her of her father's death. Each time she put an album on the turntable and heard the scritch-scratch of a needle, she would see her father thrash as Cammie drove a stake in his heart.

Cammie doubled over and wrapped her arms around her head, as if the action would squeeze the thoughts out. She hadn't meant to kill a child's father. She hadn't meant to kill a person at all. She was killing an animal, something that preyed on human beings and lived off the blood like a wild thing. She hadn't known. . . .

Slowly, ever so slowly, she stood up. The room looked bare except for the pink bed and the record player sitting on the carpet. What kind of terrors had happened in this place? How many sleepless nights did that little girl have, waiting for a man who reeked of blood to come through that door and—

Cammie couldn't finish the thought. Her shoulders were so tense that even moving her arms made pains shoot into her neck. She glanced over to make sure she had closed the window. She had. Now all she had to do was carry the toys to the car.

Just to be safe, as she entered the hall, she opened the remaining door. Two twin beds with satin comforters were separated by an end table. The window had blackout curtains. The room was dusty and unused. Good. No more children in hiding.

She hurried down the hall, past the vampire's room. The stench seemed to have grown. She had to get back to the Center. The second team needed to get here before the neighbors. They wouldn't tolerate the smell.

Cammie opened the front door. The stoop shaded the sunlight. She picked up the suitcase and the garbage bag and walked to her car.

The air was cool and refreshing. Some of the tension leaked out of her back. Maybe once the child was over the shock, she would feel better about leaving. Cammie certainly did.

She opened the back door of the Mazda, placed the suitcase on the upholstered seat, and the garbage bag on the floor. Only two more trips.

Only two more trips and she would be free of this place.

When Cammie arrived at the Westrina Center, the parking lot was full. Whitney had parked the van near the children's entrance. The building was long and flat. Built in the late sixties out of brick, additions branched off it like legs on a spider. Cammie wove through the circular driveway and parked beside the loading bay.

She walked up the ramp and knocked on the metal door.

"Yeah?" a man yelled from inside.

"Cammie," she said. "I got stuff for a kid Whitney brought in. I'm leaving in half an hour. Think you can have it unloaded by then?"

She didn't wait for an answer. Chances were when she returned, she would have to do the unloading herself. The dock crew spent most of their time sitting in the break room drinking coffee and playing cards. They did some of the janitorial work and most of the heavy lifting, usually vampiric remains. Anita was reluctant to push them hard because she had trouble hiring people to fill the position.

Cammie took the steps off the bay and walked to the concrete sidewalk leading to the front. Green shoots of grass had sprouted here, but most of the trees still had buds. The only lilac bush stood in the garden out back, and probably hadn't bloomed yet. Odd how spring made its way slowly across the city.

Large windows covered most of this wall. Many had thin blinds. Most of the rooms in this wing were offices. Administration had grown as the Center had grown.

The Westrina Center had been the first to pioneer eradication as a means of dealing with vampires. The Center's lobbying group had passed several bills in the Wisconsin legislature defining states of undead, and establishing legal guidelines for eradication. So far, none of the laws had been tested in court. The American Civil Liberties Union, which had taken on all kinds of odd clients in the past, had been strangely silent on these laws. The Center expected the lobbying and legal wings to grow over the next few years, as more and more states adopted the same legislation.

Cammie rounded the last bend in the sidewalk and found herself in the front of the building. It had a fifties feel, even though she knew it had been built ten years later. The pale brick and the wide glass double doors were taken from the remodeling plans from the first Westrina Center, located just off-campus, in a building long since abandoned.

When she had first been hired, she had been proud to work with the Westrina Center. It was the first organization of its kind in the world. Europe had had vampire troubles throughout most of its history and had dealt with them primarily through war—which, until the twentieth century, drove the vampires back underground. America didn't have a vampire problem at all until World War I veterans brought the infection back with them. Still, the infestation wasn't identified until a Milwaukee lab, specializing in blood diseases, traced the strange anemia veterans of W.W.I and W.W.II suffered to vampiric records. Those identified were treated, usually ineffectively, and asked to remain near the hospital. Slowly the disease spread across the Midwest, largely going undetected because a vampire in its first thirty years of existence rarely showed any overt physical signs of vampirism.

Vampirism got labeled the hidden disease. Its practitioners functioned well enough in society; its victims rarely died of blood loss. Sometimes they were beaten to death. More often they remained alive as codependents who helped the vampire survive by covering for it during the day and feeding it at night.

Codependents. Children. Cammie shuddered, and paused, her hand on the cool glass door handle. She had to have learned about this in class. Odd that she didn't remember it.

She didn't remember it at all.

But she knew about the Westrina Center. It had opened its doors in the fifties in the heart of vampire country, organizing groups, using abstinence and mutual support to break what it saw as an addiction. That method had failed miserably in the early sixties, and the Center had gone on to develop a more radical treatment.

She pulled open the door. The rubber mat covering the tile squished under her shoes. Muddy footprints covered the mat. The lawn maintenance people had been here. Spring at last.

A large, glassed-in formica counter led her to the tiny oak desk at the end. Behind the enclosure, data entry workers and secretaries pounded numbers in computers and answered phones. A door led to more secretarial space beyond.

DeeDee, Cammie's favorite receptionist and her closest female friend, was bent over the desk, stamping "closed" on a series of file folders. She held the stamp awkwardly between her thumb and forefingers, careful not to press a red nail against the folders themselves. Her phone bank sat to one side, five lines blinking, and two new plants made the desk seem even smaller.

"Hey, DeeDee," Cammie said. "Anita in?"

DeeDee looked up and grinned. Her lipstick and blush matched her nail polish, and her hair—blonde—this week poofed out in a new perm. "Hey, Cam. Crash Test Dummies tonight at the Club de Wash."

"I'm broke. But thanks." Cammie leaned over the desk. "Say, where's Anita? I got to talk to her."

"She's in new arrivals. But she doesn't want to be bothered." DeeDee set the stamp down. A frown made a dainty crease between her bleached eyebrows. "You okay?"

Cammie shook her head. She glanced past the glass

to see if anyone was watching. "Have you ever worked in the children's wing?"

"Nope. Don't want to either. Those kids are psychotic. Last week some brat tried to torch his room."

"Jesus."

"Yeah." DeeDee looked over her shoulder too, then focused on Cammie. "Odd thing is, we would never have heard about it if the cops hadn't come to the wrong entrance. We get rumors a lot, but that's about it. We don't even get to see the kids' files."

"Why not?"

"Confidentiality, Anita says. I say it's more. We deal with confidential stuff all the time—eradication folders, surveillance, setup. I mean, what's so different about the kids?"

Cammie tapped a blunt nail against the closed stamp on the nearest file. "They're alive."

DeeDee shrugged. "Maybe. Feels like more, you know? Or maybe the job is finally getting to me. I look at my neighbors sometimes when I go home and wonder which one is going to get it next."

Cammie's mouth went dry. She had the same thoughts sometimes. That was why most of her social activities were with the Center staff. They, at least, were safe. "Do you know when Anita's going to be back?"

"Nope." DeeDee picked the stamp back up. "Tell you what. Sarge is in. Why don't you go see her?"

Cammie made a face. The suggestion made sense, but she didn't like it. Sergeant Judith Applegate, Retired, was the second in command (her terms) at the Center. But she and Cammie didn't get along. Sarge always made physical contact, and it was rarely pleasant. She would tap Cammie in the small of the back and tell her to stand up straight, or she would place a hand on Cammie's shoulders and order her not to hunch. Around Sarge, Cammie always felt twelve years old.

Still, it didn't matter who she saw. She needed to talk to someone.

Cammie pushed away from the desk. "Have you got a ride to the Club de Wash?"

DeeDee rolled her eyes. A fleck of mascara fell from one eyelash. "I know security procedures. And I promise, Mom. I won't go home with any strange men."

Cammie frown in mock-Sarge imitation. "See that you don't."

"Yes, sir!" DeeDee saluted.

Cammie smiled as she headed down the hall. Her smile faded as she turned into the administrative wing. It had a faint scent of chalk, like the classroom of the first-grade teacher everyone hated. Most of the doors were closed, their blond wood looking forbidding against the white walls. Portraits of past directors and award-winning staff members lined the walls, small gold plaques labeling them underneath. Most were women, and all had stern nineteenth-century expressions, even though the oldest photograph dated from 1945.

Sarge's door was open. Her walls were lined with books—alphabetized according to category—and her plants stood at attention on the wide windowsill. One file sat on her desk. Her out basket was full, and her in basket was empty. The cursor blinked in a new file on her computer screen. Sarge sat in her overstuffed office chair, her white blouse starched and immaculate despite the late afternoon hour. She held the phone receiver against her ear with one hand and waved Cammie in with the other.

". . . not allowed to operate outside the state, Senator." She smiled and waved her hand again until Cammie sat in the straight-backed chair in front of the desk. "I know. You'll need to get someone in Massachusetts to investigate. We may have a listing in our files. . . . Yes, sir. I understand the necessity for discretion. The family is well known and a scandal like this— Yes, sir. But I cannot authorize out-of-state activity. That would subject us to federal regulations and so far, those regulations do not protect us like the State of Wisconsin's do. . . . No. There is no center like ours there, but some of our former people do independent work. I'll have my secretary fax you a list. . . . Thank you, Senator. I'm sorry we couldn't be of more help."

Cammie sat at the edge of her chair, conscious that her posture was straight.

Sarge hung up and leaned forward, each movement precise. She was a small woman—some would even describe her as delicate—if she didn't have the grace of a natural athlete. Her hair was blunt cut, short behind her ears, and she wore no makeup. Two tiny pearl earrings were the only concession she made to her femininity. She made a quick hand-scrawled note on the pad before her, then smiled at Cammie.

"Camila. It's been a long time since you have come to see me."

Cammie didn't move. Any movement felt like a betrayal of her own emotions. "I've been out of training for almost three years."

"And since then, you have been working with Anita." Sarge templed her fingers and leaned back in the large chair. Even that movement had a military precision. "Don't worry. I'm not offended. Most of my students turn to her. The good ones anyway. My job is to instill fear and precision. Those qualities do not inspire confidence."

"In certain situations, they do, Sarge." Cammie would rather have Sarge at her back in a dark house than Anita. Sarge's discipline would protect them both.

A half smile played at Sarge's thin lips. "Don't patronize me, Camila."

"I'm not, sir," Cammie said, falling back into old speech patterns. In training, Sarge had insisted upon "sir" as a sign of respect. She licked her lips and decided to plunge right in. "I had an eradication today, sir, and something about it disturbed me. I was going to talk with Anita, but she's not in."

"Two points for honesty," Sarge said.

"Sir, Whitney and I received a standard briefing before we went into the house. We followed procedure, found the vampire in his bedroom, and staked him. Then we heard a small sound, and turned to find a child. She lived there."

A silence hung between them for a moment. Sarge folded the temple of her hands and clasped them together. "The problem, Camila?"

A shock ran through Cammie. "That is the problem, Sarge! That little girl."

"It's not standard to include information about children in an eradication package. They are just something an eradication team might expect to encounter."

Cammie swallowed. "You never told us that. No one did."

"Camila, we had an entire unit on children and childhood procedures. It is one of our most important studies."

Cammie felt a chill run up her back. The dark slate of a blackboard covered with diagrams flashed through her mind, but was gone too fast for her to catch. "I don't remember that. I must have been sick."

Sarge folded her hands on her desktop. "You never missed a class, Camila. Or a training procedure."

"Then you skipped that section with us." Cammie's voice rose. Why didn't anyone understand that she hadn't been prepared for this? No one had worked with her on it. No one had warned her.

"I covered it, Camila," Sarge said, her voice soft. She leaned forward, her expression less rigid. "You probably just don't remember it."

"I would remember it." Cammie's whole body was shaking. "I hate being surprised on an eradication."

"It happens," Sarge said. "People often forget part of their training."

"I didn't forget anything."

Sarge nodded and sighed. She whirled her chair away from the desk. "If you don't forget anything, do you remember how Manguoso complained when I forced you all to read the handbook from cover to cover that first week?"

Cammie hated being tested. She wiped her hands on her jeans. "Should've been a sign right there that Manguoso would never make it as an eradicator."

"Did you read your handbook?" Sarge asked in an odd voice.

"You know I did."

"Then you knew, Camila. It's in the handbook." Sarge opened a door and pulled out a blue book, thumbing to a center page. "See?" She spun it around. " 'Vampiric families: A male vampire can father a child within his first year of change—' "

"I've never seen this," Cammie said. She could barely breathe. She swallowed and made herself take a deep breath. She was getting dizzy. "It's not in my handbook."

"It's been in every handbook from the beginning," Sarge said. Her gaze was sympathetic, her tone soft. "Why does this bother you so?"

"She watched us kill him." The answer came out fast, accompanied by the image of small hands, covered in blood. Cammie shook the image away.

Sarge closed her eyes and sighed. Then she nodded, and opened them again. "It happens, Camila."

"It's never happened to me before. If I had known that there could be children around, I would have at least closed the damn door. But I didn't. And I don't like being surprised like that. I was never taught to expect children. Not by you. Not by anyone."

"Camila," Sarge said, "You don't remember. Sometimes that happens. It's part of the process."

Cammie froze. "What process?"

"I can't answer that question until I check your file." Sarge swung the chair around and typed Cammie's name into the computer. "ID number?"

"What do you need my file for?" Cammie asked. Her hands were clutched into fists, the nails digging into her skin.

"Come on, Camila, don't be difficult." Sarge kept her fingers poised over the computer keyboard. She spoke without looking at Cammie. "You know about security clearances. I don't know your clearance level. I can't give you privileged information without knowing your background. Now, give me your ID number."

Cammie recited it with the rapidity of years of practice. Sarge typed it in. She moved the monitor so that Cammie couldn't see what was on the screen. Sarge tapped a button, then another, reading to herself.

After a moment, she closed the file and turned the monitor to its original position. She had gone pale. "I am sorry, Camila. I can't explain this to you."

The anger was back, making Cammie's shaking grow worse. "I have a high security clearance."

Sarge nodded. "I know. But I am not equipped to discuss this with you. You'll need to talk with Anita."

"Anita's not here."

"Then you'll have to come back." Sarge reached up and shut off the computer screen. "I'm sorry, Camila."

Sarge's fingers toyed with the edge of the file. Cammie stared at them for a moment, trying to control her breathing. When she felt as if she could speak without shouting, she said, "I feel like this has suddenly become a very big deal."

"It is a big deal," Sarge said. "It has always been a big deal. The first rule of eradication, Camila. We have been given the power to destroy. We should not use it lightly."

"I have never treated eradication lightly," Cammie said. "I feel like you people are, sending us into places with children, where children can see an atrocity they're not prepared for."

"Camila, we deal with children all the time. The children's wing is for the victims of vampires, whether they lived with the vampire or not."

Cammie's light-headedness grew. She had never thought about the children's wing. It had been part of the Center that hadn't concerned her. How odd that she had not considered it at all.

Sarge ran a finger along the top of the files. "What did you do with the child?"

"We took her to Dr. Eliason, and then Whitney brought her here while I collected her stuff."

"Then you followed procedure." Sarge picked up the folder, tapped its edge against her desk, and set the folder back down. "In these cases, sometimes, that is all you can do."

"You're not going to tell me why this is normal to everyone but me, are you?"

Sarge looked up at Cammie. For the first time, Sarge seemed small. "No. You need to make an appointment with Anita. I'm sure DeeDee will help you with that."

"I'm sure she will." Cammie spun on the balls of her feet and marched to the door. Once there, she stopped. "What's in my file, Sarge?"

Sarge's face was reflected in the glass pane of the door on the other side of the hall. Her expression became tight, and she suddenly looked older than she was. "Your entire life is in there, Camila. Your entire life."

Chapter
Four

Ben stopped in front of the address Steve had given him. This couldn't be right. A renovated five-story building stood in front of him. It had a black façade with gargoyles peering down from the roof. Most of the windows had black shutters which were closed against the light.

On the first floor, red-carpeted steps led to an Italian restaurant. The prices, posted on a menu in a window at street level, made dinner for one cost more than the average hotel room.

A foghorn sounded in the bay. The mist had grown heavier. Dusk triggered the streetlights. A wet halo circled the eerie glow. Water dripped from nearby trees. If it weren't for the rushing of cars, the entire neighborhood seemed as if it belonged in the nineteenth century.

Ben went around the carpeted steps. Another door, recessed into the building, had a wrought-iron gate before it. Forbidding place, and odd. Ben never expected a friend of Steve's to have money.

Ben rang the bell that corresponded to the apartment number Steve had given him. After a moment, he heard a ping, followed by "Who is it?" The voice was clear as a voice on a phone line. None of the scratchy intercom garble that usually came out of such equipment.

"My name is Ben Sadler. Steve Henderson gave me your name."

A brief pause made Ben look around. Should he have pressed a talk button? Had he missed something? Had they heard him? He didn't know why it suddenly felt important that he meet with these people.

"Fifth floor, third door on the left."

"Okay," Ben said, trying to keep the relief from his voice. The wrought-iron gate rose and a buzz let him know that the inside door had unlocked. He pushed it open as the gate slid back down and stepped into the hall.

It was dark and cool. A thin brownish light created more shadows than illumination. The walls were paneled—mahogany, if he guessed correctly. A corridor ran down one side. The hall smelled of oregano and tomato sauce. The Italian restaurant was on the other side of the wall.

Circular stairs with more wrought iron swept up to the second level. The elevator, off to his left, was the old-fashioned kind that was wide as a service elevator and had an elaborate double gate that operated as its doors.

He had walked all afternoon. He didn't want to take the stairs. He got inside the elevator instead.

The elevator too was dark, except for a service light that shone down from five stories up. Instead of worrying him, the dark eased him. He hadn't realized how much the gray mist had hurt his eyes. The floor buttons were red and they jutted out of the panel, unlike the modern computerized lights. When he pushed the fifth floor, a tiny light bulb inside the button illuminated the five carved into the front of the plastic. The doors closed with a metallic bang, and with a whir and a thump, the elevator shook its way to the fifth floor.

The inside gate revealed the other floors as they passed. Each grew more elaborate. The second floor looked like a fancy hotel, with red patterned carpet and matching wall paper. The third had orchids sitting on glass tables outside the door and a couch for relaxation. On the fourth, the elevator opened into a lounge lit with muted red lights.

The fifth floor was completely dark. Ben hesitated for a moment after the elevator door opened. His eyes adjusted quickly—more quickly than he remembered them doing before. A wave of sexual desire hit him, combined with a memory—the rich scent of Candyce's blood as it smeared his face. He took a deep breath, made the memory go away, but the blood smell remained like the faint odor of tobacco in a smoker's home.

He stepped out into another lounge, this one with leather furniture. The leather scent was as heavy as it was in the leather store at the mall, and it made him want to sneeze. The soft leaf of a fern brushed against his face.

His heart was pounding. What kind of weirdness had Steve gotten him into?

He made his way out of the lounge area, avoiding the darker shadows that indicated tables and chairs. A wet bar stood against one wall, and from it, he could smell the tang of wine. His stomach growled again, and he put a hand over it. Maybe Steve's friends would give him something to eat.

A wide corridor opened to what appeared to be an endless hallway. The third door on the left looked no different than all the other doors.

The blood smell grew stronger.

Ben knocked. The door opened, sending light, sound, and smell at him in a dizzying rush. Incense, cigarette smoke, alcohol, and something heady, even more intoxicating, filled the air, followed by incandescent light that seemed bright after the darkness of the hallway. The music dominated everything—Allanah Myles at full volume, her scratchy Joplinesque sound overpowering everything.

Odd that he hadn't heard it through the door.

A man stood in silhouette against the light. He was tall, broad shouldered, and dark. "Oh," he said, his voice penetrating even over the too-loud music. "You can find your way through the darkness." He stepped aside. "Welcome to the light."

Ben hesitated. What was he doing here? Then the scents pulled him inside. His stomach growled, and his arousal grew.

The man shut the door. A metallic thud that Ben felt rather than heard explained why he had heard nothing in the corridor. The entire upper floor had been soundproofed.

The man was tugging at Ben's raincoat. Ben let him pull it off.

"London Fog," the man said. "It'll do, I guess."

Ben turned to look at him. The man was tall and thin, with high cheekbones and bloodshot eyes. His lips were too red and his hair had the plastic look that some people achieved with too much mousse. He looked younger than Ben expected, someone in his early twenties, close to Ben's own age.

"This your place?"

The man laughed. His teeth were stained. "Should it be?"

The man made Ben nervous. He backed farther into the room. People leaned against the wall, talking. Some smoked cigarettes. Others sipped wine. Ben could barely see the furniture, because there were so many coats, blankets, and bodies covering it. He had been to parties like this in college, only the rooms didn't have original artwork on the walls and the stereo system was not so elaborate.

The rich, iron smell drew him farther into the room.

Between two couches, four naked women—one black, one Asian, and two white—and two naked men— both white—lay on mats. Their hands caressed their own bodies languidly. Occasionally, one of the dressed party goers would crouch over them, cup genitals with a free hand, or kiss their necks.

Ben walked closer. They looked stoned. Their eyes were glazed, their mouths half open. The women were beautiful, their bodies almost too slender, their breasts full and rosy. The black woman attracted him most. He had never seen a black woman naked before, had never realized how the dusky color of her nipples accented her skin.

"How long has it been since you've eaten?" The man had come up behind him. The press of the crowd forced the man's body against him. The warm touch of another being felt good.

The music sent a pulsing through him. It took a moment for Ben to realize he was hard. And hungry. So very hungry.

"I don't know," he said. "A few days, I think. Maybe a week. A hamburger. I had a date."

"You had a—?" The words eased out of the man. Then he gasped, and laughed. "A virgin. My god."

The music got louder, wail of guitars and the heavy pounding of the drums. Ben inched closer to the woman.

"We have a virgin," the man repeated to someone else. The word spread with the drumbeat: virgin, virgin, virgin, virgin. The man's hands slid around Ben's stomach, unbuttoning his shirt and holding him back at the same time. The touch felt good. Part of Ben's mind tried to pull away—he hadn't liked male touch before—but the rest of him kept straining toward the woman.

Another man, older, with dark, almost black eyes, followed Ben's gaze. The man sat on the mat beside the black woman. He ran his hand up her sleek thigh, then stuck his finger inside her. She moaned and reached for him. The man ignored her.

Ben's shirt was off. The man behind him ran his hand along Ben's hardness, and unzipped his pants, pulling them down. His penis bounced out, full and pulsing. He had never been naked in front of a crowd before.

He didn't care.

The other man pulled his finger out of the woman. It was covered with blood. He licked it off. "She's ready for you," the man said.

Ben didn't care if she was. He pushed the other man aside, fell to the mat, and slid inside her. She was wet. Wet with blood.

Blood. That was the smell. Blood. Like biting Candyce, and the warm fresh taste of her. He had forgotten how it tasted, how nothing had tasted good after that. He slipped inside the woman, moved against her, her breasts rubbing his chest. Around him, the virgin, virgin, virgin chant continued. An orgasm built, but stalled. He was hungry, so hungry . . .

Finally someone shoved him. He fell against her, his face lost in her neck. She had bite marks, and her skin was covered in blood. He licked it. The orgasm held. He had never been so aroused. He licked more, then finally bit her. The blood pumped into him as semen pumped out, and the orgasm seemed to last forever.

"Enough," someone said.

He kept sucking. Finally, something that tasted good.

"Enough. She's mine. He'll ruin her. That's enough."

Two strong hands pulled him away. He popped out of her, his penis covered in blood. His mouth was covered with blood, and so were his hands. Blood was matted against his chest.

A woman ripped the cuff off her blouse and pressed it against the black woman's neck. The black woman's eyes were half open. "Again?" she whispered.

He would have gone back if the hands hadn't held him in place.

"Any more," said the man who let him in, "and you'll get sick."

"Any more, and he would have killed her," said the man who had tempted him.

"He's a virgin," the woman said. "Let him alone."

The other party goers turned away from him. His pounding heart had slowed. He was coming back to himself.

He had an awful headache.

The black woman writhed on her cot in some kind of high he didn't recognize. The other woman had let go of the black woman's neck. The cloth still clung there, held in place by clotted blood.

He had attacked her. She was in a stupor and he had used her like she wasn't real. He had—

—sucked her blood—

—and the thought made his penis bounce to life again. What had happened to him? Since that night with Candyce, everything had changed.

"Feeling better?" his host asked.

"I don't know," Ben said. He waved a hand at the woman. "I just—"

"It's okay," the man said. "That's what she's for. She likes it. You gave her a high she can't get anywhere else. A virgin is the most potent. Not many cows get virgins these days."

"Cow?" Steve had used that word. It made Ben uncomfortable. "You mean she's a whore?"

"In a manner of speaking, I suppose you could use that term. Only she gets her drug fed directly into her veins. No money changes hands. Simpler that way."

Her hand reached down to her crotch. She was having her period. The blood flow was too regular to be anything else. He got harder. He wanted her again.

His host slid his hand down, and caressed Ben's penis. The touch made him squirm: the feeling was closer to pleasure than he liked. "You're young, boy," his host said. "That's good. But not tonight. Your body needs to get used to the changes. There's a shower down the hall. Use it and wait for me in the library. Steve never told you what was happening, did he?"

"Steve?" For a moment, Ben had forgotten about him. He caressed his own penis. If only they would let him go. He would try one of the other women.

"No, I can see that he didn't." The host snapped his fingers and a slender man appeared beside them. "Take our young virgin to the showers, and make sure he doesn't come out until he's pliable again."

Hands gripped him and lifted him. He tried to pull away. One more time. Just once more. But the hands carried him out of the room, the smoke, and the incense.

The hall was cooler and brought the stabbing pain back into his head. The lust drained out of him. There was a bitter, vile taste in the back of his throat. Already his mind was shoving the incident with the woman into the place it had shoved Candyce. He hadn't done that. It had happened to someone else. It hadn't felt good at all.

He shook himself again. "I can walk by myself."

"Don't try nothing." This man's voice was deep. He let go of Ben. Pain seeped into Ben's arms as the blood started flowing again.

"What is this place?" Ben asked.

"Mikos will answer your question after your shower." Mikos. The man who had touched him. The man who had given him that woman.

Suddenly Ben wanted nothing more than to get into the shower and wash the memory away. The blood had dried into a sticky mass on his chest, face, and hands.

He glanced about for the door leading to the bathroom. The hallway was lined with oil paintings, most done by surrealists. He didn't get close enough to see if he recognized any names.

The hall was wide, with gold fixtures. Antique-looking sitting benches, with ornate woodwork and thin cushions, lined the walls. Incense and cigarette smoke drifted in from the main room.

The crawly feeling was inside his arms. He shivered, realizing that he was naked. "Where's the bathroom?"

"One door down, to your right," the man said.

Ben rubbed his hands on his arms and walked on the thin blue carpet. The man followed him.

"I can go alone," Ben said.

The man smiled. "I gotta see that you do."

The hairs pricked up on Ben's arms. He found the door—white crème with an ornate gold door handle—and let himself in. A large smoking room with plush couches and easy chairs of flowered blue silk were grouped around glass tables covered with vases full of irises. Ben started to back out, but the man put a hand on the small of his back and pushed him forward.

"Keep going."

Ben moved away quickly. He didn't want that man to touch him. He no longer wanted anyone to touch him. The arousal that had built in him was gone, leaving an exhaustion he hadn't felt before. The carpet in here was a thick shag that soothed the bottom of his tired feet. He opened the far door.

The bathroom was the size of two of his old dorm rooms. A toilet and a bidet had their own alcove off to one side. A Jacuzzi bath dominated the center with two wine goblets sitting near the push-button water controls. Towels covered a nearby table. A vanity, covered with more flowers, and a hand-painted brush and comb set, stood across from the bath. Another door led to a shower the size of a walk-in closet.

"There'll be clothes waiting for you out here," the man said, and closed the bathroom door.

Ben swallowed, trying to get rid of the vile taste. In the room with the toilet and bidet, he found a sink and drank water greedily. The minute it hit his stomach, he felt nauseated. The water didn't taste good. Only blood tasted good. He stopped drinking and waited a moment before his stomach settled down.

Something was odd about this room other than its

incredible luxury. He scanned it, bare feet turning to ice on the smooth blue tile.

No mirrors. No mirrors in the sitting room. No mirrors in here. Not even reflecting glass. The fixtures were made of a burnished gold. How did a man shave? He ran his fingers along his chin. Did a man have to shave? He hadn't in days and he had no whisker growth at all.

What was happening to him?

He sat on the cold side of the Jacuzzi bath and closed his eyes. Images of Candyce rose, her face flushed, eyes bright: the flush ran all the way to her breasts. The first time—the only time—they made love. He touched her all over, then buried his face in her neck—

He opened his eyes. His penis was hard again. With a simple movement, he could be back out there, past the guard, to those women and try any of them. Any of them. It would feel so good.

He gripped the cool edge of the tub, breathing heavily. He had made love to girls before, and each time it had gotten better, but stranger. His friends, at first anyway, seemed to enjoy it more than he had: the simple touching, the feel of a girl's breast against his hand, a wet kiss. Each time, he felt a new power come into him, and by the time he met Candyce, he loved to lean against a woman's chest, believing he could hear the sound of blood rushing through her veins. He wanted to slice through skin, feel the blood pulse, but he had restrained himself.

Until Candyce.

Since then, everything seemed different.

He couldn't eat. He couldn't drink. His hearing had improved so that everyone's blood flow became audible. His sense of smell was so acute that he could scent someone with an open wound from three blocks away.

He covered his face with his cold hands. They still carried that raw scent, and it made his mouth water.

This thing was controlling him. With Candyce he had lost himself, and with that woman—

He stood and climbed into the shower.

For a moment, he stared at the controls. Buttons again, labeled "steam," "heat," "spray," and "mist." After he closed the door, a light blinked above a line that asked him to select temperature. Finally he just punched "spray" and hoped whoever had set the water temperature before him had not left it boiling.

The temperature light winked out and water sprayed him, not from a nozzle, but from small holes placed all over in the shower itself. The water was hot, painfully so, but it cleared the blood off. The red swished down the white drain, reminding him of Janet Leigh's death scene in *Psycho,* black water swirling, swirling, swirling against porcelain.

He grabbed soap and rubbed it all over his body. The sensual feeling was back. The thing he had never admitted to himself about Candyce was that he had never felt more alive, more in touch with his body, than he had with her. The same thing had happened with the woman tonight. What bothered him was that his body seemed to control him, but the others didn't seem to have that problem. Except the people on the mat. And Mikos had called them cows.

Needles of spray bit into his shoulder, his back. The sensuality frightened him. But what if it didn't? What if he learned to control those increased senses? What if he learned how to have pleasure any time he wanted it?

Perhaps, instead of letting his body control him, he could control it, and slip into the pleasure like some people slipped into an old pair of shoes.

The blood was gone. He felt clean for the first time in days. He paused for a moment, unable to find the off button. Finally he hit spray again, and the water stopped as silently as it had started.

He stepped out, grabbed a towel, and dried himself

off. The nerves in his skin were more alive than they had ever been. Even the towel felt good. Yes. He could get used to this.

He left the towel hanging over a gold burnished rack and opened the door to the sitting room. A long black kimono had been tossed across one of the chairs. No other clothes were in sight.

The kimono was made of silk. He slipped it on. It slid against his biceps and moved with the contours of his body. Everything here was designed to make him feel good.

He opened the door to the hall. The man was waiting for him. "Feeling better?"

Better? He had never felt so good in his life. "We're supposed to go to the library?"

"Yep. Looks like you're ready."

They moved quickly down the hall to the end. The man opened the double doors with a flourish. They opened inward, revealing a room done in red carpet and mahogany. Books rose an extra level, and a thin balcony jutted out on each side. A fire burned in the fireplace on the far wall, and sofa groupings huddled in small alcoves. A large desk made of the same mahogany stood in front of the fireplace.

His host—Mikos—leaned on the desk. Ben finally got a good look at him. Mikos was tall, with swarthy skin and thin features. Each strand of his black hair was in place. His dark eyebrows rose like wings above his eyes, giving him a foreign look. He had changed into a black sweatshirt and black jeans. The sweatshirt sleeves were pushed up revealing his wiry, muscular arms. "Thank you," he said, dismissing the man who had brought Ben there.

The man bowed again—an odd movement that seemed less like a servant's and more like a suppliant's—and backed out of the room.

The fire added only a minimal heat to the room. Ben's feet were cold by the time he reached the desk.

"Okay," he said, clasping his hands behind his back. "That has to be the weirdest thing I have ever experienced."

Mikos smiled. "We don't get many virgins at our parties. They're mostly for the old timers. You gave us a treat. Something we can remember. How the world was once fresh and young."

Ben swallowed. The coppery taste had left his mouth. "Who are you? Why did Steve send me here?"

"You would have died if Steve hadn't sent you." Mikos crossed his arms in front of his chest and leaned against the desk. "Tell me about yourself."

"Look, can we sit down? My feet are cold and I've been standing all day."

Mikos's smile grew. He stood up, then walked around his desk. Behind it, two overstuffed chairs framed the fireplace. The room was bigger than Ben had originally thought. He sat in one of the chairs. The heat from the fireplace finally reached his toes.

Mikos sat on the arm of the other chair. His body never appeared to be at rest. He would settle for a moment, then shift slightly. "Comfortable now?"

Ben nodded. "It's better."

"Good. Then talk to me."

A flutter grew in Ben's stomach. "What do you want to know?"

"I don't want games." Mikos's voice had grown harsh. He took a deep breath, and the calmer voice returned. "I would like to know about you. I want to know what led you here."

Ben had already told him about Steve, but Mikos didn't want to hear facts like that. Mikos wanted more. "I tasted blood for the first time last week, and"—he dropped his clasped hands on his lap to hide a growing erection—"I haven't felt the same since."

"Last week?" Mikos stood and held his hands over the fire. The flames reflected through his long nails. "You have been different longer than last week."

"No," Ben said. "I went to college and high school, and my parents were married my whole life. I'm about as normal as you can get."

Mikos laughed. The sound reverberated in the large room. "Your favorite color is red. You like odd foods like haggis and Turkish blood soup. As a little boy, you got punished for biting. In school fights, you always felt better if you got covered with your opponent's blood. You developed a taste for red wine young, and while it made your friends drunk, it didn't affect you at all. You are drawn to women at certain times of the month. Your wet dreams are violent, and in them, you get more pleasure for the things you put in your mouth than the things you touch with your genitals. As you have gotten older, you have less tolerance for sunlight. Regular sex has never felt good to you, and the first time you truly enjoyed an orgasm was last week, with some poor unsuspecting soul."

Ben's hands were trembling and his throat had gone dry. The erection was gone. He didn't like the way this man saw him. No one should be able to see that clearly.

Mikos turned. "I'm right, aren't I?"

"Is that what happened to you?"

Mikos rested against the arm of the chair, his eyes sparkling. "You're good, boy. Very good. And no, that's not what happened to me. I met a woman nearly fifty years ago who, as I look back, must have been a virgin. She nearly drained me of blood and left me for dead without sealing my wounds. As you will learn, that turns some humans. It turned me. Now I feed off other blood to live."

"Vampires?" Ben whispered the words. Vampires were derelicts with a taste for blood. Skinny, pathetic people who couldn't hold jobs and who barely had the strength to find an evening meal. Young vampires quit their jobs and hung out in bars, like Steve, unable to control their impulses, sucking the blood from willing victims. Vampires didn't have homes. They didn't have families. They didn't go to college. They were weak people who had been seduced by other weak people.

No one had sucked his blood. No one had ever touched him—until today.

Vampires. He had not let that word into his mind since he had arrived. In fact, he had been avoiding it since he last saw Candyce.

He couldn't be a vampire. He was young. He was smart. He was strong.

And he loved the taste of blood.

"All of us here are vampires," Mikos said. "Except the people on the mats. They were merely—dessert—until you came along. After they've been cows for a while, they get a sweet high. It makes them completely sexual, and completely passive. We stimulate their pleasure centers better than any synthetic drug, and if they lose their will, well, they would lose it on more dangerous drugs also."

"I've never been drained by anyone. I've never been left for dead," Ben said.

"No." Mikos's eyes had a brightness that Ben had never seen in anyone's eyes before. They were compelling. Ben couldn't look away. "You are a rare creature. You are a hereditary vampire, with a taste for blood from birth. Only since you've become sexual have you felt the need."

"My parents aren't vampires."

"Oh?" Mikos sat in the chair and stuck his feet out as Ben did. "Then how do you explain that little incident in the other room? No human can do that. It sickens them. But you. You couldn't get enough."

Ben looked at his hands. If he closed his eyes, he could feel the woman's body beneath his. She had tasted so good . . .

He kept his eyes open. "Human beings can do that."

Mikos laughed. "Ah, denial." He leaned forward. "Yes, human beings can probably do that, and some of them may even enjoy it. But it does not fall into the DSM-IV's category of normal human responses. That's the first item under the DSM-IV's category for vampire."

"DSM-IV?"

"Diagnostic and Statistical Manual, Number Four, which is, unless I'm mistaken, the current volume psychiatrists use to diagnose mental and psychological aberration."

Ben sat up straight. His feet were getting too hot. "You're saying I'm aberrant?"

"They say you're aberrant. For a human." Mikos stood and paced around his chair. He pushed up his sweatshirt sleeves, then rubbed his hands together. "But I'm saying you're not and never have been human. You've been a vampire your entire life, and for a vampire, at least one who has been trying to live with the very thing it eats, you've been surprisingly normal."

"I never heard of hereditary vampirism."

"Of course not," Mikos said. He crossed his arms. "You have believed the TV movies of the week about the vampire plague among the homeless. The sick, weak-minded creatures that prey on children. The pathetic vampire, mouth covered with blood, staggering with the weight of its evening meal. The discussions on *Donahue* and *Oprah* about the men who were once loving and who have become violent, hateful people who only go out at night. The women who don black miniskirts and cruise the street, coming home at dawn with bloodstains on their lips. If vampires were that stupid, we would not survive for centuries, Ben. A few cows become the chosen, like I did, but most can't handle it. Society deals with them. It rarely finds the successful chosen. I have enough money to live the way I want and not be questioned. I do not let my addictions interfere with my desires. And if you listen to me, neither will you."

Ben moved his feet away from the fireplace. Sweat ran down his back. This was too much for him. People did not suddenly become vampires.

—His fist connected with little Tommy Stonner's face. Pain ran from his knuckles to his wrist. Blood spurted from Tommy's nose and the crowd of boys on the playground cheered. Mrs. Deely grabbed Tommy and pulled him away. Ben licked his fist. Tommy's blood was sweet—

"That woman wanted me to do that," Ben said, banishing the childhood memory.

"Of course she did," Mikos said. "She got the most exquisite sexual high of her life."

"Why do you always have an answer for me?"

"And why do you try to minimize what you just did?" Mikos asked. "You're rested now. If I gave you any of the others, the women, the men, you would react the same way you did in front of all my friends. You would shred the neck and drain the blood if you could."

Ben clasped his hands tightly over his lap. The lust was back. Jesus, did they drug him? "No, I wouldn't," he said. "This is just hormones. I'm only twenty-two—"

Mikos closed the distance between them faster than Ben had ever seen anyone move. He grabbed Ben's arms and shoved his hands aside. Ben's erection popped through the kimono, and before Ben could move, Mikos went down on it, nipping at the base.

Ben cried out and tried to twist away. Mikos grabbed him and held him in place, and sucked. It felt good. It felt too good. Mikos was male. Ben leaned forward to push Mikos away. The cords in Mikos's neck stood out, and without a second's hesitation, Ben stuck his head in Mikos's neck and bit.

Mikos's blood was thinner than anything Ben had ever tasted before, but it had a sparkle to it like a fine champagne. Mikos's mouth was warm and wet over Ben's penis. Ben arched into Mikos, letting the sensation take him. He drank and drank, and then another orgasm—better than the first—rippled through him. Mikos pulled away from Ben's lap, mouth bloody, forcing Ben to sit up.

"Why deny what you are?" Mikos asked, running his tongue over the blood. "If you accept yourself you have so much more control."

Ben swallowed the last of Mikos's bubbly blood. His heart was pounding faster than it ever had before, and his body felt stronger. If he got up, he could run across half of Seattle and not get tired. "Control?"

Mikos nodded and stood. The fire played against his thin face. "Control. Of yourself, of your body, and of others. The vampires the humans see have lost control. They are pathetic victims of their blood lust. You could join them, or you could determine when you would feed, instead of letting your body choose for you."

"Control," Ben said. Think of it. He could choose when to have that delicious experience. He could do it every hour or every week, depending on his mood.

"Control," Mikos said, "is the beginning of power."

Ben frowned. He hadn't expected that. "What would I want with power?"

Mikos smiled. His teeth were stained with Ben's blood. "Ah, my boy. Someday you will crave it. Someday you will crave it more than the blood. And unless you control it, you will do anything for it. Just like tonight, when you did anything I wanted to get blood."

Ben froze. Mikos had steered him since Ben had arrived in the apartment. Ben had not questioned a thing. He had done what he was told. He had never been like that before. "That's not how it's done?"

Mikos shrugged. "Does it matter how most of us do it? Right now, I could bring you a real cow, with four feet and hooves, and you would hump it and try to suck its blood. Virgins have no control at all."

"Then why are you interested in me?"

"Because your friend Steve sent you to us without explanation. If you had been his protégé, he would have kept you as a young cow until you completely turned. But you are turning on your own. I told you that hereditary vampires are rare. They also have the capability of being the most powerful among us." Mikos bowed at the waist, his expression mocking. "It suits me, Master Ben Sadler, to serve you."

Chapter Five

That night Cammie dreamed:

She was lying across her bed, reading. Forbidden sunlight warmed her feet, her back. She didn't dare make any noise. Daddy was sleeping. He hated to be disturbed while he slept, especially after a night out. Lately he had been insisting that she sleep in the daylight too. She hated it. Sometimes she would fall asleep near Daddy, and he would get angry. He wanted his children on the same schedule that he was on. That way he could spend more time with them. But what he called time was mostly watching television, sipping wine, and waiting for him to go out on his nightly food run. He always came back with groceries and cooked them a large dinner which he never ate. Once she asked him why he didn't like food. He had smiled and said the wine was enough.

She sat bolt upright in her bed, arms wrapped around herself. Her heart was pounding as if she had awakened from a nightmare, but the dream itself had not been frightening. She even knew the dream's cause—the vampire and his little girl.

The bedroom was dark, hot, and too small. A thin light filtered through the blinds onto the hardwood floor. She had bought white blinds—the better to see shadows—and never kept them fully closed.

She sighed and threw back the covers. Maybe she should have gone with DeeDee to take her mind off that little girl. That breathless little cry. *Daddy.* Even now Cammie didn't want to acknowledge the pain.

The floor was cool against her bare feet. She slipped on her ancient terry cloth robe as she walked to the window and peeked through the blinds. The streetlight guarded her window like a sentinel. Cars lined the curb on the street below. The ranch houses across the street were dark except for that of Mr. Simmons, whom she had already had the Center check out. He was an elderly man with a sleeping disorder he had acquired in the war.

Night terrors. Seems he saw vampires whenever he closed his eyes.

Cammie let the blind drop. It rattled against the window frame. Poor Mr. Simmons. No one had believed him when he came back from Germany. But Germany, Rumania, Russia—all of eastern Europe and most of northern Europe had vampire problems. Recent studies had shown that Kaiser Wilhelm and Hitler had both had vampiric family members and were probably vampires themselves. Stalin had trained a special force of vampiric ghouls to carry out most of his more bloodthirsty orders. Vampires had run the POW camps in World War II. Mr. Simmons had been among the troops liberating those camps, and he had seen things that Cammie didn't even want to guess at.

No wonder he stayed awake at night.

Just as she did.

Her throat was dry and her hands were shaking. The heat in the room made the garlic even more pungent. She flicked on the hall light and turned down the thermostat.

In the thin light of a sixty-watt bulb, her hall looked like something out of a bad horror movie. Dust bunnies floated across the hardwood, a testament more to her mental state than her cleaning abilities. The light bulb hung from a cord, and no pictures covered her white walls. The tiny bathroom barely had enough room for her in it, and she had not cleaned it since she moved in. The bedroom was small, but the living room/dining room was big, and the kitchen was an extra room, a luxury in an apartment as old as this one.

She didn't get paid enough for the work she did. The Center ran on a limited budget, financed by a mysterious source of Anita's, donations from various organizations, and private funds. Once, the Center had made its money on its rehabilitation program, but since that failed, Anita had had to find more creative ways to keep the Center alive. Underpaying its staff was one of those ways.

Cammie could have had a better-paying job out of college, but she had owed the Center. They had given her a $1000 scholarship to attend the U.W. back when $1000 had been a year's tuition. The Center chose only about ten likely candidates a year to give scholarships to, with the recipients guaranteeing that they would work for the Center for at least a year after graduation. Cammie, like most, had stayed on.

Maybe now, though, she should move on to another job where she would make more money. She struggled to make the rent on this place, and each month she tried to set a little aside to buy a new piece of furniture or even a nice item of clothing. So far, it had not worked.

The living room carpet needed vacuuming. She padded across it, noting that nothing had disturbed the strands of garlic hanging around each window. Despite the Center's insistence, she did not hang crosses in her home, although she had them stashed in case of emergency. The Center's history suggested that vampires would try to kill eradication teams, but the last such attempt occurred in the seventies. Still, Cammie felt she couldn't be too cautious.

She flicked on the fluorescent light in the kitchen. It

crackled and spit, something that made her very nervous, especially since the accident last year. Her upstairs neighbor, a college student at the U.W., had gone to bed drunk, leaving the water running in his sink. It flooded the floor and eventually caved in part of Cammie's drywall ceiling, making her wake up screaming and grabbing in her top drawer for the squirt gun filled with holy water. The new plastering job was makeshift, done by her landlord's brother. It had taken him two weeks and two complaints to the Housing Authority before she had a kitchen again.

The stained brown kettle still had some plaster dents. She poured the water out of it, filled it, and turned on her top burner. At moments like this, she wanted a microwave, just a small one, to heat water and TV dinners. A small one would cost about a hundred dollars. Maybe, after this child thing had blown over, she would ask Anita for a raise.

Cammie put the tea kettle on the burner, pulled a mug off the rack, and stuck a peppermint teabag inside. Then she pushed newspapers aside on her kitchen table and sat down to wait for the water.

Nightmares. One step beneath night terrors. The report on Simmons said that he couldn't sleep more than a few hours without waking up screaming. Two wives had divorced him because they couldn't sleep—even in separate bedrooms. Years of V.A. sponsored counseling only seemed to make it worse.

All because Simmons wouldn't discuss what he had seen over there. It was too awful. He had refused to give himself permission to remember.

Cammie put her head on her arms. The little girl—Janie—she would remember. And even if she didn't, Cammie would. That soft, plaintive *Daddy* would haunt her for the rest of her days.

Cammie managed to get three hours of sleep before her appointment with Anita. Still, as she walked through the front door of the Westrina Center, she felt as if someone had dumped two tons of sand in her eyes.

"I hope to hell it was a guy," DeeDee said as she looked up from her desk at Reception. This morning, she had her hair pulled back in a big red bow that matched the candy-striped shirt she wore. She had redone her nails in red and white stripes to match.

"Only if you count Zolton Tor. Thirty-nine, built, blonde curls—"

"And the hero of that Katherine Neville book I gave you for Christmas. Jesus, Cammie, you weren't up all night reading?"

"Nope. I was up all night pacing. I started reading *after* the sun came up."

"Such an exciting life," DeeDee said. "The Crash Test Dummies were worth it."

"Yeah. Now I'm sorry I missed them."

"Me, too." DeeDee leaned back in her chair. "Anita's waiting for you. She actually beeped down a few minutes ago to see if you were here. Something heavy is happening, isn't it?"

"I don't know," Cammie said. "You're the only other person who thinks something out of the ordinary is happening."

DeeDee nodded. "Well, you hang in there, girl, and if you need anything, you just call me. I may not be able to talk to you about it, but I can at least fund your entertainment."

"Reception doesn't get paid more than Eradication."

"That's right," DeeDee said, "but we know how to manage it better."

Cammie rolled her eyes and started down the hall. Strange how her good moods would evaporate after she left DeeDee. Cammie brushed a strand of hair from her face. This morning she had been so tired she had left her hair loose. Now she regretted it. The hair constantly tumbling over her eyes made her feel like more of a mess than she was.

Most of the doors in the administration wing were closed—Thursdays were field days—but Anita's stood open. Her office's fresh minty scent covered the chalky metallic scent that normally filled the hallway. Plants hung around the door, and more hung inside, giving Anita's office a humid, junglelike interior. The carpet and curtains were forest green, and the overstuffed furniture matched, from the long couch squeezed beneath the bookshelf to the four easy chairs scattered around the room. Anita had her desk to one side, so that it was unobtrusive: she preferred her office to be more like a room than a place of power. Tiny statues peeked out of the plants, adding a touch of whimsy, and anatomically correct cloth dolls rested on a pillow.

Anita was sitting on the window seat. She was a heavy woman who looked even more solid because of the dark tunics she wore. Her salt-and-pepper hair was swept back in a bun, giving her the look of a dowager duchess from an era gone by.

The window seat was one of Anita's favorite spots in the complex. She usually sat there when she was working. She had had it specially designed when the Administration wing was added. Plants stood on a sill that rested about shoulder height. In the dip, beneath the plants, a cushioned seat whose prints matched that of the other furniture provided a comfortable, cozy, and warm seating area. Cammie had sat on it once when Anita was out of the room.

"Sarge tells me you were very upset yesterday," Anita said. She was picking dead leaves off an African violet. She didn't look at Cammie.

Cammie closed the door. She didn't want to sit down. "Finding that little girl was a bit of a surprise."

"Yes." Anita tossed the leaves into a round metal garbage can. They made a small ping as they landed. "Sometimes it can be."

"That's not what I mean." An anger Cammie didn't know she had rose inside her. "No one ever warned me about children. Ever. No matter what Sarge says."

Anita rose. Her round face was covered with a thin webbing of lines. The dimples in the corners of her mouth had become slashes that made her look as if she were constantly frowning. "What did Sarge say?"

"Not enough. She said I should know about these children. That everyone in eradication knows that vampires can have children. No one told me, Anita. I don't like that kind of surprise in my work."

Anita nodded. She ducked under a spider plant and stopped beside one of the overstuffed chairs. "Surprises like that ruin concentration, don't they."

"They're dangerous," Cammie said.

"Dangerous? Did the child interfere with you finishing your task?"

Cammie clasped her hands together. "No."

"Did she try to hurt you in any way?"

"No."

"Did she get between you and her father?"

"He wasn't her father," Cammie snapped. "He was a vampire."

Anita's gray eyes met Cammie's. "He was the only father she ever knew."

"That's what Eliason said. I think it's a crock based on supposition."

Anita shook her head. "No supposition. I did the initial interview. That little girl thought of him as her father. Why is this so difficult for you, Cammie?"

"No one told me—"

"I don't think that's what you're angry about." Anita leaned against the chair. She looked matronly standing there, matronly and safe.

"How do you know what I'm angry about?"

"You've had trouble with procedure before. It has never made you this angry."

"I never encountered a child before."

Anita nodded once. "No. I suppose you haven't." She sighed, and stood upright. "Come with me. I want to show you something."

She grabbed a ring of keys off her desk and led the way out of her office. Cammie followed, pulling the door shut behind her.

The hallway was cold compared with Anita's office. The spring sunshine filtering in through the tall windows looked thin. If she wasn't angry about procedure, what was she angry about? And why did she have to listen to Anita about her own emotions?

Anita's rubber-soled shoes squeaked on the tile floor. The keys jingled in her hand. Cammie followed, her own footsteps silent, as Sarge had trained them to be.

When they reached the end of the administrative wing, they turned right instead of left. Cammie held her breath. They were walking into a part of the Center Cammie rarely entered. Surveillance had one wing off this hall, Research had another. At the end of the hall, behind a double-locked door, was the Children's Wing.

Anita walked to the door, but did not open it. Instead, she unlocked a small wooden door. It opened to reveal a narrow staircase. Cammie frowned. She had always thought the door opened into a closet. More secrets in the Center. She wasn't sure she liked that.

Anita gripped the wooden railing with one hand. Her body brushed against the wall as she walked. Cammie had to bend as she went through the door. She was not all that tall—the staircase had been a later addition.

When they reached the top, Cammie gasped in surprise. A row of windows covered the left wall. Light filtering in from the Children's Wing provided the only visibility in the corridor. Painted backwards on the window were figures from storybooks—some permanent ones, like the Wild Things Maurice Sendak had consented to paint when he visited the wing—and some appropriate to the season. The Snow Queen had just disappeared, replaced by a half-finished portrait of Glenda the Good Witch from the Oz books. The children saw only a highly placed mirror with paintings on it. Cammie had never suspected that the adults could watch everything that happened through it.

"How long has this been here?" Cammie asked.

"Since we moved into the building," Anita said. "We need to know how the children interact without adult supervision."

The hall was filled with riding toys: child-sized mechanical cars, tricycles, wagons, and big wheels. On the other side of the reception desk, someone had built cushions into the wall and roller blades were lined up on a bench according to size. One little boy skated alone, with the receptionist keeping an eye on him. He skated in a circle, never stopping, never smiling, hands clasped behind his back, and eyes down.

The upstairs corridor branched off. Anita unlocked another door and stepped inside.

The room was larger than the narrow hall. Chairs were lined up against the window, and behind them was a desk with a computer on top. The computer was on. It hummed and the cursor blinked on an empty screen.

"This is the observation deck," Anita said. She slid into one of the chairs near the window and indicated that Cammie do the same. Cammie did not. She examined the computer, and found it to be standard issue, with a net link to the other computers in the building. Then she went to the window itself.

The room below was a playroom done in bright primary colors. Large windows opened to the garden outside. The sunlight filtering into the playroom looked as bright as the yellow on the carpeting. Toys covered the walls, and big foam cushions served as chairs on the floor.

In the center of a pile of cushions, surrounded by an army of stuffed animals, Janie sat. She clutched her stuffed dog against her chest. Her thumb was in her mouth, and she rocked back and forth as she stared at the sun.

"She's asked about the record player," Anita said, staring through the window at the brightly lit room below. "I assume you left it."

"She'd been listening to it when we got there. I thought it would hurt her."

"I'd send Whitney for it, but they've already sealed up the house." Anita leaned back, her face half in shadow. "You can't preguess another person's pain."

"But—"

"Don't but me. I've seen three generations of children through this place. We need to help whatever way we can."

"I'm sorry."

Anita nodded once. "That's better. I want you to get the court order and move through the red tape. The record player has to be here by this afternoon."

Cammie clenched her fists. "Is that why you brought me up here?"

"No." Anita waved at the chair. "Sit down."

Cammie didn't move.

"Sit down. You can't see from that height."

Cammie straightened her shoulders and eased the tightness in her hands. She grabbed the edge of the chair and pulled it back, sitting in it, but not resting. "All right."

Anita leaned forward again. Down in the room, Janie curled up inside her pile of stuffed toys. "Tell me what you do know about children and vampires."

Cammie swallowed. "I know that female vampires prey mostly on infants and children under five."

"And male vampires?"

"Kill men, mostly, and occasionally create a female vampire."

"But what do male vampires do with children?"

"How the hell am I supposed to know?" Cammie kicked against the wall and pushed her chair back. Janie looked up, her expression startled.

"It's not completely soundproofed up here," Anita said. "She can hear when you pound the wall. I don't want her any more frightened than she is."

"Sorry," Cammie said, not feeling sorry at all. The little girl had lived with a vampire. She hadn't turned him in. She hadn't tried to run away. She was as guilty as the vampire for the man's crimes.

"During the first thirty years of a male vampire's existence," Anita said, as if Cammie hadn't interrupted them, "he still seeks companionship. He tries it first by creating female vampires, and when that fails, he adopts children. Sometimes, he can father them—especially if he tries in his first year. As his addiction grows, and his humanity breaks down, he abandons the children more and more, until finally, he either uses them as prey or he creates younger, more powerful vampires. Do you understand what I'm telling you?"

"You're telling me I did the right thing."

"No." Anita put her hand on the glass, as if she were trying to touch the little girl. "I'm telling you that your actions yesterday ended a relationship. The vampire was still young enough to love this girl and treat her like a daughter. She lost her father—"

"Bullshit." Cammie whispered the word, then repeated it louder. "Bullshit. You people sent me over there. You told me to kill that vampire."

"Yes," Anita said. "And now I'm showing you the consequences of your action."

Cammie clenched her hands again, half wishing for a stake to drive through Anita's frozen heart. "Why?"

Anita reached out to her—first touch—and Cammie backed away. "Because you need to see it," Anita said.

"I need to see it?" Cammie took a deep breath. "I knew what I was getting into when you hired me for eradication. I knew that I would be slaughtering something that might or might not be alive. I never knew that it could have a family or be anything more than a creature that fed off us. Sarge promised us that we were not killing human beings."

"Since when did having a family make something a human being?" Anita asked.

Janie had fallen asleep, her head pillowed on the stuffed dog, thumb still in her mouth. "That little girl is human, isn't she?" Cammie asked.

"For now," Anita said.

Cammie finally sat down again. Her body felt heavy. "What do you mean?"

"We don't know when she was fathered or how she was raised. With luck, one of the psychologists can pull that information from her. If he was her true father, and he fathered her after he became a vampire, she will have hereditary tendencies that may not show up until her sex drive is in its peak—in her thirties. Usually we're lucky. Usually those tendencies show up much earlier."

"Then what do you do? Stake the kid?"

"Nothing so crude as that," Anita said. "She will go to live in a protective enclave where she will learn self-reliance and a way to survive without stealing blood. If those lessons do not take, the eradication team will have to take her."

"What if she doesn't have those tendencies?"

"Then she will have other problems, problems we can deal with here, and her new foster family will deal with on the outside. Over seventy percent of the children of vampires become vampires themselves. This is what we are trying to prevent. It is the most important work that the Center does. If we can stop the vampirism now, we protect everyone's future." Even though it was clear that Anita had said those words before, she didn't make it sound like a speech. Here was her passion. Here was the thing that drove her.

"If it's so important," Cammie said, "how come I've never heard about it until now?"

"Cammie," Anita said, "there has been no conspiracy of silence against you. You simply don't remember this part of your training."

"I remember my entire training. I also remember the two semesters I had when I got my psychology degree on vampirism and its history. Nothing mentioned children."

"They did, Cammie. The children of vampires are as big a societal problem as the vampires themselves." Anita held out her hand to Cammie. Cammie didn't take it. "We have counselors here at the Center. I think it's time you saw one. And remember, you can talk to me at any time."

Cammie stood up. "I don't need a counselor."

Anita sighed. "Getting help is a personal decision. But people repress things for a reason. You have blocked all information about children raised by vampiric men. Do you know why that is?"

"I never learned about it."

Anita put her hand on her knee. "Check your textbooks, Cammie, then see one of the counselors. Please."

Cammie nodded. She wasn't going to see anyone. She didn't need help. She never had.

Anita studied her for a moment. Something passed across Anita's face—a bit of a frown, an assessment. "No matter what you do for yourself," Anita said, "I still expect you to work unless the counselor says you can't. I want that record player. I've already told Judge Myerson that you would be there with a petition."

Cammie nodded. She didn't want to go back into that condo—alone, with the rich smell of decay all around her. The record player hissing and popping.

Him. Sleeping in the other room.

She couldn't go.

But she had to if she wanted to keep her job.

She glanced through the mirrored window at the little girl huddled on the stuffed animals, sucking her thumb. They were linked, somehow. Janie's destiny was part of Cammie's.

And Cammie wanted that link to end.

Chapter
Six

He came to consciousness slowly. His tongue felt as if it were glued to the roof of his mouth. Something had died in the back of his throat. His head was cushioned on a satin pillow, and the blankets covering him were made of the same smooth material. He blinked his eyes open. It was still dark.

His head throbbed. He brought a hand up, felt the warm skin of his forehead. What had he done last night? Had he had too much to drink? He didn't remember—

—thin, bubbly, like champagne—

—orgasm rippled through him, stronger than any since Candyce—

He sat up, swaying a little with the dizziness. He couldn't have done that. He must have come in, had too much to drink, and had nightmares. Nightmares. That was it.

He reached over to the bedside table and turned on the light. It had a soft glow that barely penetrated the darkness. Black curtains hung over the windows. The sheets were black, and he still wore the black kimono.

He reached under it and fingered his penis. Against the base were two tiny scabs. It had all happened. It was real.

The door opened and a slender woman of about

thirty came in carrying a tray. She wore a tank top tucked into tight jeans. Her black hair was piled on top of her head, revealing a long and slender neck. She was tiny and lean. The black top revealed muscular arms without a trace of fat. Her breasts were small and compact. Even though she was no bigger than a twelve-year-old, she moved with power.

She set the tray beside the bed.

"Hair of the dog," she said. She had a slight accent. She trilled her 'r's and clipped the back of her words. German? Russian?

He reached for her. She laughed and sat down just outside his grasp. "Not me," she said. "The glass."

The crystal goblet beside the bed was filled with a thick, black liquid. He picked it up and the scent brought his erection back. Blood. He drained it in a single gulp and wiped his mouth with the back of his hand.

The taste was gone, and within a second the headache was, too. She placed a finger on the tent his erection made of the covers. The slight touch made him harder. She grinned. "Virgins."

Her face was pleasant but not pretty. All of her features were tiny, and her eyes were so dark he had to strain to see the pupils. She smelled different from any other woman he had known—a faint odor of healthy sweat combined with a cinnamon scent. And something was missing.

He couldn't hear the whisper of her veins. She didn't smell of blood.

She leaned back. Her nipples stretched the cotton top. He longed to touch them.

"I am Vangelina," she said as he reached for her again. She slapped his hand. "And stop that. I am old enough to be your grandmother."

"My grandmother is seventy-two."

"I was born in 1863," Vangelina said. "That makes me old enough to be your great-grandmother."

"1863?"

"Darling, get used to us. We are not human and we can live forever if we have enough blood." She took the goblet from him and licked the rim. Her tongue was gray. "Mikos has asked me to train you."

"Train me?"

"Early on, there are ways to survive and ways to die. You must learn how to survive and be strong. You must learn what you can and cannot do. You cannot, for example, treat your hosts like you treated that woman last night."

"Hosts?" he asked. "You mean that cow?"

She pursed her lips and set the goblet down. "Cow is an inaccurate term. Humans are not stupid. They are different. We are parasites that feed off them, and we are better off if they live. Humans kill cows and eat them. The analogy breaks down rather quickly."

"Mikos calls them cows."

She slid her hand along the sheet covering his penis. Her touch made him throb. He could barely catch his breath. "Mikos is not always right."

He was salivating. His mouth was filling with water. She stroked him. The satin fabric made him ache. He leaned toward her neck but she moved away. When she took her hand off his penis, he felt a physical loss.

"You are putty," she said.

He licked his lips. The desire for her—for blood— was so thick he could barely think. "Please," he whispered.

" 'Please'?" She reached over, yanked his penis and twisted it. The pain knocked the air out of him. He couldn't even scream. "Your lust controls you. I could kill you if I wanted."

The lust was gone. Adrenaline flowed through his body. He inched away from her.

She smiled. Her teeth were small, white, and perfect. "I will not kill you. I am not stupid. Had I wanted to, I would have done so while you slept." She leaned toward him. "Now. You will listen to me when I talk to you. You cannot treat your hosts like you treated that woman last night."

"What did I do?" he asked.

"You almost killed her. If we left bodies around, the humans would find us, and we are very vulnerable when we sleep." Her smile grew.

"Oh," he said. The pain in his groin was beginning to subside. He blinked, trying to clear his mind. Vampires. He still did not believe that he was one of them. He had been president of his high school class. He had graduated from O.S.U. with honors. Vampires hid in the dark. They weren't human.

Humans don't respond like that.

"It is hard to get used to, is it not?" She ran a hand along his leg. He flinched. She gripped his thigh. Her fingers were surprisingly strong. "When I turned, I was eighteen. The man who turned me had not planned to. He wanted me as host. Then he had to deal with me as a contemporary. It lasted nearly a year before he disappeared and left me on my own."

"In 1863?"

"No, darling. I was born in 1863. This was 1881 in Prussia. A woman alone was not tolerated well in those days, and I had to do what you would expect." She arched, and ran her free hand along her breast. He felt himself grow hard. He had never had a sexual response so soon after being hit in the groin. She noticed, and smiled. "I did quite well, and it worked delightfully. Humans get a sexual high from the right kind of blood loss. My brothel had the best clientele in the entire country."

"I don't understand any of this," he said. If only he could think clearly. He would feel better if he could think.

"Of course not." She took her hand off him, and turned on the other light. "Get dressed. You overslept. It is nearly midnight."

"Midnight!"

"Your sleeping habits were bound to change. Why stay awake in the light if it bothers you? There are clothes in the closet. Something should fit you. I will be waiting in the kitchen, which is down the hall and to your right."

He nodded. He was beginning to feel alive again. The throbbing in his head was gone, but he did want to brush his teeth.

Vangelina let herself out of the room. He lay back for a moment, waiting for his erection to go away. He couldn't live like this. Ever since Candyce, his life had been hell. He had always controlled his body. He had controlled everything.

Now his body was controlling him.

He had to make it quit. Perhaps Van would help him.

He got out of bed and pulled the covers back where they belonged. He slid open the closet doors. A long rack of men's clothes faced him, hung according to size and formality. The suits were on one side, and older clothes on the other. Tie-dye, fringe, black turtlenecks, and dark jeans were along the other wall. In the center were sweats, regular jeans, and sweaters. Unopened packets of underwear lined the closet walls like a display in a department store. He had never seen anything like this before.

He opened a packet of briefs and put them on. Then he pulled out a pair of jeans and a gold sweater made of lamb's wool. They fit rather well. He found no socks and no shoes, so he padded barefoot across the room.

When he opened the door, the scent of incense, cigarettes, and blood teased his nose. He glanced down the hall, recognizing the way to the entry room. A thrumming of a loud stereo came from in there. If he followed that trail, he would find more women. He could do what he wanted—

—and Mikos might throw him out. Vangelina said

that he could die at this stage. Mikos said Ben would have died had he remained on his own any longer.

He followed Vangelina's instructions, finger combing his hair as he walked. The kitchen doors were open. The room was done in blue tile. The stove and refrigerator were spotless. Dusty pots hung from the rack above the oven. The clear glass cabinets were filled with goblets. Only a handful of dishes filled one of the shelves.

Vangelina opened the refrigerator as he walked in and pulled out a wine bottle. She uncorked it, and poured into the two goblets she had placed on the counter. "Rule number one," she said. "You must drink constantly. It is the only way to maintain control." She handed him a glass. "Control is everything. Without it, as you will see, we will be killed."

He took the glass. Blood. The rich scent of it made his mouth water. He started to drain it as he had before, but she grabbed his wrist.

"Sip," she said. "Control is everything."

Sip. Sipping felt impossible. He wanted to drink it all. But he made himself take just a taste. It was too cold. He liked it better hot and fresh. His hands were shaking as he set the goblet down.

"Good," she said. She grabbed his glass and took it into the dining alcove. A glass table with a large vase of roses in the center dominated the room.

She sat and put his glass down at the place across from her. She shoved the roses aside. "Lesson number one. Food."

He took the glass and gulped. She yanked it away from him.

"No more until you listen," she said. "This is your survival we are talking about."

He clasped his hands on his lap, tightly so that he could hold them in place.

"Since you have done your first feeding, your metabolism has started to change. You probably noticed that what humans call food now nauseates you."

He remembered the borscht, its wonderful red color and its rotted taste.

"You may eat human food—a small taste here and there as a decoy. Humans believe that we cannot eat. Swallowing their overcooked concoctions proves to them that you are human, even though you are not."

Ben stared at his goblet. His mouth was watering. "I've eaten their food all my life."

She rubbed the glasses between her fingers. "Since you had fresh blood—during sex, no?—you have been unable to keep human food down."

"But you say I'll be able to eat it."

"Enough of it to convince them that you are human."

He swallowed the excess saliva. "You make this sound so important."

"It is your life we are discussing," she said. "Any mistakes and they will put a stake through your heart."

Her tone was calm. She hadn't moved as she spoke. Ben flinched. How had he gotten here? Had Steve done something to him?

"Mikos says I'm a hereditary vampire."

She nodded. "I am afraid so."

"Why? How do you know that Steve didn't just"—he closed his eyes —"do something to me."

"You are too strong," she said. "And you act like a virgin. From your own report the change came over you quickly. When a human turns, it happens slowly and there is rarely a sexual response. But you, your desire to live activates your sexuality, and will do so during the few years that you are fertile. It is an evolutionary response. Your species tries to survive just like all the others."

"My god." His species. He closed his eyes. His mother made roast beef on Sundays, and they all went to church. He was human. He had to be. "My parents eat real food."

"Really?" she asked. "How do you know they are your parents?"

—It's too loud! His breath was foul in Ben's face,

his eyes bloodshot. With a single, quick movement, he
pulled off his belt and it howled through the air be-
fore connecting on Ben's back. "You're supposed to be
quiet when I sleep!"

Ben winced and rolled. "Sorry," he said, but it did
no good. The belt flew again—

He pushed his chair back. She slid the goblet to him.
He drank until the contents were gone. It soothed him,
pushed the memory away. When he finished, he glanced
at her. She was staring at him as if she understood what
had happened.

"Control," she said. She took the glass from him and
carried it to the refrigerator. The refrigerator hissed as
she pulled it open and poured him another glass. "Let
us finish with food. Do not touch anything with garlic.
It will cast you into the same kind of stupor you found
in those hosts and that will allow a human to overpower you. Even the scent of garlic, in strong amounts,
will give you an instant high. It is very dangerous."

He took the goblet from her. The sides were cold. He
wasn't as hungry now. He had time to wait for it to
warm up.

"Water is poison. It will dehydrate you, and you will
slowly starve to death."

That explained the taste in his mouth when he woke
up. The water he had had after—once he got into the
bathroom.

"Drink only blood," Van said. "The fresher the better.
Human blood if you can get it. If you need to drink and
there is no blood, red wine will do. It will not harm
you, but it will not help you either. Is that clear?"

He nodded.

"Good," she said. "Now, we will move to behavior—"

A thud resounded behind them. "What are you doing?" a male voice demanded.

Ben turned. Mikos stood there. He wore a gray flannel suit, his long hair pulled back into a ponytail. He almost glowed with energy.

Van stood and faced him. Although she was much smaller, she moved with an equal power. "I am training him."

"He doesn't need training."

Ben frowned. Van had told him that Mikos had asked her to train him. Had she lied?

"You have never worked with a hereditary," she said. "They destruct in this modern world."

"Ben won't destruct," Mikos said.

"He has a hunger like none I have seen."

Mikos smiled. "Excellent. We will need it tonight."

Vangelina lifted her chin. "You will not take him anywhere until he is ready."

"It is my decision, Van. We need a virgin's strength."

Ben took a sip from his goblet, set it down, and resisted the urge to finish it. He couldn't deny what he was. Not when the blood tasted this good to him. "What do you want me to do?"

"I want you to put on a suit and meet me in the front lobby."

"Mikos, he has no control. He does not know what to say and how to use his body."

Ben's heart was pounding. Vangelina made it sound as if they were going to do something terrible.

"He knows how to use his body well enough." Mikos gestured with his thumb. "Go, Ben. Change clothes."

Ben picked up the goblet and finished the contents. He wiped his mouth with his hand, then licked off the excess blood. Strength throbbed through him.

Van put a hand on his arm and stopped him. "Mikos, this is wrong. He is not a dog for you to command."

Ben shook her off. He didn't need anyone defending him. He stood and walked over to Mikos. They were almost the same height. "You still haven't told me what you need me for."

"We need you to be yourself," Mikos said. "You are a predator. It is time you learn how to act like one."

Chapter Seven

$$\boxed{\textbf{i}}$$

Stop him!

    Cammie knew the voice belonged to her dream, but she couldn't wake up. She could see the faded night-gray of her bedroom, and over it, the forbidden sun-filled room of her dream. The voice came from down the hall: a man's voice, deep and angry.

Stop him!

She was holding a child, a little boy, clutching him to her shoulder, pressing his face against her skin to stifle his tears. She was lying alone in the safety of her own bed, knowing that what she was feeling wasn't real.

Stop him now!

"Shush," she whispered in both worlds. "You don't want him to get up, do you? Please be quiet. Please."

The little boy snuffled once and then was silent. In the night-gray of her bed, she clutched the sheets and willed the fear to go away. The pressure of a little-boy body eased and then faded into nothing. She was completely alone. No dreams. No phantoms. Just her.

She got up and went into the kitchen. Without turning on a light, she made herself a cup of tea and sat at the table. The nights had grown longer. And each night, phantoms and dreams about vampires' children. She had had Whitney check for a boy-child in Janie's family. There was none. The little boy was an addition from her subconscious, another child to protect, a child who was not herself. But she wanted to protect no one. She wanted to go back to her job, to go to work without seeing the face of a little girl whose father she had murdered, or the nonexistent, frightened face of a dream boy who needed her strength.

Reality. She woke up with the word at the front of her mind. When images, dreams, and fiction become more important than the here and now, a person needed a bit of reality. She had to break out of the dreams, and only one person could show her that she did not understand the life of a vampire's child.

She dressed without showering, drank a cup of English Breakfast tea while standing in front of her sink, ate half a donut and grabbed the car keys. The morning was cold for this late in the spring. A layer of frost covered the fresh new grass. She hoped the cold wouldn't kill the flowers.

The car started sluggishly. It needed maintenance— another expense that she couldn't afford—and she kept putting it off. She stamped on the gas pedal until the engine rocked to life.

She pulled out of her parking space and followed the drive by rote. On University Avenue, she realized she didn't remember how she got there. She vowed, at the stoplight leading to Westgate, that she would pay attention. The next thing she knew, she had pulled into the driveway at the Westrina Center.

It was still early. Only a handful of cars were in the parking lot, Anita's and DeeDee's among them. Cammie drove around back and parked near the entrance to the Children's Wing.

This wing had a different look from the rest of the building. Frost-covered flowers bloomed all around the windows. The gardening staff maintained the look so that the children had flowers from first thaw until the snow came. Even then, they had small evergreen bushes and pine trees to add a touch of green.

The outside doors were done in glass and gold, with more flowers painted on the surface. Visiting hours were marked in small letters, along with the words *Visitors must check in. Camera monitors will record any intruders. Unauthorized personnel will be subject to fines and trespassing charges.* The Center wanted no interference with the children, from family, from friends, or from creatures of the night.

Cammie pushed the door open. She was authorized. She had ID in her wallet to prove it.

The Children's Wing was warmer than the rest of the building. The heat felt good. Her tennis shoes left tracks on the highly polished floor. No toys were out yet—it was probably too early to allow children to make noise on the floor.

She walked up to the reception desk, rapped on it, and waved when Maria Applegate lifted her startled face from underneath the counter. Maria was a sturdy, well-built woman with a round warm face. The kind of woman who made children think of good meals and safe nights. She got to her feet, holding a handful of spilled papers.

"Who signed your pass?"

Cammie was already past the desk and making her way down the hall. "Whitney and I found that little girl from West Towne."

Maria nodded. Teams often dumped extra supplies on the children they found and would not always know who signed the executive orders. "Anita is in charge of that one. She's worried about her. Little girl's taking it hard. Anita's having us all watch her like . . ."

The words faded behind Cammie as she walked

down the hall. Most of the doors were closed. Little name labels had been stuck inside metal holders. Some bore only first names and ages, while others had full names and no ages at all. Still, the wings were grouped by sex and age. Janie's room would not be near anyone named Charles, who was eight.

Cammie rounded the corner. In this part of the wing, the walls had cuddly stuffed bunnies painted on them. The young wails and cries told her what the walls did. Infant care. These children were the most fortunate. They were usually adopted away, while the older children went to orphanages or a series of foster homes.

Finally, she found the right hallway. Some wag had made the walls light pink. Pink and blue beach balls followed a dotted line across the wall. On one panel, a small terrier jumped for the ball. On another a little girl in a too-short dress and matching panties ran after it. All of the children in this wing had no last names. Janie's door was the third on the right.

A light shone from under the door. Cammie knocked, then pushed the door open.

Janie sat on the bed, staring at the window. Her toys covered the shelves, except for the stuffed animals. They were tucked under the blankets, with their heads on the pillow. The dog was in her arms and the larger toys surrounded the bed like an armed guard.

Peppermint and child sweat gave the room a musty odor. Beneath it, Cammie thought she could still catch a faint whiff of rot.

Cammie pulled up a standard-issue blond wood chair. Its legs scraped the tile floor, making a shrill sound not unlike the squeal of hands along a blackboard.

Janie whirled. Her eyes grew wide when she saw Cammie. Janie bit her lower lip. Even with the pressure of her teeth, it was trembling.

Cammie slid closer. This wouldn't be easy, but she

had to try. "Hi," Cammie said. "I want to talk to you for a minute."

Janie's teeth bit into her lip so hard that blood ran down her chin. She grabbed a button beside the bed and started pushing it.

"It's okay." Cammie stood up. Maybe if she touched the little girl, showed Janie that she meant no harm—

Janie screamed. Her teeth freed her bottom lip, and blood sprayed Cammie and the bed. Janie grabbed all of her animals against her and screamed again, louder this time.

Cammie backed away. She could hear the sound of running feet in the hallway. "It's okay," she repeated.

Janie's screams echoed in the wide hall. Anita, Maria, and two orderlies appeared at the door. "What are you doing?" Anita snapped.

Cammie said nothing. Her body felt heavy.

"She didn't show me a pass when she came in. I thought something was odd," Maria said. "I didn't think that she'd do anything, though."

"You were right to call," Anita said, stepping into the room. "She wasn't authorized."

Cammie glanced at Janie. The little girl had stopped screaming. Blood had coated her chin red. Her small arms gathered the animals tighter. She was protecting the last thing of value in her world.

"I'm sorry," Cammie whispered, and ran past Anita.

The halls seemed longer than they had as she walked there. Her shoes made squishing sounds against the tile. A little boy opened his door as she ran past. His hair stuck up in clumps and he had two long scratches tracing one cheek. "Mommy?"

Cammie couldn't look at him. She didn't stop. More doors were open, with children standing behind them, watching with wide-eyed fascination.

She turned the last corner and stopped at the empty reception desk in front. Her breath was coming in huge gasps. All she had wanted to do was talk to the child, apologize, and perhaps gain a little understanding. The understanding she had gained—but she hadn't expected the cost.

She buried her head in her arms. No need to run any farther. They had seen her. Anita would fire her now.

She listened as another pair of rubber-soled shoes squeaked their way down the hall.

"What the hell were you doing?" Anita asked.

Cammie looked up. Anita stood beside her, arms crossed, the matronly look gone. "She okay?"

"I've got one orderly with her now and I've got a call in to Dr. Eliason because he's the only one she trusts." Anita's face was red. "Don't you understand? She hates women. Her father taught her that women are dangerous and you proved it by killing him. What were you trying to do?"

"I was trying to—" Cammie stopped. She couldn't explain, not the dreams, not the desire to get Janie out of her head. "—to talk to her."

"Well, don't," Anita said. "You've got another eradication tomorrow and I want you thinking about that, not some little girl whose life is no longer your concern. And I don't ever want to see you in this wing again. Do you understand that?"

Cammie nodded. She was trembling. Apparently Anita wasn't going to fire her—at least not yet.

"And, Cammie?"

Cammie froze. She stared at the stacks of papers with children's names on them behind Maria's desk.

"If you have not chosen a counselor after that eradication tomorrow, I will choose one for you. Is that understood?"

"Yes." Cammie's voice came out small and timid. She felt like a child herself, a child who expected to be punished. She couldn't stay any longer. No matter what Anita wanted her to do, Cammie couldn't. She had to get some air.

She walked slowly down the hall, feeling Anita's gaze

on her back. It was the first mistake Cammie had ever made, but it was a big one.

The glass door was cool to her touch. As she stepped outside, the air felt brittle. Still, the sunlight was warm and soothing against her face. Dream image. She tried to shake it, but couldn't. She turned back for Anita in time to see Eliason go through the side door. She clenched her fist and leaned against the small oak that they had built the sidewalk around. She could talk to Eliason. She would wait.

Chapter
Eight

Ben found a black silk suit that fit as if it were tailored for him. From what he could tell, without a mirror or any sort of reflecting glass to confirm, it made him look taller and older. At least, he hoped it did. All this training and explaining, the uncontrollable instant erections, and his confusion had all made him feel about thirteen. He needed something to give him a little age and dignity.

The argument between Van and Mikos left him unnerved. Van had been right about control, but Mikos seemed to be in charge. Ben didn't want to do anything to get thrown out of this place—at least, not until he understood better what was happening to him.

The clothes felt good against his body. If this was vampirism, no wonder the vampires didn't want the humans to know what it was really like. All of his senses were stronger, and he had never been able to achieve such ecstasy before. He doubted many people had that chance. He would learn control from Van, but he would never forget how to lose himself completely in the moment.

Someone had left a pair of socks and dress shoes outside his door. He put them on. The socks were made of a soft wool. The shoes were too narrow, but he could wear them. He would ask for a proper fit later.

The party sounds had grown even more wild as he made his way to the front lobby. The music beat had a sexual rhythm to it, and the raw fresh scent of blood had overtaken the cigarette smoke.

The haze began even before he found the open door leading into the party area. Laughter and light talk filtered around the music. He recognized some of the faces from the night before. Most were well dressed, holding goblets like Vangelina had taught him. Some had their hands on glassy-eyed people who swayed to a rhythm all their own. A naked man grabbed Ben's crotch.

"Please," the man said. "You're the virgin. Please."

Saliva dripped in Ben's mouth. He ran his tongue along his teeth. They seemed sharper than they had before. The man's hand got tighter, and Ben's penis sprang to a kind of life. The smell of fresh blood made him crave.

A hand clasped his shoulder. "Found him." His guard from the night before. The guard was blond and slender as a woman. He didn't look as if he had any strength at all. Ben reached up to caress the guard's cheek, but the guard caught his wrist. He dragged Ben away from the naked man. More men than women lay on the mats tonight. Ben looked at them with longing. Maybe when he got back, he would have a chance—

"Thought you said Van fed him," the guard said as they reached Mikos in the front foyer. "I saw him groping some sick cow with maybe a quarter ounce of blood in him."

"Hungry already?" Mikos asked. Mikos was wearing a suit as dark as his hair. It gave him a brooding look and accented his long features.

Ben glanced back at the crowd. One of the women writhed on her mat, hands playing with her own breasts. "I'd prefer to stay, sir," Ben said.

Strong fingers grabbed his chin and turned his head. Mikos's face was so close that Ben could feel warm breath on his cheeks. Mikos smelled of mint. No blood at all tonight. "First," Mikos said very softly, "you do not call me sir anywhere. We look to be the same age to the outside. Second, you will control your lusts. If you cannot, I will control them, which will be both unpleasant and painful. Do I make myself clear?"

Ben's groin tightened with the memory of pain. He tried to nod, but couldn't. "Yes," he said, lisping the s because of the pressure of Mikos's fingers.

Mikos let him go. Ben staggered backwards and caught himself against the wall. "Tonight," Mikos said, "you will do everything I tell you."

Ben nodded. They had to get out of there. If he didn't leave soon, he would go back to the cots, no matter what Mikos said.

"I don't think this is a good idea," the guard said.

"Shut up, Josef."

"The last newbie we took nearly got us all killed," a male voice said. Ben turned. This man was short and dark with muscles that matched Van's. He looked as if he were in his teens, but his eyes had the weariness of age to them.

"This one's different. He'll listen to me, won't you, Ben?"

Ben met Mikos's gaze. Mikos's eyes were as bloodshot as they had been the night before. "We'll be coming back here when we're done?"

Mikos smiled. The smile did not reach his eyes. "I'll pick out something special for you myself—if you still want it."

The phrase made Ben frown. Were they going to change him? After working so hard to make him like them? Was there something more going on here?

"Come on." Mikos opened the door and they stepped into the dark hallway. No lights illuminated the passages, but Ben could see better than he could the night before. When the door closed behind them, the sounds of the party became a thin bass thud from behind the walls. Four men walked with Ben and Mikos—Josef, the man who had spoken, and three others Ben didn't recognize.

They stopped in front of the elevator. Mikos pushed the down button. "All right," he said, rocking back on his heels. "Ben, these are my companions. You have met Josef. Meet also Dolph, Ernst, and Sven."

The three men made no movement to acknowledge their names. Dolph was the man who had spoken to him. Ben could not tell the other two apart. They were dark and powerfully built. Their suits matched. They looked like secret service agents he had seen on television—their physical appearance identical so as to make them difficult to identify.

"They will listen to me, about everything, as you must. This has to go quickly. We must return with plenty of time before dawn."

The elevator's iron doors creaked open. The men got inside. With a quick glance back toward the apartment—he wanted to be back sooner than dawn—Ben followed.

They went below street level to a parking garage. Their shoes clicked against the pavement. They stopped beside a black Lexus with tinted mirrors. With a chirrup, the alarm went off and Dolph got in the driver's side. Mikos and Josef crowded into the front seat. Ben found himself in the center back, straddling the hump, his suit being crumpled by two men twice his size.

The car purred to a start. They wound their way out of the garage and into the dark streets.

After midnight, the downtown streets were empty. A foghorn sounded in the bay. Eerie white streetlights cast ghostly reflections in the fog.

"SeaTac, Dolph," Mikos said, and leaned back in the front seat, apparently unconcerned.

Dolph turned on a narrower street and followed it to the freeway interchange. The freeways floated above like an elaborate maze from a science fiction movie. No one spoke. The only sounds were the car's wheels on the pavement and the whoosh of other cars as they passed. By the clock on the dash, they had driven for more than a half an hour by the time Dolph started following signs leading to SeaTac International Airport.

"Southcenter," Mikos said.

The car hissed along smaller roads that led to a fifties suburban housing development. Ranch-style houses built to accommodate starter families had been modified and refurbished to fit families that had never moved out of them. Mikos gave quiet directions, interrupting the silence with a "left" or "right next block." Finally he said, "thirteen-thirty-two" and Ben took a moment to realize that Mikos meant an address.

The men beside Ben stiffened, and the temperature seemed to rise. The car stopped in front of one of the ranch houses. In the glare of the porch light, Ben noted a redwood deck that ran around the house. Aluminum siding gave the house's sides a shiny appearance. The two-car garage was open, and a Porsche was parked to one side. Oil stains showed where another car should have been.

"He here?" Josef asked.

"He's here," Mikos said.

They got out of the car. The slamming doors echoed on the quiet street. Down an alley, a dog barked, the sound deep and throaty, almost threatening. Mikos led the way up the driveway. Before Ben could follow, Dolph grabbed his arm. "You do anything wrong," he said, "and I will hurt you in ways you have never heard of before."

The threat was soft. "I'll be careful," Ben said.

The crawly feeling had returned. When Dolph let go of him, Ben rubbed his arms. A jittery sense, too rough to be adrenaline. The last time this started, he had gotten dizzy and weak.

He and Dolph followed the group into the garage.

Mikos stood back as Josef worked the lock. The door opened easily and they stepped inside.

The house was dark and reeked of unwashed dishes. Still, Ben could see. The kitchen had also been remodeled. A stove island that was not part of the original plan stood in the center. Pots and knives hung from the ceiling of the bar. One of the knives was missing.

Ben could also smell a faint trail of dried blood that ran from the kitchen to the living room. Mikos followed the scent and turned on the living room light.

"Have you reconsidered?" His voice was soft, urbane.

Ben rounded the corner into the living room. One of the other men was closing the curtains. The room was done in stark whites. A fireplace stood at one end, and above it, a Miro. Ben recognized it from his three semesters of art history.

A balding middle-aged man wrapped in a blanket sat in a rocking chair next to the fireplace. He was overweight, the flesh on his face hanging in folds. His skin was an ashen gray, his eyes glazed—not with a sexual high, like the people at the party, but with exhaustion. Bloody handprints smeared the blanket and a small pool of dried blood had formed beneath the chair.

"Couldn't face me alone?" the man asked. The words were muffled through his swollen lips. "Had to bring reinforcements?"

"I could have killed you this morning," Mikos said. "But I value you, Ian. We have worked well together."

"The money is gone, Mikos. I can't raise that much in twenty-four hours."

"It doesn't look as if you tried," Mikos said. "I left you in that chair."

"I need a week," Ian said.

Mikos reached over and put his hand on the back of Ben's neck, pushing him forward. "Ian, meet my newest associate, Ben. Ben, Ian. Ben is a virgin, Ian."

Ian's body tensed. His grip on the blanket tightened.

"Before I found him, he had been starving."

"I barely stopped him from draining Sheila last night," Josef said.

"He's had two glasses of 'wine' today. Not quite a pint. Just enough to whet his appetite."

The saliva was back in Ben's mouth. The man in front of him was human. He could hear the blood whispering through the man's veins.

"I am not lying to you," Ian's voice was shaking. "I will have the money for you in a week. You can have anything you want until then. I have more paintings in the back—"

"What use do I have for excellent forgeries?" Mikos asked. "Really, Ian. You know me better than that."

Ian threw off the blanket. He wore only a pair of shorts beneath it. As he struggled to get to his feet, he wobbled. His knees were flattened and bruised. He had bite marks all over his chest and neck.

Ben trembled. Part of his mind noted all of this and was appalled. But his body smelled the blood. His body controlled.

"Please, Mikos," Ian said. "Please give me time."

"I gave you time," Mikos said. "I want the money now."

"If you kill me, you'll never get it," Ian said.

"Ah, but I will. It is so easy to get control of your holdings." Mikos let go of Ben's neck and pushed him forward. "Just a sip, Ben. Just a sip."

Ben collided with Ian. He wasn't going to bite him—the man was begging—but the scent of dried blood filled him. Ian pushed at him weakly. Ben's teeth brushed Ian's shoulder, then he sank them in. The blood was fresh and thick. He tried to stop at a sip, but it tasted so good. Ian squirmed and with one hand, Ben held him back. Another erection built, but Ben ignored it. He didn't want to be sexual with this man. He wanted one sip. One long sip.

Finally he pulled his head away. Ian had stopped struggling. He lay on the chair, eyes half open. Mikos and the others stood around him.

"I tried to stop at a sip," Ben said, his words slurring. God, he still wasn't full. He had never been so hungry in his life.

Mikos did not smile. "You have more control than I expected, boy. You were supposed to kill him."

The words sent something free in Ben, something that rational voice in his head had held back. "Kill him?" he asked, and without waiting for an answer, lunged against Ian, ripping into his neck, tearing the flesh back and drinking, drinking. This time, he did free his penis and played with it with one hand while he sucked. The blood-coated flesh tasted good too, and he ripped at it, taking huge chunks and swallowing them.

Finally he bit into an artery, and the blood spurted down his throat. Someone else grabbed his penis and stroked it, and more hands covered his body until he was all taste and sensation, nerve endings alive and tingling and throbbing. The blood inside him gave him a warmth he had never had, and hands on him made him feel so wonderful. As the last bit of blood pulsed into him, he felt an orgasm build. He arched, anticipating it, and the hands let him go. The disappointment stalled the orgasm and he looked up, bloody and confused.

Mikos's cool hand cupped his cheek. "You're not done yet, boy."

They stood him up and gave him a towel so that he could wipe off his face. Mikos kept one hand on Ben's shoulder. When the trembling in Ben's body ceased and he became flaccid, Mikos turned him toward the rocking chair.

Ian's hair twisted crookedly on his head. The left side of his face was gone. Clean white skull shone through the gaps in the skin. A flap on his neck had been ripped back, and the tendons stood out. Large, gaping wounds flayed his chest.

The blood churned in Ben's stomach.

"Such lovely work," Mikos said. "Imagine what you would have done if you were starving."

"I didn't do that," Ben said.

"Ah, but you did." Mikos's voice was soft and mocking. "And you enjoyed it."

Ben shook himself free of Mikos and walked over to Ian. The smell of blood made him want to bury his face in those awful remains.

"They are prey. They are cows. They are dinner," Mikos said. "You see them as important and that is wrong. They are nothing compared to us. They are nothing like us."

"What did he do?" Ben asked.

"Do?" Mikos laughed. "He got in my way when I needed an example. He didn't *do* anything."

"I killed a man for nothing?" Ben whispered.

"You killed a man for supper and learned the extent of your powers." Mikos slid his arm around Ben's shoulder. "You needed to know what kind of damage you could inflict. If your intelligence is appalled, you will learn control. If not, you will have a short, but sensual life."

Ben glanced back at the body. The fresh scent of blood had become tainted, almost like spoiled milk. He was appalled. He was. He had to be. "Van called me your dog," he said. "You're not going to make me do this all the time, are you?"

Mikos laughed. The sound was deep, throaty, and charming. "Ah, Ben, you must learn. I have not made you do anything. You have chosen to do it all yourself."

Chapter Nine

i

Eliason had not turned on his car alarm. Cammie was in luck. She glanced around the Center's parking lot. The Children's Wing looked empty. Everyone must have been focusing on Janie—on Cammie's mistake.

She picked the lock on Eliason's ten-year-old Ferrari, and slipped into the passenger seat. The interior still smelled of leather and gleamed as if someone had done a recent polish. Only the analog systems on the dash and the wide construction made it look like a car from the early eighties instead of one built in the nineties.

He remained inside a long time. She dozed off and awakened several times before she heard his footsteps on the walk. She braced herself. When Eliason yelled at her, it was worse than Anita. He knew how to get to her.

He unlocked the driver's door and slid in. "Hope you didn't damage the lock," he said.

She didn't look at him. He brought the scent of light cologne mixed with rubbing alcohol into leather mix. "I was trained by the best."

"Does that mean I sue Sarge if the lock's broken forever?"

"Nah," Cammie said. "I'm richer than she is."

"Probably." He ran his long, slender fingers on his jeans. "You been out here all morning?"

"I didn't expect you to be inside so long." She closed her eyes, waiting for him to launch at her. She had given him the opening.

"Neither did I." He slid the keys into the ignition. "They warned me in med school, though. They said that good doctors rarely had days off."

The engine purred to a start. He reached over and put his hand on hers. His fingers were warm. "You want a cup of coffee? I haven't had lunch yet."

"Me, either." Her hand felt trapped beneath his, but she didn't move. She glanced at him sideways, wondering what was wrong with her. He was intelligent, attractive, and well off. They shared the same taste in books, films, and food. They had wonderful discussions. He had worked for the Center longer than she had, and she had never seen him do anything violent. He was safe. He was smart, he was gentle, and he scared her.

"Ovens?"

"Okay."

He put the car into gear and spun out of the parking lot. As long as she had known him, he drove fast cars with an assurance only good drivers had. He never endangered her life, but he always made her feel as if she had just helped him qualify for the Indy 500.

He steered with his left wrist resting on the wheel. His right hand balanced on the gear shift. "Know a good toy store?"

Cammie's shoulders tensed. He was asking for Janie. "Puzzlebox on State."

"I'd forgotten about that. They have lots of stuffed animals?"

"The entire back of the store. Mostly spendy ones, like Gund."

"It's okay. She treats them well." He spun the car onto University and half slid across the divider into the Shorewood shopping center. He parked around back so no one would see the bright red car.

They got out, and this time he turned on the alarm.

He took her arm as they walked along the narrow sidewalk, past the gallery, to the restaurant.

The Ovens of Brittany had several restaurants in town, all of them good. Cammie loved the one on Shorewood, though, because they had put their bakery by the entrance. Three chefs in white worked on morning buns. One rolled the dough up front, another basted them before putting them in the large ovens, and a third put the finished buns on a cooling rack. Cinnamon and baking bread filled the air. Cammie's stomach growled.

"I'm hungrier than I thought," she said.

"When was the last time you had a meal?"

She frowned. She couldn't remember. Eliason sighed. He put his hand on her back as he opened the door. A Mozart piano concerto tinkled overhead. The warm scent of baked goods mingled with wine from the bar, a mingling of roasting beef from the kitchen.

A slender hostess grabbed two menus and held them to her chest. "Usual spot, Brett?"

"Yes," he said. He hadn't let go of Cammie's back. The hostess glanced at her, then looked away. She led them down a short flight of stairs, so that they sat beside a quietly running fountain filled with pennies. The water and the music made some of the tension leave Cammie's shoulders. The hostess handed them menus and walked back up, saying nothing.

A busboy set water glasses with a slice of lemon in front of them. Cammie set the menu aside without looking at it, already knowing what she wanted.

Eliason glanced at his, then set it on top of hers. They said nothing as they waited for the waitress. Cammie ordered a vegetarian omelet, a small morning bun, an orange juice, and an espresso. Eliason asked for a chicken potpie.

When the waitress left, Eliason leaned forward and took Cammie's hand. She smiled, just a little, and pulled her hand away. "How bad did I fuck her up?"

Eliason sighed. "You didn't help her. I finally had to

give her something to calm her down. You're the last person she should have seen."

He made the comment calmly, with no judgment at all. Cammie squirmed. She wanted him to yell at her. She had been stupid and she wasn't sure why. "Is she going to get better?"

Eliason shrugged. "I don't know what better is in this case. Technically she was better when her father was alive."

Cammie unfolded her linen napkin and snapped it on her lap. "The Center sent me to his house."

The waitress brought the orange juice, morning bun, and a salad for Eliason. "I know they sent you," Eliason said.

"Then why is everyone acting like I did something wrong? Whitney was there too. We were doing our jobs."

"No one has said that you made a mistake." Eliason picked at the lettuce. "He would have turned on her. They always do. This one's bothering you too much, Cammie."

She took the bun and put it in front of her. It was warm. She ripped its edges into small pieces and buttered them. The bun didn't look as good as it had a moment ago. "No one ever warned me about children."

"No one thought they had to."

She glared at him. The waitress set down two steaming cups of espresso. Eliason took his, filled it with cream and sugar, and stirred it as if nothing were wrong.

"You don't know the history of the Westrina Center, do you?" he asked.

Cammie took a bit of the bun. Rich and sugary mingled with just enough butter. It tasted wonderful. She spoke between bites. "It's been here forever, and about twenty years ago, it changed buildings after this rehabilitation program started."

Eliason picked at his salad and pushed it away. "Nice, encapsulated, short, and straight out of the manual. Ever wonder why they train so many people like you?"

"Because there's so many vampires."

"There's not that many vampires."

Cammie finished the bun. She put the plate on the edge of the table. A busboy whisked it away. "They already told us when they recruited us. High burnout. People last about three years."

"And you've been here, what?" Eliason sipped his expresso. "One?"

"Over two."

The waitress brought their food. Cammie's omelet took up half the plate. Cheese smothered the vegetables, and homemade hash browns covered the side. Eliason's chicken potpie was baked in a puffed pastry. They ate for a moment in silence. Occasionally, he would look at her as if measuring her. Finally he set his fork down.

"When did the dreams start?" he asked.

Cammie jerked, nearly knocking a bite of omelet into the fountain. Eliason's eyes were dark brown and very intense. She had never noticed that before. "I've always had dreams," she said.

"But you're having nightmares now."

She swallowed. His voice was soft. Her eyes burned and she longed to rub them. She took a deep breath, and made herself look at him. "Anita's making me see a counselor."

"I think that's a good idea." Eliason said. "Janie doesn't hold the answers for you. She's got to search for her own when she's ready. You, on the other hand, already know how to search."

Cammie felt a blush build on her cheeks. She hadn't meant to disturb the child, but Eliason was right. She hadn't been thinking of anyone but herself. "I don't know what I'm searching for," she said.

"I think you do," he said.

She glanced at her hands. The nails were flat and cut close to her fingertips. "I went back to my textbooks last night," she said. "They did have passages on children and vampires. They said that every child of a vampire had a high chance of becoming a vampire too. The chances went up if the child was natural, not adopted."

"I know, Cam." Eliason's voice was soft.

"I didn't remember any of that." She took a sip of her espresso. It was warm and rich, just the way she liked it. "There's a lot of things I don't remember. My whole first grade year is gone. I can't even tell you where I went to school."

"You should work with a counselor on this," Eliason said.

"I don't want to work with a counselor. I don't want to pay someone to talk to me!" Cammie's voice rose on the last sentence. The young couple at the next table looked over at her. She avoided their gaze and ran a finger along the rim of her demitasse cup. Eliason wasn't going to listen any more than anyone else was. She pushed her hair away from her face and changed the subject. "Why did you ask me about the history of the Center?"

"Because," he said, his expression not changing. "About twenty-five years ago, when the rehab program failed, a number of the counselors became vampires themselves. Too many vampires to stop in such a short period of time. The people left worked on keeping the threat from spreading, not at taking care of the vampires who already existed. They lived mostly in the Willy Street area, and no one went there, and no one left, not even the children who lived with a vampire, like Janie did. Do you understand me?"

"Not completely." The food churned in Cammie's stomach. "The children had to fend for themselves?"

"Everyone did, until the Center finally decided on eradication in all cases."

Cammie had finished half of her omelet. That was enough. She drank the fresh squeezed orange juice as if she had just come off a marathon, then cupped the demitasse cup in her right hand. She was still trembling. "Must have been pretty ugly."

"You tell me," Eliason said. He finished the last of the potpie.

"Me?"

"Sarge tells me you were sick on the day she took your class to the Old Westrina Center. The only sick day recorded in your entire file."

Cammie nodded. She remembered that. She had awakened with the worst case of stomach flu she had ever had. "Twenty-four-hour bug."

"Was it?" Eliason asked. "Or was it nerves?"

"Nerves?"

"What would you do if I took you to the old Westrina Center this afternoon."

"This afternoon?" She was parroting him. She hated doing that, even to stall. "I haven't had much sleep, Brett. I—"

"Do you even drive by it? When was the last time you were on East Wash?"

"I don't live in that part of town." She frowned. "What are you getting at?"

"Come with me, Cammie." His voice was gentle. He held out his hand and this time she took it. "I'll keep you safe."

Her throat got dry as they rounded Capitol Square. East Washington Avenue had more lanes than she remembered, but the near east side still looked as it had in the fifties. Warehouses, dilapidated storefronts. And there, off to her right, the oversized fortress that had once housed the Westrina Center.

She didn't know how he had talked her into this.

In the late forties, the Westrina Center had taken over the building that had once housed Madison East High

School. The school moved its headquarters farther out to accommodate the children of the workers at the up-graded Oscar Mayer plant. The old building, built in the teens, was too large for the Center, but they quickly filled it with function rooms and bunks for the children.

Cammie put a hand to her forehead. Amazing the information she had picked up and hadn't realized she had.

"You okay?" Eliason asked.

Cammie nodded. She was dizzy, but she wasn't going to tell him. Visiting a part of town she hadn't been in shouldn't be hard.

Eliason swung the Ferrari into the empty parking lot. Broken glass littered the cracked pavement. He drove to the main entrance and parked in front of it. "I'll wait here if you want," he said.

Cammie sat for a moment, waiting for the dizziness to fade. Then she grabbed the door handle and let herself out of the car.

The sun was half hidden behind the tall buildings of the university, casting the school in shadow even though it was mid-afternoon. Cammie's shoes crunched on the glass.

A padlocked wire fence surrounded the building. Obviously not designed to keep vampires out. It kept humans from prowling the grounds. Still, the vampire defenses remained. The large wood double doors had ancient garlic nailed to them. All the windows were barred with small crosses and none had been broken.

The old Center was not as big as she expected it to be. Still, as the shadows made their way across the lawn, the Center loomed, holding a power the new, modern facility didn't have.

He's just a baby. I take care of him!

The little girl's voice was insistent. Cammie put her hands on the cold wire, but could see no one.

I need to see him. Nobody else knows how to take care of him. . . .

She wandered around to the side of the building, saw the half-ruined remains of a playground. The swings were mere chains and the teeter-totter had rotted into the earth.

I don't want to play. I want to see him . . .

And then the scream, so long and shrill that she had to close her eyes. The sound ripped the pain from her belly, let it rise into her neck and mouth. She leaned her head into the wire, feeling the metal dig into her forehead.

She had clutched her little brother's hand tightly, as two people, smelling of blood, led her into the Center. As they walked into Reception, she was surprised to see how many people waited for her, how quiet they seemed. She said nothing. A slender man knelt beside her, pried her brother's hand from her own. She looked at her brother's face, the face she had protected all this time, and was startled at the blood on it. Blood spattered all over his clothes. Tears built behind her eyes, but she didn't let them fall. She hadn't wanted him to know, but there he was, blood-covered and frightened. She reached out to him, but the man picked him up and carried him away.

And she never saw him again. They told her she was too dangerous. Too unstable. Too frightened.

You might hurt him. You wouldn't want to do that, now, would you, honey?

She pushed herself away from the fence. Her forehead ached and her entire body shook. She wiped her face with her sleeve, and then looked up. Eliason leaned against a tree, his arms crossed.

"You followed me," she said.

He nodded.

"And you knew."

"Yes," he said. "Current rehabilitation theory. You can't do anything for the parents, but you can save the children."

"I don't feel saved," she said, and pushed past him.

"Cammie—"

His voice echoed behind her, one of many trailing into the growing twilight. Her father had called her Camila, her brother Cam-Cam. She had adopted Cammie because it brought no pain.

Until now.

Chapter Ten

X The arm felt heavy across his neck. Ben pushed it away and sat up, his naked body sliding on the satin sheets of his bed. The woman's long red hair covered her face, but the two gashes he had opened in her neck showed. He leaned over and sucked a bit more, just enough to clear his head and give him the strength to get up.

He stretched. Amazing how quick he could get hungry again. The redhead had been his third the night before— all young, new cows themselves—and his third orgasm too. Van said the sexual stimulation would ease, but so far it had only gotten more intense. He had slept through the day, as he was supposed to, and awoke hungry again.

This time, he would pick his own cows. Mikos had a reason for giving him these young things, but two of them had been very frightened. Ben had had to hold them down until the drug in his saliva had worked its way into their system. The redhead was the only one who seemed to be familiar with the routine.

He got up, grabbed his kimono off the chair and slapped the redhead. "Wake up," he said.

She shook her head and pushed her hair back. She would have been pretty if it weren't for her glassy eyes.

"Come on." He picked his wallet off the night stand and pulled a ten from it. "Here. Get yourself some breakfast. Mikos will probably want you again tonight. Your clothes are on the floor."

She sat up and squinted at him.

"Hurry. You've been here too long already."

He turned on the light beside the bed and tossed her clothes at her. Then he tied his kimono and left the room.

The party hadn't started yet. After three nights, he no longer slept as long as he had in the first. He was also learning how to stop himself from taking too much from one cow. Mikos had been right: killing Ian had cured Ben of that almost immediately. They had only had to push him off one more cow, and that had been just after, when the killing lust still ran through him.

The kitchen light was on. Van sat at the table, playing solitaire. She had her hair pulled back, away from her face, and the harsh light gave her an odd beauty. Ben opened the refrigerator and poured himself a glass of house wine. The barriers were coming down. A week ago, he had been appalled at sucking someone's blood. Now he looked forward to it.

"You are not dressed yet," Van said.

"Soon." Ben sat across from her. He took the eight of hearts, and the four cards spread beneath it, and set them on the nine of spades.

"I would have done that," Van said.

"You didn't see it." He sipped the wine. The coppery taste soothed the jitters running through him. "Answer some questions for me?"

"Maybe," she said.

"Where's the money come from?"

Van didn't look up. "Investments."

"What kind?"

Van set the cards down and looked at him. "Most of us here have been alive for a long time. The longer you live, the wiser you get. The wiser you get, the more money you make."

"You didn't answer me," he said.

She smiled. "I know. It is not any of your business. Mikos will take care of you."

"Like he took care of Ian?"

She picked up the cards again, and started going through the pile. "Ian made his own mistakes."

"What was Ian? He wasn't a vampire. He wasn't a cow."

"He was a servant who bit his master." Mikos stood in the doorway, his hair tousled from sleep. He was wearing jeans, no shirt and no shoes. His torso was flat and bare. His ribs were outlined beneath his skin. "You ask a lot of questions, Ben. Most people who come here are content to eat, and fuck, and sleep in luxury, in return for a few odd favors that I ask."

"Should I shut up?" Ben asked, having no such intention.

"No. I like an inquiring mind. I have missed it." Mikos crossed the room. He opened the refrigerator and took a bottle of wine for himself, then came to the table and sat beside Ben. "Haven't you, Van?"

"I like things quiet."

"I'm sure you do." Mikos kicked back and put his bare feet on another chair. "Van made the mistake of getting too involved in our last project. She barely escaped with her life."

Van scooped up the cards and shoved them to the side of the table. "Ben does not need to know this."

"I think he does." Mikos took a swig from the bottle, then wiped his mouth. "I think he needs to know modern history—from the correct viewpoint."

Van stood up. "I think you are deluding yourself. The way you are teaching him, he does not need to know anything. He will be dead soon."

"Then how did he learn control so quickly? He had a willing cow in his bed when he woke up, yet he's here, sipping—sipping, mind you—from a goblet. How long did it take you to learn how to drink in a civilized fashion?"

"I do not remember," Van said with a firmness that implied that she did. "It was over a hundred years ago."

"It took me nearly a year." Mikos took another swig and faced Ben. "Most vampires die in that first year because they get caught. They get caught because they cannot control themselves. You have extra strength, and have taken more blood than I have seen any virgin take, and yet within a week, your body is under control."

"Hereditaries are different. They may seem in control, but the power overtakes them," Van said.

"Just because you saw it once doesn't mean that it will always happen." Mikos set the bottle on the table with a glass thump. "His body will develop differently from ours. It has been preparing for this from birth."

"The humans think they can reform hereditaries." Van's slender fingers played with the back of the chair.

Mikos gave Van a slow, cold look. Ben didn't understand the undertones of the conversation. They were fighting about something. With him as the focus. "I would wager," Mikos said, "that our Ben was on the forefront of the reform movement." Without taking his gaze from Van, he said, "Ben, who was the first vampire you ever remember meeting?"

—breath foul. He scooped Ben up and tucked him under his arm, carrying him to the kitchen. Ben kicked, but did not cry out. "Daddy," he whispered. "No . . ."—

"You're the first vampire I ever met," Ben said. The other memory was strong, but odd. The man who had carried him across the room had not been the father he had left in Oregon. "Although my friend Steve was one."

"Your friend Steve." Mikos's tone was mocking. He took a sip from the bottle. "Remember Steve, Van?"

"He was a fool," Van said.

"He was once human."

"Does that mean someone turned him?" Ben asked.

Mikos nodded.

"No one turned me, but I changed." Ben frowned. This was making no sense to him.

"Humans call it puberty," Van said. "Only in the hereditary vampire, it lasts nearly ten years, until the vampire is strong enough to survive on its own. Tell me, Ben. Did you kill the woman?"

Ben took another sip from the goblet. His hand was shaking. He hadn't killed Candyce, but he had come close. Too damn close.

He still wasn't completely under control. The thought of Candyce made him want to grab that redhead before she left and drain her.

He didn't move. "No," he said.

"No?" Van asked. "You took your first blood without killing?"

Ben nodded. Van's eyes were wide. She appeared to be seeing something beyond him.

"I told you," Mikos said. "He's strong."

"He's dangerous," Van said. She grabbed Mikos's bottle and stalked out of the room.

"What's with her?" Ben asked.

"You terrify her. You bring back memories she would rather forget."

"Memories of what?"

Mikos grinned and caressed Ben's cheek. "In time, *caro mio*. In time. Let's start with your questions instead."

Ben finished his glass, got up, and poured himself another. He would rather have asked these questions of Van. Mikos was too smart. He would understand that Ben's questions weren't all innocence. Then Ben would not play the innocent.

"I have never seen a setup like this before." Ben returned to his chair and straddled it. "Do you own the building?"

"And the Italian restaurant, complete with garlic." Mikos smiled. "It's a nice front."

"For what?" Ben asked. He took a sip. The wine tasted good.

"Not much really. You see most of what we do. It's an idle time. We've been waiting for something to change."

"Who was Ian?"

"Bothers you, doesn't it? Killing a man."

Ben shook his head. "I enjoyed it." The words were hard to get out. He had enjoyed it. Sometimes, when he thought about it, he was surprised at his lack of shock, his own ability to adapt so easily.

Mikos took his bottle and set it on his lap. For the first time, he seemed to be measuring Ben. "No qualms?"

Ben paused. He should have had them. The life his parents had taught him, the career track he had been on, all those petty concerns about legalities and good grades and other people—it was as if they had never existed. As if that life had belonged to someone else. That Ben would have been horrified at his actions with Ian. This Ben felt a faint stirring of sexual desire.

"It's not something I would do every night," Ben said, "but I don't regret it. I want to find out what's happening here."

"Van didn't lie to you. The money comes from investments made a long time ago. I have more assets than I care to think about. Ian helped me manage those, until I caught him embezzling from me. Stupid human. He had two weeks to get the money for me. He did not. He seemed to think he was invaluable."

"Was he?"

"Very few people are essential to any operation. Ian was not one of them." Mikos took a swig from the bottle. "I am smart enough to keep the people I need alive."

"Where did you get your money?"

Mikos smiled. "That is an indelicate question."

Ben stood up. Someone peered in the kitchen door. He walked over and shut it. "You talk as if I am the person you've been waiting for. I have no clue if you give this speech to every new recruit. But the lifestyle I have

adopted thanks to you does not allow me to live the life
I had planned. I can't go to law school in the daytime. I
can barely be around humans now. Sunlight always
bothered me, which was why I was going to stay in the
Northwest, but now even daylight makes me queasy. My
body brought me into this, but since you have helped
me regain my mind, I want to know everything I can
about this operation. You make the trains run on time.
That question got answered right away. Now I want to
know how you afford it."

"You are a good American boy. You will not like what
I have to tell you."

"I killed for you. I think that no longer makes me a
good American boy."

Mikos set the wine bottle down and ran a hand
through his hair. He leaned back. "I left Germany in 1944
when it became clear that nothing would save the Nazi
cause. Most of us supported Hitler, and there was even
talk that he was one of us. When Hitler came to power
in the early thirties, I already had a good economic base
from investments, stolen money, years of careful planning. The Nazis gave me the opportunity to kill with im-
punity as long as the dead belonged to the prescribed
groups. I started early and made sure that most of my
victims' assets became mine."

"Jews?"

"Some. The richer ones. A few Catholics, and a number of gypsies. I invested in Sweden under various
aliases—a smart move, as it turns out—and in motion
pictures here in the States, again under different names.
Some of my money remained in Germany and it is now
gone."

Ben started to ask a question. Mikos held up his hand
to stop it.

"In 1944, with the help of friends, I left Germany. My
friends got me to Alaska, where I lived for four barren
years. When it was safe, I settled in Chicago and spent
the next twenty years bringing over my friends. The

Midwest got wise to us by the mid-sixties, and the stupid newbies started dying. I moved West, bought up much of Seattle, and have been here quietly ever since."

"You have lived like this for decades?" Ben was growing bored after three nights. He needed something to stimulate his mind, to keep him active. The sex was wonderful, but sex and food were not all there was to life.

Mikos corked the wine bottle and set it on the table. "I was tired of running, and I am also not the kind of man who lets his reach exceed his grasp. Too many of us do that, and then we die rather spectacularly."

"I don't understand," Ben said. "You speak of living quietly and then you talk of high hopes for me. Is that what you tell each virgin?"

"Ah, no." Mikos got up and ran his hands in Ben's hair. Ben let Mikos touch him, although the instant arousal from a few days earlier was gone. "You shall save me from dying of boredom."

"Me?"

"Yes. The children you will father will have a power beyond even our imagining. We must guard and protect them for they are worth more than we shall ever be. The children of hereditaries have twice the strength of their parents. *Twice,* Ben."

Mikos slid his hands inside the kimono. Ben caught them. Mikos sighed and returned to his chair. He took a sip of his wine before continuing. "But even before you have children to raise, you will have something to do. Most hereditaries live in Europe and die when their natural inclinations show themselves. The Europeans believe that vampirism caused much of their problems in this century. In many centuries. Examine history closely, my friend. Our race began in northern Europe. The wars there were bloody, often focused on exterminating the foe. Even the World Wars sought to annihilate. Many of our people died—too many. For a while, we wondered if the race would survive—the real race, not those like me who had been turned, but the powers, the hereditary vampires who could concern themselves with more than eating and fucking."

"I grew up here," Ben said.

"Yes, but where were you born?"

"The Midwest."

Mikos nodded. "We have seen a handful of hereditaries come out of there. Children of vampires. Some were immigrants—children of hereditaries. But others were children of the turned. We are an amazing race, for we can create more of our kind. And you, I will wager, are the child of a hereditary. An immigrant, perhaps—or a late developer whose father had fought in one of the World Wars. Did your parents have an accent?"

—too much noise—

"I don't remember," Ben said.

Mikos took another sip of wine. "We'll see what you remember. The Midwest housed most of our people for a long time. There and northern European settlements in the East. Most vampires die, rather brutally. Slayings by former vets who served in the World Wars. Curious, don't you think?"

Ben closed his eyes. The afternoon in high school when the coach had kicked him off the basketball team for pummeling an opponent until blood sprayed everything, the girls who refused to date him again because his love bites were too painful. The signs were there. "I'm sure someone would have noticed me. How come I made it up here?"

"Because," Mikos said, "someone was thoughtful enough to ship you out West. When I came here there were no vampiric enclaves. The vets forgot what they saw in the war, and chalked it up to war crimes. It has only been in the last two decades that our numbers here have grown."

"No one understood?"

"And if they did, they were not paying attention. Vampires are not a problem here. Life is good. You have heard that as often as I have. Westerners have a strong regional snobbery that makes 'diseases' of the east an impossibility."

Ben grabbed Mikos's wine bottle, uncorked it, and drank down nearly half. When he finished, he wiped his mouth off with his hand.

"You are part of a new generation," Mikos said. "The first hereditaries to become adults in the United States. With the freedoms granted by this country, the court systems, and the protections for individuals, we have an opportunity we have never had before. If we are careful in the West, unlike other parts of the country where we are already known, we can establish ourselves completely. I have the money, Ben. As soon as your body adjusts, you will have the energy."

"To do what?"

"To gain true power."

"Political power?" Ben cupped the bottle against him. Power. He loved feeling a cow beneath his fingers. Political power was that sexual feeling on a grand scale. Excitement whispered through him.

"But Van said we can't go in front of cameras. Mirrors and stuff."

"Power is never held in the political arena. Power is money, Ben. The people who control the economy control the politicians. And we have some evidence that hereditaries can be photographed. We will experiment with you."

"People with the money have power," Ben repeated. He set the bottle on the table and twirled it, making a chiming sound. *"You* will have the money."

Mikos smiled. "I like your mind, Ben."

"Then you will not serve me, as you said."

Mikos shrugged. "We shall see, won't we?"

Chapter
Eleven

Another night without much sleep. Whenever Cammie dozed, she felt forbidden sunlight on her back, heard the door open, and her father snap *Camila!* Ben was crying. Ben was always crying, and she couldn't shut him up. She grabbed the dowel Mr. Conner at the corner drugstore had whittled down to a point *(just in case, Cammie)*—and woke herself up.

Over and over again.

Once she had picked up the phone to call Eliason. She let his number ring twice before hanging up. This was hers. She had to deal with it.

Alone, as she always had.

Dawn found her at the kitchen table, skimming Laura Kinsale's *Flowers in the Storm,* a novel Cammie had read four times because, she knew now, it was about someone who survived against incredible psychological, physical, and emotional odds. The book gave her no comfort now, but she tried to escape anyway. Still, that deep, angry voice echoed in the back of her head:

Camila!

Camila, how's a man supposed to sleep around here with that racket?

Camila! Shut him up. Shut him up or I will!

Finally she set the book down and turned on *Good*

Morning America, not because she liked the program, but because the *Today Show* reminded her of breakfasts at her foster home, long, tedious breakfasts in which her foster father read the paper, her foster mother cooked, and Cammie dutifully ate everything from burnt waffles to runny eggs. Even now, she could taste the fake maple syrup.

She shut off the television. Her brain would give her no peace now. The secrets were out. She could no longer hide them, even from herself.

She sighed. She had taken the Westrina Center's scholarship because she had needed the money. She had shown an aptitude (not surprisingly) for psychology with an emphasis on vampires, and the major had interested her. Nothing else really had. She thought she had found her calling. Instead the Westrina Center had sought her out because they knew what she was. She had joined them because she had no choice, because she was doomed to reenact her past until she could escape it.

Damn Anita for using her. Damn Anita for using them all.

In the name of healing.

I can't say any more, Sarge had said. *This is Anita's baby. You'll have to make an appointment with her.*

Sarge didn't like it. Sarge had never liked the program, and that was why it had suddenly become a very big deal. Not because of Cammie's reaction, but because Sarge was again confronted with Anita's program of self-healing.

All those eradicators. Cammie watched colleague after colleague grow quiet, or haunted, and then disappear. She had always thought they went into counseling because they had trouble with the violence. Instead they had gone because their memories were returning.

People never last longer than three years, Eliason had said. *When did the dreams start?*

It was a pattern. A pattern no one wanted to discuss.

They wanted to shunt her away to someone she didn't know, someone who would tell her this was normal.

It wasn't normal. Cammie had a 78 percent chance of becoming like the people she staked.

You need to remember, Anita had said.

Cammie remembered. She remembered the house and the smell of blood and the dowel—

She stood up. In an hour, she had to meet Whitney. She turned on the radio to WORT—a station she rarely listened to—because it played music that she wouldn't associate with anything. She made herself a breakfast that she didn't eat and changed into a dark sweatshirt and dark pants. Her gloves were still in the van, but she supposed that blood from one eradication wouldn't hurt another.

Cammie purposely left so that she would hit the worst of rush hour. Driving kept her busy. She felt dizzy, distant from herself, as if everything worked on automatic pilot. When she pulled into the Center's parking lot, she had no memory of the journey there at all.

Whitney was standing at Reception. He was wearing his black clothes, but his bright red hair stood out in contrast. He turned sharply as Cammie pulled open the double glass doors and DeeDee looked down at her desk. They had been talking about Cammie.

So everyone knew. And everyone had understood, except Cammie herself.

"I thought you wouldn't come," he said.

"Been talking to Eliason, huh?" Cammie's voice was flat. Eliason was just like everyone else. He played a good game, but in the end, he only cared about himself.

Whitney shook his head. "It's just happened to me before. I recognize the signs."

Cammie glanced at DeeDee. "So that's what you were talking about? 'The signs'?"

"Come on, Cam," DeeDee said. "Child stuff is confidential."

"My file's on the computer. Sarge called it up."

DeeDee grabbed a file from her desk. When in doubt, act beautiful and brainless. It didn't work with Cammie. Cammie knew DeeDee had a brain.

"Don't deny it, DeeDee. You've been poking around in confidential files."

"I asked her to call it up," Whitney said.

"You?" Cammie whirled. "What gives you the right to investigate my life?"

"My survival. Cammie, you acted pretty fucking weird at the last eradication."

"That doesn't give you any right to dig into my business."

Whitney ran a hand around the back of his neck. He sighed.

"Three years ago, Whitney had a partner who lost it in the middle of a staking," DeeDee said.

"DeeDee—"

"She asked what gives you the right. I think the fact that you nearly died once because of Anita's save-the-children program gives you the right to dig when no one talks to you." DeeDee jabbed the files against her nails to punctuate each word.

"I don't get it, Whitney," Cammie said. "What makes you stay when everyone else seems to disappear?"

"I guess I'm one of the ones who doesn't rehabilitate." He shrugged. "This is the only place I've ever belonged."

Cammie shifted from one foot to the other. Her anger was dissipating. "Your last partner nearly got you killed?"

Whitney shook his head. "My fault really."

"Yeah, his fault." DeeDee set the file down. "He was staking and this kid walks in. His partner, LeeAnn, goes into this extended flashback and starts freaking, and the vampire manages to pull Whitney's hand off the stake. Had him by the throat and was ripping away skin when the kid conks his old man with the hammer. LeeAnn kept screaming. The kid was the one who called the paramedics."

"I should have been more careful," Whitney said. "No vampire should be able to grab someone during a staking."

"Sarge taught us that vampires can do anything. Your partner is your second," Cammie said. She shoved her hands in her pockets. She would deal with all of this later. When she had time to think about it. "Ready?"

Whitney studied her face for a moment. "You going to cop out on me?"

"I'm here. I'll work," she said.

"Great reassurance," DeeDee said.

"Look." Cammie's voice was low. "I have a perfect service record. I have never fucked up in the line of duty. Ever."

"You never visited the Children's Wing before either."

Cammie could barely breathe. "I thought you were my friend, DeeDee."

"I am. I don't want you to make any mistakes. Whitney nearly died the last time his partner recovered memory. I don't want that to happen again. To either of you."

They stared at each other for a moment. DeeDee's bright blue contacts floated across her pupils. Cammie was trembling. She had to find some way to get rid of this energy.

Whitney tapped her shoulder. "If you're ready to go, Cam, so am I."

She broke eye contact with DeeDee. Whitney's face seemed to have more lines this morning. If he believed in her, that was all she needed.

"Okay."

They walked, their footsteps in unison, to the end of the hallway. Whitney opened the door and Cammie walked through it, as if she were part of a couple on the first date. They had never been this formal together, not even the day they got assigned.

Their blue-issue van stood at the end of the parking lot. Whitney checked the equipment before getting into the driver's seat, something he hadn't done in a long time. Cammie didn't question it. She had lost everyone's trust by approaching Janie the day before.

The van's plastic seat was cold. Cammie tugged on the sleeves of her sweatshirt and closed her eyes. She knew what section of town they were going to; she didn't want to see the drive. Perhaps then she would be able to concentrate on her work.

Whitney didn't talk except to swear as traffic forced him to make an occasional defensive maneuver. Cammie was so familiar with his curses that she could guess when he got cut off or when some idiot drove too slowly in front of him.

The eradication was scheduled for the near East Side, on Williamson Street, just past the co-op. When the van stopped, Cammie grabbed her duffel and opened the door before she looked at the neighborhood. It had been years since she stood here, on the wide tree-lined avenue. Her father's house had been two blocks closer to the Fauerbach condominiums—which were nothing more than warehouse space in those days. The house had been like the one she stood in front of, a white, two-story farmhouse, with a wide porch and a long backyard. The eaves shaded the windows and the thin fence prevented neighbors from getting too close.

Perfect vampire country.

Whitney juggled his lock-picker's tools. "Last chance, Cammie."

"I'm going," she snapped.

He yanked his duffel up and climbed the crumbling concrete steps two at a time. Cammie followed, her nervousness like a stone in the center of her stomach. Perhaps she shouldn't have come. If she screwed up, made one single mistake, she would lose her life along with Whitney.

Perhaps that wouldn't be such a bad thing.

She shook the thought. She had to go in with an attitude of strength. In the daylight, she had more power than a vampire. In the daylight, she was the one who brought death.

Whitney scanned the outside wall for a security system. Seeing none, he tried the outside door. The knob turned easily, and the door swung open, revealing a narrow, badly lit hallway. A flight of stairs went up to the left, and to the right another door beckoned. Whitney went to it. Cammie pulled out her flashlight and illuminated the lock while Whitney picked at it.

The door opened before he could finish. Both Cammie and Whitney backed up. A little boy stood there, his face a mass of bruises, one eye swollen shut. He wore a ripped T-shirt and jeans one size too small. "My daddy's asleep," he said, his voice tight with fear.

A rotted-blood smell seeped into the hallway. Cammie felt nausea return and stifled the urge to bolt.

"Take him to the van," Whitney said. He must have seen Cammie's expression. DeeDee's talk about Whitney's previous brush with death had spooked him.

Cammie had to convince him she was all right. She was going to go through with this. It was her job. "Either we both do or neither. That's procedure and you know it."

"Daddy says no one can come in. And I gotta stay." The boy barely spoke above a whisper. "He's asleep."

"And you're not supposed to wake him," Cammie said. How well she remembered those instructions.

The boy nodded. A tear slipped out of his swollen eye.

"Go sit on the couch," she said. "We'll be out in a moment."

She slid the door open gently—quietly—and walked past the little boy. Whitney followed. Cammie knew this house. She had grown up in one so similar. Light seeped through the back bedroom door, but the other rooms were dark. She followed the smell to the vampire's room, paused for a moment to remove her mallet and stake, then eased the door open.

Dark. And smelling of rot. *Not supposed to go in there.* The little boy's voice or her brother Ben's? She didn't know. Her hands trembled, like they had before. It was the only way, the only solution. If she didn't, he would hit Ben again and maybe kill him, like he had killed that woman in the parking lot—like he had threatened to kill her.

Her eyes slowly adjusted. Pictures hung on the wall. The windows had been boarded up. No light fought its way into the darkness.

"Wait, Cammie."

Cam-Cam, wait up.

But she couldn't wait. She held the stake and the mallet (dowel and hammer—too big for her small hands) before her like torches. The bed dominated the side of the room. She could barely see it in the dark.

A thin light came in from the hall, providing just enough illumination. Cammie walked to one side of the bed and saw him sleeping there, so peacefully, his hands clasped over his belly, his feet crossed at the ankles.

His lips were parted slightly. In sleep, he had no wrinkles at all. He was as handsome as he was in the picture she kept in her bureau drawer, the one of him holding Mom's hand. She kept it because Mom was smiling.

Cammie knelt. A hand touched her shoulder. She didn't turn, didn't want to see Ben. She placed the dowel over the vampire's heart and brought the hammer down with all of her strength. He roared and sat up, foul breath covering her, stolen blood spattering walls. She pounded again, ignoring the nails raking into her skin, the too-strong hands yanking at her wrists. She had to keep going. She had to. For Ben, if not for herself.

He thrashed, kicked, his foot connecting with her shoulder, nearly knocking her off balance. But she clung to the dowel, kept pounding. Blood gushed from his mouth, through his fanged teeth and across her hands. Still she pounded, thinking it would never end. The stories were wrong. Vampires never died. They sucked life's blood forever.

Then he stopped. His hands slid down the bed's side and shredded, skin drying and flaking, the bones yellowing with age.

Behind her, a child cried. A little boy. *Ben.* But she ignored him, leaned her head on the dowel and took a deep breath.

"Daddy," she whispered. But he didn't answer. He would never answer. He had been dead a long time.

She rocked back on her heels, turned and saw Whitney staring at her, his skin white. He clutched the little boy against his chest.

"The child shouldn't have been here," Whitney said.

"He would have known anyway," Cammie said. She stood up and wiped the blood on her jeans. Her last vampire. Now, finally, she could move on. "Let's get his things, take him back to the Center. Anita will take care of him."

She restrained an urge to reach out to the child. She had done that once, with Ben a long time ago. It was one thing to see your father killed. It was another to be held by his killer.

"He'll survive," she said. "We did."

Then she left the bedroom to wash the blood from her hands.

"Ben?"

She came home from school to find the curtains up, sunlight beaming into the living room. It looked dusty and shabby in the bright light. A doll poked out of a sofa cushion and a Matchbox truck was parked beneath the legs of the television.

The house was silent.

"Ben?"

She didn't dare yell too loudly, in case her father was asleep in the other room. She went into the kitchen. The table was covered with Cheerios and dried milk. A half-empty bowl sat beside the counter. The back door was open, the screen swaying in the wind.

She shut it before it could bang closed.

The backyard was empty. The grass was nearly waist high and a layer of mud covered the picnic table. The Hibachi was rusty.

"Ben?"

She left the kitchen, skirted the table—it spooked her for a reason she couldn't name, the long crack on the side, which had been there almost since the table got purchased, made her shiver—and hurried into the hallway. The bathroom door was open, the toilet lid up, the bowl stained yellow. Ben hadn't learned to flush yet. She put the lid down, but didn't press the handle. If her father was asleep, she wanted him to remain so.

"Ben?" Her cries were whispers now. Her father's door was closed—it was open when he was awake. Ben wasn't in his room. The covers on his new bed were pushed back, the **race-car-patterned** sheets scrunched against the matching comforter. She made the bed, picked his clothes off the floor, and glanced in the closet.

No Ben.

Maybe he had done something wrong. Maybe her father had made Ben disappear as their mother had so long ago.

"Ben!" Her voice came out louder than she wanted it to. She clamped a hand over her mouth. The hand was shaking. He was supposed to be here when she got home. He knew that. Mrs. Peterson was supposed to drop him off after preschool and he was supposed to turn the television on low and wait.

He had never disobeyed her before.

Usually she found him asleep in front of the set, his hand clutching his ratty blue blanket, thumb in his mouth, sucking until he drew blood.

Her room. The last room to check. She opened the door. Sunlight felt welcome in here. She kept her blinds up all the time. No dust covered the surface; even the rug was clean. She made her bed with military precision—like they talked about in the movies—and the quilt her mother had made was folded at the foot in case the nights got cold. Arfie, her favorite stuffed dog, waited on the pillow for her to wrap her arms around him and forget the day.

"Where's Ben?" she whispered.

Arfie didn't answer.

Her throat had gone dry. He couldn't have wandered off, could he? He was barely three. Not really old enough to be by himself.

She ran down the hall, losing her footing and careening against the side. She winced at the thud as her arm collided with the rough surface. The basement.

She had warned him not to go down there, but maybe he was bored. Maybe—

"Cam-Cam?" His little voice was faint, hoarse. It came from below. She hurried back into the kitchen. The basement door was closed. She tried the knob and pulled but the door only opened a crack.

"Cam-Cam?" Ben sounded frightened. What had he done?

She looked up. The hook lock near the ceiling had been attached. She dragged over a kitchen chair and stood on her tiptoes, but still couldn't reach the hook. What had he done to deserve this? Her breath whistled in her teeth. She got down, grabbed a knife off the counter, braced the door and climbed back on the stool. Then she shoved the knife at the hook. After a tense moment, the hook popped free. The door opened inward and she nearly toppled down the stairs.

"Cam-Cam!" Without the door blocking the sound, Ben's cries had become shrieks.

She jumped off the chair and ran down the stairs, flicking the light switch as she went.

His left foot was tied to the ratty tan couch that used to be in their living room. A wet bandanna lay in a circle on the floor. He had red welts on both cheeks and tear tracks that went to his chin. His fingernails were raw from scraping the thin rope. He didn't have the skill to untie complex knots yet.

"Ben." The relief echoed in her voice. He started crying again, little hiccups accompanied by dime-sized tears. "What happened?"

"I had the TV too loud," he said. "I didn't mean to, Cam. Honest."

"I know," she said. Sometimes too loud was too soft the day before. "Did he hit you?"

"No, but he put that on my mouth. It hurt." Ben pushed at the bandanna with his fingers. Then he wiped his face with the back of his hand. "I didn't mean to, Cam-Cam."

"It's okay," she said. She couldn't work the knot either. Luckily she had brought the knife with her. She sawed at the rope until Ben broke free. Maybe when their father was in a better mood, she could get him to take the rope off Ben's foot.

Ben launched himself into her arms. He was half her weight now, but she could still carry him. He held her so tight that it took her breath away.

Footsteps echoed above. Ben stiffened in her arms. "Quick," she whispered. "Get down."

She set him on the floor and sat in front of his leg, so that it looked like he was still tied. The wooden steps creaked under their father's weight.

He was gaunt and pale, his hair tousled from sleep. Bruises had formed under his eyes. His hands shook. Cammie sat in front of Ben, protecting him as best she could with her body. Their father was always the most dangerous when he had just woken up.

"You made a lot of noise, Camila," he said.

"I couldn't find Ben. I thought maybe something had happened to him."

"He didn't let me sleep."

"I thought maybe you had taken him somewhere."

To her surprise, their father smiled. "Not today, Camila. But someday. Someday he will follow me wherever I go."

PART TWO

PART TWO

Chapter Twelve

$$\boxed{\text{i}}$$

Eliason hunched over his desk. Unopened boxes of medical samples sat on the floor around him. The medical texts in the bookshelf were out of order, and the latest copies of *New England Journal of Medicine* covered the only other chair. He pulled off his reading glasses and rubbed his eyes.

The chart in front of him was sparse. His new receptionist, Sandi, had downloaded the little girl's files from her doctor at the West Towne clinic. Eliason had had to call him to get permission. The man had gotten on the phone, defensive and rude. *I had no idea her father was a vampire,* the man said. *The child arrived late one afternoon. I checked her foot and gave her a tetanus shot, then sent her home.*

Eliason had thanked him, but still requested the file. He was glad he did. The doctor had remembered the child, now almost a year later. He had talked to Eliason without checking his notes. If he had checked the notes, he would have upgraded and changed the files as so many other doctors had—to cover accusations of malpractice or worse, evidence that he didn't care about his patients. Eliason rarely reported other doctors. General practitioners were a dying breed and so overworked that they might have had good intentions but not followed through on them. Children got bruised; it was part of growing up. But palm prints and facial contusions like the ones the doctor had reported were not normal. The only thing that gave Eliason any sympathy at all was the note at the bottom of the page.

Have Lydia contact Social Services. Hold child should she come in with similar bruises again.

No wonder the doctor had been defensive; he had known something was going on and he had forgotten—failed to act. Eliason had done that only once, back in Iowa, when he was interning. The little boy had died: beaten to death, drained of blood and thrown into the garbage like a day-old pile of meat. That little boy had died, but if Eliason could help it, no one else would.

He picked up the file and walked to examining room three, down the hall. The little girl inside was blonde. Her hair was stringy and unkempt. She wore a blue dress covered with the ghosts of old stains and white knee socks that looked new. Her tiny blue Nikes were covered with mud. She had her back to the door, but she jumped when it opened.

"Hi," he said, deliberately taking the seat farthest from her. "I'm Dr. Brett."

"Mary Jo," she said, still not looking at him. A circle of bruises lined the delicate skin along her jaw.

"I guess the last time you saw a doctor was just before Christmas. You stepped on a rusty nail?"

"At school." She picked at some lint on her hem. "He gave me a shot."

"Did it hurt?"

"No." Her tone was flat. "I could take it."

It had hurt her a lot then. Tetanus shots sometimes did. "We won't give you any shots today. I just want to look at those bruises."

"Lady poked my finger."

The blood test. He hoped Heather was gentle. "Then she gave you a Hershey's kiss, right?"

"And this." She extended her hand. On the middle finger, a Band-Aid covered an oversized cotton ball.

"Well," he said, still after all these years unused to the

matter-of-fact tone the badly abused children used. "I promise. No more needles. I just want to look you over, then we'll take you to a safe place. Did you bring any toys with you?"

She shook her head. "Daddy says toys are for babies."

Eliason bit back the anger that surged through him.

"He's dead now." She finally looked at him. A fist-sized bruise ran from her temple to her cheekbone. Her left eye was black-and-blue. "Isn't he?"

Was there hope in that empty voice? He couldn't tell. "He's dead now," Eliason said.

"Those people made a big mess, but I guess he won't get mad, now, will he?"

"No, he won't," Eliason said.

She ran her tongue along her lips. They were chapped. "He's gone. He's never coming back."

"That's right," Eliason said. "How do you feel about that?"

She touched the side of her face, then brought her hand down. Her gaze never left Eliason's. "He bought me a doll once. It was soft and had red hair and buttons for eyes."

"Raggedy Ann?"

She smiled, just a little. "Yeah." Then she rubbed her face again. "She's dead too. Daddy killed her. He said she was just stuffing. Not real at all. But I heard her scream."

Her voice wavered. Eliason waited a moment, to see if she was going to say anything else. When she remained silent, he said, "He hurt her pretty bad."

Mary Jo nodded. "Sometimes she couldn't even get out of bed to go to school."

"What did her teachers say?"

"They thought she was sick a lot."

"But really her daddy hurt her?"

"She wasn't doing anything. She never did anything. He would come home all mad and he would pick her up and throw her—" Her voice broke, but she still didn't cry.

Eliason didn't move. "Would you like a hug?" he asked.

She nodded. He approached her slowly, knowing any sudden move would ruin the tentative trust. He gathered her in his arms and held her against his chest, careful of her bruises. She grabbed him with strong fists and shook. Finally she pulled away. Her eyes were still dry.

"Raggedy Ann never went to school," she said.

"I know." He smoothed a strand of hair from her forehead. "It's okay to be angry at him. No one has the right to hurt you. I'll make sure no one hurts you again."

Her eyes were wide and she didn't move. She didn't believe him. They never believed him this early on. But she would later, after she had the care of the Center, after they found her a proper home.

"I want to check out your bruises," he said. "I want to make sure they won't get worse, and then I'll put some lotion on them to make them feel better. It might sting a little at first. Is that okay?"

If a child said no, he would save the examination for later. Trust was the most important thing for a child like Mary Jo. She nodded. He started with the visible bruises on her face, holding her where the skin was unmarked. No punctures, no deep bleeding. The eye would be okay. Then he checked her arms and her legs. Her right arm was a mass of welts that ran into her dress.

"What happened?" he asked, reluctant to touch.

"Fell off my bike," she said.

Bikes didn't make welts that looked like the business end of a belt. He opened a drawer and pulled out a paper dress. "I want to check your shoulder and back," he said. "I'm going to leave the room for a minute. When I come back, will you wear this instead of your dress? That way I can look without bumping any sore places."

"Okay." Her hands were shaking. He didn't want to know if her daddy made her take off that dress especially for him. "Be right back."

Eliason let himself out of the room. He leaned on the

door, and let out a sigh. Damn them. Damn them all. The Center could only do so much. He wanted them all to disappear right now, so that he would never see another child whose body had more colors than a painter's palette. He would have to stop at the gym tonight and see if he could use the punching bag. He had to get rid of some of this anger.

He went back into his office and buzzed Sandi. While he waited, he typed the details of his conversation with Mary Jo into her computer file. He would back it up with X rays and photographic evidence, in case someone decided to go after the Center for wrongly killing her father. Nothing wrong with this eradication. If anything, the child's teachers had waited too long to report this one.

"Yes?" Sandi stood at the door. She was thin and trim, but young. Sometimes, after a patient left, she locked herself in the ladies' room and cried. Eliason hoped she would never lose that compassion. He needed it, especially when the anger at all those creeps seized him.

"Phone the Center," he said. "She needs a private room with nothing from the house unless she asks for it. And—" he frowned, considering "—a Raggedy Ann doll waiting for her on the bed. Okay? And set her up for X rays tomorrow. I think we might find some evidence of improperly healed bones."

"Is she all right otherwise?" Sandi asked.

"As all right as we can expect at the moment," Eliason said. He reached over to his desk, picked up his glasses, and put them in the case. "What have we got the rest of the afternoon?"

"A sore throat, a physical, and a baby with a runny nose." Sandi adjusted her blouse. "And you have a pile of messages."

"Anything important?"

"Another callback from University Hospital. They need the Ledyr file."

"Did we get consent from the wife yet?"

Sandi shook her head. "And Cammie Timms has called three times this afternoon."

Eliason frowned. "She say what it's about?"

"No," Sandi said. "She just says you should call back when you can."

"Thanks." Eliason turned the reading lamp on over his desk. He had to get back to Mary Jo, but he would take a moment to call Cammie. She never called him at work, and she had never left more than one message on his home machine. He didn't know what the appeal was with her. He usually tried to keep his relationships with Center employees impersonal. He didn't need the extra baggage—the emotional entanglements that usually came with survivors.

But Cammie. Cammie had been special to him from the moment he saw her. She had been slight and fragile, like little Mary Jo, only with a strength underneath it that showed in every movement. Cammie held herself away from others, avoiding any involvement at all, dealing with everything herself. It had taken all his persuasive skills to get her to see the counselor Anita had assigned. Even then, he wasn't sure it was doing much good.

He dialed the number from memory. After three rings, a sleepy voice answered.

"Cammie? It's Brett." He was hunched over his desk, protected against bad news. They hadn't been lovers, only friends, but still the idea of something happening to her made him ache.

"Hey, Brett, thanks for calling back." She was speaking slower than usual. Not sleepy. Tired. "I was wondering if you wanted to do dinner tonight."

He froze. He had never had dinner with Cammie—at least, not an official dinner. Not planned. Even though he had wanted to. But she had been so reserved, as if she had a part he would never reach. "I'd love to," he said.

"It's business, so I'll buy. I'll meet you at the Imperial Palace at seven."

His favorite Chinese place. He knew she meant the one in Shorewood. She rarely traveled to the East Side.

"Let me pick you up," he said.

"The way you drive?" Her voice was gaining more life. "Nope. I'll see you there, boy-o. If you're more than a half an hour late, I'm going to order sweet and sour pork—deep fat fried."

The thought turned his stomach. He hated Americanized Chinese food. "They won't make it that way."

"We'll see," she said, and hung up.

He stared at the phone for a moment. Cammie. Asking him out. On business. He sighed. They only had one kind of business in common. Vampires.

He stood up. A little girl was waiting for him. Eliason had to see how much damage her father had inflicted upon her before he died.

In the days before it became a Chinese restaurant, the Imperial Palace had been an ice cream and sandwich shop. Eliason had discovered it with one of his favorite young patients, an eight-year-old boy named Ryan who covered his grief with the pretense of boundless joy. They had just come back from a Madison Muskies game, in the early days of the baseball team, and stopped for an ice cream soda. Ryan had a double fudge tin roof, with a chocolate malt on the side. He had gotten sick in the bathroom, and Eliason had learned that children who smiled all the time weren't always happy. Sometimes they covered their pain with food and a happy-go-lucky grin.

Maybe that was why he liked the Imperial Palace. Not just because of the food, but because within this building, he had learned something new. Something important.

He pulled the Ferrari to the side of the building and got out. The restaurant was part of a marginal shopping center that some developer had built backwards. The easiest entrance was in the back, away from the street. Most of the stores had sidewalk entrances, however. Those that hadn't died within the first six months of operation.

Inside, the scent of ginger, onions, and incense hit him even before the door closed. The owner, a small woman who spoke broken English, waved at him from her perch behind the cash register. She slipped out and gestured that he follow her. Before they stepped into the restaurant proper, she put a hand on his chest. He leaned over. Many years of dining here had taught him that when she spoke, she expected his full attention.

"Next time when you ask young lady, you bring her in that car. She will be impressed!"

He laughed. "I'll remember that."

The Ferrari was his one indulgence, although he could afford more. He had found it at a used car lot specializing in expensive cars—poorly tuned, poorly maintained, with a cracked interior and overpriced. He had talked them to low blue-book way too easily, leading him to think that they still made a considerable profit on him. Then he dumped an equivalent amount of money into fixing the car up. Every sixty days, he paid his mechanic to keep the thing in top running condition. What money he had that didn't go to the kids went to the car.

The owner led him past the dark booths in the front, filled with suits at the end of a long day, up the stairs, and to the back. Cammie sat at a table for two, the candle illuminating her small, cat-like face. She wore black trousers with a matching silk blouse. Silver crosses, earrings he had given her last Christmas, graced her ears. She had pulled her long hair into a bun that emphasized her long neck. He had never seen her dressed up. The outfit took his breath away. It made her look frail and feminine at the same time.

"Cammie?" he said as he sat down. He had worn jeans, expecting to have a dinner battle as they usually did. Maybe she hadn't meant business. Or maybe she had said that just so she could pay. He smiled to himself. Cammie would never have that kind of change of heart.

She looked up. Her eyes were wide on her narrow face. "Thanks for coming, Brett."

He didn't see her as often since she had moved from Eradication to Records. Often, when his Ferrari pulled up in the parking lot at the Center, DeeDee told him that Cammie would suddenly find a reason to lock herself in the data rooms.

"You know I can't resist you," he said. "You look great."

She smiled, but the look didn't reach her eyes. She had never liked it when he gave her compliments. At first he had thought the problem was his skin color— perhaps she had never dated a man who was black— but later, DeeDee told him that Cammie didn't date, period. She had never spent private time alone with a man, and any man who was too forward never saw her again.

Eliason always made a point of letting Cammie know his interest and of letting her know that he would be her friend even if she never dated him. Sometimes he was relieved that they would never become intimate. Underneath that reserved exterior was a frightened little girl who carried as many bruises as young Mary Jo.

"What's up?" he asked.

"I ordered wontons. I hope that's okay," Cammie said. "And a Diet Coke for you. We've got tea coming, too."

"Sounds good," he said. "Mind if we order something other than an appetizer?"

"I was thinking maybe the pepper steak and kung pao chicken."

He set the menu aside. Cammie was rarely this forward. "Okay."

The owner waited on them herself. Cammie ordered and the owner disappeared quickly. She had never seen Eliason in here with a woman. He often came alone or with some of the kids—especially those who had poor appetites. They usually hadn't encountered Chinese food before and the food had no association for them. They found that they could eat an entire meal without feeling ill.

Cammie's fingers toyed with the linen napkin. Finally she placed it on her lap, poured herself some tea, and sat back. The wontons arrived and Eliason took one, dipping it in the sauce before taking a bite.

He would wait her out.

The wontons were warm and crispy, just the way he liked them. He was hungrier than he realized.

Cammie took a wonton, poured sauce on it, and swirled it around on her plate. "I asked you here, Brett, because you're the only friend I have."

He probably shouldn't argue with her—arguing only silenced the children—but Cammie was an adult. She had to know that she wasn't as alone as she thought. "You've got DeeDee and Whitney too. And Sarge, if you let her."

Cammie shook her head. "DeeDee and Whitney can't keep secrets."

Secrets. He tensed. So important to a vampire's child. Keeping secrets meant surviving. DeeDee and Whitney kept secrets, but now was the time to stop arguing and start listening. Cammie had asked him here for some kind of help, not to correct the way she thought.

"So this conversation is confidential?" he asked.

"Please," she said. "I don't want anyone else to know about it."

"All right." He took another wonton. Cammie still hadn't touched hers.

She took a deep breath. "I found him. My brother. I know what they did with him."

The shock went all the way to his toes. No one was supposed to trace the records. Children who were sent away from the Westrina Center were given new identities and new lives. They were able to start over. "Those records are purged," he said.

"Off the computer," Cammie said. "Anita keeps the disks in her office under lock and key."

"You raided Anita's office?"

"Give me a break." Cammie finally took a bite of the wonton. "Not only is the lock tough, but she has an elaborate security system inside. Even if I got past the alarms, I couldn't disable the camera. No one except Anita knows its location."

Eliason finished the wonton and put the plate aside. He nodded, indicating that she could go on. His heart was pounding hard. He wasn't sure he liked this.

"Ben and I were there before the Center was computerized. There are boxes and boxes of unentered files in the basement. When they computerized, they put me in the computer because of what I did—"

It took him a moment to realize that she meant because she had staked her father. He wasn't used to euphemisms from Cammie.

"—and because I never had a permanent home. They were always tracking me. But Ben got adopted out. He was three—young enough that some family in Oregon wanted him. His file was in a large box with all the other unentered files from that year. They sent him to Eugene. A family named Sadler."

Eliason gripped his Diet Coke glass. The sides were cool and damp. "He probably has no memory of this, Cammie." Or worse. A child's personality was formed by the time he was four. Little Ben might have had a memory—and acted on it.

"Maybe," she said. She finished the wonton and took the next, breaking it into little pieces as she spoke. "But

I do, now. Every night I dream about him crying in the next room. I try to keep him quiet, but my father hears him and gets up—"

That flat tone he had heard Mary Jo use had crept into Cammie's voice. He had never paid much attention to the adult children that Anita brought in. He knew that they were all tough and sarcastic, with odd fears that crept into their movements, but he had never thought—until Cammie—about how those childhood experiences still affected their adult lives.

Cammie snapped the wonton into a pile of little pieces. "I killed him before he killed Ben. You know that, don't you?"

No, he hadn't realized that, but it had been in her file. She spent the first three months in the Center, trying to escape and find her brother.

She had been eight years old.

"Cammie, that was twenty years ago. Ben is an adult now."

"I know." She ate the little pieces of wonton, one at a time. Then she sipped her tea. Her movements were sharp and automatic. "Counting my father, I have killed thirty men and thirteen women, all of whom were vampires. Forty-two were certified by the Center as dangerous and in need of eradication. My father had thrown Ben down a flight of stairs the day before I staked him. It was lucky Ben didn't die from that fall. So I waited until the middle of day, took a sharpened dowel—"

"Cammie." Eliason held up his hand. He knew the story. He had read the file when he found out Cammie was in Eradication.

"—and staked him in front of Ben. Because of that, they took Ben away from me. I saved his life and they took him away from me." The flat tone was gone, replaced by a rise in level. The owner had stopped near the door of the kitchen, steaming food on top of a round tray. Thank god the woman was discreet. "I need to know if he made it. I need to know if it was worth it."

Eliason nodded to the owner to bring the food now. She did so, setting a huge platter of pepper steak and steamed rice in front of him. She put the kung pao chicken in front of Cammie, and left as quietly as she had arrived. Eliason put steamed rice all over his plate and spooned the entrees on top of it.

He wasn't sure how to handle this. Cammie wasn't thinking clearly. She knew that Ben had a more than fifty percent chance of becoming a vampire himself. "Cammie, you have saved countless lives, not just your brother's. You know the early history of the Center. Vampires can't be rehabilitated. But we can stop them from killing more people. And we can protect the children."

Cammie took the rice from him. She wasn't meeting his gaze. "Each time I staked a vampire, I did it because I believed he was evil. Each time, I reenacted the day I tried to save my brother."

She had been talking to the counselors. They were trying to ease her past the recovery of memory and into a way of dealing with emotions behind it.

"That's why Anita puts former children in Eradication, so that they can work until something sparks the memories."

"I know the theory!" Cammie snapped. She served herself some beef and then some chicken before continuing. "I don't care how many lives I've saved. All I care about is Ben. That was all I ever cared about. If I know he's okay, if I know he made it, then I can let all of this go."

"What does your counselor say?"

"She says it's enough to know he's alive out there somewhere. But how do I know that? How do I know that the Sadlers weren't vampires in waiting?"

"Because the Center did a thorough check. They always do. They also send children to areas that aren't as infested."

"In 1974, the area wasn't infested," Cammie said. "But what about now?"

"You don't know where he is now."

"That's the problem," she said. "He could be in all kinds of danger."

"Cammie, he's a grown man now. He's capable of taking care of himself. You're still stuck back there, trying to take care of him. You have to let him go."

She took a bite of the chicken and made a face. She paused, and pulled a pepper from her mouth. "If I let him go, what do I have left, Brett?"

He reached out a hand, wishing she would take it. "You have yourself, Cammie. You need to take care of yourself."

"Finding Ben is taking care of myself." She looked up. "Don't you see? If I know he's all right, I can sleep again."

Eliason rubbed his eyes. The literature didn't have much on this kind of obsession. He sighed. "Cammie, what if he turned on his own?"

"He wouldn't!" She pushed the plate away. "Any more than I have."

He stared at her. Her eyes were too bright, and her cheeks were flushed. He had made sure she read the literature on Adult Children after she recovered her memory. She knew that she still hadn't reached her danger point. "You can't know that," he said, unwilling to argue further. "You haven't seen him since he was a little boy. He is a very different person from the one you remember. He's an adult."

"I know," she said. She picked up her tea cup, drained it, and filled it again from the metal teapot. "But he's my family. My only"—she half-chuckled without humor— "blood relation. Maybe if I can salvage that, maybe if I can have a real relationship with him, then the nightmares will go away."

"You can't look outside yourself, Cammie," Eliason said. "You're gambling too much on Ben." He stopped himself before he could say any more. If she was going to look outside herself, he wanted her to look to him.

"Maybe," she said. "But I am going to do this thing."

He took a deep breath and leaned back. She was putting him on notice that he couldn't change her mind. Maybe she was right. Maybe she needed information. There were ways to do it without jeopardizing her own safety. He took a bite of the pepper steak. It was good. "So hire a private detective."

"I did."

Eliason looked up. He didn't know she had that kind of money.

She caught his surprised glance. "Anita had the money in trust for me. My father's ill-gotten gains. She kept it, untouched, until I was able to remember and then make an educated choice. Seems most of us refuse the money. I'll use it. I'll use it to find Ben."

Eliason had heard of these trusts, another service that the Center provided. Much of the money went to support the child's care at the Center. Whatever was left over became part of the scholarship the Center would award at the end of high school. In some cases, a very few, there was money remaining. It went into a trust that the Center gave to the adult child upon recovery of memory. Sarge complained about the trusts, saying the money should legally go to the children when they turned eighteen. Anita insisted on waiting until the children could make the informed choice. Some "children" never got the money at all. If there was excess money for Cammie, what had happened to the money for her brother?

Eliason hated thinking about the trusts. It was another aspect of the Center's policies that he found a touch too shady for his own tastes. Anita ran the place like a dictator and had since the collapse in the early seventies. Because she got results, no one questioned her. No one wanted to see the Center's work end.

If Anita used the trust money to benefit the Center,

someone would have stopped her. But the trust funds sat in a separate bank, gaining interest for the children, but never giving money to the Center itself. Anita's plan did work though. Most of the adult children gave their money right back to the Center if they decided to do anything at all.

He finished the pepper steak and started into the chicken. Very spicy. Just the way he liked it. "What did the detective say?"

Cammie started eating again. "His report made Ben sound like a saint. Straight-A student, good athlete, never in trouble. He graduated with honors from University of Oregon in pre-law, of all things."

"Sounds like you have the answers you need." Eliason grabbed the pepper steak platter and refilled his own plate.

Cammie shook her head. "He's disappeared."

Eliason set his fork down. He needed to pay more attention to this conversation. "How does your detective know that?"

"That's all everyone talks about. He had a date one night with a girl and she comes home in tears, and he leaves town. No one has seen him since. The detective spent two weeks trying to find Ben. He couldn't. Ben just dropped from sight."

Eliason's hands started shaking. She had to recognize the pattern. This was how it started. But she was a survivor who had just recovered memory. It would take years for her to work through all the denial she had lived with.

He rubbed his hands on his jeans, then took a sip from the Diet Coke. It was lukewarm. He would help however he could, but he wouldn't tell her what he thought. Telling her wouldn't break through the denial. She had to break it herself. "Why was the girl crying?" he asked.

"She never said. Her mother thinks he raped her, but the girl won't press charges. Besides, everyone says it's not in Ben's profile to rape a woman."

Perhaps not. But it was in Ben's background. "Who is this 'everyone' that you keep quoting?"

"Family. Friends. I'll show you the report if you want."

This was a mess, and Cammie would get nothing more than hurt from it all. He had led her to her memories. Now he wished he hadn't. "Cammie," he said, leaning forward. "Ben is an adult. Adults have the right to leave a community without warning. You never know what people are thinking."

"Maybe something's happened to him. Maybe he's hurt, or dying or—"

"Or maybe he waited until he was twenty-three to run away from home."

"Maybe," she said. "But people don't understand that."

He gripped the edge of the table to brace himself. He was probably wrong saying this, but he couldn't keep silent. She was purposely walking into a death trap, because she had been raised that way. And she wasn't seeing it. "Cammie," he said slowly. "The girl's mother thinks the girl was assaulted. Ben is at the peak of his sexual prime. Sweetie, he could have turned. They don't have the experience in the West to understand some facets of vampirism."

"His parents do," Cammie said. "They would know. They don't believe he's a vampire."

"They might be in denial," Eliason said. *Like you are.*

Cammie frowned. "He's not. I know he's not. He saw what my father did. He would know how awful that is. He wouldn't do that to anyone." She leaned forward. "I need your help, Brett. I'm going to go find him, and I need someone back here whom I can trust. Someone who will dig through records for me. Someone who will go head to head with Anita if necessary."

God, she was going to go through with this no matter what. He pushed his plate aside. He had to stop her. Any way he could. The anger he had felt with Mary Jo rose again. He clenched his fists beneath the table. Think. He had to think. He had to find a way to get through to her. "Cammie, you're going to go to a community you've never been to, disrupt people's lives, bring them a part of the past they're not supposed to see, and for what?"

Cammie grabbed the teapot and poured herself a cup. She took a very loud sip before answering him. "You said it yourself. I need to do things for me."

"Like visiting Janie?"

Cammie nearly spat out her tea. Her face got red, and she choked before she swallowed. Eliason almost reached over to pat her on the back, when she opened her mouth and took in air. "That's not fair," she said. "It's not the same thing."

"It is the same thing. You bulldozing into a place without consideration for the people who already live there."

"I didn't ask you to judge me. I asked you to help me."

Eliason put his hands on his knees. "I have helped you. From the start. But there are some things that I will not do. You're wrong, Cammie. You're going out there on a mission that will destroy everyone, including yourself. You're reenacting your past again, only this time, you get to play the daddy."

She stood up so quickly she almost knocked the table over. Water splashed out of his glass and onto his lap. The other patrons looked over, and the owner watched from the kitchen door. Still, when Cammie spoke, her voice was low. "Of all the awful, hurtful things you could say, that was the worst. I wasn't going to tell anyone about Ben's past. I wasn't going to get involved in their lives. I was just going to do some work. For me. I'm not reenacting anything." She pulled a twenty from her purse and slammed it on the table. "I guess I was wrong. I thought you were my friend. But all you're interested in is sex, just like every other man in the world. Well, this was not a date, Brett. You can't sleep with me. I asked you for help and you're not willing to give it."

As she went by the table, he caught her wrist. "Friends tell friends things that no one wants to say. I care about you, Cammie. I probably even love you, if the truth be told. You're going to get hurt, and I want no part of that. I want to protect you from hurt. Cammie, stay here. Work with your counselors. Face this stuff and put it behind you—"

"What the hell do you think I'm going to do?" she said. She yanked her arm from his grasp. "And I'm going to do it without you."

She stomped out of the restaurant, leaving him there. He wiped the water off his jeans. His food had congealed on his plate. Still, he couldn't get up, couldn't follow her. It wouldn't be right. He had the training. He understood the tough love theory. He knew what to do.

It was what Sarge had told him when Ryan refused to listen to Eliason about eating disorders. *Sometimes,* she had said, *people have to hit bottom before they can change.*

The problem was, he didn't want to see Cammie hit bottom. She was the daughter of a vampire. Approaching thirty. A woman's sexual prime. If she was hereditary, some latent tendencies might appear. Bottom for a vampire's child was blood lust.

And once they gave in to that, there was never any turning back.

Chapter Thirteen

Candyce took a bite of the deep fried cod and the fresh homemade tartar sauce. If she couldn't drink Steelhead's excellent micro-brewed beer, she could at least treat herself to their wonderful food.

The bar was just beginning to fill up with the after work crowd. She had arrived early enough to get a table with one of the large overstuffed chairs. She had ordered a homebrewed root beer with her fish and chips and was nursing that like the best stout money could buy.

She also had to hold the table until Ben got there.

The thought of him made her queasy. She had agreed to meet him in a public place because she never wanted to be alone with him again. Her mother was convinced he had raped her, but he hadn't. Candyce had been willing. She had consented. She had wanted him until the moment he bit her when he entered her.

She had to choke down the fish. Better to clear that memory from her head. She took a sip of the root beer and leaned back.

Behind her, a table of emergency service personnel laughed over a pitcher of beer. She recognized one of them; the man who always acted as the spokesman for the evening news. Two young businessmen huddled over another table, and to her right, four men wearing Star Trek T-shirts kidded the waiter about avoiding their memorabilia shop in the Oakway shopping center.

Everyone's life seemed to be going well but hers.

The pub's door opened and she sat up as she had each time it had opened in the last half hour. She tugged her favorite black turtleneck over her jeans—her dumpy look, so that she would appeal to no one—even though her mother once said it set off her leggy figure and blonde hair to advantage. So far, not a soul had noticed her, although she scanned the face of each person who entered the door. This time, she froze.

Ben stood there. His suit had the shine of silk. His topcoat was unbuttoned, and he had wrapped a scarf carelessly around his neck. She had never seen him so dressed up. He was still the most handsome man she had ever seen, with his dark hair curling about his collar and his black eyes snapping with intelligence.

Other women watched as he searched the room. A redhead near the door smoothed her hair back. A slender dark-haired woman reached out to him, but he didn't seem to notice. Conversations slowed until Candyce could hear the basketball announcer from the overhead television set.

She didn't wave. She waited until Ben saw her. He crossed the floor in three long strides and pulled back the chair across from her. He was not smiling as he sat down. "Steve said this was important."

Somewhere, in the last few months, he had gained confidence. His voice had a mellifluous flow it had never had before. He looked older. Lines had formed in the corners of his eyes, giving him a rakish appearance. A flush rose in her cheeks. Even now, he attracted her. Despite the fear she had felt that night.

The waiter stopped at the table—a big, sensitive man who had hovered over Candyce earlier as if he had known something was wrong. "Get you anything?" The waiter's tone was curt. He was not going to be as nice to Ben.

"Red wine," Ben said without looking up.

The waiter met Candyce's gaze. He frowned just a little, as if to ask if it were okay that Ben was at her table. She nodded once, a small movement. The waiter frowned, then went to fill Ben's order.

Ben ignored the interchange. He waited until the waiter was gone. "Well?"

Candyce swallowed. She hardly knew how to talk to him. Best to just get it over with. "I'm pregnant."

"Pregnant?" Ben sat back and ran a hand through his perfectly combed hair, messing it. The self-confidence disappeared and something else flashed through. His calculating look. Finally, he was beginning to look like the man she remembered. "Are you sure it's mine?"

The flush grew deeper. She could feel it heating her face. She gripped the arms of her chair, holding herself back and forcing herself to keep her voice low. "I'm positive. You were the first, and probably the last, for me."

He grinned and ran a callused hand over her cheek. "Ah, now, Candy, I wasn't that bad."

"Bad?" She pushed her chair back so that he couldn't touch her. "I still have scars." She pulled open the collar on her turtleneck to reveal the pink scrapes on the side of her neck.

He examined them like a jeweler appraising a diamond. His fingers were gentle, his breath smelling faintly of cinnamon. "Hmm. I was a little rough, wasn't I?"

"A little? A little?" Her voice was rising. She looked down and caught hold of herself.

"And for two days afterward, you were so horny you couldn't sit still."

She brought her head up in surprise. She hadn't told anyone that.

He was smiling. The warmth in his eyes reminded her of the night they went up to the top of Skinner Butte in her old Pontiac. They had walked around the path overlooking the city, and kissed—just once—as twilight fell. "It happens that way sometimes," he said. "Especially with virgins."

She frowned. She knew sex was painful at first, but she hadn't thought it would be that painful. Still, he probably knew better. She took a fry off her plate. "I was wondering if you would put up some of the money."

"Money?" He had moved closer. She didn't remember him changing to another chair. He put his hand on her leg. Her blood turned to liquid heat. The aroused feeling she had fought after he attacked her was back, stronger than it had ever been.

"I don't want to raise a child alone."

His hand had moved its way to her groin. His fingers pressed against the stitching in her jeans. A small moan escaped her. Hard to believe she had ever been frightened of this man. He leaned forward, cupping her cheek with his other hand, and then his lips brushed hers, gently, so gently. She didn't want gentle. She wanted more. She opened his mouth and tasted it. So sweet, so good, like a rich wine going down. She pressed against his hand, wishing he would unzip her jeans. There was room on the table. All they had to do was push the plate aside . . .

Then he pulled away. His smile was soft. "See how different it is after the first time? I'm sorry I scared you."

"You ran away. I thought you didn't want me."

"That much passion scared me too. I should have come for you sooner. I'm sorry." He stood and extended a hand to her. She stood beside him, never taking her gaze from his face. She had forgotten how long his lashes were, how bright his eyes.

He pulled some money out of a money clip in his pocket and tossed a number of bills on the table. Then he extended his arm. She took it, feeling the others in the pub watching her. She had caught this beautiful man. He was taking her away from here.

He pushed open the double doors and led her into

the cool, rainy night. "I have a room at the Hilton," he said. "Come with me?"

"Oh, yes." It was like a dream, like something in those romance novels her mother had forbidden her to read. Raindrops sparkled on the newly planted trees along Fifth. The light from the Oregon Electric Station Restaurant was soft, bathing the entire neighborhood in a yellow glow.

Ben glanced at no one. He put his free hand over hers. His expensive shoes clicked on the pavement. Her tennies were silent in the wet.

When they crossed the street against the light, the traffic stopped. People in Delbert's Cafe across from the post office all looked out the window as Candyce and Ben passed. The Hilton was only half a block away, but that was half a block too far. She wanted him now.

They ran across Sixth, past the valet parking and into the front door. Piano music echoed across the lobby. A group of overdressed men laughed near the front door. A young couple wearing formal dress were waiting for the elevator. Ben pulled a key from his pocket and stopped beside them.

The girl flushed when she saw him. Her boyfriend pulled her closer. Ben ran his hand along Candyce's arm. Little tingles ran all the way to her feet.

She barely noticed the elevator ride. They got off on the eighth floor, and she pushed past Ben as he unlocked the door. By the time he closed it, she had pulled off her clothes and was waiting for him on the king-sized bed.

He took off his overcoat and scarf. He crouched over the bed, caressing her neck, her breasts. "I had forgotten how beautiful you were," he said.

Each touch made her body explode with little bursts of pleasure.

He cupped a breast. "It's bigger," he said, and kissed it. "The baby?"

Baby? She had forgotten about the baby. He put his

hands on her hips and kissed her stomach. Then he stood and peeled off his clothes. His body was leaner. He sprawled across her, entering her swiftly. An orgasm rippled through her. She had never had one before. It left her breathless.

He smiled, then plunged deeper and at the same time sank his teeth in her neck.

She had a moment of panic, but it eased and she lost all thought. Her body was nerve endings only, and all she wanted was him. She touched him everywhere, having orgasm after orgasm as he suckled at her neck. She moved and he remained completely still, until suddenly he bit harder, his body curled and convulsed.

He lay on top of her and she wondered how she had ever feared him. He hadn't hurt her. He made her feel alive. She wanted to feel that way again.

But he pulled away. "No," he said. "We can't hurt the baby."

Baby? "Who cares about the baby?" she said, reaching for him. "We're going to get rid of it anyway."

He grabbed her wrist and pulled her up against him. She was melting. If only he would touch her breasts, her hips, her mouth again—

"No," he said. His voice was firm. "We are not going to get rid of him. You're coming with me, tomorrow."

"All right." She leaned against him. She didn't care as long as he made her feel alive. She tilted her head, so that he could sink his teeth into her neck. "Again?" she whispered. "The baby's too small to get hurt."

This time, when he sank his teeth into her neck, her entire body alighted in flames.

Chapter
Fourteen

Cammie had been traveling for the better part of the day. She had had a two-hour layover in O'Hare, and another two hours to walk around Denver's new airport. Still, nothing had prepared her for the airport in Eugene, Oregon. At first Cammie thought they were emergency-landing near a warehouse. The man beside her, who was flying in from New York City on business, called it a Tonka Toy airport. She couldn't agree more.

The building was a deep forest-green. When the plane landed, Cammie waited until almost everyone had disembarked before struggling with the overhead baggage. The flight attendant said good-bye to her, and the pilot smiled at her. She smiled back hesitantly. She wasn't used to getting such attention from service personnel.

The walkway into the building was short. Ahead, she could hear laughter and growing conversation. The air felt dry and cool, despite the hot temperatures the national papers had reported for the area. She walked through the steel doors into the gate.

For the first time in her life, she had arrived at an airport with no one waiting for her. Still, she scanned the faces crowded around the counter, glancing hopefully at each person who deplaned. Most of them were white, some were dressed in late sixties garb, and all but the man from New York wore casual clothing. Despite her jeans, Cammie felt just as out of place.

She didn't know anyone in this crowd of friendly people. People who greeted each other while they waited for family or friends. People who teased across the crowded area. The entire group would erupt in laughter at the smallest thing, and cooed in delight as a small girl launched herself at the man in front of Cammie, wrapping herself around his legs and nearly tripping him. He scooped her up in one arm—the practiced parent—and went to hug his wife.

Cammie felt a pang. No one had ever held her like that.

She adjusted her shoulder bag and followed the crowd. The waiting area narrowed into a hallway with two shops and an open bar. The green carpet looked and smelled new. People were talking and laughing ahead of her, and she tried to tune them out. As they rounded a corner, she stopped. A photographic mural dominated one wall: people—she assumed they were all locals until she recognized Garrison Keillor's face—flying. Some, like the tiny baby boy near the end, had wings. Others merely had their arms outspread, their travel bags balanced on their backs. It was cute and reinforced the sense of warmth she had felt since she got off the plane.

The mural turned into windows above the escalators, but another mural on the left-hand wall—this one obviously hand painted—depicted Northwest scenes. Below was another restaurant, and beyond it the rent-a-car companies. They were right next to the single baggage claim track. The track wasn't running yet. She would pick up her car while she waited for her oversized suitcases to emerge.

The woman behind the car company counter moved like an athlete. Her face had a shiny fresh-scrubbed look, and she pulled her long hair back. She smiled when she saw Cammie. "Help you?" she asked.

All day, Cammie had not seen an airport person smile with such sincerity. Perhaps it was the lack of traffic here, and thus the lack of pressure. "I have a reservation for a mid-sized car," she said.

As they went through the procedure, the woman talked with Cammie about options and saving money—not in a salesman sort of way, but as one friend to another. She explained how to get to the car, then handed Cammie a map. "Anywhere you need to go?"

"I want to stay in a nice hotel downtown," Cammie said.

"Downtown?" the woman asked, a small frown between her eyebrows. "Or on campus?"

"Downtown," Cammie said.

"There is only one nice hotel downtown. The Hilton. But there are some nice places near campus, too, and some near Valley River, our local mall."

"Downtown," Cammie repeated.

The woman took her pen and marked the route on the map, added the text of highway signs and local landmarks. Then she pressed the map, the rental agreement, and the key into Cammie's hands. "Enjoy your stay," the woman said.

Cammie smiled. "I will," she said. The friendliness was infectious. In the Midwest people were a lot more reserved than people appeared to be in this airport.

She had expected an airport like the Dane County airport—several gates and rude attendants who were used to dealing with both students and government officials. The Eugene/Springfield area had the same size population as Madison, and it had a university, yet, judging from the airport, the place felt like a small town.

That might help her.

By the time she was done with the car, her luggage was the only set remaining on the revolving luggage track. She rented a cart and towed her luggage outside. The rental cars were on the left side of the parking lot, only two rows of them—an unusually small number to her eyes. She found hers easily, a late model white Ford sedan. It took a moment to load the car, locate all the essentials (like the lights), and spread her map before her. But soon she was outside the terminal, and following the rent-a-car clerk's instructions to the Eugene Hilton.

The airport was located in an area of fields and farms, much like the Dane County airport had been ten years before. Only the developers seemed to have missed Eugene. Her headlights swept no building newer than the early eighties and many, in the early part of her drive, needed repair. Little hairs rose on the back of her neck.

Vampire country.

But it couldn't be. Before she left, Cammie had tolerated a long lecture from Sarge on the history of vampires in the West. A few vampires had emigrated to Hollywood before the war, but most were arrested, then killed as Nazi collaborators. The great eastern and northern European immigrations to the United States had centered in the North, East, and Midwest. Few made it South, and even fewer to the West itself. Because vampires were rarely mobile, the Center assumed that vampiric activity remained confined to those regions, although no one had done any official studies.

Cammie wasn't sure she believed Sarge, but since she had made the decision to track Ben, she had done some research. Not only did she find a startling lack of vampire-related crime, she found in the Pacific Northwest lower crime statistics all around. The statistics disturbed rather than pleased her: she always feared under-reporting instead of the good life. The area's reputation for independent people and rugged lifestyles made under-reporting very probable.

The Eugene City Center turn-off was well marked just as the clerk had told her it would be. Cammie followed the trail of lights to a four-lane one-way street in the heart of the city.

Two- and three-story office buildings surrounded her. Only one building rose taller than five stories on the skyline: the hotel itself. Even the city's architecture was small town. Except for the broad one-way street, the roads had a 1950s urban feel—simple cloverleafs and two-lanes ending in stop signs. She felt both comfortable and a little unnerved at the same time. Places with this kind of population should look like cities, not small towns.

She followed the signs that led her around the block to the Hilton's guest registration parking. A large, well-lit overhang protected the area from bad weather. A valet parking attendant met her at the door. She handed him her keys just as a bellhop with a gold cart pulled open the car door. She thanked them both and went inside.

Piano music tinkled in from the bar. A group of men were laughing as they went around her through the double doors. Once the doors closed, she stopped: the prickle was back, tingling down her neck. Something subtle this time—something that her conscious brain couldn't detect. She glanced around the lobby, with the two elevator banks in front of her, the coffee shop on the left, and the registration desk off to her right. The area smelled of pastries and conditioned air and, aside from the staff, she was the only person in view. Perhaps the staff contained a vampire. She frowned, checking her watch. It was eight P.M.—too early to have a vampire hidden in the shift. This crew would have started duty in the daylight.

Cammie adjusted her duffel and made her way to the desk. Her hands were shaking and her nerves were on alert, but she didn't see what was causing the problem. A slender woman, with clear eyes and a clean complexion, checked her into a room on the eighth floor. The bellhop was waiting by the elevator when she got her key. He smiled at her. His face had none of the vampire's distinguishing marks either.

Not that she could always recognize them. Early vampirism never showed in the body. Only with age and time did vampires develop their gauntness, pallid skin, and red eyes. A few young ones would bloat from overindulgence, but often the signs were difficult to detect in the first fifty years.

The thought did not comfort her.

She smiled back.

They got into the old elevator together and it wobbled its way to eight. As the door opened, she took a half step backward. The air smelled of blood, fresh and rich, mixed with a taint of rot.

"You okay?" the bellhop asked.

She couldn't get off on this floor. She couldn't cross the threshold that divided the elevator and the hallway. Her entire body had gone rigid.

The door started to close, but the bellhop caught it with his left hand. The smacking sound echoed in the enclosed space. "Ma'am?"

What could she do? Reach into her duffel and take out her stake and hammer? Oregon had no eradication laws on the books and even if it had, it would take a concentrated investigation—one she was not qualified for—to certify the vampire to death.

"Do you smell that?" she asked.

The bellhop sniffed, a slight frown creasing his brows. "I don't smell anything, ma'am."

She made herself sneeze—partly to clean the blood scent from her nostrils and partly for show. "I'm deathly allergic to perfume," she said. "And someone on this floor bathes in it. I'm going to have to go back down and get another room."

The bellhop nodded gravely, as if she had just told him that her grandmother was dying. "Whatever you want, ma'am."

And he was probably thinking that she was crazy to switch rooms so easily.

The elevator took them back down to the lobby, and Cammie switched her room on eight for one on eleven. No faintly rotten odor greeted her here, only the processed air mixed with the slightly damp scent of an older hotel. The bellhop let her into her room, placed her suitcases for her, and eased out almost before she could hand him his tip. She hadn't behaved that oddly— at least by Midwestern standards—but she was beginning to realize that Midwestern standards might not apply here.

The door clicked shut and she collapsed on the flowered spread. The mattress beneath it was firm, just the way she liked it. The room was a standard size, with an oversize dresser and a huge TV complete with remote. Two chairs and a table stood near the curtained window, and she resisted the urge to get up and see what was outside.

She had imagined the smell.

Sarge had said there were no vampires in the Northwest.

But how would Sarge know? Sarge had never been here.

It made sense: the prickling from the moment Cammie had walked in. The scent would have been fainter in the lobby than it was on the floor where the vampire was staying. Or maybe he—or she—was just visiting, staying to service someone before going back to his or her lair.

She had no authority out here. She didn't dare get mixed up in this, and she wasn't sure she wanted to.

She wanted to find Ben, reassure herself that he was all right, and then go home—wherever home might be.

Still, the idea of a vampire in the same hotel made her feel eight again, on the edge, restless and powerless at the same time.

She got up, locked the deadbolt, pushed in the security button, and secured the chain. Then she leaned against the door, listening for a moment. Nothing. Even if a vampire were in the next room, he wouldn't know she was there, ripe for the plucking.

Before she realized what she was doing, she reached into her duffel, removed two strands of garlic. She hung them over the curtains, and placed a single bulb on the door. Then she hung the little silver cross earrings that Eliason had given her from the top of the mirror. She put the stake and hammer under her pillow.

There. She was as safe as she had ever been.

Which meant that she wasn't safe at all.

Chapter Fifteen

The sun across his face felt like a pan of boiling water. Ben sat up. His skin was steaming. Wisps of white were actually rising from his pores. The pain was intense and he could barely move. He pulled up a blanket and held it against the light to give himself shade. Each movement made the pain sink into his bones.

He kicked the cow beside him. "Wake up!" He kicked her again. "Wake up, damn you!"

She rolled away from him and toppled off the side of the bed, taking the covers with her. The pain was back, full and scalding.

She brought her hand to her eyes. He leaned over and grabbed her wrist.

"Stop that!" His voice was too loud. He would attract attention. But he had to get her to move. "Close the curtains. Hurry, you stupid bitch!"

She scrambled to her feet and pulled the curtains closed. As the sunlight disappeared, the worst of the burning stopped. His skin still steamed, though. He collapsed against the hot sheets, willing the pain to go away. Jesus. He had never experienced anything like that.

It had been as if his body had been on fire.

"Ben?" She picked up the covers. "Are you all right?"

He couldn't deal with her. Of course he wasn't all

right. Had she ever seen anyone's skin steam? Cows were so damned stupid.

He rolled out of bed and staggered into the bathroom, not flicking on the light, in part because he was afraid of the brightness and he was afraid of what he would see. Something had changed. He had never had such an intense reaction to sunlight. When he had gone to Seattle, he had been able to walk in it.

He had changed.

He turned the shower on cold and stepped inside, almost slipping on the bare tile. He couldn't see in the stall, so he felt for the handicapped bar and held it as the icy water soothed the fire in his skin.

If the cow hadn't been there, he would have died. From his own foolishness. He had been so wrapped up in seducing her that he had forgotten his own safety. Not good. Not good at all.

As his body temperature returned to normal, his wits returned. He had kicked Candyce. He had kicked Candyce and she had fallen out of bed. He leaned forward, bracing his arm on the slick tile wall. She could have lost the baby. Still might, if he had actually hurt her.

He shut off the water and grabbed a towel, drying himself off as he pushed back the curtain.

"You okay, Ben?" Her voice sounded hollow.

As he stepped into the bedroom, he reached beside the bedside table and turned on the light. The brightness made him wince. His skin was bright red and it looked freshly healed. He touched her face. She looked okay—a little scared, maybe, but okay. He had to play this right.

"Oh, man, baby," he said. "Bad dream. I'm so sorry. Did I hurt you?"

She bit her lower lip. The wariness was back in her eyes. "Surprised me."

"Yeah, me too." He lowered his head and licked her nipple, then cupped the swell of her belly. She didn't move.

"You know I would never hurt you," he said into her breasts. He slid a hand down to her pubic hair and she arched. Good.

"I love you, Ben," she whispered.

"I know," he said, and slipped inside of her. One more time, and she'd be his.

It was over quickly because he had no energy, and then he slept, his teeth still embedded in her neck.

Hours later, he woke up suckling. She was arching and cooing and rubbing herself all over him. Her skin was the color of wax paper, and through it he could see her veins pumping as they emptied into him.

God, the baby.

He rolled away.

"Don't stop." Her voice was slurred, filled with the drugs he had forced into her from his saliva. "Oh, Ben. Please. Don't stop."

He got up and walked away from the bed. She stuck three fingers inside herself and continued to roll on the bed. He looked away.

Candyce had been pretty once. He had actually thought of marrying her. But seeing her like this, her eyes glazed, her body raw from too much of his kind of sex, made him vaguely ill. She had no more control than the rest of them. From now on, all he would have to do would be to kiss her once, let her taste that saliva, and she would fuck him until she died.

Literally.

He had to be careful. That baby was more precious than all the blood in the world.

Candyce cried out as an orgasm shook her. She turned her head toward him, her eyes bruised and her lips bleeding. "Ben—"

The blood looked so tempting.

"Get up," he said.

She didn't stop. Another orgasm rippled through her.

She licked her lips, then ran her free hand across her breasts. "Look, Ben. We'd have so much fun—"

"No." He made the word harsh. "Get dressed. We're leaving."

He went into the bathroom and closed the door. His body was shaking. She might be his only chance for progeny, and he had nearly killed her. Another hour and she would have been dry, the baby dead.

They needed that child. Mikos had stressed the importance of hereditary vampires. They were the strength of the clan. They were the leaders. Like him. It wouldn't be long before Ben's strength completely overpowered Mikos.

Ben was soft now and able to pee. The only change he really hated: the thick fluid that smelled of death and turned the water in the bowl tarry black. It had frightened him the first time, and disgusted him even now. Mikos had called it a reminder that Ben would never again be human.

"Ben?" Candyce's voice had a plaintive note it had never had before. He sighed. He would have to get used to it. "I'm dressed now."

He flushed and opened the bathroom door. She was dressed, wearing the same jeans and turtleneck she had worn the day before. But she didn't look like the same woman. That woman had strength and fire, intelligence glowing out of her eyes. This woman looked like she hadn't eaten in a week and like she had borrowed someone else's clothes. He had been very careless. He would have to treat her cautiously from now on.

"Sit down and wait for me. I'll just be a minute."

She sat and clasped her hands on her lap, as if taking his orders were as natural as breathing. Stupid cunt. Didn't she realize she was reacting to a drug?

No, of course not, and with luck, she wouldn't realize it until long after the baby was born and she was thrown back into the bar where he had found her. Until then, he could do whatever he wanted with her, as long as he didn't harm the child.

He put on his suit and called down for the car. Then he gathered his belongings and let himself out of the room. Candyce followed.

He was glad Mikos had talked him into responding to Candyce's call. The trip had been a profitable one, after all.

Chapter Sixteen

Cammie sat in her car, across the street from the Sadlers' house. Her briefcase was open, and she was rifling through it, looking for her Westrina Center ID. She knew she had brought it, but it wasn't in her purse. That meant, she hoped, it was in her briefcase. She couldn't go into that house without identification.

The Sadlers lived on top of a large hill on the south side of town. The roads curved and wound through this section. The houses were mostly two story, modified ranch houses, built in the sixties and kept up. Trees hid the homes from each other, but the neighborhoods had a suburban, chummy feel. The cars that remained in the parking lots were minivans and BMWs, second cars, most of them, in a middle- class community that wanted to keep its roots and be upscale at the same time.

Ben must have been happy here. Cammie had always wanted to grow up in a place like this. Instead, she had gone from home to home in the communities around Madison, fighting for her place among other foster children and already-established household patterns.

Still, she had been thinking about what Eliason had said. Perhaps Ben had hurt the girl. Cammie believed, as Eliason did, that children's personalities were formed by the time they were four years old. Their father had been abusive. Ben had been three when he finally got out of the house. Maybe he had learned that pattern. Maybe Cammie's arrival would help him overcome it.

The ID was tucked in the bottom of a side pocket. She pulled the card out, made sure the dates were current and that it read "Investigator." Then she slipped it over the generic Westrina Center card that was in her wallet, and got out of the car.

It had been years since she wore a business suit and heels, not since her secretarial stint in college. Walking across the sloped concrete was difficult, especially since she wanted to look as though heels were her natural garb. The panty hose itched and the crotch had worked its way to her mid-thigh. Fortunately the sensible gray skirt went to her calves.

The lawn was a cultivated mass of flowers and shaved grass. The faint scent of grass mixed with rhododendrons drifted over to her. Cammie walked on the brick sidewalk, stifling a curse as her heel caught in the dirt between bricks. The carved oak door had no bell, just a gold knocker that read "Sadler." She was about to reach for it, when the door opened.

A thin, fortyish woman with ash-blonde hair stood at the door. She had an athlete's body—she probably ran every day—and her face glowed. Only the shadows beneath her eyes marred the healthy effect. She wore tight blue jeans and a white silk blouse.

"I'm Cammie Timms from the Westrina Center." Cammie pulled out her wallet and flashed her identification. The woman studied it with a surprising intensity, considering that Cammie had made an appointment with her before she left Madison.

"Come on in," she said. "I'm Donna Sadler."

She backed away from the door and Cammie stepped inside. The interior smelled of bay candles underlaid with an odor of wet dog. Odd. She hadn't heard any barking. After being attacked by a German shepherd on one of her early runs, she was always cautious of dogs.

The small foyer opened to a staircase and a living room on the left. The house was immaculate. Magazines were scattered around for effect. Flowers from the yard stood on the coffee and end tables as well as the fireplace mantel. The furniture—a sofa, two love seats, and an overstuffed chair—was cream and rose, its color scheme enhanced by the flower arrangements around it. A stereo hid in a cabinet beside the fireplace. No television. The living room had to be for guests and for show. There had to be a den somewhere else—and it had to be a lot more comfortable.

Mrs. Sadler led her into the living room. Her movements were quick and nervous. "I took the liberty of brewing some French roast. Would you like some?"

"Please." Cammie stood in the center of the room, uncertain about where to sit. Mrs. Sadler brought a silver coffee set over on a silver serving tray. Bone china mugs and two matching plates completed the look. In the center of the tray, a lemon tea cake had been neatly sliced. Mrs. Sadler set the tray down, sat on a love seat, and immediately poured the coffee. The fresh scent of the blend was soothing.

Cammie put her briefcase down and sat on the sofa across from Mrs. Sadler. Cammie sank into the thick cushions—the comfort a surprise.

"I've been expecting you," Mrs. Sadler said. "In fact, I was surprised it took you people so long to respond."

Cammie froze as she reached for the coffee cup. She made herself follow through with the movement, taking the delicate cup and saucer and holding them over her lap. "I'm sorry?"

"Well." Mrs. Sadler set a piece of tea cake on each plate, then picked up her own coffee cup. "I sent the first letter right after Ben disappeared, almost six weeks ago."

"I'm sorry, Mrs. Sadler," Cammie said, "but I'm not familiar with any letters. I came out here because we had seen the newspaper articles about Ben's disappearance. We thought that we should follow up."

"I guess there is a first time for everything." Mrs. Sadler sipped her coffee. She still hadn't met Cammie's gaze.

Cammie stiffened. "Ma'am, are you unhappy with the Westrina Center?"

Finally Mrs. Sadler looked up. Contacts floated on her gray pupils, supported by too much tearing. "I wasn't until Ben disappeared. You people stayed in the distance, offered support where you could, and never interfered. But when I wanted your help, you didn't give it. And from what I know, it's not the first time."

Cammie's hands were shaking. She had to set the cup down to keep it from rattling. "I thought you hadn't contacted us before."

"I hadn't." Mrs. Sadler broke a piece off her tea cake and wiped the powdered sugar topping on a napkin. "But a number of other parents had. In the same situation. When they saw that Ben was adopted, they contacted me because they wondered where we had found him. When they heard about the Westrina Center and the fact that no one had responded to my letters, they told me that was normal."

Cammie frowned. "I don't understand. You're saying that there are other missing children?"

"Not children," Mrs. Sadler said. "Adults. That's why the police didn't get involved for forty-eight hours, and I assume why the Center won't help either."

Cammie hadn't expected this. It was odd. She picked up her briefcase, opened it, and took out her notepad. "Could you give me the names?"

"Better yet," Mrs. Sadler said. "I'll give you copies of their letters." She got up and walked down the hallway behind the stairs. Cammie made herself breathe. Ben was not the first Westrina transplant to disappear. How odd. Too odd. Or maybe not. She had no idea how many adults stopped communicating with their families after college. Perhaps these adoptive parents just worried more than most.

The French roast tasted as rich as it smelled. She broke off a piece of her own tea cake and ate it. The cake was light, the lemon not too powerful. She had eaten half the piece by the time Mrs. Sadler came back into the room.

She gave Cammie a packet of letters. Cammie thumbed through them and found some dating back five years. She frowned. "None of these people have been found?"

Mrs. Sadler shook her head. "None of them. And the Center did nothing to help any of the parents."

"May I keep these?" Cammie asked.

"They're copies," Mrs. Sadler said. She ate the piece of cake she had broken off previously, then took another sip of her coffee.

Cammie put the letters in her briefcase. She closed it, leaving the notebook on her lap, and then picked up her own cup. She felt as if they were little girls who didn't like each other, trying to have a tea party. Only she did like Mrs. Sadler. The woman's determination and obvious affection for Ben impressed her.

"Let's go back to you," Cammie said. "I would like to know as much about Ben as I could."

Mrs. Sadler softened. "He was three when he came to us, you know, and very frightened. At first, he couldn't even sleep at night, but after a while he calmed down. He was such a sweet little boy—quiet, never complaining. He did his homework, had nice friends, and graduated at the top of his class. He was very determined. Whenever he set his mind to something, he accomplished it. We were so proud of him. We thought he was going to do great things."

Cammie took another sip of coffee, making sure she remained calm. Ben was quiet because she had trained him to be that way and he never complained because their father wouldn't listen anyway. Their father believed that babies, after they were fed and changed, needed no other care.

Mrs. Sadler took another bite of the tea cake. "He started to change in college. He didn't write or visit often, and when he did, he would stay out all night and party with his high school friends. They had never done that in high school. He was always irritable, and toward the end, his grades started to slip. If the slip had started any sooner, he wouldn't have graduated with honors."

Cammie finished her coffee and set the cup down. It sounded suspicious to her, but she had found that over the years she tended to suspect everyone of hiding something. "Teenagers often go through phases like that."

Mrs. Sadler nodded. "I married Gary in one of those phases. Fortunately it was the right choice." She pushed back a strand of hair. "I would have thought nothing of it if Ben hadn't stopped caring about what I considered to be Ben sort of things."

"What do you mean?"

"He was always considerate. Not just polite, but really kind. If he saw someone having trouble getting comfortable in a chair, he would bring over a pillow. If a homeless man needed money, Ben bought him coffee and a donut and then gave him five dollars. He was kind."

Cammie's hands had turned cold. "He stopped being kind?"

Mrs. Sadler's eyes flashed. "He stopped being *considerate*. He would still be polite, but he wouldn't do that extra thing. He wouldn't look at people anymore. He didn't seem to care about them."

"Did he do drugs?"

Mrs. Sadler shook her head. "I thought of that first." She smiled. "I'm a product of the sixties, I guess. But he was intellectually clear and always bright-eyed. He didn't even drink much, if at all." She looked down at her hands. They were well manicured, and the fingernails were covered with light pink polish. "I even searched his room and found nothing. At his age, I wouldn't have survived a search like that."

She may not have known where to look or what to look for. Drugs changed across generations. "Did he have any new friends?"

"Some college buddies, but they weren't close. They never came here, even though he was only going to school across town. No. He got into trouble with his old high school friends—boys who had never been rowdy before. And then there was Candyce."

The soft tone of Mrs. Sadler's voice alerted Cammie. "Candyce?"

"They were dating for a long time. Then one night, she said he hurt her pretty bad." Mrs. Sadler rubbed her hands on her jeans. "I wouldn't have believed her if it hadn't been for the bruises all over her arms and on the side of her face. Her mother says Ben raped Candyce, but Candyce doesn't. She said they were having fun, and then he changed, got real angry and hurt her."

Cammie sighed and looked away. She had to stand up. She couldn't sit any longer. "Before Ben came to you, he lived in an abusive household. Perhaps he learned some of those patterns—"

"My Ben would never hurt anyone!" Mrs. Sadler said.

"You just told me that he did."

"Candyce said he did. I never talked to him. He disappeared the next day."

"He disappeared?"

Mrs. Sadler shrugged. "He never came home that night. Then when Candyce's mother contacted me, I got worried. I thought maybe"—she looked down, and adjusted the tray—"maybe he *had* done something and run away. Or maybe something else happened. Maybe Candyce was lying and someone else hurt her and Ben tried to defend her." She sighed. "I just don't know."

Cammie walked to the window and peered out. More flowers covered the backyard, and a garden took up the left corner in front of the fence. On the right side, an ancient swing set rusted against a backdrop of tall trees.

An elderly dog lay underneath the weathered picnic table near the back door. "What do the police say?"

Mrs. Sadler wrapped her arms around her chest, hugging herself. "They say that there's no evidence of wrong-doing, except by Ben, and that he ran away to protect himself. I get the feeling that if Candyce prosecutes, they'll try harder to find him."

Cammie touched the curtain. It was satiny and soft. From all appearances, Ben had had a home here. He certainly hadn't wanted for anything. Maybe something had happened, something unexpected, something Candyce wouldn't talk about and Ben couldn't talk about.

"I would like Candyce's address and phone," Cammie said, "as well as the names of those high school friends you mentioned. I would also like to talk with your husband. When do you expect him back?"

"He'll be here tonight," Mrs. Sadler said. "You could come back about eight."

"I will."

Mrs. Sadler got up without looking at Cammie and hurried into the other room. Cammie returned to her briefcase. She picked up her notebook. Only a few notes. *Candyce → disappearance* was in the center of the page and circled. The other notes had bits of Mrs. Sadler's story and the few names she had mentioned.

"Here." Mrs. Sadler handed Cammie the names and numbers on a sheet of notepaper labeled in bold letters Mind Your Own Doggone Business. Cammie suspected that Mrs. Sadler didn't even see the irony.

Cammie tucked the paper beside the letters in her file and then put her notepad inside. "Thanks," she said. "You've given me a place to start."

Mrs. Sadler nodded. "I know I . . ." she looked around as if the flowers in the room might aid her. "I know I seem ungrateful, but he's been gone so long now and everyone acts as if it's normal. It's not. He wanted so much. He was going on to law school. I actually thought maybe he would be in politics or go on to become a famous lawyer. And now all that seems to be gone." She bit her lip before adding softly, "I'm so afraid for him."

Her eyes teared and her nose turned a delicate shade of pink. For a brief moment, Cammie thought Mrs. Sadler was going to cry. Cammie didn't know how to act if Mrs. Sadler cried. Was she supposed to pat her shoulder? Hug her? Stand there in mutual embarrassment?

Then Mrs. Sadler sniffled and smiled a brave little smile. "Maybe you can help him. I keep thinking that someone from his past will find him and hurt him, you know? But how could they? He was just a little boy, without anyone to love him."

Cammie felt her face heat. "Even then," she said. "People loved him."

She spun and walked through the narrow foyer. Mrs. Sadler held the front door as Cammie left. "I will be back later," Cammie said, unable to keep the coolness from her voice.

When she reached the car, she got in and leaned her head on the seat. She had loved him. Everyone seemed to have forgotten that. She had loved him so much that she had done the unspeakable to save him. That had to count for something.

I keep thinking that someone from his past will find him and hurt him.

No. Cammie wouldn't hurt him. She had come here to help him.

Whatever that took.

Chapter
Seventeen

The bar was on the wrong side of Burnside, closer to the Mission District than Portland's downtown. But Ben was gaining an instinct for these kinds of places. He drove right to it, although he didn't remember Steve's exact instructions from the first time.

Most of the cars parked along the street were twenty years old, dented and the size of small boats. The men who appeared under the glare of the streetlights wore too many clothes for the warm spring night. Their hair was matted and their eyes empty from too many drugs, too much booze, or an encounter with the wrong kind of people. The Targa, with its shiny black paint job, was out of place here.

Candyce sat quietly in the passenger seat. She had said nothing in the two-hour trip north from Eugene. Occasionally, her left hand would caress his leg and move up his thigh. He would clasp his own hand over hers before she could move it higher.

Her touch disgusted him.

The bar was in the middle of the block between Rick's House of Sleaze and the Ruby Chasm. Ben didn't give them a second glance, any more than the men who clustered outside gave him.

Candyce didn't move, waiting for him to tell her what to do.

If he left her there, she would become prey to any lowlife who passed. If he took her inside, the baby might not survive. The Targa didn't have a real backseat, so he couldn't tell her to lie down and stay out of sight.

Damn. He hadn't realized traveling with her would be this annoying.

"Come on," he said as he got out.

She opened her door and got out of the car. She didn't even move like Candyce anymore. Gone were the quick, confident movements, the comfortable ease that made her seem so intelligent. Instead she hunched, just a bit, and watched his every move.

"Stay beside me." He took her arm to protect her from the men. They watched her walk. One man licked his lips. Another reached for her breasts. Ben gave him a look that made him change his mind.

Candyce didn't seem to notice.

The name of the bar had once been the Keg, but someone had removed the letters and not replaced them, leaving a ghostly imprint above the door. A dirty bulb burned beneath a boarded-up window, providing a thin light. Ben led Candyce down the five stairs and yanked the wood door open.

The noise hit first—Springsteen at top volume and a hundred voices trying to shout above it. Then the smell—smoke, beer, fresh meat and blood. Candyce moaned. Ben slipped his hand from her arm to her buttocks and squeezed. He liked this place.

Amazing how his tastes had changed in the last few weeks.

The light bulbs had been painted red, so everything had a red tinge. Faces looked like they had been smeared with blood. Candyce clung to him and he shook her off. There would be more entertainment here than he had found since he arrived in Seattle.

A statuesque woman wearing black leather—her breasts and buttocks sticking out, nipples covered with steel points—passed, a whip in her right hand, a chain in her left. A handcuffed man wearing a pinstriped suit followed her. They disappeared into a side room.

Regular patrons sat up front. They smelled slightly sour, as if they had been overused. Some drank. Others held their glasses and watched the back of the room with furtive glances. Ben followed their gaze into the pit.

Three male vampires sat against the back wall, all of them showing the effects of years of indulgence—the too-thin bodies, the too-red lips. One of them humped a woman while sucking on the wrist of another. The other two males were engaged in conversation with the people around them as if nothing were happening. Another male vampire appeared from yet a different side room. His male cow, swaying beside him, was drained to the point of coma.

"In the back," the bartender yelled at Ben in the break between songs. "I don't want you near the customers."

Ben frowned and wondered how the bartender knew. But even new vampires had a certain air to them—a confidence and sensuality that most humans didn't have. Most people didn't notice, but folks who had been around vampires a long time got an idea. He glanced at the patrons up front. Customers, eh? Good plan by the bartender. Make them pay for the use of the bar, and the vampires. Good drugs, of all kinds.

He walked to the bar, dragging Candyce beside him. "She's stoned, but I need to take her with me. Anywhere I can leave her?"

The bartender glanced at her. He was an overweight pimply man whose alert gaze and ruddy skin marked him as a leech—a human who made money off a vampire. He clearly wasn't drugged—he looked too healthy to be someone's cow—and he didn't have that air of authority that most vampires had. He probably acted as human cover for the vampire who owned the place. "Have her take that stool by the waitress station. But be sure to collect her when you go."

"I will." Ben pulled a fifty from his money clip. "Make sure nothing happens to her."

"What do I look like, the police?" the bartender asked, but he pocketed the bill.

Ben propelled Candyce to the empty bar stool and sat her there. The bartender put a glass of water in front of her. "Wait here," Ben said.

Candyce nodded. She reached for him, but he moved out of her grasp. Others, having seen her reaction, grabbed for him as he passed, knowing that he could give them the kind of release they wanted.

The back room of the bar smelled of blood instead of beer, incense instead of smoke. A female vampire, in the dark left corner, was sucking the penis of a male cow. Judging from the pasty color of his skin, he would be dead before the night was over, but he would die in ecstasy.

He glanced back until he saw a bouncer, a big man dressed in all black. Bouncers had a different function in these bars. They got rid of the unwanted bodies, usually by dumping them in the Pacific. There were several places along the coasts of Oregon and Washington where a body dropped into the ocean would not be recovered or ever seen again.

Doors led to private rooms. Most of the vampires took their cows inside, preferring not to perform in public. The male vampire with the two cows had brought a third over. The women were servicing each other, using him as a toy, while he sampled from each neck.

In spite of himself, Ben found the scene erotic. He was tempted to find a cow of his own, take her to the back room, and drain her completely. He was hard. He would wait fifteen minutes and then take a cow of his own.

He scanned the faces of the vampires in the room, but recognized none of them. He slipped into a chair, deciding to wait. Steve would be here. People said he never left.

Ben couldn't be in a place like this all the time. Not even when he first succumbed to the blood lust. And now, now Mikos had been flaming another lust, the lust that had made Ben pursue pre-law in the first place.

Power.

It wasn't enough to have the sexual mastery. He knew himself well enough to know that he would tire of it. No. He wanted to live longer than Mikos had, to be wealthier than Mikos and to control the world around him.

Ben was young and fresh and unknown. He had the ability to do that. The bass line of the music thudded along his spine. He found a chair that faced the other vampires, his back to the cows. He didn't want to see them. Smelling them was hard enough. He made himself watch. Mikos had told him about these places, where less successful vampires spent their time. Mikos had called them dangerous, claiming that eventually some unconnected, zealous human would find them, and kill all associated with them.

Ben was amazed no one had found this one yet.

The smell and the sexual energy was making the wait unbearable. He needed to see Steve, to talk with him about that fuck-up, the one Mikos had punished Ben for, but Ben needed the release too. Screw the back room. He would have his pleasure and wait for Steve. After a moment, he stood, adjusted his pants leg to relieve the pressure and walked back to the customer tables. He grabbed a slender black-haired woman in a miniskirt. She didn't have a visible mark on her bare skin. He gripped her wrist and dragged her into the pit.

She was breathing heavily, and she licked her lips like one anticipating a snack. He sat back in his chair, keeping his gaze on the doors to the private rooms. He unzipped his pants and pulled his penis free. Then he hiked up her skirt, pleased to note that she wasn't wearing any underwear. He grabbed her hips and forced her down. She was already wet.

God, she felt good. The orgasm wasn't far away. She pushed up her leather top, and then he saw the marks—bruises lining both breasts. He no longer cared. He bit into one of the blue veins visible near her nipple and sucked.

Her orgasms were strong. She had been a cow for a long time. He could hear her cries over the music. Her blood was warm, and a bit sour—not nearly as fresh as Candyce's.

Then he exploded into her, burying his face against her breast. He kept sucking, feeling himself grow hard again, before he remembered Steve.

He pulled his teeth out of the holes he had made next to her nipple and licked the blood off the wound. She put her hands under her breasts and extended them to him. "Oh, God," she murmured. "You're young. More. Give me more."

He swallowed. He was losing track of his purpose.

Control, Van had said.

He grabbed the woman by the waist and yanked her off him. His body still throbbed. If he had known that vampires had this kind of sexual staying power, he would have sought this out.

But he had to concentrate, and the cow wasn't going to let him.

"That's it, darling," he said.

She started to go down on him, but he caught her chin, and dug his fingers into the sensitive flesh. She cried out, but not with pleasure.

"I said that's it." He tossed her away like a used condom. She tumbled onto the bloodstained floor, skirt still hiked up over her perfect ass. She pushed herself up on her elbows, staring at the other vampires, seeing if one would take her.

Ben was soft. He tucked himself in and zipped up. So far the cow hadn't found any takers. Ben looked away, just as a back room door opened. Steve came out. He looked pudgier than he had before, his long brown hair curling behind his ears. He wore faded jeans and a leather bomber jacket. The two women with him were habitual; their drained faces were filled with an obvious ecstasy only an overexposure over a long period of time could give.

He patted them affectionately on their asses and pushed them away.

Ben was out of his chair and across the room before Steve had a chance to move. As Steve looked up, Ben caught him around the throat and pushed him back against the wall. The loud thunk echoed over the music. The conversation stopped. Heads turned among the vampires to see what was going on. Most of the waiting cows didn't bother to look.

"You had no right," Ben said, his face inches from Steve's, "to tell anyone where I was."

Steve's teeth were stained brown and his skin was bloated. He overfed. No wonder he had never gone beyond places like this. He put his hands around Ben's wrists and tugged, unable to free himself. "It was just Candyce, man," he said, his voice hoarse from the pressure. Ben could feel Steve's Adam's apple moving beneath his palm. "I thought you would want to see her."

"The next time you think something," Ben said, "you call me. I'll tell you what to do."

He let go of Steve's neck. Steve rubbed his throat. "Who the hell do you think you are?" Steve asked. "Two months ago, you didn't even know what you were."

"A lot changes." Ben tugged his silk suit coat. Then he adjusted Steve's collar. "At least for some of us."

Steve slapped his hand away. "I could work with Mikos any time I want."

"Oh, really?" Ben asked. "Then why don't you?"

"His place is dull. Those weird parties night after night."

"Mikos said he made you leave," Ben said. The blood lust was still flowing through him. He was shaking. "He damn near made me leave after Candyce called me. 'Damaged the integrity of the Nest,' he said. But I swore on *my blood* that I didn't tell her anything. Now she tells me she found out from you. I'm going to make sure you never fuck me over again."

The conversation around them had resumed. They had lost their focus as the center of attention when their moment of anger had not erupted into a fight.

"I was right to send you to Mikos." Steve smiled. He touched the corner of Ben's mouth with one dirty finger. It came away covered with blood. Steve licked it off. "Never thought you'd be able to function in a place like this."

"You were wrong," Ben said. He felt as if he had aged years since he last saw Steve. Steve had been the wise one then. Ben was now. "And you were wrong to tell Candyce how to find me. If she told anyone else—"

"She didn't." Steve smiled. "I *told* her not to."

Ben froze. "You told her. How exactly did you tell her?"

Steve seemed to be standing up straighter. "Don't worry, man. I already knew about the baby. I wasn't going to mess what was rightfully yours."

"How did you tell her?" Ben moved closer.

"You know, hurting each other is against the rules," Steve said. He leaned against the wall, as if it would give and protect him from Ben.

"Really?" Ben asked. "There are rules?"

Steve nodded. "Lots of rules. Don't they teach you anything up there?"

Ben took another step forward. His body leaned against Steve's. "They didn't teach me some silly ass rule like that. It wouldn't serve any purpose, now, would it?"

"It keeps our clan going," Steve said.

Ben shook his head. "We have to cleanse the clan of those who aren't worthy of it."

"I didn't do anything wrong." Steve pushed on Ben's shoulders. Ben took a step back.

"You told Candyce where to find me," Ben said. "Now look at her."

He gestured toward the bar. Steve followed Ben's movement. Candyce was facing the bartender, swaying and singing to herself. She had the same distracted air the other cows had.

"Jesus," Steve said.

Ben saw the disgust travel across Steve's face. The three of them had grown up together—had considered each other good friends. This change in Candyce would affect Steve as much as it affected Ben.

"See?" Ben said. "If you had called me instead of trying to control things yourself, I would have told you to keep an eye on her, and let me know when the baby was born. Then I would have taken the child from her. But as it is, she has to spend the rest of her term like that, with me."

"Jesus," Steve said again. "You learn fast, don't you?"

Ben looked around the bar. Another vampire had moved into the back corner, helping the female drain the man. A small shudder ran through Ben. "It's the only way to survive," he said.

Steve got a half smile on his face. "You haven't survived yet, man. It's only been two months."

A cow walked behind Ben and trailed a hand along his buttocks. Instantly his erection was back. Control. Only for a few more minutes and then he could ease himself again. Since he was here, he might as well take advantage of it.

But first he had to finish the conversation. He would do as Mikos asked. He would spread the word, although he doubted that there would be many who would want to go beyond living for the moment.

He said, "If you got any friends who are looking for something to keep their minds busy as well as their mouths, call me. I might be able to use them."

Steve grabbed the cow that was feeling up Ben and

yanked her beside him. She rubbed against him like a cat. "What kind of busy?" Steve asked.

"I need people who can think, Steve," Ben said. "It's time we move beyond cheap little places like this one."

Steve brushed the cow's hair away from her neck. "I don't want to move beyond this, Ben. That's Mikos's problem. He wants to rule the world. But he doesn't realize that we already do."

He buried his teeth in the tender skin that joined her neck to her shoulder. Ben couldn't take it any more. His mouth was full of saliva. If he didn't have something right now, he would burst.

He glanced at Candyce. Even drugged and disgusting, she was beautiful. He had loved her. He really had. If she didn't have that precious little being in her belly, he would take her here. Now. But he couldn't. He had that much restraint.

He went over to the cow section and picked two young women, then took them into the private room Steve had vacated. Ben would use them until he couldn't anymore. He had to leave Candyce alone. That's all these places were good for, to funnel off excess hunger. Ben was going to use that hunger and gain a different kind of power, a kind that humans could only wonder at.

They would never know what hit them.

Chapter Eighteen

Cammie sprawled on her bed in the hotel room, papers scattered in front of her. Her high heels were off, one lying near the door, the other near the dresser. She lay on her stomach, her nylon-stockinged feet crossed at the ankles and swaying in the air.

She felt more comfortable in the hotel than she had the night before. The smell had disappeared, at least from the elevators. She had avoided the eighth floor. Her floor smelled clean—of conditioned air, lemon-scented polish, and that slightly damp odor she was beginning to associate with the Northwest.

The Northwest surprised her. It was fifteen degrees warmer than Madison had been when she left. The sunshine was crisp and clear, providing a view of the Cascade Range to the east, and the Coastal Range to the west. The large butte near the hotel beckoned her invitingly. Maybe, before dinner, she would see if she could drive to the top.

She had expected rain, but the woman at the desk told her that most of the rains came in the winter. Even then, the woman had said, the sun shone every day. What a change from the Midwest, where grayness could last for weeks at a time.

Despite the comfort she felt, she had kept the garlic

on her door. The maid had not touched the garlic on the curtains when she cleaned. That had reassured Cammie as well. A vampire's attraction to garlic would have made the vampire remove the garlic, even a vampire young enough to be seen in the daytime.

She rubbed her eyes and poked at the papers in front of her. The letters that Ben's adopted mother had given her were in seventeen piles, one for each family. The most typical—and the most interesting because it contained the first letter that went to the Westrina Center—came from the Ellis family.

July 11, 1990
Anita Constantine
Westrina Center
Old Middleton Road
Madison, WI 53711

Dear Ms. Constantine:

Nineteen years ago, my husband and I adopted our son, Jeremiah, through the auspices of your agency and Oregon Infant Services. Two months ago, Jeremiah disappeared. The police have found no leads.

Harold and I have hired private detectives and have had little luck. The detectives recommended that I see OIS for background material on Jerry, since he was four when he came to us. Lynette King from OIS gave us what information she had, and then referred us to you.

Would you please send us the files on Jeremiah? I have enclosed the proper release forms.

Thank you for your assistance.

Sincerely,

Katie Ellis

Katie Ellis's letters grew more insistent as time passed. Finally, in frustration, she contacted *The Oregonian,* the state's largest newspaper. It printed a story of her hunt for her missing son. That article (which Mrs. Sadler had enclosed) put her in touch with three other families. Over time, and with the help of the private detectives and OIS—which, despite its name, was a private adoption and foster care organization—they located the remaining families.

The last letter in the Ellis pile read:

January 20, 1992
Anita Constantine
Westrina Center
Old Middleton Road
Madison, WI 53711

Dear Ms. Constantine:

My son, Jeremiah, has now been missing for two years. To my knowledge, sixteen other children adopted through your center are missing as well. Even though the other parents and I have written over a hundred letters to your organization, we have had no response. We believe that the children's disappearance has something to do with the Westrina Center. Your lack of acknowledgment has given us no choice but to contact federal authorities. They have advised us to work through an attorney. Therefore, all future correspondence will come from him.

Sincerely,

Katie Ellis

Cammie leaned over the side of her bed and opened her briefcase. Inside were the remaining letters, all from the attorney. She pulled them out and sat up to read them.

The attorney, Lionel Jones, worked for Stein, Steaggerglass, Simpson and Cohen. He did have his name on the stationery, but nothing other than Attorney at Law followed his name. He was not a partner, junior or senior. Cammie had enough lawyer friends to realize that the families had made a mistake by not hiring a lawyer with more clout.

The attorney wrote four threatening letters to the Westrina Center, receiving no reply to any of them. He then wrote a letter to the families:

Dear Friends:

Please forgive the impersonal nature of this letter, but I felt it best to reach all of you at once. The Westrina Center has not responded to our demands. As I told you when you hired me, they are fully within their rights to do so. Confidentiality laws vary from state to state; Wisconsin's laws protecting children are stringent. By not responding to our letters, the Westrina Center has passively shown that they are protecting their clients' right to privacy.

We could continue to fight this, but we have no real case. Suspicion that the disappearances are linked to the children's histories does not substitute for actual proof. Without some kind of documented link (other than a shared past), a judge would throw any action we attempt out of court.

For the time being, I will cease writing letters to the Center. I suggest that you hire DeFreeze and Garity, the best private detective firm in the state, to establish a current tie between the Center and your missing children. I have enclosed their business card. If they can establish such a tie, I will move this case forward.

I am sorry that I cannot do more. In the area of adoption, children, and privacy, the law can be strict.

I remain

Your humble servant,

Lionel Jones

Attorney at Law

No business card was enclosed with this copy of the letter. It had been dated two weeks before. No wonder Mrs. Sadler had been so willing to see Cammie. She had thought the fight was over.

Cammie sighed and stretched. Nothing in her training explained these disappearances. The material the counselor had given her on Adult Children had been sparse as well.

It's a new field, the counselor had said. *The literature only covers the basics.*

Anything could have happened to those children. In addition to their vampiric heritage, most came from abusive backgrounds. If they had grown up, as she did, learning to keep to themselves, they might have had a bad turn of events and think nothing of failing to contact their adoptive parents.

But not sixteen children. Not at the same age.

The parents were right. It did seem odd that the adopted children disappeared, all in their early twenties. Most of them were probably survivors of the vampire epidemic. Perhaps something about being a vampire's child predisposed them to leave the people they loved.

Was it the violence? Mrs. Sadler had said that Ben had

left after he had hurt his girlfriend. Or perhaps he hadn't hurt her at all. Perhaps someone had attacked him, hurt the girlfriend, and then taken Ben away. But that didn't explain why the girlfriend said Ben had done it. Was there a vampire loose here, a vampire that was tracking down children of the Westrina Center? How would it know?

Had one of the adult children become a vampire?

Cammie closed her eyes and rested her forehead on her arms. She breathed in shallowly. The books the counselor had given her had had disturbing things in them. The most disturbing was the quiz at the end of the most recent book called *It Could Happen to You.* The quiz had a list of twenty items, such as "are you attracted to the color red?" If the answer to more than three was yes, then the respondent was at risk of becoming a vampire.

Cammie had answered yes to ten items.

She pushed the thought away. She had never drunk anyone's blood. She never planned to. She knew the harm it caused.

She was under control.

The others would be too.

Perhaps. Or perhaps one of them wasn't. The one who had really hurt Candyce. The one Ben and the others were protecting.

Cammie rolled back and dialed DeeDee's number. As the phone rang, she checked the digital clock radio beside her bed. Four-thirty in the afternoon, Pacific time. Just enough time to catch DeeDee at home before she went out for the evening. After six rings, someone picked up. "Gorham House of Joy. Joy's busy. DeeDee speaking."

Cammie smiled. She loved the different ways DeeDee answered the phone. "DeeDee, it's Cammie."

"Hey, Cam! How's life in the wild, wild West?"

"Getting stranger and stranger." Cammie tucked a pillow under her head. It felt odd to talk to DeeDee, as if she were reaching back to another life. "I need your help."

"Shoot, pudding."

Pudding? That was new. The sun ducked behind a cloud, making the room suddenly chill. Cammie pulled the bedspread over her feet. "It's something that may get you in trouble at the Center, so think before you answer me."

"You found your brother?" DeeDee's voice had gone quiet and serious.

"Not yet, but I have a weird lead. I don't want to say more unless you think you can help me."

DeeDee paused. "How much trouble?"

"They might fire you."

"Oh, great. Lose twenty grand a year plus bennies over some wild goose chase?"

Cammie closed her eyes. She wanted to grab Eliason and say, *See? I told you you're my only friend.*

"What do I get if I win?"

It took a minute for Cammie to understand what DeeDee meant. "My undying gratitude," Cammie said.

"How about a belief in me? That maybe I really do care about you?"

Cammie opened her eyes. The ceiling was made of thin tile. She frowned at how close DeeDee's thoughts were to her own. "That too," Cammie said quietly.

"I already know the basic poop," DeeDee said. "Don't tell anyone what I'm doing and don't get caught. Now, what am I going to do?"

Cammie took a deep breath. If DeeDee reported her, the Center could do nothing. She was half a continent away, and there would be no proof she had done anything wrong. "Okay," Cammie said. "Remember the conversation we had about kids and confidentiality?"

"Jeeze, yeah," DeeDee said. "Seems like a long time ago."

"Doesn't it?" The sun came back out, brightening the room. Cammie scooted down so that the light covered

her bare legs. "In Records, I found out that pre-1975 inactive files are stored in the basement, along with a
bunch of other stuff. Fairly easy to find. That's how I got
as much on Ben as I did."

"Okay."

"I want you to go down there and pull the files on
the seventeen names I'm going to give you, then photo-
copy the information and send it to me. Also, check
the active files, just in case something else has happened."

"God, Cammie, seventeen! This isn't something I can
do in an hour."

"That's right," Cammie said. "But I need the information as quickly as you can get it to me."

"What's going on out there?"

"Ben's not the only one who has disappeared," Cammie said. "Sixteen others have as well—at the same age.
The parents have been writing Anita, but she won't send
any information."

"Then I can't either," DeeDee said.

"I'm not going to give it to the parents." Cammie's
mouth had gone dry. Maybe she had made a mistake. "I
just want to see if there's any link besides the Center."

"You think this will help you find your brother?"

"I hope so," Cammie said.

"God." DeeDee paused. In the background Cammie
could hear the Temptations, and dishes banging. "You
better give me more than belief, then. I guess undying
gratitude will become essential."

"Wonderful!" Cammie felt as if a weight had been
lifted off her. "Let me give you my address and fax."

She gave DeeDee the names of the missing, the address and fax of the hotel, and made DeeDee promise to
send whatever she had found within a few days. Dee-
Dee promised. They chatted for a moment about mutual
friends, and then Cammie hung up.

Good first day of progress. But she still wasn't done
yet. She had to go back to the Sadlers to talk to the fa-

ther, Gary. And she wanted to start setting up appointments for the next day.

She got up, smoothed the bed, and took the addresses Mrs. Sadler had given her out of the briefcase. Then, picking up the phone, she dialed the girlfriend's number.

"Hello?" she said when a woman answered. "I'm trying to reach Candyce Holloway."

"Who is this?" The woman's voice shook. Cammie's shoulders immediately tightened.

"My name is Cammie Timms. I'm with the Westrina Center in Wisconsin. Mrs. Sadler gave me Miss Holloway's name. I need to speak to her about Ben Sadler."

"Ms. Timms." The woman took a deep breath. "Candyce went to meet him last night. I'm very frightened. She never came back."

Chapter Nineteen

Vangelina wrapped the thick white towel around her neck. Sweat trickled down her back. She adjusted her spandex tights and pulled off her cotton T-shirt, wiping her face with it. The Lycra bodysuit stuck to her breasts. She was breathing heavily.

The workout felt good. It amazed her that only a few of Mikos's friends took advantage of his weight room. But some vampires felt that if they exerted themselves, they would harm themselves. Foolish thought. It left them at a disadvantage when faced with strong prey.

She wiped down the handles on the Soloflex, and ran a towel over the bench. Then she moved the free weights back to the rack on the side of the room near the exercise bike. The air here still smelled of fresh plaster, like a new car, and sometimes she wondered if Mikos himself ever came down here.

He had had a fear of basements since those last years in Germany. His delicate constitution was not suited to bombing raids. *A bit of shrapnel through the heart, an accidental decapitation—for the first time, Van, we can die easily.*

That was why he was supporting this Ben. On the mistaken belief that vampire leaders in this country would never make errors that would lead to all-out destruction. Van glanced around the room. She was comfortable here. Everything she wanted was within reach. Even meals were easy. But she might have to move on if Mikos insisted on being noticed.

Above her, the security system buzzed, then the elevator whirred and banged. The house was waking. Soon the regulars would arrive for the nightly debauch.

Van never participated in the parties. She picked a human host (she hated the word cow) and took it to her room for a quick and tender dinner. She had too much living to do to concentrate solely on eating, sleeping, and sex. In that way, she did not belong with this group. And that attitude probably explained why Mikos had opposed her training of Ben.

She shivered. The heat she had generated during her exercise was gone now, leaving only her damp skin in the too cold room. She opened the metal door and let herself into the poorly lit hallway. The storage unit near the elevator was full of restaurant supplies. Once she had been trapped here for hours because some idiot had left a case of minced garlic at the front of the unit. She had approached it warily ever since.

When she pressed the only elevator call button, the car clanged into life from Mikos's floor. She wrapped the towel around her shoulders for added warmth and waited.

Mikos had been cool to her in the last few days, since they had had that fight in front of Ben. Hereditaries were trouble. They grew too strong too fast, and thought they knew too much. Very quickly, they would take over a nest and run it into the ground with their lack of knowledge. Or their naive mistakes.

The double elevator doors slid open. When Van stepped inside, she frowned. Someone new had been in the elevator. Not vampire, but tamed human. She recognized the scent of most of the regular hosts, and this was not one of them. Whoever had brought the new one in had best know what it was doing.

It was probably Ben, who didn't understand the rules for bringing home a new host. The host had to be addicted for over a month. If not, the drug might wear off, and the host could bring other humans—sentient humans—into the nest during the daytime. That could mean death for all.

The elevator wasn't moving fast enough for Van. She paced the wide interior. When it finally stopped, she bounded out and let herself into the apartment.

The moment the door opened, she heard the shouting.

"—no right to bring someone here. It is my home. I have say!"

"I will do whatever I please."

The living room was empty. It looked barren and slightly dumpy without the dozens of bodies that she usually saw in it. The couches sagged and had blood-stains on the fabric. The mats were rolled and stored in a corner. Cigarette burns marred the varnish on the tabletops and the stereo was covered with fingerprints.

"We have procedures for this. It takes time to adopt a cow."

"I didn't have time."

Mikos and Ben, just as she suspected. The voices came from the end of the hall. Not the library, where Mikos usually held his private conversations, but the kitchen. Ben must have surprised him. That, and the silence in the entire apartment. The rest of the nest was probably still asleep.

Fortunately for Mikos, vampires slept like the dead.

She did not smile at her own quiet joke. Instead, she crossed out of the living room into the expensively decorated hallway. Mikos kept his nestlings happy and well fed by throwing parties in the front rooms, but few of the casual participants ever got to see this part of the apartment. No need to have Seattle's entire population know the kind of money Mikos had gathered over the years. Hers was even more hidden. Mikos liked fine things. Van owned nothing except her clothes, parcels of land all over the world—and the wealth she had stored under a hundred names in a hundred banks.

"I do not want her here," Mikos said. "It's too dangerous."

"She will not leave unless I do," Ben said.

The kitchen door was open. Van slipped inside. Mikos and Ben faced each other across the table. A woman stood behind Ben, her face blank. She had blonde hair and high cheekbones—a white American beauty. Her clothes looked as if she had slept in them, but they still accented her long, slender figure. Her arms were crossed in front of her chest and her left hand teased her right breast. He had done a good job luring her. The question was whether or not she would remain lured.

Mikos was breathing heavily. He was considering Ben's statement. Ben did not understand the danger he posed with this woman. Then, how could he? No one had explained it to him.

Van closed the kitchen doors behind her, making her presence known. The men turned, both their faces flushed with anger. The woman didn't move. Only her thumb, circling her nipple, showed that she had any awareness at all.

"The entire nest can hear you," Van said.

Mikos shrugged. Ben turned away. Van pushed past him and walked to the woman. She was very young, her face unlined, eyes empty. An ugly bruise, only partially hidden by the turtleneck, decorated the left side of her neck. Ben had been careless. He had nearly drained her. Her hair still had shine, though, and her clothing was expensive.

"Old girlfriend?" Van asked.

Ben started.

"That's worse!" Mikos pushed at the table, but the glass top didn't move. "You still have human attachments to her."

"It's not what you think," Ben said.

Van pushed at the woman's arm. It was cool. Too much blood loss. The woman finally turned her head. She opened her mouth slightly, and Van could feel the force of her longing.

"She should not be here," Van said. "She is too new. And she is the wrong kind. She looks like she had some sort of intelligence. She could have served instead."

"She's pregnant." Ben yanked the woman beside him, as if he were afraid that Van would seduce her.

Mikos tilted his head. "Yours?"

"I wouldn't bring her here if it weren't."

Van ran her hand over the woman's stomach. It was slightly mounded, but firm. The woman moaned at the touch. Van felt a faint stirring. It had been a long time since she took an innocent. "How do you know the child is yours?"

"She told me."

Van smiled. "Naive boy. She was yours when you disappeared. She probably just wanted you back."

"Her body's different. She's pregnant." He had an eagerness that she didn't like. Mikos had explained the importance of children, then. She sighed. Ben responded too well to Mikos's power madness.

Mikos was staring at Van with an intensity she hadn't seen in years. She turned away, keeping her hand on the woman's firm belly.

"Yes," Van said. "The girl is pregnant. But there is no guarantee that it is yours."

Ben's posture grew more rigid. He pulled the woman so close that she ran her hand along his ribs until he caught it with one of his own. "But there is. She's the reason I left home. I nearly killed her that night and showed up here days later. When I first saw her in the bar two days ago, she didn't want to get near me. The memory was not pleasant, and it was not something she wanted to repeat."

Van closed her eyes. Perfect candidate for a drug reaction. The woman would not hold on long. At some point her loathing would break through. "You almost drained her in the last twenty-four hours."

"I won't do it again." Ben clasped his hands together. His eyes were too bright. He obviously wanted this. "I've never had to be restrained before. I will be now."

"Perhaps," Van said. "But that may not help. She may need to be drained to remain in her stupor. You do not know all the rules for hosts. Some never take to the experience. Some fight. She has the earmarks of a fighter, or she would not have been repulsed by you in the bar."

Mikos approached the woman and took her away from Ben. He examined her eyes, then squeezed both of her breasts before taking off her shirt.

"Hey," Ben said. "She's mine."

Mikos ignored him. He examined her bite marks, the expanded veins on her breast, and the now-obvious roundness to her stomach.

"Hey!" Ben said, reaching for Mikos. "Stop that."

Van grabbed Ben's wrist. "You forget," she said. "We share."

"She's pregnant," Ben said. Jealousy. It would harm the nest. The boy had no idea what he was playing with.

"Yes. The sperm is lodged. Mikos will not change that." Van could not keep the contempt from her voice.

Mikos touched the woman's breasts, then leaned over and licked the wounds on her neck without breaking the skin. The woman moaned and arched toward him.

"She doesn't act like someone who'll break out," Ben said.

"Shut up," Mikos said. He hefted a breast as if it were a melon and weighed it in his hand. "She's breeding, and it's a hereditary, child of a hereditary. Such power we could have, Van."

His movements were titillating. A pregnant woman's blood had a potency that no other being had. Van swallowed the saliva building in her mouth. "She cannot stay here," Van said. "It is too dangerous."

"She'll need to be guarded by everyone. We need to hang on to this child," Ben said.

"Aren't you strong enough to hold her?" Mikos asked. He stopped touching the woman. She grabbed his hand and tried to put it back on her body, but he shook away. "We will find you both a place."

"No," Ben said. "I want her here."

Van smiled. The young vampire wasn't as in control as he thought he was. He was trembling. "Are you afraid that you will drain her, virgin?"

"I'm not a virgin," Ben said.

"Anyone who cannot control himself is a virgin," Van said.

"We will find you a place," Mikos repeated. "She is too new to stay here and too precious to lose. Someone could drain her by accident, and then where would we be? By tomorrow night you will have a home of your own."

Mikos circled around the table. Ben started to call after him, but Van tightened her grip on his arm.

"He has made a decision, and it is best for the rest of us. Do not fight him," Van said, "or I will make sure that you get tossed out of here with nowhere to go at all. We do not need you. We now have a child we can raise to our own specifications."

Ben shook himself free. Mikos had left the room. "The child is mine," Ben said. "Not ours, not the nest's. Mine." He grabbed Van's face. His fingers had a strength she didn't expect. Still, she didn't move. The bruises would disappear with her first feeding. "I will not forget this, Van. Someday, you will understand what an awful mistake you made."

He pushed as he let go, probably hoping to make Van stumble backwards. She held her ground.

"Come along, Candyce," he said. The woman followed, leaving her shirt on the floor where Mikos had tossed it. Her heavy breasts bobbed. Hereditary, child of an hereditary. They were powerful, out of control, and dangerous. Mikos might think one valuable, but Van didn't.

She could stop this nonsense tonight, if she planned carefully enough.

Chapter Twenty

Cammie got lost as she drove into the south hills after dark. The winding roads followed no logical pattern and the houses were hidden by shrubbery. The darkness made her inability to judge spatial relationships even more acute. She turned on the wrong street time and time again. When she finally found the Sadlers' road, she was nearly fifteen minutes late.

It had been a frustrating evening. Candyce's mother had no information, other than Candyce's word that she had reached Ben, and that they were going to meet. Candyce had been gone over twenty-four hours, and the police were not yet involved.

Cammie didn't like the coincidence. Had the couple seen something that night? Had Candyce refused to discuss what happened? Or was she telling the truth? Had Ben hurt her and then disappeared? Why would someone whose life seemed so good go through the changes Ben had?

Cammie had advised Mrs. Holloway to go to the police. Since Ben was missing, the police might take Candyce's case more seriously. Mrs. Holloway promised she would. Cammie agreed to meet her the next day.

She still had the meeting with Ben's adopted father to get through. She had to circle once for a parking

space—apparently this part of Eugene was very nine-to-
five. Parking places that had seemed plentiful in the
morning were nonexistent now. Finally, she parked on
the curbless hill half a block away.

She got out of the car and locked it. Her purse and
briefcase seemed heavy as she walked up the slight in-
cline. She had put her heels back on, but now she
wished she hadn't. They would slow her down if she
had to run. She didn't like walking in the dark—it made
her feel vulnerable and wide open. But the neighborhood was silent, except for the blaring television coming from the house near her car, and had the illusion of
safety.

Two cars were parked in the Sadlers' driveway,
sedans with different license plates that were, on in-
spection, both issued by the state of Oregon. The garage
doors were closed. The porch light was on and the front
door stood open. Only the screen door prevented unwanted visitors from just walking in.

Voices floated across the lawn as Cammie approached. She knocked on the screen door. Its banging
rattle stopped the conversation. Then she saw Mrs.
Sadler. Her hair was brushed back and she had changed
into dress slacks and a white blouse.

"Sorry I'm late," Cammie said through the door. "I got
lost."

Mrs. Sadler smiled. "It happens a lot around here." She
pulled open the screen door. "We're on the back porch."

Even though the weather was warmer here than it
was in the Midwest, it was still too cool, in Cammie's
opinion, to sit outside. She followed Mrs. Sadler down
the wide hallway decorated with pictures of Ben at various ages. Cammie longed for the chance to gaze at
them. The old ones were the Ben she remembered, all
pudgy cheeks and round eyes. The new ones only had
glimpses of the little boy, mostly in the wide-eyed look
that had faded by the time he posed for his high school
graduation photo.

The hallway opened into a sitting/dining/kitchen area. The kitchen was spacious and modern, with a stove-top island and gleaming copper pots hanging above it. Mrs. Sadler led her through it to a room surrounded on three sides by floor-to-ceiling windows. The back porch.

The furniture here was wicker, with blue and green flowered cushions. Four middle-aged men wearing jeans and dress shirts sat around the wicker table. A woman in a flowered caftan was sitting on the wooden slatted swing couch, and another woman wearing shorts and a tie-dyed shirt sat in an overstuffed lounge. The third woman, whose jeans and striped dress shirt matched one of the men's outfits, stood with her back to Cammie, staring out the window.

Cammie's entire body stiffened. She had come to interview Mr. Sadler, not greet a crowd.

Mrs. Sadler noticed the change in the tension in Cammie. "I'm sorry, dear," Mrs. Sadler said. "A few of the others wanted to speak with you."

The other couples were introduced as the Ellises, the Steins, and the Caldicotts. Katie Ellis was the woman standing in the window. She turned for the introduction. Her hair, once black, was now silver, although her face appeared young. She had a figure that Cammie associated with a mother—curved and rounded, not athletic and anxious like Mrs. Sadler's.

Cammie waited until the greetings were done. She made polite responses and then turned to the only unidentified male in the room. "Mr. Sadler?"

To her surprise, he stood. He was long and lean with a sun-weathered face and faded blue eyes. "Gary," he said. His voice had a twang that sounded half Texan and half Hollywood's idea of the Ozarks.

"May I speak with you alone?"

"Certainly." He picked up a stained and chipped mug that read WORLD'S GREATEST DAD, and followed her into the living room.

He had to flick on a light switch from the hallway. In the light of two soft incandescents, the room lost its formal look. It actually felt like a place to grab a book, lie back, and read until dawn.

Cammie took the spot she had had in the morning, across from the love seat. Gary sat in the easy chair in front of the cold fireplace.

"Did your wife describe our conversation this morning?" Cammie asked.

"Yes," he said. His accent bothered her. She wished she could place it. "She said you took the letters."

The couple seemed very concerned with solving the group's problems. Cammie found that odd as well. "What do you think happened to Ben?"

Gary pulled a pipe from his pocket—surprising Cammie because the house did not smell of tobacco—and set it in his mouth. "I think he got himself in trouble." Gary's voice was low, as if he didn't want his wife to hear. He shook his head. "I just don't understand why he didn't come to me."

"What kind of trouble?" Cammie asked.

Gary pulled the pipe from his mouth. He made no motion to light it. "I don't know. I've always been a little worried about him." He glanced down the hall, then looked back at Cammie, apparently satisfied that no one was there. "He was always a bit off, you know? His mother never really knew. I made sure I always handled it."

Cammie swallowed. "What kind of things?"

"Fights in school. All boys do that, but not usually quite so violently. And he had girlfriend troubles. He played a little rough. More than once he and I talked about the way he should treat women." Gary half smiled, even though he did not appear to be amused. "It was sex. Something about sex triggered that response. Until then, he was the model of politeness. He and I had so many talks. He was as uncomfortable with it as I was."

Cammie nodded. She didn't want to interrupt the flow.

Gary ran a hand across his face. "I blamed it on the way he grew up. The adoption counselors told me what he went through, and they warned me that he might have difficulties."

Cammie's entire body had turned cold. "What had he gone through?"

"His father was a monster. They think he murdered the wife, beat the kids regularly—Ben was a mass of scars and bruises when we got him. I guess it got real bad one night, and the oldest girl killed the father rather messily in front of Ben. He used to have horrible nightmares. I would go in and turn on the light, and he would scream at me to turn it off, that it might wake Daddy, and so I got to the point where when he screamed, I would just go in and hold him." He pulled a pouch of tobacco out of his other pocket, filled the pipe, and tapped it on the table. "I never told Donna any of this. She didn't need to know."

Cammie was motionless. The shock of hearing her own past from someone else's lips made her feel weak. "What else didn't you tell your wife?"

Gary put the pipe back in his mouth. He gazed out the window. Cammie followed his look. All she could see was their reflections in the glass. "When he was a little boy," Gary said, "he would get cut a lot and lick the blood away. It worried me. His father was a vampire— that's how the Westrina Center got involved in the first place—and I was so afraid Ben would go down that road."

—bloody finger in the baby's mouth. "He's mine now."

Cammie closed her eyes against the memory. When she felt calm, she opened them again. "Did he?"

Gary shook his head. "By the time he got into junior high, he seemed okay. Good grades, lots of friends. Even his raging tempers had faded. He had trouble with the girls for a while, but that faded in high school. College changed him, but it changes every kid. That extra measure of responsibility makes it tough for them. Then this thing with Candyce." Gary's voice trailed off. He got up, and went to the window, his back to Cammie. "I keep seeing her battered face over and over in my mind, and I remember waking up in the middle of the night, going to Ben when he screamed, and he would flail and kick and hit, and I wonder if it was just something innocent, like they fell asleep together and he had a bad dream, and hurt her before he woke up." He leaned his head against the glass. "I even asked her, but she said nothing. Nothing at all."

He blocked his own reflection. Cammie saw hers, her face too pale, eyebrows creased into a frown. "She's missing, you know."

Gary whirled. The movement was so sudden that Cammie leaned back in the couch as if she were expecting a blow. He was too far away to hit her. "Candyce?"

Cammie nodded. "Her mother said she was going to meet Ben yesterday and she never came back."

"Going to meet Ben—?" he repeated the words as if he didn't believe them. "Donna! Donna!"

Mrs. Sadler came running into the room. She hadn't been that far away after all.

"You got Candyce's mother's phone number?" he asked. "Candyce is missing."

She shot Cammie a glance as if it were all her fault, then disappeared into the other room.

Gary approached her, his tread heavy on the thick carpet. "Why didn't you say anything? This could be important."

Cammie refused to shrink farther into the couch. "I thought you probably knew. Besides, Mrs. Holloway has already called the police."

"The police." He set his pipe on the table. "The police aren't doing anything."

"I've dialed!" Mrs. Sadler yelled from the other room. "Pick up."

He went to the phone on the small writing desk and picked up. "Lita? Gary Sadler. I understand your daughter heard from Ben. . . . Yes, she's right here. . . . No, we haven't heard anything. . . . Where did she go meet him? . . . You're sure it was him? . . . She called him? How? . . . Steve. I had forgotten about Steve. . . . No, you're right. When was she due back? . . . Well, maybe she and Ben just ran off together . . ." He held the phone away from his ear. Cammie could hear a shrill voice berating him. When it ceased, he put the phone back. "I know. But strange things happen. I mean, she called him . . . Oh." He put a hand over his face and sat down on the narrow desk chair. It bowed beneath his weight. "I had no idea. Why didn't you come to us?" He sighed. "Listen, we have some detectives we've hired. We can put them on this. We'll find them, whatever it takes." His entire body hunched over. Cammie gripped the side of the sofa. He was obviously getting more information than she had. "Look, Lita, I'm sorry all this happened. Let's hope there's a reasonable explanation. . . . Me too. I'll be in touch soon."

He hung up and didn't move. His wife's voice spoke lowly in the other room. She must have been listening on the extension. Cammie stood and walked over to the desk, leaning on the wall beside it. "All I learned was that she planned to meet Ben, and now she's missing. But Mrs. Holloway told you more, didn't she?"

For a moment, Gary didn't move. When he did, his body was shaking. "She's pregnant," he said, his face ashen. "Candy's pregnant."

Cammie closed her eyes, glad for the wall's support. The news made her feel hollow, light-headed, and she didn't know why. She took a deep breath to banish the light feeling. Then she opened her eyes. Gary was staring at the backs of his hands as if he had never seen them before.

"She also told you how Candyce found Ben."

He nodded. "Ben had a friend who moved to Portland

during their last year of high school. He was the only one we never thought of, the only one we never mentioned to the detectives. Steve Henderson. I guess he knew where Ben was all along."

"He's still in Portland?"

"I guess so." Gary stood up. "I've got to call the detectives. Please, could you give me a minute?"

Cammie nodded. She needed a moment to think herself. If she went back to the hotel now, she might be able to track Henderson. She picked up her briefcase just as Mrs. Sadler walked into the room.

"You're not leaving yet, are you?" she asked. "We have a lot to discuss."

No one else had come down the hall. Gary picked up the phone and shot an exasperated glance at his wife. Cammie felt the need to move as much as he did. She wanted to find Henderson before the detectives.

"I've already contacted the Westrina Center about the letters," she said. "I hope to hear in a day or so. Then I'll meet with your friends."

She hadn't planned to talk with them at all, but it might not hurt. Something was going on there too, and she didn't like it.

"Ms. Timms—" Mrs. Sadler started.

"Let her go," Gary said as he dialed. "She wants to find Ben as much as we do. Let her do her job."

Even though his words were kind, Cammie felt that his desire to be rid of her was something more. She was an unknown quantity, someone who appeared from an organization that had given them no help in the past. He wanted to work with the detectives, whom he trusted, in private.

Mrs. Sadler glanced at her husband. She bit her lower lip, as if she didn't know what to do. Cammie could feel her reluctance. Mrs. Sadler didn't want to let Cammie go—probably afraid she would never see her again.

"I will call you as soon as I hear," Cammie said. "Thanks for your help."

Gary nodded and waved absently. Apparently someone had answered on the other end of the line. Mrs. Sadler stood in the center of the room, her hands clasped tightly before her chest.

Cammie didn't wait for a response. She let herself out the front door, pulled off her shoes, and ran down the walk. Gravel bit into her feet, but she didn't care. The quicker she moved, the quicker she would get information.

The drive out of the neighborhood was easier than the drive in. It took only a few minutes to make it to Willamette Street, and then she knew where she was. The rows of restaurant chains mingled with family-owned businesses. The traffic was heavy here—for Eugene—but the area had a pretty, sparkling feel, almost as if she had stepped back in time, when the world was a safer place.

But it wasn't safer. Ben was missing, and when he was supposed to reappear, his girlfriend disappeared as well.

It took ten minutes to drive from the Sadlers' house to the hotel. The lack of sprawl here surprised her. In Madison, it would have taken half an hour to go from the far south side to the middle of town. She parked the car and hurried up to her room, ignoring the stare the bellhop gave her in the elevator because she was carrying her shoes.

She let herself into her room, tossed her shoes in a corner, and pulled off her shredded panty hose. The hose were black—she supposed the bottom of her feet were too. She sat on the bed, dialed information, and got a phone number for Steve Henderson. It was easier than she had expected.

The phone rang five times before a groggy male voice answered.

"I'm calling for Steve," Cammie said. Then she held her breath and hoped.

"Je-sus Christ." The voice sounded a bit wider awake.

"Steve's outta here. If you got any of the money he owes me, I'll talk to you. Otherwise try him at the Keg."

He hung up. After a moment, the line disconnected, and a dial tone hummed in her ear. The Keg. She called information again, got the bar's number, and dialed.

Someone picked up after two rings. Madonna pounded in the background, and laughter filtered into the phone. Cammie could almost smell the cigarette smoke. "Yeah?" The voice was male and abrasive. "Whattya want?"

Cammie swallowed. "Is this the Keg?"

"Guess so."

"I'm calling for one of your customers."

"We don't talk about who's here and who ain't. You could be an ex-wife or something."

"I'm not." Cammie balled up her free hand into a fist.

"How'm I supposed to know that?"

Talking to him wouldn't work. She would have to go herself. She glanced at the clock. Nine P.M. Portland was two hours away. "What time do you close?" she asked.

"Two."

"I'll be there," she said, but by then the line had already gone dead.

Chapter Twenty-one

The clock radio came on with a soprano screeching Wagner. Van winced. Her eyes felt gummed together. She hated Wagner. It made her think of the bad times. She reached up with one hand and slapped the radio off.

She stretched against the flannel sheets on her futon. One disadvantage to being a vampire was that she woke up cold. The blood running through her system had thinned. She would need food before she did anything else.

A thin ray of gray light eked through the shade. Her room was small, and she had never had the windows boarded like the others had. Some ancient hope let her believe that someday she would be able to tolerate light. She funded research in sunblocks with some of her excess money. With humans suddenly so afraid of the sun, vampires might find the protection they needed against the harmful rays.

Modern times. She still could not get used to all the conveniences. The world was changing too quickly for her. She tried to keep up, tried to act like a woman of her physical appearance should, but at times she wanted to let it all go. Mikos teased her because she had not completely lost her accent. She never told him that she had also kept her old world loves. The memen-

tos were merely stored where Mikos could not find
them.

She rubbed her eyes and sat up. She had kept something from each era, but some eras had appealed to her
more than most. And some she hated more than others.
Since the thirties, though, she felt as if the world was
getting ahead of her.

The thirties were heady years. Mikos had smuggled
them into Berlin in 1933, just as the economy started to
turn around. He made Nazi friends, and soon it became
clear that much of the upper crust were vampires. Hitler
himself was hereditary, but remained a virgin until 1943.
Being a virgin allowed him to be photographed and to
experience sunlight. He changed after the assassination
attempt, though. He had been more badly injured than
the media reported, and someone—probably Mikos—
had decided that Hitler needed to activate his own healing powers. One of the conspirators died first, and from
then on Hitler was crazed and uncontrollable. He hated
avoiding sunlight and worried that he would lose the
support of the people, not realizing that the support
was already waning. Eva hated the change too. She was
a fighter, and Van often wondered if Eva had put the
stake through Hitler's heart herself.

Van's hands were shaking. The memories were not
easy ones. The thirties were heady, but the forties were
hell. She had to hide her German accent as best she
could, protect her wealth, and run for her life. In '42, she
met a vampire more powerful than she could even
imagine. He raped her and nearly drained her, even
though her blood was of no use to him. He had been an
hereditary too, and he was doing his best to keep her in
line. Ever since then she had avoided hereditaries and
kept herself in superb physical condition so that she
could outmaneuver everyone, hereditary or not.

She pushed a strand of hair from her forehead. She
was wasting too much time thinking. She only had a few
hours before the nest woke up.

She rolled off the futon, pulled on her black spandex, and piled her hair into a knot on top of her head. Then she went into the kitchen and drank just enough to keep her levelheaded. She put the bottle back in the refrigerator, washed off her hands, and headed down the hall to Ben's room.

The boy had the same arrogance that she had seen in the hereditary who attacked her. He listened to no one and thought he knew it all. Ben would have to learn that he could not do as he pleased, that part of being in a nest was cooperation. It did not matter that he had the potential to be more powerful than all of them. What mattered was who he was now.

She would show him that he still had a lot to learn.

And she would make sure that an hereditary, child of an hereditary, would not come into the nest.

Over the years, she had learned how to move without making a sound. When she reached Ben's door, she grabbed the gold-plated knob and turned it so slowly her hand began to sweat. The small click as the tongue swung back echoed in the silent hallway. She pushed the door open and slid into the room.

Here the darkness was complete. The coppery scent of fresh blood filled the air. Her stomach rumbled. After a moment, her night vision began to work. Ben slept with his arms over his head. The girl huddled against him, as if she craved touch even in sleep.

Van pushed the door closed behind her. Another click, as loud as a rifle report, echoed in the small space. Ben did not move. Poor boy. He even slept like the dead. Strong vampires had to train themselves to snap awake at the slightest sound.

Van worked her way around the bed. She ran a hand along the girl's arm. Still warm. The girl arched and moaned. Her blood whispered in her veins, and the scent of it covered her. Van licked her lips. The girl was still fresh, and with the baby, she would be delightful. But not yet. Van let her hand drop. She made her way to the closet and slid between the half-open doors. Then she huddled up in the back, on a pile of dirty shirts, to wait.

The sound of a creaking bed woke Van from a doze. She checked her watch: she had been hiding for nearly two hours. She leaned against the cool wall, hoping that Ben would not turn on a light.

The rustle of satin sheets, and then the girl's voice, inaudible at first. Ben mumbled a reply, and the girl said, "Please?" quite clearly. Van knew what the girl was begging for. They all did, at this stage.

"Go back to sleep," Ben said, disgust in his voice.

Van frowned. Not good. If he were going to keep this girl lured for nine months, he had to treat her well. She was not a traditional host. She would fight, if not for herself, then for the child. Ben had not yet reached that stage where the loneliness overwhelmed him. His actions toward his primary host would change then.

Carpet-muffled footsteps edged closer to her. Van held her breath. The closet door swung open and Ben stood in front of her in all his naked glory. He had broad shoulders and narrow hips. He was fortunate to turn when he was young, before the flabbiness of middle age showed in his naked form. Had he been human she would have been interested. But he wasn't, and his body was only a curiosity.

He took a silk shirt off a hanger, then pulled down a pair of newly laundered blue jeans. He grabbed socks and underwear from a pile beside her, his hand nearly brushing her thigh. Van did not move, did not even flinch. He closed the door tight, barring most of the noise from Van.

"Please, Ben," the girl said.

"Later," he said. "I want you to sleep now."

Command tones. She was still new enough that they would work. That, plus the blood loss and the surging hormones. Everything was working in Van's favor.

The slamming of the door shook the entire room. Van climbed out of her hiding place and bent over, peering under the crack in the closet door. Only one figure on the bed. The door was closed. The rest of the room empty.

Van pushed the closet door open. The girl sat up. "Who're you?"

Van smiled, even though she doubted if the girl could see her face. "My, you are pretty, child," Van said. She climbed into Ben's side of the bed. The sheets were still warm from his presence. The girl hadn't moved. She was wary. Van touched the girl's right breast. The shock of sexual desire was so strong it felt like a separate presence in the room.

The girl arched, but moved no closer. "I don't—I never—"

"Liked women?" Van licked the nipple. It was salty with sweat. "Have you ever tried?"

The girl moaned her response. Van kneaded the other breast, then nipped her way up to the neck. So easy. Easier than she had thought. The girl thrust her pelvis toward Van. "Please," the girl said.

So she liked a true orgasm. Well, Van would give her one. Her last. Van kept her thumb on the girl's clitoris, then shoved three fingers inside, playing until she found the spot that made the girl tremble with desire. Then Van bit the jugular with all of her strength.

Orgasm after orgasm shuddered through the girl. Her blood pulsed into Van's mouth. Fresh, untainted except for a faint hint of decay that had probably started with Ben. Van's hunger took over and she sucked until she could no more. The girl yelled her pleasure, and then the sound trailed off as the strength left her.

The orgasms stopped, but Van didn't. She kept drinking. She hadn't had a pregnant woman in decades. The brightness of the blood teased her, fulfilled her. She had kept herself deliberately hungry and she didn't want to stop.

The door slammed open, banging against the wall as the light clicked on. "Jesus, Van!" Mikos said.

"What the hell is she doing?" Ben asked.

Van didn't look at them. She sucked harder, working to finish. The girl's body was cold and limp beneath hers. She kept her fingers in place, though. A bit of pleasure was barely enough payment for a meal like this.

Hands grabbed her shoulders and yanked her backwards so hard that she would have tumbled off the bed if she hadn't been holding the girl's pelvis. Van caught herself and stood. Ben was slapping the girl, trying to get her attention. Her eyes were open and glazed. Blood trickled from the gaping hole in her neck.

"What were you doing?" Mikos asked.

Van shrugged, trying to keep her voice calm. "I had not eaten in twenty-four hours. She smelled fresh."

Ben turned, hands clenched. "She was mine."

Van wiped her mouth with her thumb and forefinger. They smelled musky. "She was in the nest."

"You knew what she was," Mikos said.

Van licked her lips. "Sometimes," she said, "even the strongest of us lose control." She started for the door. Ben flew past Mikos and tackled her, wrapping his arms around her waist and shoving her to the ground. The flat carpet scraped her back. She kneed him in the stomach, then kicked him in the groin. As he cried in pain, she pushed him off her.

"She had no place here," Van said. "She was unprepared, a fighter, and a danger to us all. If you had not drained her, she would not have let me touch her. She even tried to protest in her drugged way. She would have broken out, *virgin*, and we all could have died. Think next time before you bring a new host into the nest."

Ben was hunched in a fetal position, clutching himself. She kicked him in the side and used all her force to push his body out of her way.

"You may be hereditary, virgin," she said. "But I

understand survival. I will not let you threaten any of us."

"He didn't know—" Mikos began.

"He does now," Van said, and left the room.

Chapter
Twenty-two

The drive to Portland was a blur of fields and city lights. Interstate 5 had enough traffic so that Cammie didn't feel alone, but the cars were so widely spaced she felt as if she were driving in the middle of the night. When she drove I-90 to Chicago, the traffic was always bumper to bumper, even at 65 miles per hour.

She fiddled with radio stations, leaving the scan function on the car stereo until she found a song she liked. Not much to do except think, and thinking was making her nervous.

First Ben disappears, then Candyce, and a number of children sent here by the Westrina Center. Something was happening, and she didn't like any of her options. Either the children had gathered on their own, or someone was systematically kidnapping them, or—

(he's mine now)

—they found an alternate way to live. All of them.

She clutched the steering wheel so tightly that her hands hurt. She had the windows down and the cool night air played with her hair. Ben would never have become like their dad. Ben was a straight-A student, with dreams and a future. He wouldn't throw all of that away. Vampires were deadbeats who turned to bloodsucking because they needed some joy in their empty lives.

Ben's life was full. She had seen to that. She had saved him that morning so long ago.

Outside Salem, the traffic became thicker. By the time she reached Portland, the bumper-to-bumper traffic she had been missing appeared suddenly on the sharp slanting curves that marked the Interstate. She followed the signs that led her to downtown.

When she had gotten gas outside Eugene, she had asked the gas station attendant if he knew of the Keg in Portland. From his startled glance, he clearly had, and hadn't expected someone to ask about it.

"Not somewhere you want to go, miss," he had said with a politeness she was beginning to associate with the Pacific Northwest. "It's not a safe place."

She shrugged and smiled. "I'm looking for someone. His roommate assures me he's there."

"Better off going to his house and waiting for him to come home," the attendant said. "Seriously."

"Tell you what," she said. "I'll drive by and if it looks more dangerous than any bar I've ever been in, I won't stop, okay?"

He frowned, but gave her directions. Fortunately he didn't know her. She had been in some of the scariest bars in Wisconsin.

Burnside led her across the Columbia River and into a seedier side of town. She took the side street that the attendant had told her of, and immediately recognized the neighborhood. Places like this existed all over the Midwest.

She hadn't expected to find places like that here. Sarge had been wrong. A shiver ran down Cammie's spine.

The streetlights reflected empty pavement, but if Cammie squinted, she could see cardboard boxes propped against buildings, boxes that shifted with their occupants. Two storefronts were boarded up, and another sold sex toys. Its flickering neon sign made it clear that the store had done business for years.

The bar had no name across its front, but the words The Keg were still visible in the faded paint. Cammie stopped the car beneath a streetlight, letting the little yellow pool of light give her some comfort. She watched the bar's door for half an hour. No one entered or left.

Not a good sign. But this was the closest she had been to Ben since she started the trip. She wouldn't leave the area without a good reason.

She smoothed her hair with one hand, grabbed her purse, and let herself out the door. She locked the car, and engaged the alarm—not that it would stop anyone from breaking in, but it would at least warn her of a problem. She longed to take off her heels, but the pavement was so filthy, she didn't want to touch it with her nyloned feet.

The night had grown chill. No one had warned her that the temperatures in this part of the country could vary forty degrees between day and night. She would have to bring a coat with her from now on.

Boxes rustled as her heels clicked on the pavement. The hair on the back of her neck prickled. She was being watched.

She took the two steps down to the oak door and was about to pull it open when the smell hit her. Blood, as thick as beer outside most bars. Blood mixed with fear.

She froze. The roommate wouldn't tell her about this place on a lark. Not if he knew what kind of place it was. He wouldn't want it raided, if he were part of it, and he wouldn't lead an innocent woman to her death if he weren't. Perhaps the roommate had no idea what kind of place this was.

Or perhaps he knew and didn't care.

Living with someone who was turning was hell. That the roommate still had bitterness in his voice meant he had survived it, but not happily.

Cammie swallowed. Perhaps she smelled the blood

because she expected to. Cow-bars like this shouldn't exist in the Northwest, not if vampires were scarce. She would check—quickly.

She pushed open the door and stood for a moment in the doorway, letting her eyes adjust to the red-tinged darkness. The smell was stronger here, so thick that she nearly choked on it. It coated her nostrils and her mouth, making her swallow to prevent herself from losing the contents of her stomach.

The people who sat closest to the door did not look at each other. No one tried to talk over the pounding music. They stared at the next room, their eyes glassy, their expressions longing. In the next room, she could get glimpses of red-tinged bodies, moving in an obscene parody of the sex act. The bartender turned to her and she stepped back, letting the door close in front of her.

She couldn't go in. To go in there unprotected would be suicide.

She hurried up the stairs, forcing herself to walk. She didn't want to call any more attention to herself by running. By hitting the button on her key ring, she shut off the car alarm. The car chirruped at her, and the sound was like the voice of a friend calling out into the darkness. She unlocked the door, got in, and locked the car again, starting it while she watched the bar in the rearview mirror.

The oak door opened, and the bartender came out. He was a stout man with pasty skin, but not too pasty. He wasn't one of them himself. He was a collaborator, a human who benefited from that kind of debauchery. She yanked the wheel a hard left and peeled down the street, driving in darkness so that he couldn't read her license plates.

She drove as fast as she could, feeling as if the hounds of hell were on her heels. But no car followed her. It was as if no one had seen her, no one had noticed. The bartender probably thought she wandered into the wrong bar by mistake.

Or maybe he remembered her earlier phone call and figured she had all the information she needed.

When she reached the downtown, with its expensive high-rise hotels and well-lit streets, she stopped for a moment and rested her head on the steering wheel.

A nest.

A functioning nest. A nest where someone named Steve spent most of his time. Steve, an old friend of Ben's. Steve, who had put Candyce in touch with Ben. Had Candyce gone in there alone? No wonder she was missing. No unprotected human would escape untainted.

Maybe Ben had gone there looking for Steve too. Maybe Steve was luring his friends into that world, bringing in easy prey for the vampires within.

Perhaps Ben had been one of those blank faces she had seen. Perhaps she had stared at her own brother and not even known it. She sat up and wiped her eyes with her left hand.

Perhaps he had been in there with Steve, waiting for his old girlfriend. Perhaps—

(he's mine now)

—he had turned too.

Oh, God. Not Ben. Not her baby brother.

She made herself take a deep breath. This was now too big for her to do on her own. She would need some help, and she would have to do some digging to find it.

Problem was, she lacked the time. If Ben were trapped in there—if Ben and Candyce were trapped in there—or even Steve, not a vampire but a host, luring his friends for his master, were trapped in there—they wouldn't last long. A place like that had a steady turnover of hosts. They died or stumbled out the back door, broken, frightened and unable to function in society again.

Cammie didn't have the strength to be a one-woman savior. Even if she did, she couldn't go after a nest alone.

The bartender would protect it in the daytime, and she wouldn't be able to kill all the vampires by nightfall.

Best to get out of Portland. She would return to Eugene, call the Center, find help, and go from there.

It was the only thing she could do.

Chapter
Twenty-three

"She had absolutely no right!" Ben slammed the library door behind him. He was shaking. It was one thing to see the body of someone he didn't know. But he had grown up with Candyce. He had loved her once. In her too-white, bruised face, he had seen the girl he had laughed with, the girl he had held.

Mikos and Van walked ahead of him, their bare feet leaving small bloody prints on the polished wood floor. They had left Candyce's body in his bed. He wanted it properly buried. They hadn't even given him time to cover her face.

No one answered him. They hadn't spoken to him since Mikos commanded them all to meet in the library. They kept walking until they reached the sitting area in front of the fireplace. No fire burned in the grate, and the room was cold. The library smelled of old books and long-dead fires.

Ben clenched his fists. He wanted to grab Van and slam her into the wall. But he remembered the ease with which she had controlled him earlier.

Mikos leaned against the marble mantel. "She had a right, Ben."

Van sank into the easy chair and stuck her feet out in front of her. Her eyes glittered. Her skin was flushed with the kill. "You brought her into the nest. We share here."

"She was pregnant."

Van shrugged. "I hate hereditaries." She kept her gaze level on his. He could feel the anger waving off her. She had done it on purpose. She hadn't picked Candyce at random.

"You had no right!" Ben stopped beside the chair. He wasn't sure he could control himself. Candyce had only been twenty-four. She had an entire life ahead of her. But he couldn't let them know he had cared for a cow. He had to appeal to Mikos. "We needed that child. It may be my last."

Mikos tugged at his black sweatshirt. His face seemed to have more lines in it than it ever had before. "It might," he said, "but you jeopardized her by bringing her here without understanding the rules."

Ben took a step toward the chair. His muscles were taunt. "I did not believe any of you would kill her. I thought we all had the same goals."

Van pushed herself out of the chair. Her movements were lithe and quick, like a cat's. "Then you think wrong, *virgin*. We form a nest for safety, but our definition of safety varies. That's why we have rules. You broke the rules. I merely restored order."

"You created chaos—"

Mikos held up his hand. Ben and Van stopped yelling. "You both hurt order," Mikos said. "Ben should not have brought that child here, and you, Van, should have talked with me before taking matters into your own hands."

"I did talk to you." Van rocked back and forth on her feet like a fighter maintaining her stance. Although she watched Mikos, she seemed to be keeping an eye on Ben as well. "When Ben first brought her here. I told you the girl was a danger. I told you that she might break free, but you said it was worth the risk. We needed the hereditary. I merely showed you that we didn't need the hereditary that much."

Ben moved within inches of her. A vein pulsed in her throat. He longed to rip it open, even though her blood would taste spoiled. He would let it run to the ground like so much poison. "You had no right to kill her."

"I had the same right as I always do with hosts in this nest. I had the right to try her. You drained her so badly that a normal feeding killed her." Van lifted her chin as she spoke. A single drop of blood had dried on her lower lip.

"It wasn't an accident, Van," Mikos said. He walked over to them, and grabbed both of their arms. His grip on Ben's upper arm pinched the skin. "Don't make it sound like one."

Ben wrenched himself free and walked over to the fireplace. He pulled the metal curtains back and grabbed wood from the pile, letting the methodical chore of building a fire calm him. Wood, kindling, paper. Wood, kindling, paper. Then he lit a match against the marble, letting the faint scent of sulfur soothe him, and touched the flame to the protruding pieces of paper. The paper caught. He closed the curtains and stood, the light heat of the paper fire warming his legs.

"I need to know what we are going to do with her," he said, "and what I can do to prevent this from happening again." Although it would never happen in quite the same way again. He had cared for Candyce for years. Odd how he had forgotten that in the last few days, and how the caring had returned since he saw her cold, still body. Old dreams. He had thought that with the child, he might be able to make a home with Candyce. But the thought had never been on the surface of his brain. He had just known that she would be beside him, raising the child, while he lived his new life.

"Know the rules." Van crossed her arms in front of her chest. The muscles rippled in her too-thin skin.

"I'm trying to learn," he snapped. He would kill her. Somehow. He would get even with her for spoiling his chance at raising a powerful child.

For Candyce.

"Nothing will happen to Van," Mikos said. He still had his arm around Van's shoulder. He would take her side against Ben. In everything. "She was within her rights."

"I wasn't referring to Van." The heat had grown more intense. Ben moved away from the fireplace. "I meant Candyce."

Van smiled mockingly and brought a hand up to her breast, mimicking Candyce's movements. Ben slapped it away.

"She's being taken care of," Mikos said.

"She's got a family. People will be looking for her."

Mikos's mouth formed a straight line. "We know what to do, Ben. We've been doing this for lifetimes."

The implication was that he didn't know. "Look," he said. "My hometown's probably in an uproar with me missing. With Candyce gone too, someone will be looking. I just wanted to warn you—"

"You should have thought of all of that before bringing her here." Van spat on the floor near Ben's feet. "You threaten us all, *virgin.*"

"Are we done talking to Van?" Ben asked Mikos. Ben couldn't stand having her in the room any longer. The bitch had ruined his life. With one simple movement. With one uncontrollable action.

"No," Mikos said, looking at Van. He drew her closer and spoke softly, like a lover. "But hear this, Van. I will not tolerate such behavior in my nest again. Is that clear?"

Vangelina glanced at him sideways through her slightly slanted eyes. The look emphasized her catlike appearance even more. "You prefer that virgin to me, Mikos?"

"We need him. He's hereditary."

"I have known you since you turned. You would throw that away?"

"We have never been on opposite sides before, Van," Mikos said.

Ben didn't move, trying not to reveal his pleasure at

Mikos's show of support. He had expected Mikos to continue backing Van.

"Then you are a fool, Mikos." Van eased out of his embrace. She shook her shoulders as if to shake the feeling of him off her skin. "You need old friends whom you can trust, not children with no knowledge of the rules."

"We have always disagreed about hereditaries, Vangelina."

"Yes, we have," she said, "but the past has always supported my argument. What has an hereditary gotten you except pain and near death?"

"They have gotten me here, to now," Mikos said. "To a future that I can control."

"Can you?" Van asked. She glanced at Ben. Ben met her gaze. She was smart and she was powerful, but he would be smarter. Someday.

"You think you can control him now," Van said. "But wait until he makes more mistakes. Wait until he exposes the entire nest."

She turned and walked along the polished floor. Her footsteps were quiet and by the time she reached the doorway, the crackling of the fire drowned out any noise she made. She let herself out and Ben felt himself relax.

"The rules." Mikos's voice boomed in the stillness. "You shall not jeopardize the nest. It is the supreme rule and central to the survival of any nest."

Ben gripped the side of the armchair. Its fabric was soft under his fingers. The fire gave off the smell of woodsmoke and warmed the room.

"You shall be forgiven this time," Mikos said, "but another infraction and you shall be thrown out without support. Is that clear?"

"Clear," Ben said. He made sure he sounded calm.

Mikos paced around the armchair as he spoke. "Humans jeopardize the nest. The only humans allowed up here are experienced cows. Cows must be in use over a month before we are sure of their strength. There are bars for cow-training, or, if you prefer privacy, you may rent an apartment, as long as you let the lease lapse when the cow leaves."

Ben nodded. So that was why there were so many vampires in Steve's bar. They were training cows.

"Second," Mikos said. "I make the rules here, and you shall listen to me. You shall ask my permission before bringing a cow up here. Any cow."

Ben licked his lower lip. His body was trembling. That rule would change, and Mikos would be surprised when it did.

"Finally, there will be no disagreements between nest members. If there are, the youngest member shall leave the nest."

"That's not what you said to Vangelina." Ben was gripping the chair so hard his nails had pierced the fabric.

"What I do with Van is my business," Mikos said. "You will not second-guess me, nor will you go against me. The second rule."

He stared at Ben, his dark eyes bright in his lined face. Ben was holding his breath. He finally released it. He still needed the nest. As long as he needed them, he would have to use their rules. Still, he could not let everything rest with orders.

"You said we would change things. You said I was the most important person to join this nest in a long time, maybe ever."

Mikos nodded. "You are important. But not so important that you jeopardize all of our lives."

Mikos walked closer to the chair. He smelled of musk and something drier, as if the age of his body affected his aroma. "You must agree to the rules or I will make you leave," he said.

"I do not understand why you tell Van one thing and me another. If what I did was so wrong, then why didn't you toss Candyce out in the first place?"

Mikos's body did not move at all. Yet his face seemed to go flat. Ben had seen that expression once before, the night he had made his first kill. Mikos did not tolerate much opposition.

"I wanted to observe her. She threatened our nest, but the child of an hereditary was fifteen times more valuable than you are, Benjamin. A child I could raise myself and train from birth had a certain allure that made your cow's presence worth the risk." Mikos shrugged by moving one shoulder. "I was willing to take that risk. Van was not. Both responses are valid. My quarrel with her comes from her disobedience, not her actions."

"She killed Candyce," Ben whispered.

Mikos nodded. "And judging by your response, it was a good thing. The cow meant more to you than a cow should. You would have gotten careless. You might have even hurt her worse than you did. You are still new. You might yet father another child. But I warn you. Any new cow you train must be raised outside the nest. I will not tolerate this kind of upheaval in my home again."

The fabric bit into Ben's fingertips. He was staring at Mikos, breathing shallowly. It would take so little to throw the chair aside, to attack Mikos unprovoked. But Van had defeated him, and Ben had surprise on his side then. He would have to wait until he was stronger, until he was cleverer. When they least suspected.

They had no right to control him.

No one did.

"Do you understand?" Mikos asked.

Ben understood. He just wasn't sure if he agreed.

"Do you understand?" Mikos repeated.

"I understand," Ben said. His tone was sullen, the tone he had used when his father made rules he didn't want to follow. Let Mikos know he was upset. Mikos would not rule the nest forever. "Aren't you going to punish Van for killing someone so precious?"

Mikos took a deep breath. "Van was within her rights, Ben. She founded this nest, not me, although she lets me run it. She is not someone to take lightly. Van and I may disagree, but we do not fight. For the good of the nest. Do you understand?"

"Oh, I understand," Ben said. The message wasn't as subtle as Mikos thought it was. He was warning Ben not to fight him too. But Ben would do as he pleased. No one had the right to kill anyone he brought into the nest. No one had the right to order him around. Someday they would all understand that.

Maybe the day he killed Van.

Mikos turned his back on Ben, and then stopped. Mikos's shoulders were broad. His body held so much power in check that it looked as if it would burst through him. "I have given you a home, food, clothing, and wealth," Mikos said. "Do not betray me. If you do, my people will slaughter you in your sleep."

If they chose to remain faithful to Mikos. Ben smiled, knowing that Mikos could not see it. "I will not betray you, Mikos," Ben lied.

Chapter
Twenty-four

The hotel room no longer felt safe. Only Cammie's exhaustion let her sleep until ten the following morning. Even then, nightmares of blood and vampires rearing out of movie-imagined coffins made the sleep restless and unfulfilling.

Before she showered, she called DeeDee and asked for any records the Center had of former employees or similar centers in the area. DeeDee put her on hold for what seemed like hours before coming back with the name of an addiction-counseling office in Roseburg, to the south, and the detectives the Sadlers had mentioned: DeFreeze & Garity. DeFreeze & Garity were not known for their vampire work, but they had handled odd cases and had a reputation for results and discretion. Other than that, the Center had no information that would help Cammie.

She was on her own.

By ten-thirty, she was dressed and out of the room. She now carried a pouch of garlic and the protection kit she used to use when she was in Eradication. When she had come West, the idea of carrying one felt silly, but now it seemed necessary. She also wore jeans and tennis shoes, much more sensible attire when vampires were in the area.

She carried her briefcase the half block to the small

coffee shop she had discovered. Delbert's was a homey concoction of tables and benches with artwork on the walls, and a knack for making delicious breakfast muffins. A comic shop graced one wall, and upstairs was a large used bookstore. The wood and brick design gave the building a noncommercial feel. She liked it better than either of the restaurants in the Hilton.

Jazz filled the air from the area's noncommercial radio station. Two other tables were full—a student sat at one, copying something from an oversized book into a yellow legal pad, and two women at another, deep in an intimate conversation.

She took a table beneath the art-covered wall and ordered an omelet, with a lemon poppyseed muffin. To that, she added an espresso, which the woman behind the counter gave her before she returned to her seat.

Cammie opened her briefcase and pulled out the letters and the Eugene phone book she had taken from the hotel room. She needed to see what sorts of self-help services were available in Eugene before she went to the police station. She really didn't want to contact the center in Roseburg if she didn't have to.

Nothing listed under vampires or addiction in the yellow pages. She turned to counseling and found more listings than she had ever seen. Most just gave a name and an address, but some counselors listed their specialties. Only one listed vampirism as an addiction. The clinics focused on drug and alcohol abuse, and a number of clinics focused on help for long-term physical pain. She wondered what kind of things occurred in the community that would call for such a clinic.

The man at the stove called her name. She got up and picked up a hot plate with an omelet pushed square against the hash browns. Ham and melted cheese oozed out of the flattened egg. Her stomach growled. She hadn't even touched her espresso, and she needed the caffeine. She took her plate back to her table, copied down the counselor's phone number, and pushed the phone book aside.

Then she started eating breakfast. The food tasted better than she expected: the egg light and fluffy, the ham warm, and the cheese mild enough not to overtake the omelet itself. She didn't remember eating dinner the night before, and the drive to Portland had left her stressed and anxious.

Through the window, she could watch the city. People threaded up the stairs to the post office, some carrying packages, others with nothing at all. Most would stop outside after they had picked up their mail, and read a letter or examine a bill. The sunshine was bright, making the green lawn vibrant against the blue sky. Such a pretty place. She had wanted to believe that there were no vampires here, that she had finally discovered a place that was safe.

The smell that first night should have clued her. This town was even farther back than Madison had been twenty years ago. No treatment centers for vampires. No eradication programs. The problem would only spread as time went on. And somehow Ben was mixed up in it. Maybe he had gone into the Keg to meet his friend Steve and had never come out.

She finished the omelet and pushed the plate aside. Then she ate the muffin slowly, letting its sweetness fill her. The espresso was warm and she sipped it as she watched. All those Westrina Center children disappearing. Some kind of revenge? Or something else?

Revenge would be difficult to encompass all those children, unless the actor was well placed in social services or with the OCS. Possible, but then the vampire would have to be a young one whose obsession had not yet affected his job performance.

If Whitney were here, he would have an opinion about what was going on. So would Eliason. Even DeeDee. Anita would tell her to let it go, but Cammie wasn't going to rest now. Things had gotten too complicated.

Cammie ripped off the sheet of notepaper with the phone number on it, grabbed a quarter, and went to the pay phone outside the restaurant door. The phone was bolted to the wall next to the stairs leading to the bookstore. It had an odd sort of privacy. Cammie dialed, leaned against the wall, and waited.

A receptionist picked up. Cammie asked for Dr. Brooker only to be told that he was with a client. "I would like to see him today, if possible."

"Is this an emergency?" the receptionist asked. Her voice had the bored tone to it, as if a life-and-death matter could not shake her.

"I'm from the Westrina Center in Wisconsin. I need to talk with him about some things going on in Oregon."

"You're here now?" the receptionist asked.

"Only for a few days." Cammie hated that tone. How could clients speak to a man who hired a woman as unfeeling as this one?

"I have a half an hour only. Two o'clock?"

"Wonderful," Cammie said. "I'll be there." She hung up the phone. The omelet turned in her stomach. Nerves. She would go into a waiting room where vampires sat. Maybe even Brooker himself had gotten contaminated. Or maybe he had a staff large enough to carry on a program like the Westrina Center's.

She put a hand over her stomach and went back into the restaurant. The clock over the door told her that she had been there nearly forty-five minutes. She packed up her briefcase and bused her dishes. She still had time to go to the police station.

The police station was only a two-block walk from the restaurant and her hotel. No wonder the town seemed small. Every important building was within one square mile of every other. The sunshine felt warm on her face. She would never get used to the feeling of light on her body. It made her feel free and joyful. No one could touch her in the sunlight. The sunlight kept her safe.

The police station was a three-story windowless building that appeared to have been built in the late sixties. As she followed the signs up a set of concrete stairs, she found herself in a small courtyard. Flowers twisted along the columns and benches faced away from the street. A rabbit's warren of offices faced the yard. The windows were here, running floor to ceiling, offering a view of the greenery and the sunshine.

Cammie went inside the reception area. It was a small room that opened into a larger area. The larger area was protected by a security door and bulletproof glass. She approached the intercom. An officer looked up. She had been stamping traffic tickets on the desk behind the glass.

"Help you?"

"I'm Camila Timms. I'm here to see Officer Thornton. She is expecting me sometime today."

The woman nodded. She had short brown hair clipped back like a man's. Her hands were stained with red dye from the stamp. "I'll let her know you're here."

She walked to a back desk to page. Cammie could hear nothing through the glass. She went to the window and looked out at the concrete garden.

Two officers were sitting on a bench, eating bag lunches. A bird swooped overhead, building a nest in a newly planted maple, and the officers laughed and pointed. A woman in a blue business suit hurried into one of the back offices and a thin man wearing ragged blue jeans emerged from the office next door.

"She'll see you." The officer's voice sounded tinny and scratchy through the intercom.

Cammie turned. A buzzer sounded as the security door was released. She pushed it open and stepped inside.

The silent room of the front office became a cacophony of voices, typewriters, and blaring radios. Cigarette smoke, old coffee grounds, and filtered air mingled. The air conditioner made the station too cold in patches, just right in others. Cammie unrolled the sleeves of her blouse as she followed the officer through a maze of large metal desks.

Most of the desks were empty. One, toward the back, was covered by a receptionist's grid. The man working it wore a headset and smiled as they passed. Other officers were on the phone. The wide communal room narrowed into a hallway that led to the interior entrances for the outer offices.

The officer stopped at a desk on the edge of the hallway. It was clear except for a file folder, and two photos, both of young children. The phone had a dozen lines, all indicated by small red lights. Most of the lights were on.

The chair behind the desk was empty. The officer pulled back a hard wooden chair. "She'll be right back," the officer said. "Have a seat."

Cammie sat down. The officer left. The file folder was full, but not labeled. The children's pictures had individual frames—the cheap silver kind found in any Kmart or Target. The green desk chair had a light indentation in its fake leather cushion.

A white coffee mug with the saying I-I-I *Like* Str-EEEE-sss slammed on the desk in front of her, steaming hot coffee sloshing at the sides. A tall, slender man with close-cropped black hair and deep blue eyes sank into the chair. Then the man smiled, and Cammie realized she was looking at a woman.

"Officer Thornton?"

"In the flesh." Thornton had a low voice that some men would have been proud of. She slurped her coffee, then ran a long hand through her hair, leaving strands of it on end. "You got something for me?"

"I don't know." Cammie extended her right hand. "I'm Camila Timms of the Westrina Center."

Thornton rested her right ankle on her left knee and balanced the coffee cup on her calf. Her blue pants leg rode up, revealing bright pink socks. "What's your interest in the Sadler case?"

Quick, sharp, and to the point. Like the people Cammie was used to dealing with. Time to be honest with someone. "Will our conversation remain confidential?"

"If possible." Thornton tugged her pants leg over the non-regulation socks. "What's in it for me?"

"I don't know yet," Cammie said. "Except that I'll share information with you as I gain it. My work here is unofficial, but I am using the Westrina Center's information base. I'm expecting some preadoption files on the missing kids in the afternoon's mail."

"Thought we were going to have to get a court order for those." Thornton cradled the coffee mug between her hands. "All right. I'll keep quiet, for a while, anyway. What's your interest?"

Cammie swallowed. She hadn't talked to anyone outside the Center about this. "I'm Ben Sadler's sister."

Thornton rolled her eyes and slammed the mug on the metal desk. The sound stopped conversation throughout the room. She sat up and leaned forward. "Guess again, honey. Sadler's an only kid. We checked him out—" She paused and didn't quite gasp. Her mouth quirked into a half smile. "Oh. You're the sister who murdered the dad."

Cammie flushed. Thornton made it all sound so casual. Not at all the gruesome, bloody event that haunted Cammie's dreams. "The Sadlers don't know who I am."

"Good thing," Thornton said. "They'd want you the hell outta here. You lie about the Westrina Center?"

Cammie shook her head. "I've worked there for nearly three years. I—uh—worked in Eradication until a few months ago. They let you do that until the memory comes back—"

"Jesus Christ, woman. You telling me you're a professional assassin?"

The conversation in the room completely stopped

this time. An officer standing near the hallway put his hand casually on his gun. Another hung up the phone, slowly, as if he expected a problem. Thornton glared at them. They returned to work, but their movements were different, as if they were listening.

"In the Midwest," Cammie said calmly, "it's like being a skip tracer."

"It's nothing of the sort," Thornton said. "I read about you folks. They call you religious vigilantes and say somehow you got the courts to agree. God, I've watched this stuff on television. It's obscene. You get to barge into people's homes and slaughter them, when our cops get nailed for busting pot smokers at the local Saturday market."

"We have state support," Cammie said. Her mouth was dry.

"Good thing, honey. Try that in Oregon, and individualists from all sides of the political aisle would nail you to the proverbial cross." Thornton leaned forward, her dark eyes snapping. "How many you killed?"

Cammie smoothed her hands over her jeans. This interview was not going as she had expected. "It doesn't matter. What does matter is that until a few months ago, I had no memory of my childhood at all. It—came back—and I decided to find Ben."

"Just like that?"

Cammie looked up. "Just like that."

"And you manage to show up when he's disappeared? Such a coincidence, Miss Timms."

"I was still in the Midwest when he disappeared," Cammie said. She wasn't sure if she liked Thornton. She wasn't sure if it mattered. "I came here to see if I could help find him."

"We've got people on it."

"People who have dealt with vampires?"

Thornton picked up her mug and took a ladylike sip. Then she set the mug down again and shoved the file aside. "I know you people like to think you have the monopoly on knowledge. But I've dealt with a few vampires in my day. So has everyone in the department. We can handle damn near anything we come across."

"I'm sure you can," Cammie said. "But Ben's not your major focus. He's mine, though. You know that his girlfriend was supposed to meet him the other day, and now she's missing. And the man she got Ben's address from hangs out in a cow-bar in Portland."

"A what?"

"A bar where vampires get easy prey. Surely you have some here."

"I never heard them called that before," Thornton said. "You sure about all this?"

Cammie nodded. "I was at the bar last night, but I didn't go in. I need some help before tackling this. We're talking about a nest of vampires. Ben might have gotten himself mixed into the wrong kind of company."

Thornton sat up and sighed. "We can't put a watch on you, Miss Timms, and we can't let you work with our people. You're better off giving us the information and letting us do the work—"

"I've already gotten twice the information you have," Cammie said. "I promised to keep you informed, but I don't know this area. What I need from you is a different kind of help. I want to know what organizations, if any, work in vampire eradication. I also want to know who the vampire specialists are here, and where I can find local nests. I have an appointment with Dr. Brooker this afternoon."

"Ted Brooker?"

Cammie nodded.

"You found our specialist. There are no eradication laws on the books in the Northwest. There's an addiction clinic in Roseburg, a few rehab clinics in Portland, and a big one in Salem connected to the state penitentiary, but they won't have anyone trained in assassination." Thornton's eyes narrowed. "That is what you're looking for, isn't it?"

"I'm looking for some experienced help," Cammie said. "But I guess I won't find it here."

She stood and picked up her briefcase.

"Wait," Thornton said. "About the information you promised. We can still work together."

"Only if you share in return," Cammie said.

Thornton studied her. Finally, Thornton said, "What do you need to know?"

"What you know. Everything you know."

"I'll need to check you out first."

Cammie nodded but did not sit back down. "Throw me a bone. Let me know I can trust you."

Thornton smiled. Her face cascaded into a valley of sun-wrinkles. Now it was impossible to mistake her for a man. "You're a tough lady."

"I'm not alone."

Thornton nodded. "All right. Sadler was sighted two days ago in the Steelhead bar a few blocks from here. He met that girlfriend of his and she left with him. They went to the Hilton."

The night Cammie had arrived. Her skin crawled. She had been only a few rooms away from him. So close and she hadn't even known it. "Where did you find this out?"

"We followed the girl's path after the mother called. We can't officially look yet, but since she's part of the Sadler investigation, we were able to fudge."

Cammie was breathing shallowly. "And?"

"He'd checked out by the time we found him. Used his family's address when he checked in. Valet said he parked a Targa with a Washington plate. License plate attaches it to an empty lot outside of Spokane."

"Ben's car?" Cammie's voice was trembling.

Thornton shook her head. "Car's registered to a William Charles Schiff. Schiff's been behind a number of other unsavory things along I-5. We think it's an alias, but for whom we don't know."

"So you haven't traced him."

"Not yet."

Cammie's shoulders hurt. She had been holding them too rigidly. "What aren't you telling me?"

"The girl went with him willingly."

"I got that," Cammie said.

"No." Thornton's voice was soft. "The next day. They drove off together after he checked out. Two different valets saw them."

"So you think it's some kind of young love adventure?"

"I would have, if it weren't for the car. Something odd is going on. The fact that you found a link to a vampire nest has me concerned."

Something heavy was pressing against Cammie's chest. She was finding it hard to breathe. "Why?"

"Because when I interviewed that girl, she claimed she hated your brother. And now she leaves with him. What does that suggest to you?"

Cammie's mind skipped over the implication. Ben wouldn't be a vampire. Not after all he had lived through. He would avoid vampires. "Maybe she was angry at him. Maybe she was lying to you." Her words didn't sound convincing.

"And maybe she wasn't." Thornton ran her hands through her hair. "We have an APB out on the car. We're treating it like a kidnapping."

"With Ben at fault?"

"He showed up here of his own free will. An adult's not missing just because he fails to tell his parents what he's doing."

Cammie's hand was trembling. She set the briefcase down. "You said Candyce went with him willingly. Why are you following up on that?"

Thornton took a sip of her coffee, winced, and set the mug aside. "Because it bothers me. The Targa bothers me. The girl's change in attitude bothers me. Something's not right, and the fact that there could be vampires involved in this mess only makes it worse. Think your brother's gone over?"

"No!" The word exploded out of Cammie. "He knew what it was like. No one would ever choose that as a lifestyle."

"Kids become their parents," Thornton said.

Cammie shook her head. "I didn't. My friends didn't. We made it out. Ben had an even better chance."

Thornton raised her eyebrows. "You made it out, huh? You just got done telling me you kill for a living. How is that different from your father, the vampire?"

Cammie felt as if Thornton had hit her in the stomach. Cammie gasped for air, then took a step back from the desk, nearly tripping on her own briefcase. "It's different," Cammie said when she could speak. "I save lives. He took them."

"Save lives by killing people, huh? Odd little sense of justice you have there, girl."

"It's legal."

"So was slavery, once."

Cammie was light-headed. She needed to get out of here. "What's your point, Officer?"

"Maybe escape isn't as easy as you thought it was. Maybe your brother is his father's son after all."

Cammie shook her head. Thornton smiled. "If you're going to investigate, Timms, then you need an open mind."

"Sounds like your mind is made up," Cammie said. "You think my brother's evil."

"From the sounds of it," Thornton said, "I don't know your brother any better than you do. You think you're a good guy, and you spend your life killing people. Wonder what he does to blow off that steam from his past? Got any idea? His parents sure didn't. They thought it was all behind him."

"He had a good life," Cammie said.

"Did he?" Thornton stood. "Or are we just believing Mom and Dad's P.R.?"

"There is no P.R.," Cammie said. "Ben survived. He had to."

Chapter
Twenty-five

For the first time since his change, Ben wished he could get drunk. Sweet, sweet oblivion, lost to him now. The only way he could lose himself would be in someone's neck. Or to take a little garlic. Just enough to put himself out. But even then, he would be in a stupor, not happy and carefree.

Maybe he would never feel carefree again.

He sat in the basement of one of Seattle's jazz restaurants. The bar down here, done in crude white plaster walls covered with serapes and Mexican rugs, catered to a new music crowd. The white-covered tables were too close together, and only the carved, cavelike booths built into the walls offered any privacy at all.

He didn't want privacy.

He sipped red wine, slowly, and listened to the five-piece band. The singer managed to fit a small piano onto the performance space, and the others circled around it, like lovers. They played a New Age kind of jazz, filled with soft chords and flowing runs. Ben's fingers caressed his glass. Every few minutes, he would scan the room for a single female, but most seemed to come with their boyfriends or other women, and the bar had no place to dance.

He had forgotten about dancing. He should have walked to a different bar, less upscale but just as nice, on the other side of Mikos's building. But he hadn't. He wanted some place where the women felt safe, some place where he could get the right kind of cow. Not the kind that had been used over and over like the ones that visited Mikos. No. He wanted someone as fresh and pure as Candyce.

Candyce. His grip tightened on the glass. She had been a mess when Van finished with her. Eyes open and staring, body bathed in blood. For the first time since he turned, the sight of blood had made him ill instead of arousing him. Maybe he still had some human traits after all.

He missed her.

Not the cow she had become, but the girl he had known. The one who had laughed with him, who chose silly movies instead of the latest foreign import. The girl who drank microbrewed beer and made sharp observations about people at the next table.

That girl had died before Van drained her body.

This was the kind of life he was doomed to lead. He would find a woman who appealed to him, sleep with her, and she would become a blind follower, with no thoughts of her own. If she had more strength of character, according to Mikos, she would turn on him and try to kill him in his sleep.

He could no longer laugh and make jokes and enjoy the company of someone close to him.

Unless he had a child. The child would have a mind of its own, as well as all of his strength. The child would become someone with whom he could have a real relationship.

The wine had a fruity, almost bloodlike odor. He sipped. The taste was bitter, like drinking overboiled coffee. Nothing tasted right anymore. Only the blood, which tasted better than anything he'd ever had.

He should have left Candyce in Eugene, but he hadn't. He had needed that child. The craving was as deep as the blood craving he woke up with each night.

The child would push him forward and give him strength. It would also make him the center of the community, because of all of them, he was the only one with the ability to still make children. He would make as many as he could before he turned completely.

Then he would never be alone again.

Now that Candyce was dead, his chances for a child had faded. He would have to find the proper woman quickly—and it would have to be a woman whose features he could tolerate. He would never again use someone he had once cared about, so his old girlfriends (what few he had) were out of the question.

He had to find someone new.

The music eased its way to an ending, and the leader announced that the band would take a short break. More couples leaned over the small candle lamps in the center of the tables. Large, rowdy groups had filled all the recessed booths. A woman sat alone near the entrance, her long fingers drumming on the tabletop. She was waiting for someone, and it looked like she wouldn't wait much longer.

Ben grabbed his glass and stood. He would lose his table, but no matter. He threaded his way through the densely packed floor. "Want some company?" he asked.

He put all the charm he owned into the question. He could feel the power flowing from him. She had chocolate-colored eyes and dark Mediterranean skin. Her hair was black and shone in the soft light. She glanced at the door as if she couldn't decide, then smiled at him. Her teeth were small and white. She was stunning.

He could look at her forever.

"Please," she said.

He pulled the chair back as far as it would go and slid into it. "I'm Ben," he said, extending his hand. When she took it, a sexual charge jumped between them. First contact made.

"Judith." Her voice was soft and deep. She smelled

fresh. Her blood would be untainted. Saliva formed in the back of his mouth. He wanted her already.

"Has anyone told you that you're beautiful?"

She smiled and then she really was. She leaned closer. Her pupils had dilated. He was succeeding. "Not today."

"You're beautiful," he said, and kissed her. The kiss was gentle at first, then he put his tongue inside her mouth and touched all corners. Finally he nipped her lower lip. Her blood was sweet, sweeter than any he had ever had, and he longed to get more. But this was just the hook.

He pulled out of the kiss. Her eyes were slightly glassy, her cheeks flushed. An overbuilt man wearing a tank top and tight blue jeans stopped beside the table. "Judith!"

It took her a minute to look up, and even longer to recognize him. "Go away, Rich." Her words were slightly slurred.

"We had a date," Rich said.

"Not anymore," she said. "I got Ben now."

Rich faced Ben for the first time. Rich's face was flushed. He looked more confused than angry. "Who're you?"

"Ben," Ben said, making his tones soft and leaving the charm in. "The lady looked lonely."

"I was just a few minutes late!"

"An hour," Judith said to Ben. Her hand was on his arm, her touch light, but her fingers kept stroking his wristbone. Definitely hooked.

"An hour's too long to keep a lady waiting," Ben said. He stood and offered Judith his arm. "Let's go, honey."

She stood too and swayed a little. Rich reached out to catch her, but Ben was quicker. He placed one hand under her elbow and steadied her.

"Judith," Rich said, "I know you're trying to make me mad, but going off with some guy you don't know is not a good idea."

Her smile had a vague edge it had not had earlier. "I know him," she said.

"Judith!" Rich grabbed her free arm. Ben stepped between them.

Rich smelled of sweat and fear. So the woman meant a lot to him. Ah, well. "She's coming with me," Ben said. "If you want, you can call and check on her in the morning."

Judith laughed, the sloppy too-high laugh of a drunk. Rich stared at him, then stepped back. Ben put his arm around her waist and propelled her from the bar. He had to get her somewhere. Once he started the seduction, he was as hooked as his cow. He wanted to taste her, to feel the dual orgasm of taste and explosion flow through him.

Outside the air was fresh. He nibbled Judith's neck so that the fresh air wouldn't free her. "You live near here?" he asked. She tasted so sweet. She was perfect.

She shook her head. "But I got my car."

He smiled. Good. "I'm not staying too far from here. Want to drive me to my hotel?"

She slid a hand down his back and cupped his buttocks. He leaned over and kissed her, nipping harder. He wanted to take her right here, right now, in full view of everyone, but he needed control. She was fresh. It would be better to take her in a safe place.

Her car was a five-year-old Datsun that needed a new paint job. Papers were strewn on the seat inside, and the car smelled of cigarette smoke. She would have to quit that habit. He had grown even more sensitive to smoke since his change.

She drove him to the batch of high-priced downtown hotels. He led her into the Sheraton, and then made a pretense of forgetting his key. He went to the desk and registered under the fake name Mikos had given him. Ben took a suite on the upper floor. No need to skimp on cash if things worked out as he expected.

She clung to him on the elevator ride. When he got to the room, he pushed open the door. She gasped at the sunken living room and the view of Seattle's skyline. The furniture had an untouched showroom look, but fresh flowers sat on the desk. "My God," she said, and was in his arms.

He pushed the door closed with his foot. The slam echoed in the suite. He bit her neck as he unfastened her blouse, then tore it as he tried to get it over her arms. Her jeans were snug and he had to struggle with them. Finally she took his hands and moved them, then wriggled out of the jeans herself. He freed himself without taking off his clothes, and pushed inside her. She was wet and waiting.

Her blood tasted of sunshine and fresh mints. It made him giddy, and he had to be careful not to take too much. She climaxed beneath him once, twice, screaming her pleasure. His orgasm was slower than he was used to, but it finally flooded through him. He collapsed on top of her, forcing himself to remove his mouth from her neck. He licked the wound and it clotted. Then he sighed.

He had noticed, in the last few nights with Candyce, that the orgasms were no longer draining, but he had chalked it up to repeat performance with her. It was the same with Judith. The orgasm hardly even felt good. It was as if something tugged inside him, trying to get free. He would rather have kept his lips on her neck and drained her dry. It was a more sensual, fulfilling experience.

Mikos had told him it would come to this.

Ben pushed up on his elbows. He brushed a strand of dark hair from her forehead tenderly. She smiled at him, her eyes completely glassy now.

"I'm sorry," he said, keeping up the fiction. "I didn't ask, and I forgot to use protection."

"I don't have AIDS," she said.

He knew that. He would have been able to smell any blood disease. He stayed clear of them. But he said nothing. "Good, but that isn't what I meant."

She frowned. Her hand was playing with his buttocks again. Women were so impatient. He wasn't ready for a second try.

"You could have gotten pregnant."

She laughed, the sound even more drunken and sloppy than it had been earlier. Was this what was going to pass for intimacy for him from now on? Women so drugged that they lived only for sex, no matter what kind they found?

"No, I couldn't." She laughed again.

He hadn't felt a diaphragm, and her blood was clear of all drugs but the alcohol. "What are you using?"

"Nothing." Her grin got wider. "Tubes tied"—she laughed—"tied for Rich." Her expression clouded. "Think he's mad?"

Tubes tied? He had wasted all this effort on a woman who couldn't get pregnant? He grabbed her shoulder so hard she gasped. Then he pushed her face into the sofa.

"What?" Her voice was muffled. "What?"

He buried his face in her neck. Wasted. An evening wasted. An entire rotten day. He lost Candyce, then spent too much time with this bimbo, a woman who couldn't help him at all. He drank and drank.

She pushed at him once, feebly, then her body started to convulse. The orgasms were deep. He could feel them around him. He was startled to find that he had gotten hard. He plunged himself into her, not going for pleasure, but for pain.

She had no right to lie to him. She had no right to lead him up here on false pretenses. His teeth ripped through her skin, but her body kept expressing its enjoyment. Her hands gripped his backside, forcing him deeper.

He wanted her to hurt, to push him away, to cry out, but she did nothing, except whisper "more, more," the harsher he got. Finally he pushed away from her, slamming her head against the sofa's armrest. Her cheeks were pasty white and her mouth slack. She licked her lips and slid a hand over her own breast.

"Please?" she whispered.

"Jesus," he said. He zipped up and went into the bathroom. The bathroom was done in gold, with gold faucets and even a gold toilet. He didn't look at the mirror. Practice made that possible. He turned on the separate handles for hot and cold, and splashed his face. The blood swirled down the marble-inlaid sink. He took toilet paper and dried his skin, then rubbed his face with a towel. No stains that way. He wiped off everything he'd touched when he had finished.

Then he checked his clothes for blood. Finding none, he went back into the main room.

She hadn't changed position. Her head lolled back, eyes half open, hand still cupping a breast. For a moment, he thought she was dead, but then she sighed, a deep contented sound.

In the morning, she would wake up and he would be gone. She wouldn't remember his name (although Rich would—Ben would have to be more careful next time), and it would all become an exciting memory. Rich would never be able to compare sexually.

Ben smiled. Their relationship was doomed. Poor Judith, forever seeking the sexual satisfaction she had found for one night only.

Served her right, the stupid bitch. Fooling him like that. It would serve her right if she paid forever.

He climbed up the two stairs and opened the door into the hallway. The whole day had been a screw-up. He would have to look harder for the right kind of woman, and before he took her he would have to be sure.

He shut the door quietly behind him. The wide tan hallway was empty.

Or maybe he would get an apartment and bring a parade of women up there. Once in bed, they would tell him if they could get pregnant. Then he would have an option. He wouldn't have to be sexual with them if they couldn't have children. He could drain them dry and let them go.

He smiled. He wasn't acting on impulse anymore. He finally had a bit of a plan.

Chapter Twenty-six

Cammie had expected the University Hill area to be near the University of Oregon and had spent a good five minutes on the wrong side of the aqueduct. Then a kind woman had told her that University Hill was near the baseball diamond. Cammie knew where that was. She drove right to it.

Dr. Brooker's office was a red brick building with matching brick sidewalk and a sculpted lawn. Willamette Street turned from one way to two way right on the corner, and the local baseball stadium was only a block away. Cammie had to drive around that stadium twice before finding a place to park.

Her meeting with Thornton had left her crabby and on edge. The officer had no right to comment on Cammie's life. Cammie's work had been perfectly legal. The Eradication program even served as therapy for adult survivors. Just because customs were different here did not allow Thornton to accuse Cammie of being no better than a vampire.

Maybe Brooker would be different. Cammie needed some help if she was going to track down Ben.

The door to the office was made of paneled wood. A small arched window stood about eye level. Cammie tried the knob. The door pushed open, and the scent of roses greeted her.

A large bouquet of white roses sat on top of the glass-topped coffee table in the middle of the room. Small pink and green roses decorated the sofa, love seat, and easy chair. A Dali original hung over the fireplace and two signed prints hung on the wall above the sofa. The room would have looked like someone's living room if it hadn't been for the oversized reception desk blocking the entrance to what had once been a kitchen.

"Help you?" The same bored voice Cammie had heard on the phone. Its owner was young—maybe twenty—with obviously dyed straw-blonde hair. The desk dwarfed her. She wore a blue cardigan sweater skirt outfit that might have belonged to Cammie's mother, and a thin, cheap diamond engagement ring.

"I'm here to see Dr. Brooker."

"Oh, the lady from out of town." The woman smiled. "Have a seat. He'll be with you soonest."

Cammie sank onto the sofa. It had a firmness that surprised her. Next to the arm was a bookshelf with psychology and pop-psychology titles: *The Dance of Anger, Adult Children of Alcoholics, On Death and Dying, Surviving Sexual Abuse,* and Rowan's classic, *The Vampire.* Cammie was reaching for one when the stout door in the hallway opened.

A woman with dark, stringy hair came out. She saw Cammie and averted her gaze, drawing her raincoat tighter as she let herself out of the building. A thin man with hair cropped too close to be an Afro emerged behind her. His suit coat hung loosely on his tall frame. His light brown skin bore traces of acne scars, and his wide eyes had an unusual warmth.

He stopped in front of her. "Miss Timms, I'm Ted Brooker."

Cammie stood and took his hand. His palm was warm, dry, and calloused. Not the hand of a man who worked indoors all day.

"I understand you're with the Westrina Center," he said, leading the way into his office.

"Yes," she said. "But I'm in Eugene on personal business."

Brooker's office was as large as the reception area. A faint odor of pipe tobacco lingered in the air. It made her want to sneeze. An oriental rug covered the brown carpet, and the sofa in here was done in deep, masculine brown. An oversized rocking chair faced the sofa, and a handcarved oak desk, covered with stacks of papers and reports, dominated the left side of the room.

Brooker sat in the rocking chair. That left Cammie no choice but to sit on the couch. This couch was older than the first and twice as comfortable. She sank into the folds and fought the urge to relax.

"How can I help you?" The warmth in his voice matched his eyes. Then he smiled. "Whatever you tell me will remain confidential."

Cammie nodded. She had expected that. "I don't know what you know of the Westrina Center, but most of its employees are children of vampires."

Brooker nodded. "Anita Constantine's work is familiar to anyone in this business. She is a pioneer."

"I've been working for the Westrina Center for nearly three years in Eradication." Brooker leaned back when he heard that. Cammie ignored the movement and continued. "When the memories came back, I moved out of Eradication and into Records. I also hired a private detective to find the brother I had protected when I was eight years old."

"I thought Anita believed in no contact with the past."

"She opposed my search." Cammie ran a hand through her hair. This man, with his calm voice and searching eyes, made her feel nervous and relaxed at the same time. "I would have quit when I found out where he was, except that no one knows. My brother is missing. I came to Eugene to track him myself, and the trail led me to a cow-bar in Portland."

"Vampires," Brooker said, without surprise.

"Vampires. I don't know how he's involved, if at all, but I do know that one of his friends hangs out there. I also know that Ben's not the first Westrina Center adoptee to disappear in the last few years."

Brooker nodded. He got out of the rocking chair, went to his desk, and filled a pipe. "Mind?" he said, holding it up. Cammie shook her head. He stuck the pipe in his mouth, held a match over it, and sucked on the end until the tobacco caught. Then he returned to the chair.

"Your problem reflects a blindness the Westrina Center has held all along," he said. The smoke smelled faintly of bay leaves. "The idea that if a person is removed from the problem, the problem will go away."

Cammie frowned. "That's not true. Eradication programs deal with unresolved memory."

"Really? Or do they take advantage of your pain to get cheap, willing labor?"

Cammie stood. "I came here for help, not for criticism of my life and friends."

Brooker waved his pipe. "I'm not criticizing, merely offering another viewpoint. Please, sit down."

She sat again. She had been reacting angrily to people all day. Maybe she should listen.

"I work with ACVs like you," Brooker said. "Many were adopted out of the Midwest by the Westrina Center. These kids—adults now—find that they share many things in common. A need for occasional violence, sleep disorders, deep unexplained fears. People whose fathers were vampires when they were born also have a longing for blood that begins in puberty and is tied to a hormonal change that we do not understand."

"There's no proof that vampirism is inherited," Cammie snapped. She had read the books. She knew the risks. But no one had used scientific data to make the connection. The data was too hard to collect.

Brooker smiled. "That's right. There is no scientific proof, but there is strong evidence. Over fifty percent of a vampire's children become vampires themselves. And that doesn't count the children who go on to work in violent professions."

"I had no blood longing in puberty." Cammie was sitting up straighter. She didn't want to let this go. It was the same point that Thornton had made. These Western hicks had no concept of true vampirism.

"The change seems to come later for women. It seems to be tied to the peak sexual drive." He put the pipe in his mouth and puffed before continuing. "I am not saying that you are a vampire."

"The sunlight confirms that." Cammie resisted the urge to cross her arms in front of her chest. She wanted to appear as open as she could, but she was wasting her time here. Brooker wasn't going to help her.

"The Westrina Center's problems have always come because they treat vampires like criminals instead of like people with an awful disease." Brooker's gaze remained on her face as he spoke.

Cammie shifted on the couch. "They tried to treat the disease in the sixties."

"Yes, by simple counseling, not by taking into consideration the physical changes the vampire goes through. Instead of examining the changes, the Center went to the other extreme. After the massacre in Wisconsin, the Center managed to get the eradication laws passed. Eradication is as ineffective as simple counseling." He puffed one more time. The pipe was annoying her. He had no right to talk about addictions when his was so obvious.

"Look," Cammie said, moving to the edge of the couch. "We disagree on methods and treatments. You clearly aren't going to be able to help me. I was hoping you had a team that would investigate the bar with me and help me find my brother. I don't want a lecture on the benefits of treating vampires."

Brooker took the pipe from his mouth and rested his hand on the arm of the rocking chair. The room was silent except for the rustle of his clothing as he moved.

"Eradication is illegal in the Pacific Northwest. No one here has the training you need."

"Which is probably why you have a problem." Cammie adjusted the legs of her jeans before standing.

"It seems you have the problem," Brooker said. He looked at the couch as if she were still sitting there. "The treatments didn't work for you. You are the one here, wrapped up in your own past, instead of moving into your future."

"Ben is my future."

Brooker shook his head. "Your future is somewhere else. Your brother left your side, what, twenty years ago? You are searching for a man you never met, hoping to find a boy that you lost. Or, perhaps, are you searching for a bit of yourself?"

Cammie stopped beside him. "The Westrina Center made sure I found every bit of myself that I needed."

"You don't sound very happy about it." Brooker leaned back and looked at her. His eyes were wide and dark. "Tell me, Miss Timms, have you ever been happy?"

For a moment, she saw herself in college, sitting on the Union Terrace, feet propped on a metal chair, a cup of tea beside her. The sun fell across her bare legs. The blue water of Lake Mendota sparkled, and nearly a hundred sailboats caught the light. She had been reading Camus, and in his bleak philosophy, had found a soulmate. Then a student crossed in front of her, blocking the sun, and the feeling passed. Nothing else came to mind. "I don't need your analysis, Brooker."

"You came to me for help," he said. "Sometimes people don't know what kind of help they need."

She smiled at him, but the smile wasn't friendly. The anger she had felt all day bubbled within her. She clenched her teeth so that she wouldn't yell. "If I needed therapy, *Doctor* Brooker, I wouldn't come to you. I'm sure that your addictive patients must appreciate the way you smoke your pipe. It must give them courage for their own recovery."

"Anger is often the first step out of denial," Brooker said.

"Perhaps." Cammie grabbed the doorknob, turning it as she spoke. "Or perhaps it's the only sane response to your particular version of hooey. I'm sorry I wasted both of our time."

She opened the door, then closed it behind her carefully so that it didn't slam and disturb the receptionist. The girl was typing on a late model IBM PC and didn't look up as Cammie made her way to the front door.

Outside the fresh air blew the stench of bay-scented pipe tobacco off her. She would have to change clothes. Time to return to the hotel anyway. The day had gotten her nowhere. She had some decisions to make.

She got into the car, and drove back to the hotel. The drive across Eugene was easier because she had done it once before. Somehow, going north worked better than driving into the south. The streets were laid out better, the one ways not as confusing as they were climbing into the hills. She passed the Safeway and the two-story office buildings. The greenery pleased her and helped her relax. Strange place, this city. The Hilton and a retirement center near Skinner Butte were the tallest buildings in the area. Most buildings were short and compact, giving the city a trim, low-key look.

When she reached the Hilton, she drove right into the parking garage and took the elevator to the main lobby. Despite the calm she had managed to superimpose on herself in the drive, her hands were shaking. Damn that man for his presumptiveness. He had no right telling her how to live her life.

A package was waiting for her at the front desk. She noted DeeDee's return address, then stuck the package under her arm. The elevator ride was interminable. When she reached her room, she unlocked the door, went inside and tossed the package on the bed.

For the second day in a row, the maid had opened the curtains. The sunlight refreshed her as nothing else could. Cammie kicked off her shoes and sat in the over-stuffed chair beside the window. She closed her eyes and willed the trembling to stop.

The Westrina Center's policies worked. They had worked with her. She was calmer than she had been, better even. Her search for Ben was something she wanted to do, not something she had to do. She wanted to know that the brother she had killed for was happy.

As if she knew what that meant. Brooker had at least been right about that.

Cammie opened her eyes, got up, and picked up the package. It was thick. She ripped the red and blue envelope, then pulled out the files.

A note, in DeeDee's flowing handwriting, said simply that she found nothing in Active, and that she hoped Cammie was well. Cammie studied the note for a long moment. What had happened to DeeDee that placed her at the Center? Did people in Reception need the same qualifications as people in Eradication? Pretty DeeDee, with her sharp tongue and expertly applied makeup. Right now, Cammie would give anything to talk to her face-to-face.

But it would have to wait. Cammie pulled out the first file and started to read. Typical case, over sixteen years ago. Single mother goes crazy, kills all her children by draining their blood. All but the youngest die. The youngest, a year old at the time, spared because his mother was already sated. Neighbors called the police. They arrived to survey the carnage and stake the mother. The infant, after a stay in the hospital, got adopted in the Northwest through the Westrina Center.

Cammie sighed and rubbed her eyes. Her stomach was queasy. She had read case files before, and all of them were personal horror stories, each graphic in its own way, each so tragic that words could barely describe them. Twenty years ago, children had no way out. Even now, it took documentation, a court battle, and pretty damning evidence to rescue a child.

Or the staking of a parent.

In front of the child.

The sun had gone behind a cloud, and the room was cold. Cammie got up to turn on the heat when she noticed the blinking light on her phone. Odd that the desk hadn't given her the message when she arrived. She and the clerk had been so concerned about the package that neither of them thought to check for phone messages.

Cammie dialed the operator and asked for her message.

"A Detective Thornton called. He said it was important."

"She," Cammie corrected reflexively. She hung up, and called the number Thornton had left. It was a direct line into the police department. Cammie went through two officers—not the switchboard—before she got to Thornton.

"Thought you weren't going to call," Thornton said, her voice even deeper through the phone lines.

"I just got the message," Cammie said. "What's up?"

"You get those files?"

Cammie frowned. "Yes."

"Your brother's in there?"

"I don't know. Let me check." She leaned across the bed, and picked up the envelope. It only took a minute of thumbing through the files before she found Ben's. "Yes. But I thought you wanted all of them."

"I do," Thornton said. "But your brother's the important one right now."

Cammie's throat was dry. "Why? What have you got?"

Thornton sighed. "I don't got it. The Seattle police do."

Cammie didn't like Thornton's tone. "Is he okay?"

"He's fine, so far as I know. But that girlfriend of his isn't. They found her in Elliot Bay, body weighted down. She would have disappeared forever if she hadn't snagged on a boat anchor."

"She's dead?" Cammie gripped the receiver, her fingernails digging into the plastic. "Did she drown?"

"Oh, no, honey. She was dead before she hit the water. Something ripped her neck out and drank all her blood, and it sure as hell wasn't the fish."

Cammie lay back on the bed. The room was spinning. She forced herself to breathe.

"You okay?" Thornton asked.

"Have you told her mother yet?"

"Not yet. That's next on my list of pleasant tasks for a sunny afternoon."

"I want to go with you to Seattle."

"I'm not going. This belongs to the Seattle police. I just thought I would send them as much information as I could. Can you get a copy of that file down here ASAP?"

"I don't think Ben did it," Cammie said.

Thornton didn't reply for a moment. In the silence, Cammie could hear two male voices argue about the best microbrewery in the city. "If he didn't," Thornton said softly, "then he might be in the bay, too. I'm sorry, honey. But the information could help."

In. Out. Breathe, Cammie. Breathe. The room's spinning slowed. "You're right," she said. "I'll be there in a few minutes. You got a copy machine?"

"Not one that works. There's a copy shop on Fifth. Easy to get to if you're walking."

"Okay." Cammie hung up without saying good-bye. She was numb. Vampires everywhere. How could Anita think this area was risk free?

Anita. Sarge. It was time for backup. Cammie could no longer face this one alone.

Chapter Twenty-seven

The nest was quiet when Ben let himself in about two hours before sunrise. The front room still smelled of blood and incense, but someone had put away the mattresses and straightened the couch. A single light burned near the hallway entrance. The silence made Ben's hair stand on end.

"Finally."

He whirled in the direction of the voice. Mikos sat on the cane-backed chair near the covered window. His body was hidden in shadow.

"Where have you been?"

Ben felt like he was still in high school and his father was interrogating him. "You said I couldn't bring a new cow here. So I didn't."

"Then you haven't heard the news," Mikos said. His voice had a flatness that Ben had never heard before.

Ben shook his head. The contentment he had felt when he left the hotel vanished. He took a step toward Mikos, unable to see Mikos's face in the shadows. "What happened?"

"The police found your little pregnant girl." Mikos didn't move. His stillness, and his tone, were eerie.

"Candyce?" Ben couldn't keep the fear from his voice. "She was alive, then, after all?"

"Oh, no. She was very dead. The boys dumped her in Elliot Bay and didn't make sure she sank."

A shudder ran through Ben. Candyce. She had been the head cheerleader in high school. Her hair caught in a ponytail, eyes vibrant and alive. She had made the other girls look like they were standing still. Her enthusiasm always caught a crowd, always caught him.

He hadn't wanted her to end up like this.

"The police found her body, then."

"My, we're astute this evening. What were we doing, sniffing garlic?" Mikos stood. His body had a power that Ben had never noted before. Mikos stepped into the light. The veneer of civilization had left his face. His features looked sharper, ragged, more dangerous. "Where were you tonight?"

"I hit a few bars, and then I went to the Sheraton."

"Whose name did you use?"

"Williams.'"

"Whose car?"

"The girl's."

Mikos let out a breath of air. It sounded like a hiss. "She still alive?"

"Yes," Ben said. "And she enjoyed it. She'll think it's some fantasy thing."

"Good." A strand of hair fell across Mikos's forehead. "We're going to dump the Targa and the Williams cards. That identity is gone."

Ben nodded. He was shaking. The police could trace him to Candyce. Anyone could have seen them. "That's not why you waited up for me."

"You're right." Mikos put his hand on Ben's shoulder. His palm felt heavy, as if he were holding Ben down. "The entire incident has me thinking. We haven't been planning your life, Ben, and we need to. We need to control your future better."

"What do you mean?" Ben wanted to pull away from Mikos's grip but knew he didn't dare. The feeling of youth remained.

"We'll give you identification, a new car, and establish a residence for you outside the nest. I want you to find a woman and get her pregnant if you still can. You need an unimpeachable history. Then we'll move forward on our plans for political gain." Mikos's fingers were digging into Ben's collarbone.

"Why now? Because of Candyce?" Ben was confused. The blood he had drunk had left him logy and exhausted. The weight of Candyce's death preyed on him.

"And because of Van." Mikos let go of Ben's shoulder and ran a hand along his neck. He traced Ben's jawline with his thumb, then moved it to Ben's lips. Ben remembered the champagne taste of Mikos's blood and felt a longing for it, even though he was full from his night out. He found it hard to concentrate on Mikos's words.

"We need to get you out of the nest until you and Van settle this thing," Mikos said. "She has more ammunition to use against you with the others now that the cow's body has been discovered. It's better to take you out of here for a while, let the entire incident cool down, then bring you back as a full-fledged hereditary, with, I hope, children."

Ben nibbled Mikos's thumb. His blood was cool, but effervescent and delicious. Compelling. "I don't want to leave," Ben said.

With his free hand, Mikos grabbed Ben's right arm and nipped the wrist. The surge of blood through Ben's own veins made him hard. He didn't want to leave. He belonged here. Like this.

"You may stay if you would like," Mikos said against Ben's skin. "I am merely suggesting a course of action. You only have a short time to get a cow pregnant—a few months, maybe a few years. You need to focus on that first, and then we begin our political work."

Ben moved his own mouth to Mikos's wrist and bit. More blood, thin but bubbly, traveled into his throat. He wasn't sure who was seducing whom, whose power flowed the strongest. "I don't want to wait," Ben said. "I want to begin now."

Mikos sealed the wound on Ben's wrist, grabbed Ben's jaw and moved his mouth away from the blood. Then he licked his own blood off Ben's lips. Their tongues met, and Ben felt a sexual need like he hadn't felt since that first night with Candyce. Then Mikos pulled away and laughed. "You are young, aren't you? Ah, Benjamin, my friend. You have a lifetime. You have a dozen lifetimes. The safer we play things, the better we will be. Do you understand?"

Ben ran a hand over his face. He did understand. Mikos was seducing him. Mikos was still the stronger of the two of them. But if Ben got away from the nest, he would be able to work on his own powers without interference. He would come back a virgin no longer, and he would control the nest. He would also get rid of Van.

He took a deep breath to control himself, but there was no denying the throbbing in his groin. Better to let Mikos think he dominated entirely. Ben unzipped his pants, setting himself free. "Let's finish it," he said, allowing his voice to be as breathless as he felt.

Mikos's grin had a joy Ben had never seen before. He spat on his hand, then grabbed Ben's penis and played with it, while biting into Ben's carotid artery. Ben's orgasm was immediate and powerful, and it continued, like the cow's had that night, long after he was dry.

Finally Mikos let him go. "I still rule the nest," he said.

Ben was weak and wasted, but the feeling he had had after the first time Mikos had fucked him was not there. Although he could feel Mikos's power, Ben still managed to retain a small portion of himself. "I'll do whatever you want," he lied.

"Good," Mikos said. He was still stroking Ben as they spoke. Ben was so sensitive that the sensation was almost painful. "I want you to leave tonight. It's best if Van doesn't see you again."

Ben nodded. He didn't want to go, to leave Mikos, but

he didn't want to remain close to Van either. The idea made sense to him. "I have no income of my own."

Mikos let Ben go. Then Mikos reached into the back pocket of his jeans and pulled out a money clip. He tossed it to Ben. The clip was full of cash. Ben flipped through it. The wad of bills was thick, and all of them appeared to be five hundreds. "You did some work for me a few months ago," Mikos said. "I never paid you for it. Use this as your stake. If you run out, you can always help me again."

The killing. Ben stuffed the money in his pocket. Mikos was telling him something. He could make money as a hired assassin. Or he could do something more creative. But Mikos was sending him out of the nest.

Second rule. Protect the nest at all costs. Mikos was seeing Ben as both an asset and a threat. Mikos was covering all angles.

"Thanks," Ben said. The sexual charge was dissipating as Mikos moved away from him. Such control. And it was only a small percentage of the control Ben had now over his cows. His control would grow as time went by.

"Find a place to live first, then a woman, then worry about money," Mikos said. "And stay in touch."

"I will," Ben said.

Mikos flicked on one more light. The room became brighter, the dirt from the night's party—the cigarette butts, the blood on the carpet—was suddenly visible. "And Ben, how did that cow find you?"

"Steve sent her to me. The cops won't follow that trail."

"Fortunately. The lure of the Keg will probably be too much for them. Still, I don't like it that you're so easy to find." Mikos stood. His eyes were dark, his lips full. Ben felt the longing surge through him again. He hadn't realized, until this moment, that Mikos had hooked him, just as Ben had hooked the cows. It would be good to get away.

Understanding the other side of that lust would probably make it easier for him to use it. He would remember this feeling. "I don't like being easy to find either," Ben said. "I warned Steve not to let anyone contact me here again."

"Good. Let's hope the warning sticks." Mikos glanced at his watch. "The sun will be up soon."

Ben nodded, glad for the dismissal. He went back to his room, slipped out of the wet clothes, and pulled on some jeans. He took a canvas bag and filled it with more jeans, underwear, socks, shirts, and one suit. Then he hurried back out to the front room.

Mikos hadn't moved. Ben slipped by him without touching him. To touch him meant that Ben wouldn't leave until the next night.

"Remember," Mikos said, so close that Ben could feel his breath, "when you're out on your own, any mistake you make jeopardizes no one but yourself."

Ben hadn't thought of that. He had made mistakes in the nest and the nest had covered for him. Now he had to cover for himself. His throat was dry. "I'll remember," he said.

Chapter
Twenty-eight

The late afternoon sunlight filtered through the double-paned windows, illuminating the streaks on the ancient tile floor. Eliason pushed open the double doors and walked into the Westrina Center. His shoulders tightened slightly, as they always did when he came here. He associated the place with problems and injured children, both of which set him on edge. The poorly designed air conditioning, which made the interior a freezer, didn't help.

He walked past the glassed-in reception area and stopped at DeeDee's oak desk. "Anita leave some files for me?" he asked.

DeeDee looked up. Her hair was orange this week and frizzed around a red bandanna. She wore matching red overalls, and the look—which would have been grotesque on any other woman—suited her. She grabbed four file folders off the corner of her desk and handed them to him.

He had never seen her so quiet. Usually she gabbed at him from the moment he entered the door. "What's going on?" he asked.

DeeDee slid back her chair. "You want some coffee? I do. I promised the girls in the back morning buns, and I've been forgetting every day. If you drive me in that great car of yours, I can be back before my break is over."

He frowned. He really wanted to see Sarge, to discuss little Lee Anderson's parents whom the eradicators couldn't find, but he supposed the meeting could wait. He had set no definite time with Sarge, and she had said she would be in the office until eight or nine that night.

"You just want a ride in my car."

DeeDee laughed. If he hadn't seen the lines beneath her eyes, he would have thought the laugh genuine. "Maybe I want to ride something else, Doctor," she said, waving at the women in the back as she went out the door. The office was used to the flirting. DeeDee and Eliason acted that way all the time. In truth, though, they didn't interest each other. After one disastrous date years before, they decided that they enjoyed friendship more.

The air got warmer as they went through the double doors. The steam heat of a hot June day coated them the minute they stepped outside. Eliason hadn't even been inside long enough to acclimatize himself to the chill, but it didn't matter. The heat overpowered him anyway.

He walked around the rosebushes and the still-green grass to his car. He opened the passenger side for DeeDee and then let himself in. The leather smelled hot, but the interior still contained a bit of the air-conditioned coolness. He started the car and put a hand over the vent, pleased that the air conditioning was still on chill.

"You really want to go to the Ovens?" he asked as DeeDee pulled her door shut.

"May as well," she said. "I don't want coffee though. It's too damn hot."

He pulled out of the parking lot and headed for Shorewood, the nearest bakery. The car purred under his hand. The heat didn't affect it at all. "Okay. I know you're not here for my great personality. What's up?"

"You hear from Cammie at all?" DeeDee asked.

The little twitch of nervousness returned. Eliason had to work at looking relaxed. "I haven't heard from her since she left. Why?"

"Stupid girl." DeeDee bit her lower lip, smearing her lipstick, something he had never seen her do. "Can I talk to you? Completely confidential? No Anita, no Sarge, no nobody?"

Since Cammie had left, he had spent most nights pacing his apartment, glaring at the phone. He had never really followed through on the relationship with her, and after the dinner at the Imperial Palace, he suspected she never wanted to see him again. Still, he wanted her to call. He wanted to know she was all right. He even called his travel agent and priced tickets to Oregon, just in case he wanted to find her. He stopped short of booking them, though. If Cammie wanted to talk with him, she would.

"I'll file the information under doctor-patient relations and no one will get it out of me," he said. He shifted slightly in his seat and braced his wrist on the wheel, steering with his arm instead of his hand. They emerged off Old Middleton Road onto University, and the traffic was staggering.

"Cammie called a few days ago and wanted information on children from the inactive files. Most of the names she gave me had files over twenty years old with no updates. I sent her a bunch of inactive files. But there were four active files, all with current eradication investigations proceeding against them. I kept those."

"DeeDee—"

She held up a hand to stop him from going on. But he could feel a flush building. She had asked him for confidentiality, but she didn't respect the privacy of others.

"The files were *old*," she said, "and there wasn't much Cammie could get from them except history of the traumas. She had already spoken to the kids' parents and knew where they got adopted out. It seems all of them had disappeared, like Ben."

Eliason turned the Ferrari into the parking lot in front of the Ovens. He left the car running. He didn't like the way this was developing. Cammie had gotten herself into something, something that might hurt her. "What was in the active files?"

"Investigation reports," DeeDee said. "All four adoptees had come back here, and all four are being investigated for vampiric connections. It seems they wanted to be part of an established community. Jeremiah Ellis, the oldest, is scheduled for eradication review in two weeks."

Eliason sighed. A woman came out of the restaurant with a white baked goods box balanced on one hand. She put the box in the Ford Bronco parked next to the Ferrari and backed out, narrowly missing the Ferrari's right side. "You haven't told Cammie?"

"I was going to today, but she was really upset when she called."

He sat up, his entire body rigid, no longer pretending relaxation. He should have kept closer tabs. Being without her, being without knowledge of her, was driving him crazy. That she had contacted DeeDee more than once bothered him. He had always thought he was closer to her.

Probably not anymore, after all the things he had said that last night. "She called?"

"Yeah, at the Center, so I knew she was upset. She wanted Whitney. When I told her he was on an eradication, she made me promise to get him to call right away." DeeDee's hands were shaking. She had now bitten off most of the lipstick on her lower lip. "But that's not the part that got me upset. She sounded funny, and when I asked her what was wrong, she said that Ben's girlfriend Candyce was found dead in Seattle. Obvious vampire killing. Obvious. Then her voice broke and she hung up, and she didn't even leave a number where I could have Whitney reach her."

"Then why aren't you still there, waiting for her to call back?" Eliason watched her out of the corner of his eye. The sun reflected off her frizzed hair, leaving part of her face shaded. The exhaustion made her look bruised. He would have been there. He would have haunted the phone until he heard from her again.

"Because I wanted to talk to you, Brett. Here's the weird part. I found a bunch of letters that those parents sent Anita. They pleaded with her for information on the kids, and she never answered. They even got an attorney to write, and no response."

"That's not odd." Confidentiality often excluded the parents. He wanted DeeDee off this trail. He wanted to hear more about Cammie.

"Yes, it is." DeeDee ran a thumb over her long, polished nails. "When those letters started coming, we already had active files on two of the kids. Maybe if Anita had written back that early, something could have been done, the investigation could have been called off, and the Ellis boy wouldn't be up for eradication."

A couple came out of the restaurant, laughing. The woman's arm was around the man's waist, and they kissed before going to separate cars. He had never kissed Cammie. Odd that he would be so tied to her. He looked away. "Westrina Center policy states that a vampire can't be rehabilitated. It might have been kinder of Anita to let the parents think the kids were missing rather than in trouble."

"It's not her decision, though, is it?" DeeDee leaned her head back.

There were no rules. The Center had been in the unique position for the past forty years of defining its own place in the world. Anita's work was unusual. The fact that she sometimes took liberties with it should surprise no one.

But Eliason said nothing. He had made it a policy to remain close-mouthed about his misgivings. That way, he could continue working for the Center and helping the children. "The Center has had a successful adoption program for twenty years."

"Yeah," DeeDee said, her voice tired. "And now that

those kids are becoming adults, they disappear or turn up with the same problems their parents had. That's not successful, Brett."

"You're only basing that on a few letters."

"No," she said. "I'm not. I went through Anita's desk last night."

He turned, shocked.

She shrugged. "Sometimes secretaries can go places no other employees can. Anyway, inside was an entire drawer of letters like those, from parents all over the West Coast. What if the program didn't work? What if those kids are all vampires?"

A chill ran down Eliason's back. Cammie. She was just old enough to be at risk. In fact, from his informal studies, she was a prime candidate. She had already spent too much time killing.

He bit his lower lip. Maybe he should have done something sooner. He and Anita had gone around and around over eradication when he first opened his practice. He refused to treat anyone on the squad, and in fact, refused for years to enter any part of the Center except the Children's Wing. "You're making too much of this," he said, and shut off the ignition. "Go on inside and get those buns. I'll drive you back to the Center."

DeeDee shot him an angry glance, but got out of the car. She adjusted her bandanna before she pulled open the large restaurant door. He wasn't fooling her. She obviously knew that her news was upsetting him. But he had to think his position through before speaking up. He couldn't risk his work with the kids. Just this morning, he had made a breakthrough with little Mary Jo. She had sobbed in his arms. Sometimes a vampire's child never learned to cry.

Behind Eliason, the traffic whooshed. A child laughed outside the neighboring store. The children were adopted out or worked in eradication. The eradication program worked for some; he had seen it, and worked with the counselors sponsoring it. The adult children were never completely whole, but they were at least able to function and to live interesting lives after they left the Center. Some, like Whitney, preferred to remain, to keep the anger under control, but others went on to be lawyers and doctors and teachers.

Of course, no one knew what happened as the years went on. Most of the known ACVs were no older than thirty-five.

And no one knew what happened to the adopted kids. Cammie's brother had been three when he was adopted out, more than old enough to absorb the life patterns of his old man. The adopted children followed the pattern of other adoptions in the country. The older the child, the less attractive it was to new parents. Infants went first, and children over five were rarely considered.

But studies were showing that children remembered those early years on a deep, nonverbal level. Traumatic experiences remained imprinted. And being raised by a vampire was traumatic, no matter how old the child was.

Eliason gripped the wheel with his right hand, his fingers sliding in the leather grooves. He had been just like all the others, believing that a child who had escaped the situation had escaped the problems and the pain. He knew better. He had seen too many battered wives, too many alcoholic men, to think that childhood problems stopped when the child left home. Sometimes the problems were just beginning.

Cammie. He had let her walk alone and unarmed into her past.

DeeDee pulled the door open and slid in. The buns smelled rich and warm.

"Cammie say why she wanted Whitney?" he asked as she slammed the door.

"No." DeeDee looked at him. Her eyes were wide on

her too-pale face. "But it's not hard to figure. He was her partner, and the girlfriend was found exsanguinated."

"Eradication," Eliason said.

DeeDee nodded. "Let's just hope Cammie doesn't do anything stupid."

Chapter Twenty-nine

i

"I realize it's late," Ben said, rubbing the sleep from his eyes. The thin plastic hotel phone barely fit between his chin and shoulder. The thin blankets and the patterned spread were barely enough to keep him warm. "I'm afraid I work until nearly ten P.M. each night."

He leaned against the pine headboard and squinted at the window. The Red Lion had blackout curtains, which was one of the reasons he chose the hotel—that, and the fact it was only a short drive from the nest. Light trickled in around the edge of the curtain. He would have to get up and fix it, but sometimes that was even more hazardous than leaving the crack alone.

The realtor on the other end of the phone was cutting him no slack. "I do not work that late, Mr. Norris. Perhaps a showing before you go to work?"

"Not unless you're up before dawn," he said.

"My goodness," she said. "The job is all consuming."

"For three weeks," he said. "Then I get two off. Makes it a bitch, though, when I have to find a place to live while working so hard."

"You weren't evicted, were you, Mr. Norris?" That was the second time she had asked the question. Obviously his first answer had not convinced her. He repressed a sigh.

"No," he said, letting his exhaustion seep into his voice. "If you must know the truth, my wife and I are getting a divorce. It's rather sudden. I'll tell you the details if you would like."

"Oh, no," The realtor's tone finally had some warmth. "I'm so sorry, Mr. Norris. I didn't realize that times were so awkward for you. Of course I can show you the house. I'll just inform the owners that we'll be arriving late due to your schedule."

"Thank you," he said. He got the address from her and hung up. Wretched woman. She was probably single too, and she would want a drink afterward, and—

Maybe that wouldn't be so bad. He would have to see. If she was young enough, and fertile, then the trip might be worth more than the house.

He rubbed a hand over his face. That had been his last phone call, and his only appointment. Finding a place to live was the most important thing he could do. Then he would worry about money. Mikos had handed him $50,000 in $500 bills, but that wouldn't last a forever, and he certainly didn't want to go back to Mikos for money. If he could help it. The realization that Mikos was controlling him like a cow had made Ben even more leery of returning.

If nothing else, he could sell the car. Mikos had given him the Lexus.

He wouldn't worry about it now. He had a house to view, and perhaps a woman to seduce. If he planned it right, he would seduce a number of them, and take the children after they were born. The nest would love to raise a group of hereditaries. Then he would keep the woman and the child who pleased him the most. He would have his own little family, something to come home to.

Like he could have had with Candyce.

He slid back under the covers and closed his eyes. Why didn't people do business at night? Things seemed so much more sensible then.

ii

A few hours later, he pulled the Lexus into the dead-end street in Olympia. The homes were new: most still had dirt for lawns. Some, along a gravel drive, were still under construction. Sleep in the daytime would be difficult.

But not impossible. A young forest graced the right end of the development, and the road belonged solely to the new homes. The house with the for-rent sign sat at the very edge of the row of homes, with all but the street side secluded from the neighbors.

Perfect. They would be able to watch him come and go, but not see him inside the house.

The lights in the house were on, and a car was in the driveway. A woman came to the door. Her blue business suit accented her Rubenesque figure, and the low heels did nothing for her legs. He smiled at her. If she wore a low-cut evening gown that revealed her décolletage, and high spiked heels, she would turn heads. She had probably never thought of that.

As he hurried up the walk, he held out his hand. "Thank you for coming so late, Glenda," he said.

She took his hand and smiled at him as they stepped into the light. Too much red lipstick and eyeliner a bit too thick. She had reapplied it just before he arrived. But her face wasn't bad. Her kind of beauty was just out of fashion.

"I'm sorry to hear about your situation," she said. "I went through that a year ago, and it's not easy."

He nodded, trying to look properly upset.

The house still had the new-glue smell from the freshly laid carpet. The walls had no scuff marks. The windows overlooked the backyard. They were too small for a house this size. They should have covered half the wall. Instead, they were the size of bathroom windows.

Glenda caught him looking at the windows. "I warned you they were tiny," she said. "The problem with this house, as you can probably tell, is that it is dark. But it's spacious and no one has ever lived in it."

"Then why did you have to inform the owners that you were coming late?"

She smiled. "Sometimes men use a late-night showing as an excuse to get a woman alone. If they think that other people are going to be there, they don't come."

He nodded. How logical. He hadn't thought of it. "Who are the owners?"

"A couple from Seattle. They own and rent several properties in Olympia. They made a mistake with this one, though. They built it, not realizing that they needed to have some input in the design. Apparently they told the contractors to do it according to the specs, which included those windows."

He put a hand on her arm. Her sleeve was warm, even though the evening was cool. "You don't have to apologize for the windows," he said. "I won't be here much during the day. I wouldn't rent it for the view."

She nodded. He explored the kitchen—with appliances so new they still bore their energy-efficient tags—and the sunken dining room. The wall begged for an opening to a deck, but none had been built in. The house did have an air of cheapness that a little more care would have dissipated.

The bedrooms were even darker, with narrow windows up near the ceiling. One room, off the bathroom, had no windows at all. "What's this?" he asked.

"Oh," she said, "You can use it as storage. It was supposed to be a walk-in closet off the master bedroom, but it ended up too large."

It was perfect. A bed would fit in there with no problem at all. With the door closed, and another bedroom set in the master bedroom, no one would figure out where he really slept. "The price you quoted me is what they want?" he asked.

She nodded.

"And it's available now, obviously."

"Yes," she said. Her voice sounded strained. She probably needed the commission.

"Good," he said. "I'll take it. Have you got a lease?"

"We do have to check references—"

He sighed. "You're going to find problems. The wife froze all my accounts and has destroyed both of our credit. You can call my place of employment, though."

"We need a valid application, Mr. Norris—"

He reached into his back pocket and pulled out his wallet. "I was planning to pay for the first three months with cash. Would that help?" He counted out six of Mikos's bills.

She was staring at the money. "One would think you made a living illegally, what with the car and the cash." She giggled, so he would take it as a joke.

"That's why I said you could call my employer." He pressed the money into her hand. "You know how it is. I managed to get my savings out before the wife took them, but I haven't had time to open a new account."

She bit her lower lip. Her gaze scanned him, obviously checking out the quiet expense of his clothing, remembering the car, and noting that more bills were in his wallet. She pulled an application out of her blazer pocket and set it on the counter. "Let's just fill this out for form's sake, Mr. Norris. We'll need a damage deposit, but otherwise, I would say you should be able to bring your stuff over tomorrow."

"What stuff there is," he mumbled. He took the offered pen, and filled out the sheet. He put Mikos's number down as his place of employment. Someone there would lie for him. David Norris was one of the nest's names.

She wrote out a receipt for the cash, then wandered around the kitchen, opening cupboards and running her hand along the sideboards, pretending not to watch as he worked. When he finished, he handed her the sheet. "Hope it works," he said.

"Me, too."

He glanced around the kitchen. It was a start. He would show Mikos and the others. He would show them that he could survive as well as they could—better because he had to make his own way. "Listen," he said, running a hand through his hair. "Let me buy you some coffee, for keeping you out this late."

The naked hope in her eyes shocked him. She looked away, and her voice carried none of that desperation when she spoke. "I'd love that."

"I'm not familiar with Olympia. Is there anything around here?"

"There's an IHOP not far from here."

"Coffee shop? Anything nicer?"

She shook her head. "It's too late, unless you want to go to a bar."

A bar would set the wrong mood. He wanted her to feel his interest. From her reaction, no one had been interested in a long time. "Come on," he said, taking her elbow and escorting her into the hallway. "I'll follow you."

They shut off the lights, and she locked the lock box. He escorted her to her car, and reassessed her earning potential. She drove a late model Paseo, red if he could judge the color in the dark. She was probably doing well for herself at her job.

Just not in her personal life.

Perfect.

He got into the Lexus and waited for her to back out of the driveway. As he followed her to the restaurant, he surveyed the neighborhood. More housing developments rose near his. No one would live in them for months. Then he would be at the center of a suburban neighborhood, complete with children and networking neighbors. He would have to decide, at that point, if he wanted to be the eccentric yuppie at the end of the block or if he wanted to move to more suitable surroundings.

There was time to make that decision.

The IHOP restaurant was an older version, done in the hideous blue and orange design he remembered from his childhood. She parked on the side, and through the wide windows he could see some old men sitting at a large booth, and a young couple hunched over a shared plate of ice cream. Glenda waited for him to get out of his car and lock it. They walked inside together.

A permanent haze of cigarette smoke made the air foggy. Coffee and fried meats added to the restaurant odor. The waitress led them to a cracked booth away from the other patrons.

"Coffee?" she asked.

Ben nodded for both of them. He looked at the menu, not at all tempted by the pictures of food. He had forgotten what most of it tasted like. But Van had once told him that he could taste anything, and so he would.

"Want a dessert?" he asked.

She patted her nipped waist. "I don't think I should."

"Nonsense," he said, with a smile. If she became permanent, he would like her to be well fed. That way, when the wasting started, it would look like a diet. He reached across the table and cupped her cheek. The softness of her skin surprised him. "You're really beautiful, you know. Don't let fashion dictate what you think of yourself."

She flushed again, unable to meet his gaze.

"How about we split something?" he asked. He pointed at an oversized ice cream dessert. "Come on. I can't eat it on my own."

Her smile returned, shy, a young schoolgirl's on her first date. "All right," she said.

When the waitress returned with their coffees, Ben ordered for them. He asked for two spoons, although he doubted he would make much use of his. "So you been on your own for a while," he said. "Does it get easier?"

"Oh, yes." She added two small containers of cream to her coffee and a packet of artificial sugar. "The first six months are the hardest, I think. After that, you kinda get used to being on your own."

He leaned back against the booth and put his feet on the seat beside her. He cupped his coffee mug in one hand, but did not drink. "Yeah," he said. "I've heard that before. But the hard thing for me is that I wanted kids. That's what the disagreement started over. Kids."

Glenda took a small sip of her coffee. When she set the mug down, a lipstick stain marred the rim. "You're young. It's not like you have a clock or anything."

"I'm not as young as I look," Ben said. He brought the mug to his lips, rolled the bitter liquid around on his tongue, and made himself swallow. God, he used to like that stuff? "And besides, there is a clock. The magazines just haven't written about it."

Glenda grinned. "You mean like male menopause?"

He shook his head. "I want to play with my kid. I want to enjoy him, have enough energy to be an interesting father. My dad was in his forties when I was born, and I never got to play with him. I want my kid to play with me."

"Yeah," Glenda said, and sighed. "I just want a kid."

Ben's body became rigid. No tied tubes. No distractions. Probably a pill that he could throw away or a diaphragm that they could forget to use. "You got time yet, don't you?"

"Oh, yeah," she said. "I just haven't had much interest." Then she blushed. "I shouldn't tell you that, I suppose."

The waitress brought their ice cream. It sloshed over the bowl onto the saucer. Fake strawberry sauce was too bright to be blood, but Ben pretended anyway. He took a large spoonful and shoved it in his mouth before he could think about it. The cold, cloying sweetness made him gag. Force of will prevented his disgust from showing.

Glenda took a large bite as well. She looked away from him, as if her revelation made her less of a person.

"I'm interested," he said, careful to keep his voice low. And he was. She was attractive enough and looked strong. Besides that, she was unattached and wanted children.

"Yeah," she said, her voice heavy with sarcasm. "A handsome man like you."

The waitress passed with a tray of steaming food. She stopped at the table behind them. Ben hadn't even realized anyone was sitting there. "You don't have a lot of confidence in yourself."

She stood her spoon up in the ice cream. "My husband—my ex-husband—took to calling me the fat pig. It doesn't do a lot for making a woman feel attractive."

"Surely you were built like this when he married you." Ben was feeling light-headed. The food was having an odd effect on him. He sat up and hoped the feeling would go away.

"I was," she said. "But we were young. He was just happy to get one with big tits. Then he wanted me to lose weight, look like those enhanced models. Skinny everywhere but up top. He didn't understand when I tried to explain to him that it didn't work that way."

Ben had never had a woman with big breasts and soft skin. It would be interesting. He took her hand. The blood rushed through her veins. Saliva formed in his mouth and, to his surprise, he had grown hard. "I think you're beautiful," he said again.

He wanted her. He wanted her right here. He moved forward, and the dizziness hit him again. Something was wrong. He wanted to take this slow, and his body was moving too fast.

"Thank you," she said.

He leaned back, then looked behind him. The woman in the other booth was reading a romance novel and eating spaghetti. With bread. Garlic bread. Good God, he was being poisoned.

"You done?" he asked.

Glenda nodded. He pulled out his wallet and put a twenty on the tab, then led her outside. Once the cool air hit him, the headache in the back of his skull dissipated. He was still aroused.

One kiss. She wanted it too. One kiss and they would be bound. He would get the house and she would come when he wanted her to. One kiss.

He leaned into her without thinking. Her soft body against his made the arousal even stronger. He wanted to touch that skin, to be inside her, to feel those over-sized breasts against his flesh. He kissed her with all the passion he felt. She responded hungrily. He slipped his hands into her suit jacket, felt the silkiness of her blouse, the ridge of her bra. He disengaged his mouth from hers and trailed down her neck, shoving the jacket back and nipping the skin of her collarbone. Small nick. In the morning it would look like a hickey.

Her blood was salty and warm, with a touch of sweetness. God, he could suck all night. Her hands slid into his pants and around the front. Behind him someone laughed.

She froze. He stood up. He was still dizzy, but not as bad. She was staring at him with half-opened eyes. Two teenagers stood to one side—boys.

"Why don't you take her home, man. It's cold out here," one of them said.

Home. Bed. Slow. What was wrong with him?

That garlic. It worked like alcohol. No inhibitions at all. Mikos had warned him of that, but Ben had never experienced it. He had to get a grip on himself. He needed control if he was going to protect himself.

Garlic. Such a small amount too.

"I'm sorry," he said, pushing the hair from Glenda's face. She really was pretty. Much nicer than Candyce. He would treat her right. Maybe she would retain enough of a brain to be more than a brood mare for him. "I didn't mean to embarrass you in public like that."

She looked away. The shy girl had returned. "You didn't do anything. I was the one—"

He put a finger to her lips, longing to follow it with his mouth. The arousal was still there, so strong that it might overpower him at any moment. "I do want you, Glenda," he said. "But not like this. I want more than one night. Tell you what. I'll pick up the keys from you tomorrow late, and then we'll go furniture shopping at the mall. It'll give us a chance to talk, to be together. What do you say?"

Her smile was thin. She didn't believe him. He could have her now if he wanted. But that wouldn't work. He needed that house worse, and she had to keep her job, at least for a while. "Okay," she said.

"Good," he said. "How about I pick you up at your office about nine?"

"Nine?" she said. "That doesn't give us much time. They close at ten."

He shrugged. "I have to work."

"Oh, yeah."

He slipped his arm around her and walked her to her car. The scent of blood on her collar made him itch. Tomorrow, he promised himself. And not under the influence of anything. She climbed into the driver's seat. He leaned over and kissed her, meaning to give her a light peck, but the kiss became something deeper again. If the door hadn't been leaning into his side, making him feel a slight pain, he would have crawled into the car with her.

Control, Ben. Control.

He came up for air, the warmth of her blood on his tongue. "Nine," he said. He would be able to handle the twilight.

She nodded. "I'll see you then." Her voice shook. He closed her door so that he wouldn't touch her again. She backed up too quickly, and drove out of the parking lot with more abandon than she had had before. He swallowed. The excess saliva in his mouth was making him nervous.

He hadn't had a reaction like that since his first night at the nest. Out of control, a slave to his body. And to think just the night before, he had wanted the oblivion of alcohol. He had gotten it without really trying. Someday, he would take a woman on garlic. It promised to be a heady, overwhelming experience.

But one he chose, not one he stumbled into. He took a deep breath, then another, waiting for his body to settle down before he went to the car. He wanted some control before he hit that singles bar he had seen on the drive over. He didn't want another corpse to deal with, just enough nourishment to carry him through to the next day.

Glenda. Already a prospect, and a good one. He hoped to hell she was fertile. He needed all the opportunities he could get.

Chapter Thirty

i

DeFreeze and Garity ran a small but successful private detective business in downtown Portland. It took Cammie most of the afternoon to reach them by phone, and another hour to find them. Their offices were part of a mirrored high rise off the Columbia River. The interior was done in a calm, studied blue with plaques, commendations, and letters of praise decorating the wall. A receptionist, who doubled as a secretary and office manager, blocked the way to the back. If Cammie had had more time, she would have picked a company whose offices were a little seedier, a company with a little more hunger and fewer commendations. A company whose owner didn't look like he spent most of his time behind a desk.

Jason DeFreeze had black hair going silver at the temples, a face flushed with too much food and alcohol, and a suit that cost Cammie's monthly salary. His office overlooked the river, and most of Portland.

"Let me get this straight," DeFreeze said, templing his fingers and rocking his leather office chair. "You want two of our men to accompany you to a bar and then stake out your hotel room in case someone shows up."

"Yes." Cammie sat on the edge of the royal blue chair, determined not to let him intimidate her. It wasn't working. "I'll pay your normal fee, plus any retainers."

"This is very short notice."

"I know that," she said through her teeth. "I can go elsewhere."

In fact, she wanted to. She had approached DeFreeze and Garity because she couldn't reach Whitney by phone, and she didn't have time to check the credentials of any other detective agency.

"No need," he said. "We have two men who can work with you tonight, and another two who can relieve them in the morning. It all just seems odd to me, Miss Timms."

She stood, unable to sit in that sterile room any longer. "I thought you people were used to oddities."

"So we are." He leaned back and the chair squeaked. "I worry about your involvement. Why don't you let us find your brother?"

"Because you've been searching for him for weeks. I have had better luck."

The ease in his body fled at her tone. Two spots of color decorated DeFreeze's cheeks. "Oh?"

"My brother is Benjamin Sadler. His parents hired your firm some time ago, or don't you remember?"

"The Sadler case has been particularly difficult."

"I'm sure it has." Cammie put her hands on the desk and faced DeFreeze. "Let me be frank with you, Mr. De-Freeze. I am singularly unimpressed with your firm, and if I had more time, I would go elsewhere. I do a much better job by myself. Unfortunately, I need backup tonight, and I think that, despite your deficits as a private detective firm, you can provide me with muscle. Now if I'm wrong, please direct me to someone who can help me."

"We can help you," DeFreeze said. He was subdued. "We will help in any way we can."

"Good," Cammie said. "I have a check for your retainer. I will pay the balance when I come out of all this. Alive."

DeFreeze opened his mouth as if to warn her, but she raised an eyebrow and he said nothing else. He accepted her check and then buzzed the intercom. "Send in Norm and John."

Cammie sat on the arm of the chair. She had let De-Freeze have the upper hand because of his expensive office and obvious success. But she needed results if she was going to find Ben, and DeFreeze had not proven those, in this case.

Two men entered the room. Both were in their early twenties. One was lean and wiry, his arms corded with muscle. The other had the look of a traditional bruiser: tall, muscular, and broad. DeFreeze introduced the lean, wiry one as John and the muscular one as Norm.

"Have you worked with vampires before?" Cammie asked.

"They're experienced, Miss Timms." DeFreeze said.

She didn't look at him. She kept her eyes on the two men. They were studying their boss. One of the men had gone pale. "You've just observed, haven't you?" she asked. "You haven't gone into a nest. You haven't staked anyone."

"You're not asking for a staking, are you?" DeFreeze said. "It's illegal in Oregon."

"I'm asking for protection," Cammie snapped. She sighed. She would have a lot of work to do with them in the next few hours.

Around midnight, John drove the battered brown station wagon to a parking spot across the street from the Keg. The neighborhood had not improved. In fact, Cammie's memory of it had been charitable. Winos sprawled on the sidewalk and derelict cars littered the alley. A faint scent of garbage filtered through the open window.

Norm sat in the back. Neither man had spoken since Cammie had gone through Sarge's eradication routine with them. "You got everything?" Cammie asked.

John patted the duffel beside him. "Put on the garlic when you leave, then decorate the car with it. Time the meeting carefully. If you haven't come out in a half an hour, go in, garlic blazing."

"With stakes," Norm said. His nervousness would be an asset. He had looked decidedly queasy when she discussed the difficulties of staking an awake vampire.

"That's right. Now be careful. Essentially you're drugging them. The secret is to have enough garlic to incapacitate rather than make them lose their inhibitions. If you come in too late, I could be dead. If I die, you don't get paid. Is that clear?" She probably didn't need to be that harsh, but she had never been in a situation like this with unreliable backup. Whitney would have needed no special instructions. Whitney would have been helping her with the plan.

Her mouth was dry. She wasn't sure if this would work, but it was the best idea she could come up with. If her brother had not been promiscuous, then maybe he would investigate her claim out of sheer curiosity.

If he had freedom of movement.

Even if he didn't, someone had sent him after Candyce. The trick had to work.

Cammie checked her ponytail, then smoothed her t-shirt over her jeans. She got out of the station wagon and hurried across the street, glancing on either side to see if she was noticed.

If she was, she had no clue. The winos didn't move, and no one emerged from the sex shop next to the bar. Her hands were shaking. Half an hour, guys, she thought. Please pay attention.

She went down the filthy concrete steps and pulled open the heavy oak door. The smell of rotting blood hit her first, followed by a musky scent she had never encountered before. Incense overlaid it all with a sweetness that turned her stomach and sent a charge down to her groin.

It took a moment for her eyes to adjust to the darkness. An old Mr. Mister song blared over the stereo system, and provided the only noise in the room. Red-colored lamps graced the tables and illuminated the drugged faces of the humans waiting their turn. The bartender looked at her, his eyes clear. He knew she didn't belong.

Laughter tinkled out of the back. A woman, swaying with desire, grabbed at the man who had led her out of a side room. Vampire and his catch. Cammie's nausea was growing worse.

She walked over to the bar. The faint scent of beer reached her. Some of the patrons held a draft. But no liquor sat on the shelves. Only a large cash register, its drawer open and brimming with money. The bartender was a large man with meaty arms. He wore a butcher's apron over his brown slacks and flannel shirt.

"First time cover charge is fifty bucks," the bartender said over the music.

The price was higher than she'd expected. But, she supposed, if a cop came in here with the thought of closing the place down, he probably wouldn't get out alive. "I'm not here for the entertainment," she said. "I have a message for Steve."

"Steve?"

"His roommate told me I could find him here. Please," she said. "It's very important."

"Yeah, sure." The bartender pulled a tap handle and filled a mug with cold beer. He set it in front of Cammie. "You know how many guys named Steve are in here tonight?"

"How many are regulars?" she asked. "How many have been coming here for years?"

"Years." The bartender squinted at her. "The drink's on the house."

"I haven't paid the cover yet," she said.

The bartender studied her for a moment. His eyes were sunken into his round face. Small lines dotted his mouth, like an inexperienced artist's attempt at shadowing. "No," he said. "I guess you haven't."

A chill ran down her back. He knew she wasn't going to host one of his vampires. Unless he forced her. "Steve," she prompted.

The bartender took the beer back and poured it in the sink behind the bar. "The one you want is in the vampire's circle. He likes 'em small and busty, like you. He should enjoy himself."

"If he does," she said. "You won't make your fifty dollar cover."

"If he does," the bartender said. "You won't care if I take your clothes, let alone your money."

The chill had grown to a shudder. She gave the bartender a saucy smile, then walked around the tables, and down the stairs to the vampire's circle.

In the corner, near an unused fireplace, two women worked on a man. One sucked his neck while the other covered his groin. The man had a listless, glazed look to his face. Occasionally, he would press one of the women's heads even harder into his flesh.

A slender woman sat in a high-backed chair by the wall. A man walked over to her, and she took his arm, sinking her teeth into the wrist. He cried out in pleasure and slid a hand to his own groin.

Cammie felt an odd detachment, as if her mind were separate from her body. She was disgusted and lost inside a wall within herself. Yet her nipples were hard, and her body trembled. She felt the arousal and tried to ignore it, thinking perhaps that it was part of the air—that they had released a chemical that triggered sexual response.

She didn't want to think that the response was hers alone.

Directly in front of Cammie, a naked woman sat on a man's lap. He sucked her breasts and she moaned in sexual ecstasy, writhing and pitching against him, as if the experience took her beyond her body.

The nausea that had threatened worked its way to Cammie's throat. She swallowed hard. A slender woman dressed in white came up to her. The woman had mahogany skin and a wide, kissable mouth. She placed a cold hand on Cammie's arm. "You could come with me if you like," the woman said.

Cammie resisted the urge to move away. "Actually," she said, "I'm looking for Steve."

The woman took her hand off Cammie's arm. "He's in that room," she said, nodding toward a beaded door on the left. Then she walked up the stairs, and took the hand of a woman waiting at one of the tables. Cammie made herself look away.

She pushed open the beaded door. The room smelled of blood and sex. Steve was on a futon, completely naked, his chest covered in blood. A man lay across him, eyes half open. The red light caught a thin, angry wound on the man's neck.

"You look fresh," Steve said, sitting up and pushing the man aside. Cammie's heart was pounding. Even if he caught her, the boys would come get her. Even if he bit her, she would survive the first time. But she had no idea what would happen next. She might die like so many others. Or her heredity might come through, and she might turn.

"I didn't come for sex," she said. "I came because I was told you could find Ben."

Steve got up and crossed over to her. He ran a hand over her breast, smearing blood on her T-shirt. Her nipples ached. She swallowed again to keep her gorge down, but let him touch. "You don't want Ben."

"I do," she said. "I'm pregnant."

Steve snatched his hand away as if he had been burned. "Randy little son of a bitch, isn't he?" Steve said. "How come I don't know you?"

"I don't know," Cammie said. His mood change frightened her more than his touch had. She backed away.

He glanced down at her stomach. "You're not show-ing. Sure this isn't some kind of trick?"

"It's not a trick!" Cammie let the terror into her voice. "He stayed with me for a few nights. He said he was coming to see you and I haven't heard from him since. Your roommate told me I could find you here."

"Fucking Scott," Steve muttered. He sat back down on the futon. The man sighed and put a hand on Steve's leg. Steve pushed it away. Steve ran his tongue over his lips. "Tell you what," he said. "You give me a free one, and I'll tell you how to find Ben."

Cammie shook her head. Her time had to be nearly up. "I'm not that way. I don't know what happened when I met Ben, because it happened so fast. But I've never been in a place like this before, and I really don't want to stay."

"Ben would probably kill me if I messed with his sport anyway," Steve said.

Cammie let out a silent sigh of relief. She reached into her back pocket and handed Steve a piece of note-paper with the Hilton's phone number and her room extension. "I don't want to keep looking. Tell him I'll wait for his call, okay? I just want to talk to him."

Steve glanced at the card, then walked over to the pile of clothes in the corner and tucked the card inside. "Don't know when I'll get a chance to call him," Steve said.

"Look," Cammie said. "I'll pay you."

Steve came back to her and slid a hand under her T-shirt. His palm was cold. His touch made her breast cold. He dug his fingers into the soft skin until she started from the pain. "I don't need money," he said. "Af-ter that baby's born, you come back to me, and give me a taste of that sweet body of yours. Otherwise I'll find some other way to make you pay. Clear?"

Cammie nodded. It felt as if he were going to rip her breast off. She bit her lip to keep from crying out.

"Okay." He let her go. She staggered back a step. "I'll find Ben for you, sweet thing."

"Thank you," she said, and ducked out of the room. The writhing couples in the vampire center looked like they were doing an odd dance. The blood smell seemed to have gotten stronger. She ran up the stairs, through the tables, and out the door.

When the fresh air hit her, the nausea took over. She vomited on the sidewalk, then leaned against a telephone pole, trying to catch her breath. So close. So very close. Now she had to hope that Steve would keep his word.

Hands touched her shoulder and she shook them off.

"Hey," a soft voice said. "It's just John. You okay?"

She nodded and stood up, then wiped her mouth with the back of her hand. John led her to the car. He smelled of garlic. They had been about to come in. She would have been safe after all.

She slid into the car next to Norm. She picked up his garlic and rubbed it against herself. She was safe.

For the time being, she was safe.

Chapter
Thirty-one

"You're hard to find, man." The gaunt man leaning against the doorjamb wore a leather jacket, torn jeans, and Nikes. His untrimmed black hair brushed against his shoulders. His teeth were stained.

Ben held the door by the edge, wondering why he had opened it. He had just woken up and had enough to drink to slake his deep thirst. But he was tired. And he had an evening to spend with Glenda before he went cruising. "May I help you?"

"Oh, for chrissake." The man pushed past Ben into the entry. A lamp burned over the deacon's bench that Glenda had insisted on. She hadn't arrived yet. The porch light illuminated the muddy footprints on the concrete steps.

"I didn't invite you in," Ben said.

"It's Steve, man. Close the fucking door."

Steve. Ben did close the door. The hair on the back of his neck rose. He hadn't expected Steve. It did not bode well.

Steve stuck his hands in the pockets of his jacket and walked into the living room. The red sectional, chosen for comfort, not appearance, dominated the room. "Not bad." He plunked onto the armchair and put his feet on the matching ottoman. "They kicked you out of the nest, huh?"

"How did you find me?" Ben stood in the doorway. Now that Steve was in context, he did look familiar. The rangy, relaxed way he used his body spoke of nights cruising the Gut in Eugene, Steve's body lounged in the back seat of Ben's father's station wagon.

"Mikos told me."

The statement made Ben freeze. Mikos had wanted to keep Ben's new nest secret. This had to be important enough to send Steve over. A car pulled up in the driveway, its hum reverberating through the thin walls. Glenda. Damn. He had only seen her once since the night they went furniture shopping. They met for drinks a few nights ago at the microbrewery near the house, but he had not brought her back. Tonight was supposed to be the full-blown seduction. The effort he was making at self-control already made him cranky.

"Is this important, or can we talk later?"

Steve put his arms behind his head. The jacket was worn and cracked on the elbows. "Odd. Maybe important. But definitely odd."

Glenda knocked on the door, then opened it. She wore a low-cut blouse with a half bra underneath, accenting her cleavage. The skirt and high heels gave her legs shape. "Hi," she said. "Hope you don't mind the intrusion."

Her grin faded when she saw Steve. Steve smiled at her, raising himself to full height.

Ben's shoulders got tight. This wasn't going to go well. "Glenda, meet Steve."

She walked over to the armchair and held out her hand. Steve stared at it for a moment, then glanced at Ben. Ben crossed his arms. Steve took her hand and shook it, keeping his gaze on Ben. "How fucking suburban," Steve said.

Glenda took her hand back as if she had been burned.

"Steve and I went to high school together," Ben said. "He showed up about fifteen minutes before you did, claiming he had important news."

"Personal news," Steve said. "Not for cow—"

Ben frowned.

"Cowards or ladies." Steve smiled and bowed at Glenda. "Maybe you can wait for him in the bedroom."

"That bar you hang out in stole your manners," Ben snapped.

Glenda wiped her hand on her skirt. "I can come back later," she said.

Ben walked over to her, slipped his arm around her, and kissed her. She tasted good. God, he was ready for her. Her body relaxed into his. "Just give us a moment, darling," he said. "You can stay, but I think Steve wants to talk in private."

"All right," she said. "But don't be long." She slipped out of his arms and went through the kitchen into the family room. After a moment, the television blared the *Tonight Show* theme song.

Ben took two steps toward the armchair. He had to breathe deep to control the arousal. He had been planning this seduction for so long that Steve's intrusion was throwing off his concentration. "What's so damn important that you come in here and meddle with my life?"

Steve held up his hands. "Hey, man. I'm just the messenger boy doing you a favor. You don't have to listen."

Ben's body was humming. He made himself step back and then sat on the edge of the sectional. Glenda's fresh scent carried from the other room. He wondered if Steve could smell it. "What message?"

"Second time in as many months, some cow comes in and tells me you got her pregnant."

"What?" Ben frowned. The Seattle cows would have gone to the nest, and the woman he had a week ago wouldn't have known how to find him. He had had other women, but he had used aliases each time. That left the woman he had fucked in Steve's cow-bar, but he didn't remember giving her his name. Maybe Steve had given it to her.

"Mr. Mighty Sperm Strikes Again." Steve laughed and leaned back. "If you got it, Budola, don't complain. It won't last."

"Who was she?"

"Didn't say. Just her phone number. Cute thing, well built. Said you spent some time with her when you were running away from home."

The arousal left him. He was on complete alert. He had spent time with no one. This was a setup. Ben ran a hand over his leg. "I never spent time with anyone."

"Someone's after you, then," Steve said. "I'd let it drop."

"Who would set me up?" Ben asked. He clenched his fist. No wonder Mikos hadn't wanted him in the nest. "How would they know to go through you?"

"I been thinking about it on the drive over last night, and I figure Candyce told someone how she found you, and that someone told the cops. They're trying to find you. That's why I came up here." Steve crossed his arms in front of his chest. People change but the old friendships never died.

"Were you followed?"

Steve shook his head. "I may act stupid, but I watch my ass."

He probably did, if he had managed to stay alive that long. Vampires like Steve usually died in their first year. Ben licked his lips. Someone trying to find him. A woman. He might be able to use that. "You check out the phone number?"

"It's the Hilton in Portland. The extension is a room number."

"Really?" Ben asked. Better and better. They wouldn't expect anything in a public hotel. "How long is she going to be there?"

"She says until she hears from you, but I think she'll leave in a week or so when she discovers the ploy isn't working."

Ben lay flat on the sectional, the crown of his head brushing against the back cushion. "I didn't say it wouldn't work."

"You're not going there!" Steve's voice echoed in the living room.

Ben sat up. Steve's eyes were wide, his face even whiter than it had been before. "Why not? What's the worst case? They catch me. Cops can't kill me in Oregon or Washington without a valid reason. They can't hold me for long, and even if they try, I'm stronger than they are. I can charm any one of them."

"They'll charge you with Candyce's murder."

Ben shrugged. "I'll wait until the night shift. There has to be someone on the force with a little blood-drinking problem. They can't hold me. They've never been able to hold any of us longer than twenty-four hours."

"And if they take you out into the sun?"

"They won't," Ben said.

"They'll do anything they can," Steve said.

Ben smiled just a little. "So they take me out into the sun. It won't kill me. It'll just cause a lot of pain. Then I get my lawyer to sue them for inhumane treatment."

"Inhumane treatment." Steve chuckled. "To a vampire. That's rich."

"Vampires are human under Oregon law," Ben said. "It'll work."

Steve shook his head. His long hair caught on his collar, making it look as if he had a pageboy. "Sounds like a lot of work for nothing."

"It's not nothing. At best, I'll be some poor innocent kid who ran away from home who's being suckered into some game. At worst, they'll try to nail me for the murder. It might work to my advantage to have my name cleared. Mikos can afford a good lawyer, and the nest most certainly can handle any jury. Lots of options, Steve, old boy, and none of them threaten me." Ben stood. The television blared studio laughter from the other room. He couldn't see Glenda. Good.

"You take too many risks," Steve said.

Risks would make Ben strong. A vampire didn't become as powerful as Mikos without gambling a bit. Ben had a feeling this might work to his advantage.

He walked over to the high windows. The lights reflected the room to him—the new sectional, the easy chairs, the stereo set. He thought he caught the edge of Steve's leather jacket, but he couldn't be certain. "How long has it been since you saw her?" Ben asked.

"She came into the Keg last night. I left and stayed at Mikos's."

"So Mikos knows about this?"

"He's the one who helped me find you."

"What did he say about it?"

"He just shook his head and said you were the most fertile vampire he'd ever met. Said he thought Van ruined your only chance at a byblow. So what happened to Candyce?"

"Van killed her." The sentence came out easier than Ben expected it to. The thought didn't bother him as much as it once had. Candyce was gone now, and he could do nothing about it. Nothing except try again.

"Fuck." Steve leaned forward and rubbed his bare chin. "And they kicked you out of the nest?"

"No." Ben came back to the sectional and leaned on it. "I left on my own. I want to try again, and I don't want that bitch Van to get at the next one."

Steve frowned. "Why'd Van go for her anyway?"

"Said Candyce wasn't ready to be in the nest, that she'd break."

"She probably would have. She always was one strong little bitch."

"Yeah, well. It's over and done now. I got Glenda." Ben rocked a little on his feet. Now that he knew what he was going to do, he wanted to get busy.

"Little heavy for my tastes," Steve said. "But she looks like a breeder."

"That's what I'm hoping," Ben said. He ran a hand through his hair. "Look, Steve, I'd offer to let you stay, but I have business in the next room that wouldn't understand."

"Jesus. Sounds like a wife, not a cow."

Ben suppressed a sigh. "She has a real-world job that I need to have her work at for a while. So I play a few other games."

Steve shook his head. "This power thing you and Mikos do makes no sense to me. It's a hell of a lot easier to go down to the Keg, get your feed and whatever other gratification you need, and pull in your half of the take. Room, board, and cash. Drugs and free pussy. What else could a guy want?"

"You tell me," Ben said. "You're the one running errands for me. And I don't even pay you."

Steve pushed himself out of the armchair. "You know," he said. "Van probably wanted you out too. You're one part brilliant to two parts stupid. And sometimes it's hard to tell which part is which."

He walked across the thin carpet to the front door. "This'll probably be the last time we'll connect, Ben," he said. "I'm not going to be your message boy anymore."

"Never asked you to in the first place," Ben said. Then he tipped an imaginary hat—a gesture from their high school days. "But I do appreciate the assistance, this time."

"Oops," Steve said, reaching into his pocket. "Almost forgot." He pulled out a piece of paper and held it out.

Ben had to walk to the door to get it. He glanced down and then smiled. "The phone number."

"All you need is that extension," Steve said. "It's the room number. And then you're home, if that's what you want to call it. I still think it's two parts stupid."

"Or maybe it's one part brilliant," Ben said. He held the door and watched as Steve hurried out of the artificial light. He didn't want to see Steve anymore either. It seemed as though every time their paths crossed, Ben's life changed.

This time it had to change for the better.

Chapter
Thirty-two

The rental car's air-conditioning system cheeped. It sounded like a small bird strangling underneath the hood. Eliason gripped the wheel, wishing for his Ferrari. This white sedan monstrosity did not move well in traffic. It had no pickup and was too big to fit into spaces between trucks.

This trip had been interminable. Losing an entire day in transit was making him crazy. He had spoken with Thornton on the phone, but hadn't received the results he wanted. Cammie had left the police station upset, but hadn't said what her plans would be.

"I think I should drive," Whitney said for the third time since the plane had dumped them at the minuscule Eugene airport. Traveling with Whitney hadn't been a joy either. Whitney refused to eat anything covered with red sauce and had asked for a special meal from the airline. When Eliason had received his tiny plate of lasagna, Whitney had made a gagging noise and disappeared to the back of the plane for a good ten minutes. Still, Whitney wanted to find Cammie as much as Eliason did.

"We should be there by now," Eliason said, ignoring Whitney. Eliason's eyes ached. He hated driving unfamiliar cars at night.

"Why? The clerk gave us no time limit on the directions. She just said the hotel was downtown. And how the hell do you know it was the right hotel?" Their panic was feeding off each other's. Whitney had never left the Midwest. Eliason had offered to go alone, but Whitney had insisted. If Cammie were in trouble, Whitney said, he would know better than anyone else how to help.

"Because DeeDee had Cammie's mailing address. I called before the flight took off. Cammie's registered." Eliason's hands were sweating. He had tried calling Cammie from the airport and had received no answer in her room. She hadn't picked up her messages either, for two days. The nervous feeling he had had in the base of his stomach ever since she left had grown worse.

The highway arched downward. He stayed in the left lane as the rental car clerk had instructed him and turned onto a four-lane one-way street near some small motels. He followed the street past a series of houses that blended with businesses. A fresh fish market stood on one corner, a law office on another. Only five other cars were on the street at all. Eugene was quiet at night.

The hotel stood next to a concrete monstrosity that the large electronic sign assured him was the area's civic center. He went around the block and ended up next to a white limo in the Hilton's valet parking area. He left the keys in the ignition and the car running.

"If they want you to move this thing," he said to Whitney, "circle around the block. I'll come get you as soon as I know something."

"Let's just go in, Brett," Whitney said. "Cammie's probably in the restaurant—"

"Probably," Eliason said. "But no sense in going through the trouble to park this thing if we'll need it again right away."

He got out and stepped up on the concrete sidewalk leading into the hotel. The double doors opened into a plush lobby. Two well-dressed couples laughed in front of the door to the downstairs restaurant. The restaurant itself looked full. A woman wearing a long black evening dress and carrying a beaded clutch purse hurried to the elevator. Eliason scanned the lobby until he saw Registration.

First he tried the small white hotel phone on the edge of the long registration desk. Cammie did not pick up, and the operator asked him if he wanted to leave a message. He declined. Then he hung up and leaned on the counter.

The man behind it, wearing a navy blue suit, was hunched over a computer screen, face flushed. He hit several keys, then sighed in frustration.

"They take more time than they're worth, don't they?" Eliason asked. He didn't want the clerk to know he was feeling panicked. People seemed to help better when they believed the information wasn't crucial.

The clerk looked up, startled. His flush grew, and then he smiled. "When they're working, they're wonderful little things," he said. "But when the entire system shuts down I remember why I hated this job when I had to do everything by hand." He stood up and tugged at his suit coat. "May I help you?"

"I've been trying to reach Cammie Timms for two days now. The operator says she hasn't been picking up her messages."

The clerk sighed again. "It's the computer system. They're supposed to be forwarded to her. She's at our sister hotel in Portland for a few days, but she left most of her belongings here. I know because I set the whole thing up a couple of evenings ago."

The counter dug into Eliason's chest. Portland. She was farther away than he thought. But at least someone knew where she was. "Did she say what she was doing in Portland?"

The clerk shook his head. "She looked pretty serious though. Said it was a family matter."

Goose bumps formed on Eliason's arms although the room temperature didn't change. Family matter. Ben. She must have found him. And she had gone without help, without backup.

"Can you tell me how to get to that hotel?" Eliason asked.

"Better than that," the clerk said. "I have a map."

He opened a drawer next to the computer and pulled out a preprinted map of the area. "Ignore the inside," he said. "It takes you to Salem. The diagram you want is on the back." He turned it over and slid it at Eliason.

Eliason took the thin tri-folded paper and slapped it against his hand. "Thanks," he said. He had to make himself walk out of the building. The time pressure that had been bothering him since he spoke to DeeDee in Madison two days before had just grown stronger. For the last forty-eight hours, he had been running at top speed, blessing the airlines for the frequent flyer miles they had given him for all those conferences he had attended, which allowed both him and Whitney to schedule the trip within a day and to fly free on top of it. Even though that had been relatively painless, changing his appointment schedule and finding other physicians to watch his Westrina Center patients had not. He had probably gotten about four hours of sleep since he left the Ovens of Brittany parking lot.

Whitney had gotten about the same. In the Denver airport they had spent their two-hour layover discussing various plans, various things they could do if they found Cammie in trouble. Neither of them had expected her to be out of the city.

Outside, Whitney had moved the car forward to allow a Subaru to pull up just outside the door. He had remained in the driver's seat. Eliason had no choice but to crawl in on the passenger side.

"What's wrong?" Whitney asked.

"She's in the Hilton in Portland, on family matters."

"Oh, God." Whitney leaned his head forward and rested his forehead on the steering wheel. "I knew I should have come with her."

"What would you have been able to do?" Eliason asked.

Whitney sat up and started the car. "Read the signs better. She's there meeting that brother of hers, isn't she?"

"That's what I figure," Eliason said.

"The brother that was last seen in the company of a girl recently murdered by a vampire."

"The same."

"The brother who raped that girl the night she got pregnant."

"She only has one brother," Eliason said.

"God, Cammie." Whitney held out his hand. "Let me see that map."

Eliason handed it over. His hands were shaking. He had known when he sent her off alone that she would hit bottom. But now that bottom was probably here, he didn't want anything to happen to her. He should have stopped her. He should have declared his undying love, locked her in his apartment, and made her stay until she vowed she would remain in Madison for the rest of her life.

But that wouldn't have worked. Cammie was a woman of action, and she had focused on her brother instead of on herself. That one error—which Eliason might have prevented if he had only talked to her more—might cost Cammie her life.

"I sure as hell hope Portland's close," Whitney said.

Eliason leaned back as Whitney turned right on the one-way street leading out of the Hilton's parking area. "An hour or two won't make any difference either way," Eliason said, trying to convince himself. "She's already been there two days."

"Christ," Whitney said. "We're just in time to pick up the pieces."

Chapter
Thirty-three

Ben pulled the Lexus into a space across the street from the hotel. The night was cool and the wind off the Columbia River was fresh. He loved Portland. He might actually move here when the opportunity presented itself.

He buzzed up the windows and slipped out of the car, leaning for a moment against the polished metal exterior. Camila Timms. The name was familiar. It brought—

(Cam-Cam!)

—odd memories into his head. Ever since he had called the Hilton and asked for the name of the party in room 361—and it had been surprisingly easy to get—a vague headache had threatened at the back of his brain. That night, he had made slow, casual love to Glenda, enjoying it in a way he hadn't thought possible, and then had had nightmares about a man with glowing red eyes, nightmares so strong they had awakened Glenda. To awaken a cow after her first time took something short of an earthquake.

Something was going on here, and it had nothing to do with Candyce.

He tugged on his pants legs and steeled himself. Then he stood and pressed the button on the key chain that activated his car alarm. The car chirruped its response to him.

The street was empty. A door banged in the breeze, and he suspected that someone was watching him through the empty windows of the office building behind him. It didn't matter. He was getting stronger each day. He could take anyone.

His leather shoes clicked on the concrete as he crossed the street. He had to snap himself into alertness. Odd memories had been flooding him on the two-hour drive.

"Mommy, what was my real daddy like?"

His mother moved sharply, a flush rising in her cheeks. She kept her gaze on the bread dough, half rolled on the counter before her. "I don't know, honey," she said. "I never met him."

Her voice was funny. Ben swung his feet. They barely connected with the floor. He hated being ten. Grownups lied to kids. She knew what his real dad had been like. She just refused to tell him.

He rubbed his eyes and stretched, half tempted to go down to Steve's cow-bar and drain some unsuspecting cow until it couldn't stand anymore. Maybe after he saw this woman. He wanted to be hungry, and on the edge when he saw her. That kept him thinking clearly and gave him an advantage if he had to attack her.

Ben stepped up on the curb and into the hotel's side door.

A Mozart piano concerto flowed through speakers overhead. The hotel smelled vaguely of furniture polish and untainted blood. Vampires rarely came in here, and never to feed.

His hunger was making his hands shake.

He climbed the green carpeted steps and glanced at the registration desk. It was empty, although a door was open to the back. Through it, he could see a young woman dressed in blue, bent over a computer keyboard.

Better that she didn't see him.

He walked through the lobby, past the closed gift shop, to the bank of elevators. He pushed the button and one opened immediately. He stopped. The interior was lined with mirrors. Good thing he was alone.

He got in and wiped his hands on his pants. Camila Timms. Cam-Cam.

(small pixieish face puckered with worry. "What did you do, Ben?")

They had met somewhere. Before he came to Eugene.

Once Van had asked him what he knew of his natural parents. Nothing, Ben had replied. His parents were good upstanding citizens. But his natural parents, the ones who gave birth to him, they were ciphers. Until he had been in the nest for a few weeks, he had even forgotten they had existed.

He pushed the button for the correct floor, feeling the adrenaline run through him, mixing with his hunger. If this was a trap, he was prepared. He would slaughter them all.

And if it wasn't, he would get some answers from the mysterious Camila Timms.

Chapter
Thirty-four

Cammie had four pillows propped behind her back, and the thin hotel bedspread over her feet. She was watching *The Unforgiven* on pay-per-view while thumbing through a translation of a nineteenth-century German text on vampirism. She had wanted that book for a long time and finally found it at Powell's Bookstore, along with four others, locally published, on vampire rehab theory. She had only seen a few texts on rehab, all of which Anita had scoffed at because she believed that vampires could not be rehabilitated.

The rehab books fascinated her. The process had gone way beyond counseling to include ways of weaning the vampire off the blood and dealing with the physical changes. Cammie promised herself that when this was over, she would visit one of the rehab clinics and see what they did.

Two days in the hotel room had nearly driven her crazy. For the most part, she kept the adjoining door open to the detectives' room, but they had started a riotous game of gin that was breaking her concentration. She had already seen the movie three times, and this fourth time served more as background noise, although she did surface for the wonderful scene in the jail with Gene Hackman and Richard Harris.

No phone calls, no nothing. She figured she would give Ben three more days to take her bait and then she would go back to Eugene and try something else.

She could no longer smell the garlic hidden in the folds of the curtain. She had buried the room in it. She wondered how the maid could stand to come in there. She wanted any vampire who entered to immediately suffer the effects of garlic poisoning, to be debilitated instead of merely intoxicated. Ever since she left the Keg, she checked the garlic. It acted as a talisman, something that would keep her safe. She had given the detectives some too, and supervised while they hung the bulbs all over their room.

She pushed the book away and fluffed up the pillows. Except for short excursions to Powell's and a local grocery store, she had spent the last two days in the room. The inactivity made her uncomfortable. It also made her reflect on her actions.

She had thought that the pregnancy gambit was her best bet. If it didn't bring Ben to her, it might bring the person who captured both Ben and Candyce. Now, she wasn't so sure. If Ben hadn't slept with a lot of women, then he would know the message for the ploy it was. He would have no reason to find her. The only person the message would bring would be the person who killed Candyce. And that person was probably a vampire.

During the middle of her vigil the night before, Cammie had nearly packed her things, called to the men in the next room, and left. She didn't want to face a vampire. She wanted to take action, but by taking action, she had forced herself into one small room with nothing to do.

Eastwood had moved to the final shootout. The blazing guns made her nervous. She hit the mute button, seeing only the flare of the muzzles and then characters falling to the barroom floor.

The day before, she had spent nearly an hour on the phone with Thornton. It seemed the Seattle police had no more news, and Thornton had moved on to a new case. She had offered to come up to Portland on her day off and help Cammie, which Cammie found oddly touching, but Cammie turned her down. She didn't need one more inexperienced vampire hunter on her team.

A knock on the door made her start. She glanced at the closed adjoining door, but the sound hadn't come from there. With the TV's sound off, she could hear the detectives' laughter. She hadn't ordered any room service. Her heart started to pound harder.

"Yeah?" she said.

"I'm responding to a message left at the Keg." The voice outside sounded male and muffled. Cammie's throat went dry. She pulled on her jeans, put on her side pack, and slipped her bare feet into her tennis shoes.

"Okay," she said. "Just give me a minute."

She opened the adjoining door. The detectives looked up from their game. She put a finger to her lips, then nodded toward her room. "We got him," she mouthed. She pulled the door closed, but didn't latch it. Then she pulled open the room door, careful not to unhook the chain.

The man standing in the hallway was tall and dark. He wore a London Fog raincoat loosely over his shoulders. His jeans were pressed and his white shirt immaculate. "I understand you're looking for Ben Sadler," he said.

"Yes." Cammie's entire body shook. He was stunning. Twenty-five, maybe younger, with flawless skin and dark brown eyes. His cologne smelled good.

"Well, you just found him. May I come in or should we talk in the hall?" His voice came from deep inside his chest. It had a richness that some of the best actors emulated.

Cammie undid the chain lock. She turned her back on the door, as if the man's entrance held no importance to her. The door's latch clicked as the door closed.

Ben. Her brother. All grown up.

"Have a seat," Cammie said. She took one of the chairs beneath the curtains, as close to the garlic as she could get. Then she looked up.

The man's face caught the light and it took all of her strength not to gasp. He had the long, narrow features of her father, with the same wide black eyes. His mouth was softer, and his skin more elastic, but this was not the cherubic baby face she remembered.

"I never saw you before in my life," he said. He sounded surprised.

"Not true." Cammie swallowed. Her throat was dry. "You spent the first three years of your life with me. I'm your sister, Camila."

He put a hand to his forehead and swayed. The frown on his face as familiar as one on her own. "Sister?" He sat down on the edge of the bed. "Cam-Cam?" Little boy's inflections in a man's voice.

She held her breath and nodded.

"Why're you looking for me?" He loosened his collar with one hand and took a deep breath. His features were gaining color. She must have shocked him. "Why now?"

She stood. He wasn't a vampire. He wouldn't have been able to stay in the garlic so long.

"Because," she said. "I finally remembered."

"Remembered," he whispered. "The dreams . . ."

She could barely breathe. Something like hope was rising in her chest. "You're having dreams too?"

He nodded. He stood up, walked across the room, and caressed her arm. His touch felt good. "I've been having a lot of dreams. Nightmares." He wiped a hand across his forehead. "This room is hot."

"No," Cammie said. "It's cool. Are you okay?"

"Dreams," he whispered. He was very close to her. "My sister." He pulled her against him. His body was cool. "Cam-Cam."

He leaned forward and kissed her on the lips. Her entire body became rigid. No. Brothers didn't . . .

. . . and then she relaxed into him. He tasted good. Very good. She slipped her hands along his back and pulled him closer. Family. They needed each other.

Brothers didn't . . .

But he tasted so good . . .

She pushed him away. He was a vampire. Jesus. The garlic was getting to him, but not like she had expected. She wiped her mouth with the back of her hand. "You're a vampire."

He tilted his head, the softness gone from his face. "What did you expect, girl?"

He thought she was too. No, he wouldn't. He would be able to smell that she wasn't. "Not this," she said. "Not—"

He grabbed her arm with his hand. The strength in his fingers pinched the bone. "I remember you," he said, his words slurring. "You pounded that stake, all the blood flying, Dad screaming. Now it's my turn, isn't it?"

"No," she said. She tried to wrench her arm free, but he wouldn't let go. "I came to see how you were doing, Ben."

"Doing?" He pulled her close. His pupils were dilated and he was swaying like a drunk. When her pelvis hit his, she realized his penis was hard. "Doing? You fucking *lie!*"

With a roar, he sank his teeth into her neck. She screamed, but he jammed his shoulder into her mouth. With her good hand, she pushed him, but he didn't budge. He was sucking. She could feel the blood draining. God, it felt good. Her groin throbbed in response. He stuck his other hand inside her shirt and pinched her nipple.

The pain aroused her farther. She arched against him, her body responding although her mind was screaming. She tried to twist free.

"Goddammit!" She sounded hoarse. "I'm your sister!"

He didn't respond except to pull her closer. A bang sounded behind them.

"Let her go!" John. His voice was shaking.

Ben turned. "All right."

He let go of her arm. She stared at it, thinking she needed to move, but she couldn't remember how. Her groin tingled and her breasts ached. Something warm flowed through her, like good brandy.

He had bitten her. Drained her. She was drugged.

Like those people in the cow-bar.

She had always wondered what would happen to her if she got bit.

Ben held up his hands. John advanced, holding up his cross and garlic. Norm stood behind him and pulled out his gun.

Not a gun! Cammie said. *I told you a gun won't work.* But the words didn't come out. She couldn't open her mouth.

Ben took another step closer, then, moving with that incredible speed, kicked John in the groin. John fell to his knees. Ben grabbed John's head and forced it against his chest. His neck broke with an audible snap.

Cammie gasped and moved, but it felt as if she were underwater. Norm leveled the gun at Ben, but Ben kept coming forward. When he reached Norm, he slammed him against the wall and buried his face in Norm's throat.

He's strong. He's so strong. Cammie licked her lips. *Stronger than any she had ever seen before.* This much garlic should have debilitated him.

Norm had stopped struggling, but still Ben ripped at his neck.

Cammie walked quietly. Her entire body tingled. Drugged. The feelings she had were not hers. They belonged to the drug Ben had put into her system. She wasn't thinking clearly. She was forgetting something. She knelt over John's body and pulled the stake and hammer from his side pack.

Ben's hand wrapped itself around her wrist. "Oh, no," he said. His words were slurred. "You're not going to do me, you little bitch. I don't know how you found me, but you were determined to destroy the men in this family, weren't you? But I'm not going to fucking let you."

He shook the stake out of her hand, then pulled her close again and kissed her, his tongue invading her mouth.

She tried to pull away but he held her tight. Then she leaned into him. Sweet Jesus, he tasted good. She never knew a man could taste like that. She slid her free arm around him. She needed him to touch her, needed to feel him all over her—

Then he pulled away, and she felt as if she had lost something important. She reached for him, but he smiled and took her hand. "That's right, Cam-Cam," he said. "I'll have you soon. Real soon."

He ran a thumb along her lip and it came away bloody. He took the edge of the bedspread and wiped her mouth, then checked his shirt. Flecks of blood marred the white. He slid his arms into his coat sleeves and buttoned the raincoat.

He pulled her collar over the warm, pulsing spot on her neck. "Come along, sweetness," he said. "We're going to have a party, just you and I."

"Wake up, sweetness. We're going to have a party, just you and I."

Cammie felt hands on her chest. She rolled over, trying to cling to sleep, but the hands forced her to stay on her back. Her feet were cold. The covers were gone, and her nightgown was wrapped around her waist.

Fingers on her face. "Wake up, honey."

The hands slid down and forced her thighs apart. The bed creaked as a new weight settled on it. Bare legs brushed hers. "Come on, little girl. Daddy needs some of that comfort you been sharing with that brother of yours."

Something hard poked her. She was suddenly wide awake and struggling to get free. The hands grabbed her wrists and held them above her head. "Oh, no, sweetness. Daddy loves you."

His whiskers scratched her neck. Then he bit her and she screamed. He brought one hand down and covered her mouth. She kicked at him, and he wrapped his legs around hers.

The warmth was spreading through her, making her tingle with fear and excitement. She was screaming against his hand. His tongue played with the wound in her neck.

Then he shoved himself inside her, and a pain ripped kitty-corner through her groin and stomach. She screamed so hard that her throat tore, but the *only sound in the room was his breathing and grunts of pleasure.*

His hand gripped her mouth so hard that she bit the insides of her cheeks. She could barely breathe. He pounded at her bottom while his teeth remained in her neck. The square light fixture on the ceiling, the one with the race cars, was only a faint shape in the darkness. It started to spin. It whirled round and round, faster and faster, taking her somewhere else, away from all this pain.

Then he fell on her. His hand went lax and slipped off her face. Her entire body was one big heartbeat. She no longer wanted to scream. No one would hear her anyway. She tried to push him off, but he wouldn't budge.

"Ah, sweetness," he said. "You're the only person in the world who tastes like honey."

He eased off her. He tugged her nightgown down, and pulled the covers over her, folding them over her chest like they did on television. He kissed her forehead. A light kiss, barely a brush.

"Sleep well, Camila," he said, and opened the door. The hallway light was bright. It made him all shadow and blackness. So big, like a monster from the dark.

"Good night, Daddy," she said, then rolled over, and tried to go back to sleep.

PART THREE

Chapter Thirty-five

Seven squad cars blocked the entrance to the hotel, their blue and red lights flashing across the brick façade. Eliason leaned against the window of the white rental car, the armrest digging into his side. His entire body was cold.

"We're not going to get in there," Whitney said. His voice trembled. He obviously was as upset about this as Eliason was.

God, why did Cammie have to go to a whole new state? If they had been in Wisconsin, they would have been able to work with the cops. Eliason swallowed. "Find a place to park."

"They're not going to let us in."

"We don't know until we try."

Whitney moved the car out of traffic and into an empty spot in front of a two-hour meter. Eliason was out of the car before it stopped. He jogged across the four-lane street, weaving in and out of the cars. One narrowly missed him and honked. Eliason ignored it. Something had lodged in his throat, and his breathing was ragged. He was too late. He had delayed too long. He was too late.

No one sat in the squads near the door. A handful of people had gathered on the sidewalk, staring at the double glass doors as if they held a secret.

"What's going on?" Eliason asked as he ran by.

"I don't know," a woman replied. No one else answered him. He pushed open the glass doors, and a hotel clerk, his face white, put a hand on Eliason's shoulder, stopping him.

"I can't let you go any farther, sir."

"You just tell me," Eliason said. "Does this have anything to do with Cammie Timms?"

The clerk's eyes grew wider. Eliason's heart felt as if it had stopped in his chest.

"Camila Timms is my wife." Eliason said the first thing that had come to mind. "You let me up there or I swear to God I won't be responsible for what happens to you."

At that moment, Whitney came through the doors. He was breathing hard. Sweat covered his forehead and dotted his curly red hair.

"Room three sixty-one," the clerk said. He stepped away as if Eliason had contaminated him.

"Come on, Whitney," Eliason said. He ran to the elevators without checking if Whitney was following. A balding man, wearing brown slippers, his red robe barely covering his paunch, strode down the hall.

"Do you know what all this noise is?" he asked Eliason.

Eliason didn't answer. He pressed the up button on the elevator. He shifted back and forth on both feet, hating the wait. Each second was another that Cammie needed him. After a moment, he looked around for a stairway. It was to the left of the elevators, beneath a large red sign marked Exit.

He yanked open the heavy metal door. The stairwell was made of concrete. His footsteps echoed inside. It was colder here than the main part of the hotel. He took the steps two at a time, and noted the yellow numbers painted on the doors on each landing. When he hit three, he pulled the door open and stepped into the hallway.

Six police officers worked the hall a few doors down. One officer crouched near the wall, scraping something off into a plastic sack. Another was taking pictures of the carpet. Voices murmured in low discussion.

"I don't like the look of this." Whitney stood behind Eliason. Eliason started at the sound of Whitney's voice. The whole thing was giving Eliason the creeps.

Eliason didn't like the way this looked either. He walked toward the cops. One of them, a woman who wore her long brown hair in a ponytail, held up her hand. "I can't let you go any farther," she said.

"My wife was in this room," Eliason said.

The woman's brown eyes met his. He recognized the look. He had used it a few times himself. "Then you don't want to go in, sir."

"Why? Is she dead?" He couldn't keep the note of panic from his voice.

"No, sir—"

"Then I'm going inside." He shoved her out of the way and went to the doorway. Whitney followed. Blood spattered the wall. A man's body was crumpled below the stain. On the floor, the coroner was zipping up a body bag over a man's face.

"Where's Cammie?" Eliason asked.

A burly man in a brown suit turned. His face was lined with stress, and he had a cigarette in his mouth. He smelled of Vicks. "Who're you?"

"I'm Brett Eliason. I'm a doctor."

"We don't need a doctor here."

"I see that," Eliason said. "I want to know where Cammie is."

"He says he's her husband," the female cop said.

The burly man assessed Eliason. "We don't know," the man said. "Some guy in a London Fog coat showed up a few hours ago. The front desk started getting complaints about thuds and screams up here. Hotel security comes up here, finds the door open and this inside. Your wife left with the guy. The desk clerk says he thought she left willingly, but she seemed odd to him. Docile, like the guy had her on a leash."

"You got film of this?" Whitney asked.

Eliason frowned, glad Whitney was along. Eliason would never have thought to ask those kinds of questions.

"Yeah. We got a few guys down with security now, reviewing the tapes. We're not going to get much. The camera was at an odd angle from the door. Maybe we'll have gotten his face when he left."

Eliason's body was shaking. "You know where she is?"

The cop shook his head. "She left with him in a Lexus. We got an APB out for him, but spendy cars aren't that unusual in this part of Portland. No one caught the plate."

"Call down to Eugene," Whitney said. "She was working with the Eugene police on a case."

A bell sounded down the hall, followed by the pneumatic sound of the elevator doors opening. A silver-haired man in a black silk suit pushed his way through the door.

"Jesus, Art," the man said as he surveyed the scene.

The burly cop looked away from Eliason. "Sorry to bring you down tonight, Jason, but these guys had your ID in their pockets. Thought maybe you might know something."

"Girl said she was looking for her brother. Easy case. She wanted them to accompany her to a bar, then guard her here."

"What kind of bar?" Whitney asked.

The silver-haired man turned to Whitney as though seeing him for the first time. "She called it a cow-bar. It's the Keg near the mission."

"A cow-bar," Whitney said.

"Vampires," Eliason said, the hair prickling on the back of his scalp. He pushed his way past the cops, walked around the body bag, and grabbed the curtains. As they moved, the garlic bulbs appeared. "She was prepared. What went wrong?"

"This guy died with a cross and garlic in his hands," the burly cop said. "The other guy had his throat ripped out."

"There's enough garlic in here to wipe out a nest," Whitney said. His eyes were wide.

Eliason glanced at him. "Then this couldn't have been done by a vampire."

"Oh, yes it could. We got one major motherfucker here. Either he's very old or he's hereditary and been at this for a while." Whitney put a hand to his face. "Jesus, Cam."

"Do you gentlemen mind telling us what's going on here?" the burly cop asked. "You're not her husband, are you?"

Eliason shook his head. Time to stop lying and start working with these people. They only had a short amount of time. "Whitney and I are from the Westrina Center in Wisconsin. Cammie put in a call to us two days ago, asking for help—"

"That's when she came to our offices," the silver-haired man said.

"She never got back to us, and we got worried. She wasn't supposed to be here at all. She was too involved. But we never thought it would end like this." Eliason rubbed his forearm with his right hand. He had never figured Cammie would get herself in this kind of mess. She had too much training. She was too cautious.

He should have thought about it.

Denial and family. It took a lot of counseling to overcome both of those things, and she had to face them together. He should have thought it through. He had failed her, and now she might die because of it.

"Look," Whitney said. "I've been vampire hunting for a long time now, and I can tell you one thing: we don't have a lot of time. He moved her from here because he felt threatened. But the first chance he gets, he's going to drain her, just like he did that guy there. He might torture her a little, which will give us extra time, but not much. He knows we're looking for him, and he'll get rid of her as fast as he can. And then we'll never find him again."

The burly cop stared at them for a moment. Then he nodded his head once. "All right," he said. "But I hope you two can think like a crazy man, because we already lost the advantage when that car drove away. Finding someone in this town is nearly impossible."

"We'll find her," Eliason said, but he didn't believe it.

Chapter
Thirty-six

He felt sick and woozy. His driving was erratic.
He had run one red light and made himself
concentrate after that. If he got pulled over and
they saw the blood on his shirt, they might
take him in.

It wouldn't be an issue, if it weren't for Cam-Cam.

He glanced at her. She was staring straight ahead, sitting primly, much as Candyce had done. Nothing about
Cam-Cam was familiar. She was too big to be his sister,
too forceful.

Too womanly.

And he couldn't keep his mind clear. Images crowded
him. *A long-haired girl with a bruised face and pale
skin drawn over her cheekbones cradled him as he
cried.*

She held a stake in her left hand.

The blood coated his father's bed.

"Daddy," she whispered.

"Daddy," he said.

She glanced at him, and he thought he saw something flicker in her eyes. She couldn't be coming out of
it so quickly. He put a hand on her leg. Maybe she
wasn't Cam-Cam. Maybe she wasn't his sister.

But he knew. He knew she was.

He had never been so drawn to another person. Not

Mikos. Not Candyce. Not even that first night with the cows. He was so aroused he thought that if he touched himself he would explode.

He had to pull over.

She was screaming. He could barely see her beneath their father. He touched his father's back, and his father roared, slamming him against the wall.

He had to get his head clear. That garlic got to him. The man he killed had held an entire bulb. Ben's hands were shaking. His entire body hummed. He had never been this out of control before. Everything was heightened and speeded up. It had only taken him a few minutes to rip that guy's neck out.

In front of her. Christ, he would have to kill her too.

They had passed Powell's and gone up a hill in what he had thought was the middle of the city. But the city seemed to have gone away. A lot of traffic, but no houses that he could see. He wished he knew Portland better. He had thought he was heading west toward the coast, but in his state, he could have been driving into the sunrise and not noticed.

She sighed. He touched her leg. It was warm. The blood flowed through it. Family blood. Like his. Jesus. She had been five years older—

(I'll keep you safe, Ben)

Five years. That made her nearly thirty. Almost her sexual prime. Family blood. Maybe her memories came back for a different reason.

His hard-on rubbed against the zipper of his pants. Soon. Soon he would have to stop and do something or he would take her while he was driving and they would get caught. He rolled down the window. The cool night air soothed him, but didn't ease the dizziness or the ache.

Finally he saw a side road. He pulled off. The road led into a stand of pine trees. As he rounded a corner, the road opened into a driveway that led to a fake Greek revival building. The sign out front identified it as a mortuary. Great. There were no other cars, and there wouldn't be any. No one came to graveyards at night.

He parked behind the building. No lights inside except the security light. He got out of the car. The cool air made his skin tingle. He walked around the car, pulled open the passenger door, and held out his hand.

She took his hand. Desire flooded through him. God, she was beautiful. He needed her. Now. He kissed her to keep her with him. She tasted of peppermint and sweet, untainted blood. He would have to be careful. He didn't want to kill her.

Then he remembered what Mikos had shown him. A vampire couldn't die when it was drained of blood. Only a stake through the heart or a cut-off head would kill a vampire.

Saliva filled Ben's mouth. He could drink until he was sated. For the first time ever.

He pulled her to the side of the mortuary, to the soft grass. It had to be perfect for her first time. Then he would show her how to live. Someone to be with him forever. Someone who wouldn't lose herself—not after he turned her. Someone to share the life with him.

The grass was damp against his feet. He stopped in the darkness and pulled her against him, rubbing her back, her buttocks. She moaned. He unbuttoned her shirt and took her right breast in his mouth. So good.

Her left hand moved to her side.

He grabbed her wrist, followed the hand, found a sidepack with weapons in it. He tightened his grip and pulled away enough so that he could see her face in the moonlight.

"You don't want to kill me," he said. "I can show you heaven."

He brushed her ponytail off her shoulder and bit into the artery. Her blood was sweet, as intoxicating as the garlic only better. Nourishing. She struggled for a moment, then moaned. He heard the burr of a zipper. With her right hand she struggled to get out of her pants.

He let go and helped her, then freed himself. He cradled her against him, his penis against the warmth of her stomach. Then he leaned her back, onto the grass.

"I'll love you forever," he said, and shoved himself inside her.

Chapter Thirty-seven

Cammie woke up in the dark. Her body was tingling. There was an odd, almost rotted taste in her mouth.

Blood. He had slit his wrist and made her drink his blood.

Her stomach turned. She rolled over and found she was on a bed. The sheets were flannel, and she was cold.

Her groin ached.

He had been inside her. And she had liked it, begged him for more. They had used each other until she passed out.

She buried her face in the pillow. She didn't want to think about it.

Stop thinking. Stop thinking. It'll go away if you forget. Daddy's a good man. He didn't mean to hurt me . . .

Voices in the other room. A woman and a man, talking softly. Something smelled good out there. Fresh. She sat up and wiped the hair from her face.

She was naked.

She reached beside the bed and flicked on a light. Her body was covered with bites and bruises. A grass stain ran from her elbow to her wrist.

Don't think about it.

It was the drug. That's what they taught in the Center. The drug seduced.

But it didn't make someone drink. And enjoy.

Over fifty percent of hereditàries become vampires themselves.

She covered her face with her dirt-spattered hands.

Don't think.

The voices were coming closer. She pulled the covers up to her neck.

"See?" the woman said. "A light's on now. Someone's in there."

"Look, Glenda, come here." Cammie recognized the male voice now. Ben. The thought of him made her giddy.

The door slammed back. A heavyset woman stood there. She wore a business suit and nylons, but she had taken off her shoes. Her cheeks were pink, and from the bed, Cammie could smell the woman's good health.

Ben stood behind her, shadows beneath his dark eyes.

The woman's expression tightened. "Who is she?"

He put his arm on her shoulder. She shrugged him off. Cammie's mouth filled with saliva. The aching in her groin had become a throbbing.

"I'm Ben's sister," she said. The words sounded alien in her mouth. The woman looked good. Too good. Cammie patted the side of the bed. A part of her mind stood distant, warning her that she was doing something wrong. "Come sit. Let's get acquainted."

Ben's hand clamped on the woman's shoulder. "She's ill, Glenda. Don't mind her. I'm going to get you something to drink, Cam-Cam."

He eased the woman out of the room. With his free hand, he pulled the door shut. Cammie started to follow them, then stopped.

The voice in her head was screaming.

She had nearly taken that woman.

Like a vampire would.

It was there. Inside her. It had been there all along.

The adrenaline rush. Ben couldn't leave her unattended, could he? She needed something.

The door opened again, and Ben stood there alone. He held a wine bottle in one hand, a glass in the other. "I'm sorry," he said. "About yesterday. The garlic—I lost my head."

He poured the wine into the glass. The scent made her dizzy and made the throbbing in her groin even stronger. She got up, not caring that she was naked, and took the glass from him. Then she drank. It tasted good. Almost as good as he had the night before. He poured her more and watched until she had downed the whole bottle. Then he got the blanket and wrapped her in it, and tenderly led her to the bed.

He brushed the hair out of her face. She swallowed, licking her lips. The calm voice in the back of her head told her to get away from him.

She didn't move.

"I've been watching you sleep," he said. "You look like my sister. I'm sorry for the rough introduction. The garlic—"

"The garlic was my fault," she said, and didn't know why she was apologizing for his action. She wanted more wine. It dulled her.

"You're new, aren't you? Never taken blood before?"

"I used to kill vampires," she said, her voice flat.

He flinched. "I'm going to give you more wine. I want you to stay here tonight. Otherwise you'll go out there and rip someone's throat off."

She remembered the longing she had, the way that woman smelled, the urge to grab her neck and bite—

"The wine will help?" she asked.

He nodded. "Then I'll get someone to train you." He stroked her face and leaned her into him as if she were a child. "You'll like this life, Cam-Cam. It's not like they say."

"Why do you care what I like?" she asked.

"Because," he said, "we can be together. Like we used to. Remember? How we protected each other?"

She remembered. Only she remembered protecting him. From vampires.

A heavy feeling of failure swept over her. She was no better than he was. No better than their father had been. "The wine," she reminded him.

He nodded and got up, taking the bottle with him. When he closed the door, she searched until she found her clothes. The sidepack was gone. She looked in the empty closet, under the bed, and on the floor. Nothing.

Then she sat down and licked the edge of the glass. No matter. She would probably have used the stake on the wrong person.

Herself.

Chapter
Thirty-eight

Jason DeFreeze was obviously shaken up. Eliason had pegged him as the kind of man who always looked neat, yet his tie was pulled away from his neck and his silver-tipped hair was mussed. He sat in the large leather chair behind the custom-made desk and leaned back, his face pale with stress. Through the tall windows, the lights of the city spread before them. Eliason could see himself and Whitney reflected in the glass. Whitney had a streak of dirt along the side of his cheek. Eliason's eyes seemed too big for his face.

"I've never lost operatives like that," DeFreeze said.

Whitney ran a hand through his curly red hair. He hadn't stopped moving since they found the bodies. "I have," he said.

DeFreeze wasn't speaking much. It was as if he had made a decision and wanted Eliason to pry it out of him.

Eliason sighed. "The notes," he reminded DeFreeze.

The notes were why they came. DeFreeze had made notes of the meeting with Cammie and of his discussion with his operatives. In there, he hoped he had the name of the cow-bar and Cammie's contact.

"Right," DeFreeze said. He swiveled the chair, pulled open a drawer in his desk, and searched. He obviously found nothing, for he stood and went into the outer office.

When he appeared to be out of earshot, Whitney took Eliason's arm. "You know what's happened to her, don't you?"

"I don't know any more than you do."

"Think, man." Whitney's grip was tight. "She's ACV. He didn't kill her. If he takes her—"

"Jesus." Eliason closed his eyes and leaned his head back against the wood of the chair. He had been avoiding thinking about that. Cammie, as lost to them as all the others.

Whitney leaned over. "You know what Center regulations are if we find her, and she's been polluted."

Eliason knew. They would have to stake her, along with the vampire that made her. "Eradication's illegal in the West."

Whitney nodded. He let go of Eliason's arm. The pressure of his fingers left warm spots on Eliason's skin. "I'm going to see how bad it is," Whitney said. "Sometimes friends help each other in mysterious ways."

Whitney's words made a chill run up Eliason's back. The West had other programs. They would try those first. Cammie had to have a chance.

"Got it," DeFreeze said. He stood in the doorway, a manila file open in his hands. The light framed him from the back. "She was meeting a man named Steve. She suspected he was a vampire. The report John and Norm filed confirmed that, although she got in and out of the bar unharmed. She was leaving a message for a Ben Sadler."

"The police are going to need that information," Whitney said. His voice was all business. He had obviously switched into Eradication mode.

DeFreeze nodded. "They're not going to be able to do much. They leave cow-bars alone."

Eliason stood. He turned his back on the windows. "We can't wait for them anyway. Each moment we delay is another moment that Cammie gets hurt. Any way we can get this Steve?"

"Oh, there's a way." Whitney picked imaginary lint off his jeans. "But it's risky."

"I sure as hell would like to get that bastard who killed my operatives," DeFreeze said. "I've done risky."

"Not this kind." Whitney kept his head down as he spoke. The curls on the nape of his neck had grown wild, as if he never had them cut. "We have to get him out of that cow-bar, and then we have to get him to talk."

Eliason frowned. "He won't talk to us."

"Not willingly," Whitney said.

"No one can make a vampire talk if he doesn't want to," DeFreeze said.

"I've done it." Whitney's voice was small. He hunched farther forward in his chair. "We actually found a vamp who had hidden his children. He wouldn't tell us where they were and Investigation couldn't find them. So my partner before Cammie, Alyse, buried the guy in garlic and woke him up. He was too drugged to move, and he answered any question we asked."

Eliason didn't like the sound of that. He had never faced an adult vampire. He wasn't sure he wanted to.

But they had to find Cammie somehow.

"The garlic didn't help my boys tonight," DeFreeze said.

"That's because this guy is a practicing hereditary— or, if it wasn't Cammie's brother, it was a vamp over a hundred years old. Despite what the media says, the old ones are rare. And smart. The stronger the vampire, the less garlic affects him. But smart vampires don't live in cow-bars."

Eliason crossed his arms and leaned against the desk. He didn't want to ruin the one chance they had. "From what you said, we have to find him when he sleeps, and there's no way to do that in a cow-bar. There should be a human guardian."

"Oh, there is." Whitney stood. He ran a hand over his hair, and looked at both men. His eyes were bruised from lack of sleep. "There's a reason smart vampires stay away. Leeches can be bribed, especially if the vampire in question is threatening the cow-bar. And it looks as if this Steve guy is, if Cammie got in."

"How much money?" DeFreeze asked.

"Ten grand, twenty grand." Whitney shrugged. "Something to make it worth the betrayal and loss of business. We'd get the coffin to a safe place, douse it, and start asking questions."

Eliason's throat was dry. No wonder Whitney was so good on eradication. He remained calm, cool, even under pressure. "How do you know all this about cow-bars? The Center rarely works with them."

Whitney's features appeared to have shrunken in on themselves. "Cammie asked me once why I stayed when others always left. I never told her the reason. I'm not really ACV. My father was a leech. I grew up in cow-bars, Brett. I know them as well as I know my own hands."

"Do you think we're going to get answers out of Steve?" DeFreeze asked.

Eliason made himself swallow. They had to get answers out of Steve. He was their only tie to Cammie, except Ben himself.

Whitney shrugged. "There's only one way to find out."

Chapter Thirty-nine

It was just past twilight as Ben led Mikos up the walk to his Olympia home. With each step, Steve's words came back to haunt him. Fucking suburban. Not at all like a place Mikos would enjoy. Good thing Ben had gotten Glenda out of there. He wouldn't see her again for a few more nights. She had been angry about Cam-Cam, and he had had to drain her more than he had planned to get her to forget that Cam existed.

But Ben couldn't forget. He ached for her.

She was beautiful.

He had gone through her possessions that first night after he had dumped her in his bed. Her identification showed that she had worked for the Westrina Center in the Midwest. It also listed her name and age.

In the past twenty-four hours, the memories were coming back to him. She was his sister.

And that didn't stop him from lusting after her.

He pushed open the door and flicked on the light. The sectionals were neatly arranged. Everything was as he had left it. The bottle remained untouched on the dining room table. Cam was still asleep.

Good.

"She'll be tough to convert," Mikos had said when

Ben told him. "You will need the protection of the nest. An eradicator has a desire to fight the intoxication."

"I thought you can't fight what you are," Ben had replied.

"No." Mikos had smiled a little. "But you can try."

Now, as he stood in the living room, Mikos nodded. "You have done well. Where's your cow?"

"At her home," Ben said. "Luckily I hadn't moved her in here yet."

"Good." Mikos brushed a hand along the velour surface of the sectional. "We can't afford distractions tonight. Show me where she is."

Ben flicked on the light and led the way down the hallway. It still looked barren compared to the home he had grown up in. No pictures on the walls, no streaks marring the white surface. Only the paint and the tan carpet. He pushed open the door to his bedroom.

The thread of light illuminated the form on the bed. Cam slept in a fetal position, her slim body huddled under the covers. She had her back to them. He loved the curve of it, the way it tapered into her buttocks.

"Delicious," Mikos said. He pulled off his shirt, then slipped out of his jeans. His penis was limp. "She needs to drink me."

Ben nodded. Just looking at Cam had made him hard. It wasn't right to lust after a sister like this. But they hadn't grown up together. And when he had mentioned it to Mikos, Mikos had shrugged.

"There are no taboos among vampires," Mikos had said. "Who knows what kind of future the two of you will create."

It was as if Mikos had given him permission. And nothing looked so inviting as the female form on that bed.

Ben undressed slowly. Mikos watched, touching Ben's erection when it popped out of Ben's pants. Ben moaned, but moved away. He wanted to save himself for Cam. He went over to the bed and crawled in behind her, pressing himself against her. She stretched against him, her body suddenly rigid.

He bit her carotid artery, sending his tainted saliva into her, and she relaxed. Her blood pumped into him, as sweet as it had been the first time. He had drained her that night, and she had filled up on him. Nothing compared with that, except this taste.

Mikos was on the bed with them. He grabbed her head with his hand and shoved it against his own neck. She tried to turn away, but he pushed. Ben almost cautioned him not to hurt her, but he didn't want to let go of the sweet liquid filling him.

He slipped inside her. She was wet. An orgasm spasmed through her. Mikos reached around her and caressed Ben's naked buttocks. Ben raised his free wrist to Mikos and Mikos bit. They were all feeding off each other. The blood loss was as exciting as the flow.

Cam-Cam's orgasms were powerful. She made small groaning sounds and she rubbed against Ben as if she couldn't get enough. A huge orgasm built inside him. He stopped moving, trying to savor it. Then Mikos's hand slid down and gripped Ben's balls. Ben sucked harder on Cam, her warm blood easing every ache inside him. Then he spasmed into her, the power of his orgasm matching her own.

Finally, Mikos detached his mouth from Ben's wrist, and rolled away from them.

"More," Cam whispered. Her words were slurred. "Please. You taste so good."

Mikos laughed and offered her his wrist. She took it and sucked greedily, the noise of her mouth echoing in the room. Through her blood, Ben could taste some of Mikos's effervescence. Another orgasm was building. He pushed against her, hard, and they came together.

Spent, Ben let her artery go. He licked it closed, then licked his own wrist. Cam's hand had traveled down to her pubic hair. Mikos caught it.

"Turn on the light," Mikos said.

Ben reached to the side of the bed and turned on the light. Cam-Cam was breathing hard. Her cheeks were flushed with the blood warmth.

"Camila Timms," Mikos said, sitting up. The bruise she had made in his neck was already fading. "Did you like that?"

"You taste good," she said, wiping her mouth.

"But did you like it?" Mikos asked.

A small frown creased her forehead. "I shouldn't," she said.

"But did you?"

"Can we do it again?" Her voice was soft.

Mikos laughed. The warmth of the sound tingled through Ben. They had succeeded, then. Mikos ran his hand along her face. "We'll do it every night, you and I," Mikos said, "Until that frown goes away."

Ben sat up. He didn't like that. Cam was his find. His to train. His to love.

"Your brother doesn't like that, Camila."

She turned to him, her eyes enormous on her small face. Her mouth was slack and blood covered. He had never seen anyone so heavily drugged, although he suspected he had looked like that on his first night in the nest. "I killed him, Ben," she said. "I was coming to take you home."

He cupped her head, his hand over Mikos's. He licked the blood off her lips. She opened her mouth so that he could taste inside. "It's better that you come home with me," he said. "I can't live with your people. You can live with mine."

"Being a vampire. 'S wrong, Ben."

"Oh, Cam," he said, stroking her breast. Her distress made him ache. "They're afraid of us. That's why they teach you it's wrong. You and I are hereditary. We can be powerful. Imagine feeling like this the rest of your life."

"'M outta control, Ben." She arched into his hand. A tear ran down her left cheek. "Never been outta control."

He slipped inside her again, just to feel her warmth. "Enjoy it," he said. "Your body is a toy. Enjoy it."

Mikos bit her shoulder from the back and her arch was stronger. An orgasm fluttered through her. She murmured as if in pain. Mikos gave her his wrist and she sucked on it, that frown still creasing her forehead. Her second orgasm made Ben sink his teeth into the other side of her neck. After a moment, her teeth brushed his skin. When she bit, he came for the third time. It was almost painful because he was dry.

She let him go and leaned on him. He could feel the total relaxation in her body. " 'S wrong, Ben," she whispered.

Mikos stroked her hair. His gaze met Ben's. "Her mind is strong," Mikos said. "But her body craves this as much as yours did. We have to get her to stop thinking."

Ben licked her wounds closed and cradled her against him like she used to cradle him. He hadn't believed he was capable of such tenderness. "What if she really doesn't want this?"

Mikos smiled. "The physical change has already begun. It's only a matter of time before she's convinced. She's ours, Ben. Yours and mine. Forever."

Chapter Forty

Her mouth was dry, her body curiously sated. She ached in a thousand places—bruises along her arms and neck—and her groin tingled. She could catalogue all those things, but they felt distant, as if they belonged to someone else. Most of her mind was engaged in doing as Mikos and Ben directed, but somewhere, toward the back, her personality hid. There was a wall around it, a glass wall so thick that nothing could get through. If she tried, she could connect herself, her mind and her body, for just a moment, and then she would get nauseous.

She followed them off an elevator into a darkened hallway. The faint scent of blood trickled to her. Her mouth watered. Jesus. Couldn't she stop the physical sensations? It was as if she couldn't get enough. And she didn't even enjoy it. It was just something she had to do, a compulsion like she had never had before.

Mikos stopped in front of a wooden door. Soft conversation echoed behind it. He unlocked the door and swung it open, bathing the hallway in light and sound.

Cigarette smoke mingled with the blood odor. Half a dozen people were jammed in the entryway. Poison played on the stereo, almost drowned out by the conversation. In the back of the room, a naked man stood on a chair, rubbing himself all over. A hand grabbed him and he toppled off.

Cammie's mouth opened slightly. They didn't have to lead her in. She went on her own, longing throbbing through her. In the glass prison, her real self cried out that she was no better than the people she had fought, but that didn't stop her movement.

A man ran his hand along her breast, and she turned so that he could feel the nipple. "Hey, Mikos," the man said. "What you got here?"

"Another virgin," Mikos said.

The crowd parted for her. She felt a hand on her back. Ben. His forehead was creased with worry. "If this is too soon for you," he said, but she didn't understand what he meant.

Then she saw them, people on the mat. Three women and two men. One of the men looked like Eliason, but as she looked closer, she realized that this man was younger. And drugged. His penis was erect and he was playing with it. The skin along his shoulder was purple with bite marks.

The smell of blood was thick. Maybe just a taste. A taste . . .

She knelt beside the man, put her hand on his chest, and leaned into his neck. As she bit, other fingers grabbed her, ripping off her clothes, positioning her over him until his body slipped into hers. It was almost painful. She was sore.

(No, Daddy. Please. No)

But still she moved, the arousal more than she could bear. His blood had a sour taste, but it was good. Not as good as Mikos's, but thicker, more nourishing. The people behind her were chanting. She rocked on the man, feeling his orgasm inside her, but not stopping. He was moaning and arching, and then he stopped. His blood was easing to a trickle.

"She's killing him," Ben said.

(Let him go)

"It's time she joined the other side of the fence," Mikos said. "Let her kill for us once."

(Let him go!)

His blood was so good. Maybe if she went deeper—

(Let him go!)

She pulled back, her own voice in her head so strong that it was as if someone had shouted in her ear. The arousal was gone as if it had never been. She climbed off the man's cool body. His eyes were open. She had killed him.

Then he licked his lips. "God," he whispered. "They were right about virgins."

Mikos was smiling at her. His eyes were red-rimmed like her father's had been. Ben touched her arm. She turned to him. He was suddenly solace in this room full of strangers. "I'm going to be sick," she said.

He nodded. He helped her up, put a hand on her back and propelled her through the double doors, down the hall and into an ornate bathroom. She went around the overlarge tub into the room with the toilet and vomited blood all over the porcelain. Then she sat, shaking, and used toilet paper to wipe off her mouth. The nausea was gone, but the disgust was still there.

Ben was leaning against the wall, watching her. "I did that after my first time too," he said. "It's like the shock as the body finishes its change or something. I don't know. Then I didn't eat for days. You need to keep eating or you'll get sicker."

She rested her cheek against the cool tile. She almost liked him. That disgusted her the most. He treated her like a lover, not a brother. Like—

(Dad had)

—the man of her dreams. Only he forced her to do things she thought only sick people did.

(Over fifty percent of vampires' children . . .)

Great. She had become a statistic now.

"You'll like it, Cam-Cam," he said. "You will. Soon you won't be able to get enough."

That was what she was afraid of. Someday she would completely cross over. Someday she would think it all right to take a drugged man's life because he offered his blood to her. Someday satisfying her own needs would become more important than anything else.

"I can't live like this," she said.

"Yes you can, Cam." He crouched beside her and held her against him. "We'll live together. Trust me. It'll be fun."

Chapter
Forty-one

$$\boxed{\text{i}}$$

The fire in the library was dying. Ben had his feet propped on a stool, a glass in his hand. He sipped, not willing to use a cow this evening. Cam's response had unnerved him, and he wanted to settle his stomach.

Mikos pulled back the wire screen and put another log on the fire. Then he stirred the embers until small blue flames surrounded the log. He propped the screen back up and wiped his hands on his jeans. "She's going to be tough, you know," he said.

Ben nodded. That was becoming clearer and clearer. He had thought after Mikos had drained her that she would be willing to be part of the nest. Her reluctance surprised him. "I was uncomfortable at first," he said.

"I worry at her restraint. She should have killed that cow." Mikos walked over to the other high-back chair and sat heavily.

"She was getting ill. She had had too much. We should have waited another night before bringing her here. After you and me together, her system couldn't take more blood." Ben took a sip. The blood in the glass was warm and barely fresh.

Mikos leaned his head against the back of the chair. "Perhaps," he said. "It makes sense. But she killed our people too long and she is older than you, Ben. She has had more time to learn about herself. I want you to lock her in her room tonight, and each night until we're sure of her."

"She didn't try anything at my place." Ben swirled the glass in his hand, watching the blood stain the sides.

"It was still too new for her. She wouldn't have. But now is the time that will tell us what our future is with her. If she crosses completely, she will be an asset to the nest. The two of you will be able to work together. If she doesn't, we will have to take care of her."

Ben closed his eyes. Cam was too special. He would take her out of the nest before he had anything happen to her. Perhaps the life here merely overwhelmed her. He sighed.

Mikos seemed to take that as a tacit agreement to the plan. "Now," he said. "Tell me again about the woman you found in Olympia."

It was nearly an hour later when Ben left the library. He was tired and a bit discouraged. The elation he had felt when he found Cam had eased into a small disquiet. The memories she brought with her were tender: full of hugs and warmth. For the first time, he felt as if someone had actually loved him. But this Cam-Cam was an adult, who had lived for a lifetime without him. He knew nothing of her and hadn't had a chance to get to know her. The garlic induced lust that had forced him to attack her had left them strangers.

Except that the lust hadn't dissipated.

It was the one thing he didn't discuss with Mikos, for Mikos saw nothing wrong with it. But Mikos didn't notice the pain in Cam's eyes when Ben touched her, or her passivity when he fondled her. She rarely took any initiative, and only then when he insisted. Despite her distaste, though, he couldn't stay away.

Not ever.

He walked down the hall to the kitchen, clutching his now-empty glass. He would have a nightcap, then check on Cam and lock her in, as Mikos suggested. The sounds of the nightly party had dimmed to an occasional drunken giggle. But from the kitchen he heard voices.

Female.

And one of them was Cam's.

"This is real wine!" she said.

"That wine, it is for the hosts." Van. Ben clenched his fists. Van was with her. He pushed open the double doors. Cam was beside the sink, Van beside her, leaning against the counter. They weren't touching.

"What's going on?" he snapped, looking at Van.

Van smiled, her small features holding a challenge. "I was explaining to your sister that she will feel better when she learns how to control her body."

"She's doing fine now," Ben said.

"Oh, no. She is disgusted with herself. She cannot stop the lust. But I have told her there will come a time when she will learn how to use it to her advantage." She ran a hand along Cam's shoulder. "Ask me, child, if you need anything."

Cam nodded. Van walked past her. Ben grabbed Van's hand. "You leave her alone," he said softly.

"Afraid that I will kill her like I did your prize brood mare?" Van laughed. "This one, she will be much more difficult to harm. I would be careful with her."

Van wrenched her hand out of Ben's grasp and went through the kitchen doors.

Ben went over to Cam and put a hand on her back. She stiffened. He tried to ignore the movement. "Did she hurt you?"

Cam shook her head. "She just told me the physical progression. She said I should ask you about it, since you just went through it."

Good. She had questions. Maybe that meant she was accepting. "We only have an hour before sunrise," he said, going to the refrigerator and pouring himself another glass, "but I'll tell you as much as I can."

Chapter
Forty-two

Because Eliason put up the money, he was the one elected to do the less dangerous job of guarding the van. The van belonged to De-Freeze. It was a black 1970s model that held more than it should. DeFreeze had built a dividing wall between the driver's seat and the back of the van. He had also customized the license plate holder so that the plate was difficult to read, even up close.

The early morning sunlight made the neighborhood outside the Keg look even seamier than it was. The paint was peeling off the buildings and litter covered the streets. A wino—or perhaps a vampire victim—slept in a nearby alley, covered with newspapers. Eliason sat in the van's driver's seat with the window down, gagging occasionally at the fetid stench that rose off the unwashed streets.

He hoped they would hurry. Waiting out here might have been the easy job but it certainly wasn't the best. If something happened to them inside he had no way of knowing. He just hoped Whitney was right about being able to buy vampires out of a nest like that. If he wasn't, they could all be hurt.

Eliason ran a damp hand along his jeans. He was tired, and sitting here quietly wasn't helping. They had stayed up all night preparing the van—the back end was buried in garlic. They had cleaned out the garlic in two local Safeways as well as used all of Whitney's stock. As the warm sun beat on the van, the heat would release some of that stench to mix with the other wonderful odors on the street. Eliason could hardly wait.

He glanced at his watch. They had been inside for fifteen minutes.

DeFreeze had insisted on it remaining the three of them. There seemed to be a tacit understanding that they might break Oregon law. DeFreeze had provided the equipment, including a gurney, Eliason was putting up the money, and Whitney was providing his expertise.

Eliason hoped that would be enough. Cammie didn't have much time.

Then the door to the Keg burst open. Whitney came out lugging the gurney up the flight of stairs. DeFreeze was behind him, suit wrinkled, and tie gone. A coffin-sized box wobbled on the gurney top. An overweight man wearing a butcher's apron stood behind them, watching.

They had him.

Eliason got out of the van and hurried around back to open the double doors. The odor of garlic was overpowering. It covered everything. Whitney was breathing heavily. His face was red with strain. Eliason helped them lift the gurney into the back, surprised at the weight, and amazed they had managed it.

Whitney grabbed Eliason's arm. "Come with me," he said. He leaned over to the side, and said to DeFreeze, "You drive."

Eliason immediately understood. They were providing an alibi for DeFreeze. *Those guys were from the Midwest. Things are different there. I had no idea what they were planning.*

Whitney stepped into the back and Eliason followed. Then Whitney pulled the door closed, and Eliason turned on the overhead light. The lid on the box had slid half off and steam was coming from inside. A man moaned, as if he were coming out of sleep.

Whitney put on thick leather gloves, then pulled the lid the rest of the way off.

The man inside was too thin. His skin had a vampire's pallor, but he had no other distinguishing characteristics. His right arm steamed where the sun must have struck it. He reached slowly to touch it as the van lurched forward.

"Hey!" His words were sleep blurred. "What gives."

"We bought you from your leech," Whitney said. He took a bulb of garlic and rubbed it along the edge of the coffin.

"Hey!" The vampire screamed and pushed back, but his movements were feeble. "Stop that!"

"Steve Henderson?" Eliason asked.

The vampire blinked at him. "Do I know you?"

"Not yet," Whitney said. He tossed the bulb to Eliason. Eliason held it like a shield.

The vampire must have suddenly realized he was in danger. He tried to sit up, but fell over against the side of the coffin. The gurney slipped along the van's floor. Eliason reached down and locked the wheels.

Whitney pulled out two small stakes and a mallet. The vampire screamed and tried to shield his chest. "Grab his hand and put it against the side," Whitney said.

Eliason did. The vampire was surprisingly weak. Whitney picked up one stake and pounded it through the vampire's palm. The vampire's scream sounded almost human, but no blood spattered either of them. Eliason was shaking. He had never intentionally harmed another being before. He had to remind himself that if the vampire lived, the wounds would disappear. This would only cause pain. Nothing more.

He grabbed the other hand and held it down while Whitney nailed it into the coffin. Then Whitney shoved a clove of garlic in the vampire's mouth. The vampire bucked and kicked with his legs, but missed them both.

The van swerved around a corner, and Eliason nearly lost his balance. The smell of garlic was making him nauseated.

Whitney held a garlic bulb in front of the vampire's face. The vampire's face had become green. "You realize," Whitney said, "that I can make you very ill with this. I read somewhere that if a vampire ingests garlic, it rots in him. You'll get very sick and be unable to eat. You'll go crazy for a few days. Loose your mind completely. One clove won't hurt you, but a bulb, well, that's another story."

"No!" the vampire whimpered. He tugged, as if trying to free his hands.

"Of course, we could just stake you here. Now. But we don't want to do that."

The van weaved all over the road. Eliason swallowed to keep his meager breakfast down. He didn't want to be part of this. He was a healer, not a man who maimed. "Look," he said. "A woman came to you a few days ago, looking for Ben Sadler. Where is she now?"

The vampire licked his lips. He tried to raise his head near Eliason's neck. He snapped at the vein, but Eliason moved out of reach. The garlic was taking effect. The vampire's eyes were rolling in the back of his head. "She was staying at the Hilton. Gave Ben the number. Sweet thing. Smelled—fresh . . . like you." He snapped again.

Whitney held the bulb over the vampire's nose. He brought his head down. "Where is she now?"

"Hotel?" The word had a mushy sound. The vampire licked his lips. "You smell good. Please. Just a little taste?"

Eliason pushed Whitney's hand away. "Someone showed up at the hotel and took her away. We think it was your friend Ben. Where would he have taken her?"

"To the nest." The vampire tugged on his arm. The stake in his right hand was coming loose. Whitney glanced at it.

"Where's the nest?" Eliason asked.

The vampire laughed. He ran his tongue over his teeth. "Can't tell you that. Mikos . . . kill me."

Whitney pounded the stake deeper into the vampire's hand. "I'll kill you if you don't say anything," Whitney said.

"Seattle!" The vampire screamed. "Seattle! The nest is in Seattle!"

"Good." Whitney leaned forward. His eyes were bright. He was enjoying this. Eliason swallowed hard. "But Seattle is a big place. Where in Seattle?"

The vampire shook his head. His tongue lolled out the side of his mouth and his eyes were glazed. "Can't . . . Mikos . . . kill . . ."

Whitney shoved another clove of garlic in the vampire's mouth. This time, the vampire bit his fingers. The vampire's teeth went through the glove but didn't break the skin. Whitney hit him with the back of his hand, and Eliason heard the gulp as the vampire compulsively swallowed the garlic.

"You're killing me, man," the vampire said. He tilted his head back. "God, I need a fuck. Some blood, man . . . please . . . a fuck?"

"In a minute," Eliason said. "First tell us where the nest is."

The vampire's eyes focused on Eliason's face. "Then you'll fuck me?" His voice sounded thick, as if his tongue had swollen in his mouth. "God, man, that's great. You're one of the most beautiful cows I've ever fucking seen. Ever. I'll make you feel real good."

Eliason resisted the urge to turn away. Whitney had done this before. Cammie and Whitney killed people like this all the time. He didn't know how they could. The vampire seemed human.

Human enough to beat the crap out of children.

Human enough to leave bodies in the street.

"The nest," Eliason said.

Whitney leaned closer. The vampire screamed. "Keep him away from me!"

Eliason nodded at Whitney. The van started bumping. They were apparently on gravel road. DeFreeze was taking them outside the city, as he had promised.

"Where's the nest?" Eliason asked.

"Promise you'll fuck me?" The vampire was whispering. "Promise?"

"As soon as you tell me," Eliason said. He needed this to end. Cammie or no Cammie, this was beyond him.

"Near Elliot Bay. Downtown." He whispered an address. "Upstairs. Third floor. Italian restaurant on the ground. Good cover, Mikos says." He licked his lips. "Now, free my hands. I promise you . . . oh, God."

He convulsed once. Red tinged beads of sweat appeared on his forehead.

"Rap on the wall," Whitney said. "Get DeFreeze to stop."

Eliason stood, glad to be away from that scene. He rapped on the van's metal side with the prearranged triple knock. Then he heard one of the most terrifying screams he had ever heard.

He turned to see Whitney pounding a stake in the vampire's heart. Blood gushed all over the back of the van, bits of garlic mixed in. Still Whitney held. The vampire's legs flailed and kicked. Whitney kept pounding.

One of the vampire's hands ripped free, and slapped at Whitney's face. Whitney ignored it. Blood was coating his skin, dotting his hair. Some splattered on Eliason and he was startled to realize that it was cold.

Then the vampire stopped moving. His skin sank in on itself and grew withered as if he had aged. The van skidded to a stop.

Eliason swallowed. He had to repeat the mantra he had learned in med-school when they opened cadavers. "You didn't tell me you were going to do that."

Whitney looked at him, expression hard. "What did you expect me to do? Set him free?"

"I don't know." Eliason ran a hand through his short, curly hair. "I hadn't thought that far."

"Well, get out, and see if we're in a suitable area. We can't let DeFreeze see this."

"Right." Eliason opened the back door to the van. They were in a forest, apparently up an old logging road. The air here smelled refreshingly of pine. DeFreeze had just come around the right side of the van. His eyes widened when he saw Eliason. Eliason glanced down at himself. He was covered in blood. He shook his head and closed the doors.

"We got the address," Eliason said.

"Good." DeFreeze's Adam's apple bobbed as he swallowed. He rubbed his hands together, and glanced around. "Old road, you know. Not really used. What do you say we clean the van up here?"

"Let Whitney do it," Eliason said. Then he pushed past DeFreeze and staggered off the side of the road. He leaned against a tree and breathed deeply to try to settle his stomach. He hoped this was worth it. If they could save Cammie, it might be. Otherwise he had just gone against all his training for nothing.

Chapter
Forty-three

Cammie woke up groggy and disoriented. She was alone in the bed and relieved to find herself that way. Ben had stayed until nearly dawn, talking with her, explaining the transition, and then he had left. He must have been a nice boy once, just as his adopted mother had described. There were vestiges remaining, like bits of youth still hiding in an old man's face.

A headache pounded in the back of her head. She rolled over and glanced at the clock. The red digital readout showed 3:01 P.M. The blackout curtains made it impossible to tell time. The sun was still up.

She put her head on the pillow. Images of the previous night flashed through her mind. The lust she had felt for that poor man lying on the mat. He had still been there when she went to bed, waiting for someone else. At least she had stopped before killing him.

At least she had done that much.

That voice in the back of her head had stopped her. It had reached through the glass walls and grabbed her back. She would be an unhappy vampire, a morose woman at the mercy of her own obsession. A future she didn't want.

They had never taught that at the Center, that some

vampires didn't want to live the life, although she had seen it in books.

In the rehab books.

Her mouth was dry. She licked her lips. Three P.M. She had awakened in the sunlight. Ben said sunlight would grow gradually more painful as time went on but right now she could still survive in it.

And the rest of the nest couldn't.

She could survive.

She stood up. Her body ached with longing. She wanted blood so badly that if she closed her eyes, she could imagine it pouring in her mouth. So easy to slide over. So easy to become one of Mikos's victims. Nests always had a leader, and that leader always seduced the followers.

But some followers broke. That was how the Center had tracked so many nests.

Some followers broke.

She pushed her hair off her face and grabbed her clothes, tugging her jeans over her hips and pulling a sweatshirt over her head. She kept her feet bare. No one would wake up. This was the time of day when the sun was reaching its zenith. She had the power, all by herself, to break free of the nest.

She went to the door, and turned the handle, but the door was locked. Damn. They had thought of that. Someone had realized she was a threat.

She had always been bad at locks.

But she had had training.

She flicked on the overhead light. Her hands were shaking. Maybe she would go to the refrigerator and get a drink. Just one. The thought calmed her. She crouched in front of the lock, remembering Sarge's instructions.

Go slow. Examine what you're facing. Remain calm.

The lock was a simple latch, not a dead bolt, something easily broken with a bit of patience. She worked it until she heard it snap free. The door eased open.

The hallway was dark. She would keep it that way.

She walked the length of the hall toward the kitchen before she stopped.

If she had a drink, she would be hooked again.

No. She needed a plan.

She put a hand over her face and thought. What would she and Whitney do? The big vampire first, and then the others, but there were too many for her to do in a single afternoon. With this blood weakness, she didn't have the strength. If one of them bit her, she would lose everything.

No. She had to destroy the nest without killing all the vampires. And that meant fire.

She would have to incinerate the place. And she didn't have her own equipment.

Think. Think. What would work? There were matches in the living room. People had been smoking cigarettes and she had vaguely noticed some incense burning before they went to sleep. The entire nest was strewn with papers, but she needed a catalyst. Something that would flame up quickly, that would allow it to spread.

Alcohol. If there was wine for the cows, there had to be something else. Something that burned well.

Like rum. Sarge had always recommended 151 Bacardi Rum as one way to start a house fire.

She went into the kitchen and stared at the refrigerator. It was a new model, with an ice maker on the side. Her mouth watered. In there was solace. In there was something that would take the ache from her body and ease the trembling in her hands.

In there was insanity.

She turned her back on it. She crouched in front of the cabinet she had seen the night before, and opened it, moving bottles carefully. It was a complete bar—and in the back, three bottles of rum. One wasn't the right kind. Regular rum wouldn't burn. Only 151.

Both of the other bottles were 151 Bacardi Rum. Her luck was holding.

She tiptoed into the living room and found a bowl of

matches on the counter. The lingering scents of blood and sex made her longing grow. She clamped down on it. This was her chance. Her only chance. She would take it.

Cammie poured the rum on a pile of papers, then left a trail of liquid that went to another set of doused papers. She continued all the way through the nest, stopping at doorways. Each time she made a noise, she jumped and waited, expecting to be caught. But no one seemed to notice her. She skipped the door that Van had said was hers—Van seemed too savvy not to investigate a strange noise—and went down the hall, ending her trail in the library at the fireplace.

Then she grabbed a piece of wood, took it into the kitchen, grabbed a knife and whittled the edge into a point. Mikos wasn't in one of the main rooms. She already knew that. He had to be somewhere more protected. Probably off the library.

She went back in. The room smelled faintly of old books and rum. She grabbed another piece of wood to use as a club. Her sense of smell was becoming more acute. She closed her eyes and sniffed, finally getting a whiff of the scent that was uniquely Mikos.

His blood bubbled in her mouth, rich and effervescent, like good champagne.

Her groin ached. She wouldn't let him touch her. She would go in commando style, as Sarge had taught her. She would stake him, then light the fires, and leave.

She didn't think of what she would do to Ben.

She wouldn't let herself.

Chapter
Forty-four

The door beside his closed. Ben snapped awake. He had been sleeping fitfully, dreaming of Cam-Cam spattered in blood. She had been screaming for him—*Ben! Ben!*—but someone was dragging him away.

He sat up. Nearly four. Not close to time to get up. Then he heard it again. The creak of a door. The sound of someone walking in the halls. Sounded like no one was sleeping well. At least Cam was in her room. Protected.

But he had better see. Van might have had other plans. Damn that woman. He would take her as soon as he got the chance. Maybe even later today.

He got out of bed and pulled on his kimono. Then he opened his door.

The hallway smelled of alcohol. A thin trail of it ran into the kitchen. Someone had let a cow loose in the building. He wrinkled his nose. Distasteful.

The door to the library was open. The alcohol trail led him in there. He followed it and saw Mikos's door standing open.

A scream echoed through the building, long, deep, and male. It made Ben's hair stand on end. Something crashed in Mikos's room, and then the scream again until it gurgled and died.

He ran to the door. Cam was there, crouched over Mikos. She was covered in blood, a block of wood in one hand and a stake *(dowel)* in the other. Mikos's body was flailing on the bed, turning to dust, disappearing.

(Daddy!)

"What did you do?" he asked.

She looked up then, obviously startled. "Ben."

"What did you do?" He would have to kill her. She had killed Mikos. She had damaged the nest.

"I—" She looked around, then stopped, the nervous movement gone. She pulled the stake from the skeletal form on the bed. "I did it for you, Ben. You need to be in charge here."

God. He wanted to believe that. But she hadn't shown any loyalty to him in the past few days. When he found her, she had been in a room filled with garlic and vampire hunters. She had killed vampires before.

Sometimes they're too strong for the drug, Van had said. *Sometimes they break free.*

He held up his hands. He would have to get her out of here. Then he would figure out what to do with her. "Cam, you aren't going to kill me, are you?"

She was frowning. She got off the bed. "We have to get out of here. He probably woke up the whole nest."

"This room is soundproofed. Whatever they heard, they heard through the open door."

She held the block of wood in one hand, the stake in the other. "I don't want to live like this anymore, Ben," she said.

He took a step closer to her. He was stronger. He would be able to get the equipment from her. "Cam-Cam, you have no choice. You can't deny what we are."

"We're children of vampires. We don't have to be like him, Ben." Her knuckles were white around the stake.

"We're not like him," Ben said. "I have learned control. You will too. We can beat this thing."

Cam shook her head. "It devours everyone in the end.

Don't you see? Eventually you'll lose every bit of caring you ever had."

He took another step toward her. "Cam, that's a myth. I care for you."

"You don't know me. It's some crazed blood lust talking. I'm going to burn down this nest, and then I'm going to leave. You can come with me if you want or die here." Her hands were trembling. Mikos's blood had dried on her face.

"And then what, Cam? You'll feed. That's how you'll survive. There is no other way." He took another step, gauging her strength, and her distance.

"They have rehab programs now."

Ben laughed. "Rehab, Cam? No matter what they do, the craving will never go away. You'll have to live with it every day, every minute."

She swallowed. For a moment, he thought he had gotten to her. Then she shook her head. "Better that than living like this. I'd rather fight myself than steal the life's blood from someone else."

"I never thought you would have a conscience, Cam," he said.

"I never thought you wouldn't."

Then he lunged for her and caught her in the waist. She slammed back against the wall, the block slamming into his back and knocking the air from his lungs. She kneed him in the groin and rolled away. Pain shot through him, bringing tears to his eyes. She grabbed the stake and brought it down. In the last moment, he managed to scoot. She caught the sleeve of his kimono. He tore it getting away.

He grabbed at her again, but she rolled. She had been trained to fight. She kicked with startling accuracy, hitting him in the stomach and groin simultaneously. He couldn't breathe. He couldn't move. But he had to. He had to get away.

He started to roll, but she brought the stake down through his chest, using both hands to plunge it through his body. Blood gushed from his mouth. Jesus. He had loved her. He didn't deserve this. He was only trying for the best for her.

He flailed at her, but the strength was leaving him. She grabbed the block with her free hand and pounded the stake in deeper.

She had protected him. She had always protected him. So why was she hurting him now?

"Cam-Cam," he whispered, through the blood. "Cam—"

Chapter Forty-five

And then he died. Cammie rested her head on the edge of her stake. "God, Ben," she whispered. If only he had wanted to change. If only he had wanted to try, she could have taken him with her. But he hadn't. They were forever doomed to be separate and different.

If only she could have seen it before.

His mouth was open, his eyes empty. His skin didn't change. His body remained the same. He was so new that the only vampiric changes he had suffered had been internal.

"Oh, Ben," she said again.

A door opened in the outer hallway. She lifted her head. She still had a whole nest of them to fight. The only thing she could do, the only thing she had time to do, was light fires and leave.

She pulled the stake from Ben's heart, and grabbed her block of wood. Then she got up and with shaking hands felt for the matches. They were in her back pocket. She pulled them out. They had stayed dry despite all the blood. She tucked the block of wood and stake under her arm, ran to the door of Mikos's bedroom, then glanced around the library. No one yet. She lit the first match and tossed it into the mess she had made near the fireplace. Then she dashed into the hall, lighting matches and dropping them as she ran, feeling the heat as the rum ignited.

The doors to the kitchen opened. Cammie turned and slammed the wood block into the face that appeared. Van. She slid backwards, not expecting the attack. Cammie stood over her, and using the same technique she had used on Ben (Bless Sarge and her training) slammed the stake into Van's heart. Van grabbed it, struggling. Fire was following the rum trails. Cammie could either finish her or get out.

Cammie was going to get out.

She ran down the hall, pausing only in the living room to light another match and throw it on the first pile she had made. It erupted into bright blue flame. Then she dashed into the hall and down the stairwell. The air here was cool. It smelled of leather, not vampires.

If she made it to the street, she would be free.

Chapter
Forty-six

It was dark by the time the van reached downtown Seattle. They had driven as fast as they could. DeFreeze had contacted both the Portland and the Seattle police, giving them the address, but not telling how he had obtained it. Eliason sat in the passenger seat, Whitney beside him, and DeFreeze driving. They had not spoken since they left the vampire's body in the woods.

They had dumped the gurney and gone to DeFreeze's secluded mountainside home. Whitney had used a hose to get the blood and garlic out of the back of the van, but Eliason was sure that it had done no good. The scent of garlic still covered him, even though he had changed clothes and showered.

That scent would haunt his dreams.

As they crossed the freeway bridges going into the city, they saw a fire lighting the night sky. "That's the direction we need to go," DeFreeze said.

He turned the van toward the lights, and within a few blocks they stopped. The police had cordoned off the area. A fire had devastated most of a building in the center of the block.

DeFreeze got out of the van. Eliason wasn't far behind him. The Seattle air was cold and smelled of sea, smoke, and ash. DeFreeze approached a cop, pulled out his wallet, and opened it to his ID.

"Jason DeFreeze," he said. "I called in with a tip earlier that there was a nest of vampires in this building."

The cop nodded. "We had a swat team ready to go when the whole upper story of the building erupted."

"Anyone get out?" Eliason asked. Whitney had come up behind him, silent. His face was illuminated by the flames.

The cop shook his head. "Not while we were here. But it had to be burning a while before it went down like that."

Red light danced across Whitney's face, making him look almost satanic. Eliason doubted they would spend much time together again. Whitney took his arm. "She got them, Brett," he said.

"How do you know it was Cammie?" DeFreeze asked.

Eliason stared at the burning building. He wouldn't find her here. He knew that. He would put Whitney on a plane in the morning and search up and down the I-5 corridor. He had an idea where she would go if she lived.

"He knows it was Cammie," Eliason said, "because there was nothing in the world she hated more than vampires."

Chapter Forty-seven

She was driving down Interstate 5 in Ben's Lexus. She had no money, and the blood smell on her clothes was driving her crazy. She had planned to drive to the rehab center in Roseburg, where no one knew her, but she couldn't. She knew she wouldn't make it that far. She was hungry and desperate and if she got close to anything human, she might take a drink.

She needed protection.

So she was going to the nearest rehab center, just inside Portland. Then she would wire for her money and her clothes and begin the day-to-day living.

Fighting the craving, minute by minute, as Ben had said.

Rehab had failed in the Midwest, but Brooker had said that was because they had only used counseling.

She hoped to hell he was right. She couldn't carry this monkey on her own.

And if she succumbed, she would have killed Ben for nothing.

Cam-Cam, he had whispered.

Daddy.

The thing they never told anyone, the thing the experts never put in the books, the thing the Center only barely acknowledged, was the love.

He had been the only father she had ever had. Despite what he did to her, she had loved him.

Just as she had loved Ben.

And she would have to live with that forever.

SCIENCE FICTION/FANTASY